MURDER IN THE LAVENDER

BOOK 18 OF THE MAGGIE NEWBERRY
MYSTERIES

SUSAN KIERNAN-LEWIS

SAN MARCO PRESS

Murder in the Lavender. Book 18 of the Maggie Newberry Mysteries. Copyright © 2021 by Susan Kiernan-Lewis.

All rights reserved.

Books by Susan Kiernan-Lewis
The Maggie Newberry Mysteries
Murder in the South of France
Murder à la Carte
Murder in Provence
Murder in Paris
Murder in Aix
Murder in Nice
Murder in the Latin Quarter
Murder in the Abbey
Murder in the Bistro
Murder in Cannes
Murder in Grenoble
Murder in the Vineyard
Murder in Arles
Murder in Marseille
Murder in St-Rémy
Murder à la Mode
Murder in Avignon
Murder in the Lavender
Murder in Mont St-Michel
A Provençal Christmas: A Short Story
A Thanksgiving in Provence
Laurent's Kitchen

An American in Paris Mysteries
Déjà Dead
Death by Cliché
Dying to be French
Ménage à Murder
Killing it in Paris

The Stranded in Provence Mysteries
Parlez-Vous Murder?
Crime and Croissants
Accent on Murder
A Bad Éclair Day
Croak, Monsieur!
Death du Jour
Murder Très Gauche
Wined and Died
A French Country Christmas

The Irish End Games
Free Falling
Going Gone
Heading Home
Blind Sided
Rising Tides
Cold Comfort
Never Never
Wit's End
Dead On
White Out
Black Out
End Game

The Mia Kazmaroff Mysteries
Reckless
Shameless
Breathless
Heartless
Clueless
Ruthless

Ella Out of Time
Swept Away
Carried Away
Stolen Away

The French Women's Diet

1

The brisk evening breeze whipped the leaves and twigs in tight vortices of smoke and dirt across the perimeter of the farm. Chantal shivered and pulled her cotton cardigan tighter around her while feeling in her pocket for her cigarettes. Her fingers touched the note he'd left her and she felt a frission of annoyance ripple through her.

Why the big production? Why couldn't he have just asked to meet up like a normal person?

She felt a flush of shame at how she'd struggled to decipher the simple note. Her reading wasn't good. And Enzo knew that. Which was probably the reason he wrote the note instead of talking to her.

To humiliate her.

A sound in the distance made her turn in that direction.

He was late but that was typical. She squinted to see the muted glow of lights from the lavender barn in the distance. Someone must be working late.

"Enzo?" she called, careful to keep her voice down.

There was no answer.

She felt a stiffness in her jaw as she pulled out a cigarette and lit it, taking in a harsh drag that brought pain and relief in equal measure into her lungs.

She hadn't gone to much trouble tonight, she was still wearing the plain dress she'd worked the field in today. But she *had* put on scent and added some lip gloss. Even if she was over him she still wanted to look good. She wanted him to be sorry they were breaking up. In fact, breaking up with him was the only reason she'd agreed to meet him at all tonight.

Enzo had chosen the spot but a remote section of the farm's already harvested lavender field was perfect for her purposes too.

She grimaced as she brought his face to mind. He'd been getting on her nerves long before now. But this latest nonsense was the final nail in his coffin.

She took another fierce drag on her cigarette, flicking the ashes into the remnants of the cut stubble of the harvested lavender. Looking at the flowers, now truncated and shorn to the ground, made her sad.

Before the harvest they had been such proud, billowing waves of vibrant purple before the harvest. She was surprised to realize that she didn't hate this job. It was hard work to be sure. Backbreaking in fact and not her sort of thing at all.

But aside from the heavenly scent and the pretty flowers, leaving was probably for the best.

She only wished she'd been the one to make that decision.

She shivered again and rubbed her arms against the chill of the late August evening.

Where was he?

It was easily a four-mile walk to the monastery dormitory and she'd counted on getting a ride back there from Enzo. But the longer she stood waiting in the growing cold, the more uneasy she found herself becoming.

She didn't love the dark but, except for psychos or old women, who did? Agreeing to meet Enzo here at this time of evening had seemed to make sense this afternoon. Now she wished she'd just sent him a text telling him they were over.

She bridled when she remembered she no longer had a cellphone. She felt her anger begin to build in her again.

How dare she? How dare that vicious cow take my phone?

She heard another noise, this time it was closer and actually made her catch her breath. The sound had been of someone or something creeping, as if to mask the sounds of approach.

"Enzo?" she said again, this time even softer than before. "Is that you?"

Only the delicate whistling of the night air sliding through the army of plane trees lining the field's border answered her.

This is nuts.

She tossed her cigarette down, pausing only long enough to stamp it out in the dirt and then spun around to head toward the village road that ran beside the field. Her movement spurred her apprehension as if the very thought of running reminded her that there was something to run from. She hadn't gone five steps when she heard the rustling sound again. This time there was nothing cautious about it.

She felt her heart thudding in her chest as she broke into a run, her eyes locked onto the old stone wall at the field's edge, her sandals sliding in the sandy soil.

It must be a dog! Or maybe someone playing a trick.

The sound of the footsteps behind her were gaining on her.

She heard her own labored breathing at the same time. She wanted to scream but couldn't spare the breath. The road was nearer now but there were no lights, no cars.

"Leave me alone!" she shrieked in panic seconds before she slipped in her loose sandals and came down hard on the ground. She scrambled to her feet.

"Please," she whimpered, trying to peer into the dark at her pursuer. "Please don't hurt me."

The shadowy figure lunged at her, grabbing her with one hand. At the same moment Chantal saw the gleam of the scythe reflected by the moon.

A moment later, the blood had stopped gurgling in Chantal's windpipe and she lay quiet, her gore saturating the ground among the lavender blossoms.

The killer waited, one eye on the farm's processing barn in the distance, before turning to glance at the road. When it was clear that Chantal no longer breathed, her killer squatted next to her and scooped up several stalks of dried lavender from the ground.

Gently, methodically, the stalks were tucked into Chantal's neckline and sleeves and between the buttons on her dress.

Then a quick reach into Chantal's cardigan pocket to retrieve the note which was then folded and tucked safely away where no one would find it.

Throw it away? Or keep it to remember her by?

Time later to consider all that.

Finally, satisfied but reluctant to leave, the killer pulled a sticky, bloodstained tendril of Chantal's hair from her face before touching the girl's lips with fingers that just barely shook, and then lightly, almost imperceptibly, kissed her cheek.

A dog's lone howl caught on the wind and carried across the field before fading in the night air.

The only thing to do now was to walk away. Invisibly. Quietly.

Quietly so as not to disturb one second more of the lovely, fragrant night.

2

Unlike in most performing arts venues in America, Maggie thought, the thing that stands out about the Théâtre d'Aix was the scent of just baked *chouquettes*. She was pretty sure the beer and wine by the glass were still the bestsellers, but it wouldn't be France if baked goods weren't involved.

She fanned herself with her program and looked around the crowded auditorium. She knew most everyone who was here. They were all parents of the other students Jemmy had taken his summer theater class with.

She glanced at her watch and twisted the wedding ring on her finger, then crossed and uncrossed her arms.

It wasn't that she wasn't looking forward to seeing what Jemmy did with the role of Puck. She was sure he'd be wonderful. It wasn't that.

"Do you know the play?" her best friend Grace Van Sant asked from where she sat two seats down. Maggie always thought that ever-elegant, beautiful Grace was her name personified. Like her namesake Princess Grace of Monaco, Grace was blond, willowy and always chic.

Between Maggie and Grace sat Danielle, an elderly family friend who lived with Grace at the bed and breakfast Grace ran twenty kilometers from Aix. On the other side of Grace sat Maggie's husband Laurent. To her right sat Maggie's twelve-year-old daughter Mila.

And the reason for her disquiet.

"*Everybody* knows this play," Maggie whispered back to Grace. "It's *Shakespeare.*"

"Won't it lose something in translation?" Grace asked with a frown.

Grace might have a point there, Maggie thought. While it was all very impressive for Jemmy's summer school theater class to put on a Shakespeare play, if it wasn't performed in English the point of Shakespeare would be lost.

She glanced around the auditorium and saw the parents of most of the other actors in the play.

But performing it in Aix to a largely French audience did make one wonder how much pleasure anyone was going to get out of the production.

Maggie shrugged and gave Grace a smile, before turning to look at her husband.

Handsome with brown hair that he wore nearly to his shoulders and dark, unfathomable brown eyes, Laurent was a large man, unlike most Frenchmen, nearly six foot five. Seated in the normal-sized auditorium chairs, he looked uncomfortable and oversized. He was looking at his phone, something he rarely did.

But Maggie knew why he was doing it now and she wasn't happy about it.

Last year after dropping their older, adopted, son Luc off at his school in Napa Valley, California, Laurent had met an American vintner who'd impressed him with her knowledge of wines, vineyard management and harvesting techniques. In fact, she'd impressed him so much that when she ran into a problem of a personal nature and turned to Laurent for advice, he'd suggested she come to France to sort out her life.

Rochelle Lando was forty-five years old and in the middle of a contentious divorce. She'd lost her job as winery manager at the prestigious Napa winery under very mysterious circumstances and neither Rochelle nor Laurent were talking about it.

To be fair, Laurent rarely talked about anything and because he was French and tight-lipped anyway, Maggie knew he believed keeping Rochelle's secret was the least he could do for her.

If that was the only thing he was doing for her, Maggie wouldn't mind a bit. But she also knew he occasionally gave Rochelle rides, he helped her find temporary work, spoke to the US consulate citizen services in Marseille about her visa, and advised her on the phone at all hours of the day and night. When she first came to France last fall, she'd moved in with Maggie and Laurent before Laurent made arrangements for her to live at the nearby monastery where she now worked.

Maggie forced herself to focus on the heavy curtain draping the stage. She tried to imagine what Jemmy was doing backstage. Was he nervous? Excited? He'd spent the week rehearsing and Maggie had enjoyed how passionate he'd been in the process.

It's nice to have a hobby, she thought. Unfortunately, Laurent didn't feel the same.

She stole another look at him and saw his eyebrows were pulled together in a frown of either concentration or annoyance.

He had invited Rochelle to tonight's play and so far she hadn't shown up.

Mila kicked the seat in front of her and the elderly man who sat in it turned and glowered at her. For a moment, Maggie wasn't sure how Mila would respond. She'd been raised to be respectful of others, and certainly her elders, but Mila was going through a stage these days that seemed to erase any and everything she'd been taught up to now.

"*Pardon*," Mila muttered insincerely, crossing her arms and looking away from the man's glare which he now turned on Maggie—who was clearly the real culprit since she'd raised such an ill-behaved child.

Maggie smiled apologetically and was momentarily glad that Laurent was busy trying to locate Rochelle on his phone. If he'd caught what had just happened, the evening would have taken a bad turn. Laurent had much less patience for Mila's rudeness—especially to people outside the family. If he'd witnessed what Maggie just had, he would have frog-marched Mila to the family car where she'd spend the next two hours waiting for the play to be over.

Maggie took in a breath to try to settle her nerves and to remind herself that this was Jemmy's big night. Just the sight of him in his Puck costume before they all left for Aix this evening had given Maggie a deep seated pleasure that had eluded her all summer long.

Laurent cleared his throat and jammed his phone into his jacket pocket, elbowing both Maggie and Danielle on either side of him in the process. He crossed his arms which further shrank Maggie's available arm space.

It wasn't the cramped seating that bothered her so much as the crossed arms themselves. They seemed to signify a stubborn resistance to the entire point of the evening.

Laurent wasn't happy about Jemmy's interest in acting.

Maggie knew that Laurent was proud of his son but Jemmy had spent a good part of the summer enthusing over a possible career on stage and that had not gone over well. Laurent was old-school in a lot of ways—or perhaps that was just the Frenchman in him—but he would always expect Jemmy to make a career in something sensible and financially advantageous, if not actually take a role in the family business.

Maggie had tried to play down Jemmy's interest in the theater but Laurent wasn't listening.

Jemmy's argument to Laurent—one that had never had any chance of being listened to—was that with Luc off to college to learn all about vineyard management so that he would someday take over the family wine business, Jemmy should be able to take up a career of his choice.

Unfortunately Laurent didn't consider acting any kind of career.

The lights in the auditorium flickered and the audience began to react with sounds of agitation as the curtain shimmered in a preamble to being drawn up.

"It's starting!" Danielle said in an excited whisper.

As the curtain began to inch its way up Maggie caught movement out of the corner of her eye at the side entrance to the auditorium.

Rochelle paused briefly in the doorway and scanned the audience until she saw Laurent. Then her face broadened into a smile.

Rochelle was beautiful. There was no doubt about that. She was blonde and tall and tan from her life in California and from working outdoors in the south of France.

Maggie felt Laurent shift in his seat indicating that he too had seen Rochelle's entrance. The lights dimmed slowly and Maggie refocused her attention on the stage and the point of tonight.

Why do I let her get to me? Why does it matter if she's late or if she shows up at all?

Because it matters to Laurent.

As Maggie focused on the setting for the first scene of the play—one that she knew did not contain her son—she scolded herself for the pettiness of her bias against Rochelle.

It's just jealousy and I have nothing to worry about on that score.

She glanced at Laurent who now seemed to have relaxed

and settled into his seat, his eyes on the stage. She and Laurent had come a long way together. Even the story of how they'd met—one unfortunately rampant with lies and betrayal—had not served to separate them. If anything, it had only underscored their deep connection to each other.

Without looking at her, Laurent took Maggie's hand and gave it a squeeze. Public signs of affection were rare with Laurent unless of course under the veil of darkness in a theater. Maggie squeezed his hand back and felt her shoulders relax.

Tonight was about Jemmy. It was an evening of guaranteed enjoyment and Maggie wouldn't let needless worries or anxiety mar the promise of that.

She turned to see that even Mila had sat up straighter in her seat in anticipation of the show beginning. Just as Maggie gave herself up to the coming pleasure of the play, her husband's warm large hand in hers, a thought came to her out of nowhere.

Would I still dislike her if I didn't know she was trying to get my husband into her bed?

3

The bistro, situated north of *Cours Mirabeau*, in a tangle of streets known as *Vieil Aix*—the old section of Aix— had been chosen by Laurent for the après-show party. Maggie had encouraged his involvement since in every other way regarding the event he'd been relatively uninterested.

Maggie sat at the buffet table in the restaurant, the remnants of a paella before her. She smiled as she watched Jemmy, his eyes bright with pleasure and pride where he stood talking to a few of his friends who had also been in the play. He practically glowed.

The play had been funny and inspiring. All the actors had acquitted themselves beautifully—especially considering the words were in English and Shakespearean English at that.

Their little party sat around a long table with Jemmy at the head of it and his parents on either side of him. Ever since he was ten he'd been allowed diluted champagne or wine but tonight Maggie thought the flush in his cheeks had more to do with the joy of recognizing his own achievement.

Laurent was proud but restrained. Maggie watched him as

he interacted with the parents of the other children and occasionally spoke to Rochelle who sat beside him.

Danielle was seated next to Maggie.

"Our boy did well tonight," Danielle said.

"He did, didn't he?" Maggie said with a proud smile in the direction of her firstborn.

"I remember when you and Laurent brought him home from the hospital," Danielle said. "I had never seen a more alert baby! He was engaged from the very start."

"Mom, can we go now?" Mila said tapping her foot near where she slumped next to Danielle.

Maggie had caught her trying to drink from Danielle's wine glass earlier and felt a burgeoning frustration that the girl couldn't behave for one evening. If Laurent had seen her do it, she'd end up taking her next ten meals upstairs in her bedroom.

Come to think of it, Mila would probably prefer that, Maggie thought dispiritedly.

"Not yet," Maggie said calmly and then turned away from her daughter.

"The evening is young, *mon chou*," Danielle said to Mila with a fond smile. "And sometimes what we think we want is not easy to see."

Maggie was grateful Mila didn't roll her eyes at Danielle's comment. Maggie wouldn't be able to let that go and she didn't want to break up everyone's fun just yet to make a point to Mila.

Maggie caught Grace's eye from where Grace sat on the other side of Rochelle. After all their years as friends in a foreign land the two of them had developed a way of communicating that transcended language.

Grace arched an eyebrow at her and then turned to speak to Rochelle next to her.

"I haven't seen you in ages," Grace said in what Maggie

recognized as Grace's for-company-only voice. "I hear you're staying at the monastery these days. Good for you."

Rochelle smiled at Grace.

"That's right," she said. "Laurent got me a bed there and I'm really enjoying it."

"Must be quite a shock after life in California," Grace observed.

"I was ready for the change. I make my own bed, work in the garden, help grow my own food, and I find the people at the monastery actually closer to my kind of people."

Aside from the order of monks who worked at *l'Abbaye de Sainte-Trinité*, the people living there were refugees or transient workers who moved from vineyard to vineyard for work in the summer.

"Really," Grace said, her smile firmly in place.

"I know it's hard to believe," Rochelle said. "Sometimes it's even hard for *me* to believe I'm living this life."

"Was California really so terrible?" Grace asked lightly.

Rochelle and Grace were not friends and Maggie could see Rochelle struggle with how to answer Grace's question.

"No, not for the longest time," Rochelle said. "But I'm where I need to be now."

Laurent stood up, a glass of champagne in one hand and looked around as everyone reached for their glasses.

"To my son," he said, lifting the glass in Jemmy's direction. "Clearly he has a brilliant future in artful persuasion."

Everyone laughed, including Jemmy but Maggie could see Jemmy was looking for all the ways that Laurent's words might be interpreted.

Relax, dear boy, Maggie urged him silently, her heart hurting just a little for him.

Just enjoy your moment. There'll be plenty of time for self-analysis and dissection in the months and years to come.

4

It was well past midnight before Maggie and Laurent began the first moves to break up the party. Tomorrow was Saturday so the children could all sleep late but Rochelle had to be at work before dawn. In addition to work at the monastery, she was cutting lavender at an area farm while waiting to work the harvest at Maggie and Laurent's vineyard, Domaine St-Buvard.

Maggie knew Laurent had the utmost respect for Rochelle's knowledge as a vintner but she wondered why he didn't think it odd that Rochelle was cutting lavender and living in a refugee dormitory in a country where she didn't speak the language. There was more to Rochelle's story, of that Maggie was sure. In the three months that Rochelle lived with them at Domaine St-Buvard, she had been fastidiously neat, always friendly—if not overly so—and vigilantly aware of every word out of her mouth.

Three months was a long time to live with someone who wasn't family. Maggie recognized that she would've pushed Laurent to have her move out sooner if it hadn't been for the fact that Rochelle seemed to have a way with Mila.

Whether it was because Rochelle had raised a daughter of her own—now in her mid-twenties—or because she wasn't apt to take Mila's near-constant complaints and disrespect personally, there had been much less tension in the family with Rochelle in the house.

As Laurent went around the room of the restaurant to shake hands and say goodbye to the other parents of the actors in the play, Grace found her way over to where Maggie stood with Danielle. Mila was already standing at the door, an impatient frown on her face and her chin jutting out in a hard line.

"She can't even talk to anyone because she doesn't speak French," Grace said, nodding her head to indicate Rochelle. "How does she manage at the monastery? And what has she been *doing* the last seven months?"

"It's harder to learn a language when you're older," Maggie said, watching as Rochelle joined Milla at the door.

"It's especially hard if you don't even try," Grace said.

"I think it is because she enjoys having her own personal French translator," Danielle said and both Maggie and Grace looked at her in mild astonishment.

"That is the first catty thing I've ever heard you say!" Maggie said with a laugh.

"But it is true, is it not?" Danielle said. "It gives her a reason to keep him close."

"I'm not worried."

"Nor should you be, *chérie*," Danielle said. "Laurent only has eyes for you."

Maggie watched Laurent clap Jemmy on the shoulder and the boy's eyes lit up. Laurent leaned over and said a few words to him and Maggie watched Jemmy nod and then turn to say goodbye to his friends.

"He really was marvelous, darling," Grace said. "Are you sure Laurent won't let him go forward with the acting bug?"

"He's pretty adamant that he'd rather go back to bilking

tourists on the Côte d'Azur than see Jemmy take up acting as a profession," Maggie said.

Before Maggie met Laurent he had made his living for years as the original Dirty Rotten Scoundrel on the Riviera. It had been skill and a lot of luck on his part that this episode of his past life hadn't ended for him in a lengthy prison sentence.

Mila squealed with laughter and Maggie turned to see what on Earth could have prompted it. She couldn't remember the last time she'd heard Mila laugh.

"And so I told the manager, Madame Tootsie," Rochelle said, "*every old fart knows there are some smells even lavender can't camouflage.*"

"Oh, my gosh," Mila said. "Did you really? What did she say?"

"She very wisely pretended not to understand my English," Rochelle said with a laugh.

Mila threw back her head and laughed until she caught sight of Maggie and then the laugh died on her lips. Maggie had heard a little about the lavender farm manager, Annette Toussaint, who was indeed elderly and who probably hadn't understood Rochelle's insult.

"We'll be leaving soon," Maggie said to Mila who promptly rolled her eyes. As Maggie turned back to say goodbye to Danielle and Grace, she noticed that Laurent was standing near enough to have overheard Rochelle's little joke to Mila.

And Laurent wasn't laughing.

Laurent took some things very seriously and mocking the community's elders was one of them. Of course Rochelle couldn't know that, Maggie thought with a throb of pleasure for which she instantly felt guilty.

She turned back to Grace and Danielle. Because Danielle lived with Grace at the bed and breakfast, they had come to the play together.

"She'll need to watch herself," Grace said under her breath, "if she doesn't want to get on the wrong side of your husband."

"I'm sure she didn't mean anything by it," Maggie said, internally wincing at her own ungenerous thoughts just seconds earlier.

Danielle leaned over and hugged Maggie.

"It was a lovely night, *chérie*," she said. "Send Jemmy and Mila to *Dormir* tomorrow afternoon. I am making *gougères* and I know how Mila loves to make them."

"Sure, okay," Maggie said, wondering if Mila still loved making *gougères* these days.

After kissing both Danielle and Grace goodnight, Maggie went to wait with Mila and Rochelle by the door for Laurent and Jemmy to finish their socializing.

It wasn't until Maggie was standing next to Rochelle that she realized that the woman must have come straight from working in the lavender field. Her jeans were not clean and the jacket she wore was missing a button.

Fighting her initial impression which was the belief that to not bother dressing for the occasion showed a basic lack of respect for her and for Laurent, Maggie smiled pleasantly at Rochelle. She reminded herself that she really didn't know that much about Rochelle.

She didn't know what Rochelle had gone through or what she was still going through. It was highly possible that Rochelle hadn't meant anything by her lack of proper dress.

Maybe, Maggie thought, like so many people in reduced circumstances, she was just trying to do the best she could.

Still, she could've at least scraped the mud off her shoes.

5

Laurent glowered at the pan of sizzling bacon on the La Cornue stove before him. He once swore that he'd never spend more for a stove than he did for an economy car but he'd not regretted it a day since he'd done it.

The kitchen itself was painted a pale ochre yellow. The wide window over the sink was as old as the house and had a deep stone sill big enough for a decent sized *potager* if he'd a mind to put one there. His *potager* was through the dining room and off the back terrace in the garden.

The window brought the Mediterranean sun into the room and altered the color of the walls depending on the time of day and season. Another feature of the window was the fact that it faced the front driveway. Laurent was able to see any vehicle coming down the length of their drive long before it arrived.

"I don't want anything savory for breakfast," Mila said, her voice screeching across Laurent's up-to-now placid countenance like carpenter's nails raking over slate.

"You're having what I make," Laurent said, not glancing at his daughter. He knew she was wearing something that would set his teeth on edge. But since she wasn't leaving the house he tried to remind himself that it didn't matter what she was wearing. She might as well still be in her nightgown.

"I love bacon," Jemmy said from where he was reading a book at the counter.

Laurent knew Jemmy was trying to soften him up to lob another appeal in his direction. It was not subtle but Laurent reminded himself that Jemmy was young.

When you're young and want something, you forget about strategy.

Laurent had never had that luxury as a child.

"You're only saying that because you want something from him," Mila said to her brother. "You're pathetic."

"Go to your room," Laurent said, without turning around. He hadn't meant to say it, it had just escaped. In some ways it was in lieu of throwing his spatula across the room. Even so, it was a loss of control that bothered him.

And of course he couldn't take it back now.

"But I'm hungry!" Mila said, her voice rising in a shriller whine.

It was astonishing to Laurent that Mila could behave like this. Not six months ago, she was eager to please and help out around the house. It was like some demon had slipped into the *mas* when they were all asleep and stolen his sweet, docile daughter and left this *monstre* in her place.

A ripple of guilt at his thoughts sifted through him. He turned to attend to the eggs in a separate pan on the stove, forcing himself not to respond to her. He knew she would escalate the argument regardless of what he did or said. Any response, no response, it made no difference.

"You have to feed me! It's the law!"

"What's all the yelling down there?" Maggie called from upstairs.

Laurent appreciated what Maggie was trying to do but no amount of distraction was going to defuse this situation. Mila was determined to have her tantrum and they were powerless to prevent it.

"Dad won't let me have breakfast!" Mila shouted. "He's being mean!"

Should I count to ten? Should I leave?

But leaving would give her the result she wanted.

And since when did I worry about not giving my precious girl what she wanted?

Since she turned into a monster who only wants to throw the family into chaos.

Carefully Laurent plated up the eggs, added two pieces of buttered toast and three strips of bacon to the plate. He set the plate down in front of Jemmy who hurriedly moved his book out of the way.

"I'm serious!" Mila said, now close to tears. "I can call social services on you!"

Laurent had actually faltered in his resolve to withhold her breakfast when he heard the tears in her voice until she threatened him. He broke a piece of toast in half and tossed a half each to the two big hunting dogs watching his every move from the dining room.

They'd recently acquired a scruffy little stray—something Mila had found in the village and begged to be allowed to keep before promptly losing interest in the animal. Laurent called the little dog to him to give her a smaller piece of toast. Otherwise the bigger dogs would never let her have it.

"I'm telling!" Mila said, her bottom lip sticking out in a pout but her eyes dry.

"Who are you telling?" Maggie said coming into the kitchen. "Mm-mm! That smells good." She kissed Mila, who jerked her face away in annoyance, and then she kissed Jemmy on the head.

Laurent frowned when he saw Maggie but not because he didn't like what he saw. She was wearing a form-fitting knit dress. He could see she'd put on makeup too.

"Where are you going today?" he asked. He was sure she'd told him but now that he saw how deliberately dressed she was, he felt a characteristic protective stirring.

"I've got a meeting with the Women's Guild in Arles," she said. "I told you."

"This is really good, Dad," Jemmy said in between mouthfuls.

Laurent turned to pour Maggie a cup of coffee from the French press on the counter.

"Will you eat?" he asked.

"A piece of that toast," Maggie said. "They'll probably force me to eat a six-course lunch and I'll never get through it all if I have breakfast."

"You don't have to eat every bite of it," he said as he handed her the coffee cup.

"You're talking to an American," Maggie said. "I eat the way I eat."

"Is nobody listening to me?" Mila said loudly. "I'm starving!"

"I thought I told you to go to your room," Laurent said, finally looking at his daughter. Sure enough she was wearing a crop top and hip huggers on her young prepubescent body.

Maggie walked into the kitchen to look at something on the refrigerator, signaling her unwillingness to jump into the fray with Laurent. He couldn't blame her.

He gave Mila his coldest most intractable look and she threw her napkin on the counter.

"I hate you!" she said, jumping down from her chair and running upstairs, her long ponytail swinging behind her.

It should have felt better with her gone, the tension dissipated, the threat neutralized, but Laurent didn't feel better. He felt angry and helpless and confused.

Maggie turned from the fridge, not bothering to ask what that had all been about.

What was it ever about?

"Dad?" Jemmy said, chewing on a piece of bacon.

Laurent grunted and went to put the frying pan in the sink to wash.

"I was just wondering if you'd had time to think about that theater school I was telling you about yesterday."

Laurent didn't respond. He turned on the water in the sink.

"Dad?" Jemmy pressed. "Madame LeBé thinks I can get a scholarship if it's about the money."

Laurent turned around.

"Did Madame LeBé suggest you might need a financial scholarship?"

Jemmy fidgeted and dropped his gaze to his plate.

"No, but she thought in case that was, you know, the reason why I couldn't go..."

"It's not the reason," Laurent said, aware that Maggie was listening to every word and frowning. "Are you finished with your breakfast?"

Jemmy dropped the bacon piece on his plate. His face red, all pretense at artifice gone.

"I guess," he said glumly.

"Then take a rake to the front drive. And let the dogs out."

Jemmy got up from the counter, his shoulders slumped in defeat. Laurent saw his son try to catch Maggie's eye which irritated him.

As soon as Jemmy had left the room, Maggie started in.

"Laurent," she said reasonably, "I'm not saying let him go but what harm would it be to hear about the program?"

He looked at her, his eyes half-lidded and baleful. He whipped the dishtowel he normally wore over one shoulder off and onto the counter and turned to push past her out of the kitchen.

"I have a busy day today," he said over his shoulder. "You will have to handle dinner alone tonight."

He grabbed his car keys and strode out the front door.

6

Maggie looked at the kitchen of dirty dishes and then turned to see the back of Laurent's Peugeot as it disappeared down the front drive.

Well, this is new, she thought.

Laurent was normally fastidious about his kitchen. Every pot and utensil in its place, every crumb wiped away, the stove gleaming. Not only had he *not* washed up after breakfast today but he hadn't kissed her goodbye either. Nor had he bothered to roll his eyes in an attempt to commiserate with her over the kids and their less than stellar behavior this morning.

She put on an apron and moved to the sink to fill it with sudsy water.

Not that she could blame him. Mila had been in rare form and Jemmy really should learn to pick his moments better.

She knew Laurent was nearly at his limit with Mila and his leaving the field of combat was likely the best thing to do given the circumstances.

Maggie washed up the two pans and Jemmy's plate before wiping down the counter of toast crumbs. The little dog, Fleur, appeared from the dining room where she had obviously evaded Jemmy's corralling of the other two dogs.

Maggie smiled at the animal, who was very sweet. *Not as smart as Petit Four,* she thought, *and not as connected to me.* Petit Four had been Maggie's personal *petite amie* for ten wonderful years.

Maggie broke off a piece of toast and the animal took it gingerly from her fingers.

They say if you're lucky you get one really good dog in your life.

She ran her fingers through Fleur's fur. This one might not be at Petit Four's level, but she was a good family dog, eager to love and to please.

You can't ask for too much more from a dog, Maggie thought. She glanced at the kitchen clock and saw she had a few minutes before she had to leave for her meeting in town.

Maggie wrote an expat blog of her life in Provence that had become popular with other expats in France and with over ten thousand Francophiles in the US and the UK. She'd been able to monetize the blog when she added ads for local artisans and specialty farmers in Arles and Marseille. Normally, the blog posts wrote themselves when describing the delights of living in the South of France.

But there had been lean years when the newsletter had done little to move the needle on local artisan product sales. And of course rather than blame the economy or the weather or a national downturn in tourism, the vendors blamed Maggie's newsletter.

Her meeting this morning was in Arles with Cosette Villeneuve, president of the Women's Guild, to discuss a promotion Maggie was spearheading for the upcoming olive festival in the village of Mouriès.

Maggie had worked closely with these ladies in the past and since she'd begun reaching out to them in person—unheard of in the world of social media and electronic relationships—her stock had begun to inch back up with the small villages and craftspeople in the area which of course was essential if she was going to continue to try to make money off of her newsletter.

She would need to leave Jemmy and Mila alone for the morning—not an unusual occurrence but one, given Mila's recent behavior issues, Maggie didn't feel entirely comfortable with. The girl reminded her these days of Grace's older daughter, Taylor. Instantly Maggie regretted the comparison.

Taylor had been a problem ever since her toddler years. Today she was in and out of drug rehab clinics and estranged from both her parents.

No, Mila wasn't in Taylor's league, thank God. Mila was a pain in the butt teenager going through a difficult rebellious stage like so many teens did. It was just hard to bear since she'd been literally an angel of a child up until now.

Maggie heard her phone ring from inside her purse which was hanging on the back of one of the kitchen barstools. She hurried to dig it out and saw that Grace was calling.

"Hey," Maggie said. "What time did you guys get home last night?"

Dormir wasn't far from Domaine St-Buvard but it was a good twenty mile drive from Aix—most of it over winding, rural roads.

Plus, at the last minute, Laurent had informed Maggie that he'd agreed to drive Rochelle back to the monastery, leaving Maggie and the kids to grab a ride home with Grace and Danielle.

That was not an unusual occurrence, Maggie had noted in her attempt to quell her irritation, but it was still an imposition.

"A little before one," Grace said. "No problems although Danielle slept the rest of the drive home."

"I can't tell you how grateful I was that you both came," Maggie said. "It made a big difference to Jemmy to have his own support section in the audience."

"Of course, darling! We couldn't have Jemmy make his big stage debut without us. Is he still basking in his triumph this morning?"

"Moderately," Maggie said as she seated herself on one of the barstools and pulled her coffee toward her. "He made the mistake of trying to talk Laurent into letting him go to some drama school in Avignon and that pretty much put the kibosh on his 'basking.'"

"Why is Laurent so dead set against it?"

"I don't know," Maggie said with a sigh. "A male thing, maybe? A French thing?"

"I would've thought with Luc all set to take over the reins at Domaine St-Buvard that Laurent would let Jemmy do his own thing."

"Yes, well, Luc is still years away from that," Maggie reminded her. "Plus he's out there in California and anything could happen. He could decide he prefers living in the States."

"God forbid. So Jemmy is Laurent's spare to his heir?"

"Something like that."

"Could you believe that getup that Rochelle was wearing last night? Does she not own any proper clothes anymore?"

Maggie bit her tongue. While she too had noted Rochelle's lack of care in her attire last night, she was working hard to cut the woman some slack.

"Danielle said she heard from Madame Bledet that Rochelle was seen at the local *pharmarcie* last week and burst into tears," Grace said. "Honestly, if she would just make the effort to learn the language it would probably help."

"She *cried*?" Maggie said, feeling a flinch of guilt at the image forming in her head.

"That's what Madame Bledet said. What is her deal?"

"I don't know. Laurent says she's not handling the divorce well," Maggie said.

"He told you that?" Grace said, her voice revealing her surprise.

"Well, not in so many words," Maggie admitted.

The fact was Laurent had very determinedly *not* said much of anything about Rochelle or what she was going through or what her life had been like back in California. When Maggie asked what the status of Rochelle's divorce proceedings were Laurent had merely grunted and said, "Ongoing."

To Maggie, "ongoing" meant roadblocks, costly lawyers, and emotional quagmires. With Rochelle's children well beyond custodial age it was hard to imagine what Rochelle and her husband were finding to argue over except money.

That age-old one-size-fits-all bedrock to every problem since time began.

"Why is Laurent so determined to help her?" Grace asked. "Why did he even encourage her to come to France? It makes no sense."

"I think he reminds her of someone he once knew," Maggie said.

This was just a guess on Maggie's part because again Laurent was not at all forthcoming about his reasons.

"Well, it's all very fishy," Grace said. "No! Philippe! Put that down!"

Maggie waited while Grace dealt with whatever was happening on her end with her five-year-old grandson. When Grace came back on the line, Maggie said, "How's he doing, your young man?"

Philippe was Taylor's child and was left with Grace when he was two years old.

"I cannot remember either Zouzou or Taylor having this much energy," Grace said. "Maybe it's just a boy thing? Was Jemmy like this?"

"Boys are different," Maggie said with a laugh. "But he's

such a sweet-tempered little fellow. Speaking of Zouzou, how's she doing in Paris?"

Zouzou had moved to Paris for the summer to take a pastry course with a group of students and a chaperone.

"Absolutely over the moon about Paris and her class and every French boy she sees," Grace said. "I can't wait for her to come back but I'm not sure how I'm going to keep her happy after this summer."

"Zouzou's got a good head on her shoulders," Maggie said. "She'll settle into the routine when she gets back."

The sound of the two big dogs barking from the back yard made Maggie slide off her barstool and walk to the French doors that led to the terrace. Jemmy must have let them out and forgotten about them, she thought as she opened the door to let them in.

Instantly little Fleur ran to them and began jumping around their knees until the older dog Buddy snarled at her.

"What's Mila done with her summer?" Grace asked as Maggie returned to the kitchen, one eye on the clock. She'd need to leave for her meeting in another few minutes.

"Pretty much been a pain in the butt to all and sundry," Maggie said. "She's decided she wants to be a fashion model."

"What a cherub!" Grace said with a laugh. "What is she, four foot two?"

"I know. She takes after me," Maggie said referring to her short stature. "And trust me I'm blamed for that on a daily basis. Still, she believes she'll shoot up."

"You have to give her credit," Grace said. "She's not giving up."

"Well, I wish she would," Maggie said. "Between her bad temper and Laurent's short fuse, it's been like a war zone around here. Let's just say Jemmy isn't the only one who wouldn't mind a sabbatical."

"Well, they'll sort it out," Grace said. "Remember how

Laurent helped Zouzou that time when she was being such a pill?"

"I do," Maggie said. "But in some ways I think it's harder when it's your own. You feel angrier about their insubordination than with someone else's kid."

The sound of something breaking upstairs was followed immediately by the distant yelp of pain from little Fleur.

"I need to go, Grace," Maggie said as she strode for the stairs. "Something's happening upstairs."

"Go on, darling. We'll see you all for Sunday lunch?"

"Affirmative. See you then."

Maggie disconnected and ran up the stairs to see what in the world had happened, knowing without a shadow of a doubt that it had to do with Mila.

7

As Laurent drove to the monastery *Abbaye de Sainte-Trinité* he passed the string of four mini-cottages he'd built to help house the refugee families staying at the monastery. Mila used to say the tiny houses looked like playhouses. She once begged to have one for her own.

Where did that girl go?

As soon as he passed through the village of Ponte l'Abbe he saw the tall church spire on the horizon which heralded his approach to the twelfth-century Cistercian monastery.

The monastery was maintained today by a dozen or so Benedictine monks with the capability for making wine and storing wine, but there was no longer any adjoining land to plant vines. Today the monastery was dedicated to caring for the streams of homeless and refugees that appeared on its doorstep with numbing regularity.

The winding drive from the village led straight to the front door of the main building—a sprawling stone structure complete with stone turrets that was visible for miles. A stone curtain wall enclosed the monastery on two sides.

As Laurent parked in the gravel lot in front, he thought of Rochelle. The woman had been through so much and yet continued to work harder and more relentlessly than any woman he'd ever met.

Perhaps that is an American trait?

Maggie was very tenacious too.

He strode through the towering medieval gates of the monastery's entrance—a gigantic structure that loomed easily ten feet over Laurent's head. It didn't take much imagination to believe that behind those doors was a microcosm of peace and serenity untouched by the outside world when actually it was almost literally bedlam.

Unlike some orders which focus on contemplation, the *Abbaye de Sainte-Trinité* sought to balance a life of prayer and contemplation with focus on hospitality and service to refugees. It headed by Frère Jean who always insisted that, regardless of the noise and chaos these guests could sometimes create, *Abbaye de Sainte-Trinité* was a place of spirituality, liturgical prayer and community life.

A small stone chapel sat next to an even older arrangement of low-roofed buildings once used as stables. Beyond that were the monastery's gardens.

Laurent had been working at the monastery with *Frère* Jean for over three years now to find work and housing for the area's transient workers and refugees. While the monk, a small balding man with a hunched back and a ready smile had had some problems in the past which led to him temporarily leaving the monastery, but later returned to his role as abbot, the head of the monastery.

Laurent would need a dozen people to work his harvest this year. Afterwards, most of them would move on after they'd been paid. Laurent continued walking to the main building which appeared to have been built several centuries after the rest of the monastery. This building contained the expansive dining hall and dormitories.

Once inside the building, the hall opened up into a communal area featuring a high-arched ceiling of rock over slate floors and stone walls with tall narrow windows through which streamed several shafts of the fierce summer sun. Children ran laughing across the stone floor throwing balls.

Immediately he saw Rochelle sitting alone at a table reading a book. She was wearing a used and ill-fitting jumpsuit which did nothing to hide her remarkable figure, slim hips and full breasts.

Laurent moved toward her and she turned to him, her face opening in a smile of pleasure at the sight of him.

"Laurent!" she said, hurrying over to kiss him on both cheeks, her hand resting against his broad chest. "I didn't expect you so soon."

Rochelle grabbed his sleeve and tugged him to one of the dining tables. It was at least an hour past breakfast and aside from Rochelle and her friend, there was no one in the dining hall.

"Congratulations again on Jemmy's performance last night," Rochelle said as she seated herself across from him, her eyes bright with happiness as she regarded him. "You must have been so proud."

"As any parent might be," he said, seating himself. He was here to talk with Frère Jean about the people he'd choose for this year's harvest. Laurent intended to make Rochelle his overseer on the job and was looking forward to having someone on the harvest with him this year who knew what they were doing.

"My kids were never into any kind of performance art," Rochelle said, almost wistfully. "Theo was all about the books. No sports or anything else. And Rachel was just too shy. She got that from Dave."

She made a face when she referenced her husband and Laurent tried to determine if it meant she wanted to talk about him or preferred not to. He wasn't as good at these guessing games as Maggie was but he could see the value in attempting to play them.

"Have you heard from his lawyer?" he asked.

"Not recently," she said. "Thank God. You know I never realized until after I'd had two children by him and lived with him for twenty-five years how incredibly selfish he is. He wants it all, you know."

Laurent did know. Rochelle had shared earlier the fact that the main hold up with the divorce had to do with the fact that Rochelle's husband did not want to share assets with his wife. They had married and lived in Alabama for their entire marriage before Rochelle had moved to California to pursue her career as a vintner.

The two of them had owned a small vineyard near Anniston, Alabama, which Rochelle's husband had sold without consulting her. That was three years ago and unlike California their assets in Alabama were not considered jointly owned.

There was every possibility that Rochelle would leave the marriage with nothing.

"But how are you, *chérie*?"

The endearment had just slipped out, something Laurent would never normally have let happen. To his discomfort, Rochelle's eyes filled with tears.

"Thank you, darling Laurent, for asking," she said reaching for his hand. "Not good, frankly. Although the work here at the monastery and the lavender field is just what I need right now. I have no time for obsessing over what I should or shouldn't be doing. And I know I have you to thank for that."

Laurent leaned away and debated easing his hand out of Rochelle's grip but decided he was making too much of it. The woman was distraught, she didn't speak the language and had virtually no friends in the country except for himself. She was just looking for a little harmless comfort.

"There is a beginner's language class in Aix," he said, patting her hand that gripped his. "It will make things much easier if you speak some French."

She shifted in her seat and Laurent pulled his hand free.

"But how am I going to get there?" she asked. "I don't have a car."

"I will take you. It is in the morning and I can go to the Aix produce market while you are at class."

"What about my work at the lavender field?" Rochelle said.

"Surely the lavender is harvested by now?"

"Just the handpicked plants for potpourri and food seasoning," she said, glancing down at her hand now alone in her lap. "Madame Toussaint will need somebody to follow behind the tractor to gather up what the harvester cuts."

Laurent frowned. "*La Lavandin* must have several workers besides you."

"Yes, of course but even if I'm not the one walking behind the tractor, there's all the sorting and stripping in the distillation facility. Madame Toussaint made it very clear that I'm needed until the middle of the month at which time I'll be working on your harvest, right?"

"*Bon*," Laurent said, standing up. "Then you will start classes at the end of the month. The Domaine St-Buvard harvest won't take four days. Then you must think of what your next steps will be."

"I know," Rochelle said, standing up too and moving closer to him. "I've been thinking of that."

Suddenly the door to the dining hall swung open and Laurent and Rochelle both turned to see Frère Luis, a tall young monk who was new to the monastery, hurrying inside.

Laurent had expected to meet with Frère Jean about his pickers and he frowned at seeing Luis instead.

"Monsieur Dernier?" Frère Luis said breathlessly. Before he had a chance to say more, three uniformed policemen stepped into the dining hall behind the monk. They marched purposefully toward Laurent and stopped in front of him. One of the police seemed to take in a covert breath at the size of Laurent.

"What is the meaning of this?" Laurent said, folding his arms across his chest.

"I will ask the questions," a woman's deep voice said from behind the policemen.

A stout woman, who was not wearing makeup and whose long dark blonde hair was tied back in a single ponytail, strode in behind the men.

Laurent knew that Margaux LaBelle had taken over the duties of Detective *Capitaine* Roger Bedard in Aix. It was unusual to see a woman at such a high rank. She was clearly eager to show she was worthy of the honor.

"Madame Rochelle Lando?" LaBelle said.

Laurent moved to stand between the two women.

"What do you want with her?" he asked.

LaBelle directed her icy blue laser gaze on Laurent but she blushed at the confrontation. He was easily a foot taller.

"Interfere with my investigation," she said tightly, "and you may end up defending her honor from a jail cell."

She sidestepped Laurent to confront Rochelle.

"You are Rochelle Lando?" she said loudly.

"I...I am," Rochelle said, the tremor evident in her voice.

Without looking behind her LaBelle snapped her fingers over her shoulder, and the two policemen lunged forward to grab Rochelle who squeaked helplessly as they turned her around and cuffed her.

Laurent forced himself to stay calm. He knew very well that interfering with a detective who had something to prove could go very quickly sideways.

"There has been a mistake," he said between gritted teeth. "You are making a mistake."

"Be careful that *you* don't make one, Monsieur," Labelle said in a threatening tone before turning to Rochelle where she stood between the two policemen, her bottom lip visibly trembling, her elbows pressed tightly to her sides.

"Rochelle Lando," LaBelle said, "I am arresting you for the murder of Chantal Lambert."

8

Maggie's mind whirled like a maelstrom as she drove down the highway. Anxiety trumped confusion and then gave way to bewilderment. She'd received the phone call from Laurent in the middle of her lunch with the guild ladies at which point she'd immediately given her apologies and left the restaurant to drive to Aix.

She still didn't know the specifics of what had happened. All Laurent would say was that Rochelle had been arrested and Maggie needed to come to the police station in downtown Aix.

What had Rochelle done? Had she graduated from crying in public retail establishments to shoplifting? And why couldn't Laurent handle it on his own?

Maggie glanced at her dashboard where her phone was vibrating and she picked it up to see Danielle's picture on the screen.

"Hey, Danielle," she said, answering the phone. "What's up?"

"*Chérie*, I have heard that Rochelle has been arrested," Danielle said.

"Wow. Way to work the grapevine," Maggie said. "I'm on my

way to Aix now where she's being held. Do you know why she was arrested?"

"Just gossip," Danielle said but from the tenor of her voice it was clear she wanted to tell Maggie anyway.

"Well, that's more than I have," Maggie said as she saw the exit for Aix coming up. "Fill me in."

"I heard this from Madame LeDonc who plays Piquet with Madame Manoff," Danielle said.

"Okay," Maggie said.

"And Madame Manoff heard it from the woman who does her cleaning who lives at the monastery."

"Rochelle was arrested at the monastery?"

"*Oui*. Not two hours ago. That dreadful new woman detective arrested her."

Maggie had had a lengthy and unpleasant run-in with the new detective the year before. Margaux LaBelle was a tough, hard-nosed policewoman who was even less interested than most cops in hearing what she had to say.

"Okay," Maggie said again, exiting the ramp toward the heart of Aix. "So what's the charge?"

"Oh, *chérie*, they say it is murder!" Danielle said.

At first Maggie didn't think she heard her correctly.

"Are you serious?"

"They say Madame Rochelle murdered a child who was living at the lavender farm," Danielle said.

This was becoming increasingly more bizarre and unbelievable. Rochelle was accused of murdering a child?

"How come we didn't hear of this?" Maggie asked. "I never heard anything about a child being killed!"

"No, nor any of us," Danielle said. "*C'est horrible, non?*"

"You could say that," Maggie said, as she tried to make sense of what she was hearing.

The cops have evidence that Rochelle killed a child? Was this really possible?

"Danielle, I need to go," Maggie said. "I'm about to pull into the police station parking lot. I'll let you know what I find out."

"*Faites attention, chérie,*" Danielle said before hanging up. *Be careful.*

~

Maggie walked into the waiting room of the Aix police station and instantly saw her husband in conference with Detective Margaux LaBelle.

Laurent was looming over the detective, his hands on his hips. Maggie had to hand it to the detective. A lesser person would have been intimidated by Laurent's physicality and size. But LaBelle stood squarely in front of Laurent, her body language confident and even combative. She wore dark form-hugging slacks and a short-waisted leather jacket even in August.

Maggie hurried over to them and Laurent turned to her.

"What's happened?" Maggie said. "Where's Rochelle?"

"As I was telling your husband," LaBelle said stiffly, giving Maggie a look of cold disdain, "Rochelle Lando will not have even the possibility of bail until at least the end of the week and I wouldn't count on it then."

"What is she being charged with?" Maggie asked, her eyes going from Laurent's face to LaBelle's.

"A woman was killed last night at La Lavandin," Laurent said quietly.

"A woman?" Maggie said. "Not a child?"

LaBelle turned to her. "Who told you the victim was a child?"

"Just something I heard." Maggie said. "Why do you think Rochelle is involved? She was with us last night."

"Apparently it happened earlier in the evening," Laurent said, his face solemn and tense.

Maggie turned to LaBelle. "So you think Rochelle Lando killed this woman and then went to a production of *Midsummer Night's Dream*?"

LaBelle flushed angrily.

"I don't care if she went to her own wedding after killing the girl," LaBelle said, heatedly. "I'm only interested in the facts."

"And you think you have those?" Maggie asked.

"Clearly I do if I arrested her."

"Where was the woman killed?"

"We are done here," LaBelle said, turning away from Maggie to continue her conversation with Laurent. "I will let you know if bail is a possibility but I would doubt it."

Then she turned on her heel and walked out of the waiting room into the hallway that Maggie knew led to the detectives' offices and conference rooms.

Maggie turned to Laurent. "Do you know anything about the victim?"

"*Non.* I never met her."

"But she lived at the lavender farm outside of La Barben?"

Laurent shook his head.

"I do not know, *chérie*. Only that she worked there."

"Why did they arrest Rochelle? Does she have a lawyer?"

Laurent jerked his head in the direction of the door to indicate they should leave and continue their conversation outside.

"The courts will assign her legal counsel," he said.

The courtyard outside the station branched off to a cobblestone street with cars parked on both sides, but very little pedestrian activity. The afternoon sun was pounding down on the normally hardy geraniums stuffed into oversized planters that punctuated the walkway every twenty feet.

"This is terrible," Maggie said as she stood on the sidewalk. She'd raced down here the second Laurent called but there was really nothing she could do.

What had Laurent hoped she could do?

"I'll get on the phone and see who they've assigned to her," she said.

"We must help her, *chérie*."

Maggie looked at him to try to interpret his expression, difficult during even the most obvious of cases, which this certainly was not.

"Of course, if we can," she said carefully.

"Rochelle is all alone, Maggie. She needs our help."

Maggie bit her tongue. While it was true she'd never particularly liked Rochelle, even she had difficulty imagining the woman could have committed murder.

"Did LaBelle tell you *why* they arrested her for this murder?" she asked. "I can't imagine her DNA is on any international database. How did they know to come for her?"

"Detective LaBelle said Rochelle was overheard saying that Chantal—the victim—had better watch her back."

"That's it?" Maggie snorted. "That's nothing."

"Detective LaBelle does not appear to believe it is nothing," Laurent said, rolling his shoulders in an uncharacteristic expression of unease.

"So Rochelle knew the victim through her work at the lavender farm?" Maggie asked.

"Presumably."

Maggie watched Laurent's face for a moment. The sky was a painful stark blue and she blinked into its glare as she studied his face.

"I'm sorry, Laurent," she said. "This is the last thing you need to be worrying about right now. You've got the harvest coming up."

"I'll talk to her lawyer tomorrow," she said. "If it's a matter of money—"

Laurent stopped walking and put a hand on Maggie's arm, pulling her around to face him. "We must help her, *Maggie*," he said, his eyes probing hers.

He rarely called her by her first name. And Maggie didn't like him doing it now.

She pursed her lips together.

"Look, Laurent, we don't even know that she didn't do it!"

Laurent dropped his hand from her arm.

"Plus both Jemmy and Mila are currently needing the max from both of us. You know that. You don't have time to deal with this. Not to mention the fact that LaBelle will *not* welcome interference from either of us."

He held her gaze for a moment before turning away.

"Laurent?" Maggie said, pulling at his sleeve. "You see that, right? We don't have all the facts and this is not the time for either of us...especially you...to get involved in this. We need to let LaBelle handle it."

"LaBelle," he said, his lip curling. "You know she only wants to close her case."

"I'm just saying that Detective LaBelle clearly has evidence which led her to arrest Rochelle in the first place. We don't know anything about the case."

"Where did you park?" Laurent scanned the parking lot for her car.

"Laurent, don't be like that," Maggie said. "I'll call the public defenders' office when I get home and see who is assigned to her. We won't abandon her."

"*Non*, we won't," he said. "Because I promised her we would prove her innocence."

9

Laurent walked Maggie to her car before they went their separate ways—Laurent to the monastery to talk to anyone who might know what happened and Maggie to *Dormir* to see Grace.

How could he even be thinking of getting involved in this? With everything that's happening in our family?

"I can't believe you made that promise to her," she said as he stood by her car, jiggling his car keys in his pocket. "But if you did promise her then you need to let *me* handle it."

Laurent raised an eyebrow at her in response and she tried to ignore his unspoken rebuke. She knew she needed to try harder not to be biased against Rochelle—or resent Laurent's feelings for her, whatever they were.

"I'm the one who has more experience working with the police," Maggie said, opening her car door. "Let me dig around and see what I can find out."

Laurent nodded and then leaned over and kissed her, surprising her.

"*Bon*," he said. "Very good. You will be careful, yes?" he said, patting her hand as she climbed into the driver's seat of her car.

"Of course," she said as he turned to head off to his own car.

But as she watched him go, his tall straight back moving away from her, she couldn't help but think that any other time with any other situation he'd have thrown a fit about her involving herself in yet another murder case.

But this time it's just "be careful."

Maggie was less than two kilometers from *Dormir* when she turned off the D7N. Once off the highway, it was a beautiful drive to Danielle and Eduard Marceau's old country *mas*. It had been transformed into *Dormir*, the modern bed and breakfast owned by Laurent and run by Grace these last four years.

The house had once been a *mas* rising majestically amid a sprawling vineyard. Home to five generations of *vignerons* who now are only remembered by a few villagers in St-Buvard.

After the last world war the owner of the house never returned from the German prisoner of war camp where he'd spent the war. His wife and two children moved to Paris and eventually sold the house to Danielle and her first husband Eduard Marceau.

Eduard had had plans to create an expansion of the vineyard surrounding his new house by purchasing the two large tracts of vineyard that abutted his property. One was owned by Jean-Luc Alexandre, an elderly bachelor, and the other was owned at the time by a recent transplant, Laurent Dernier and his American wife.

When Eduard died his land passed to Danielle who had by then married Jean-Luc, Danielle sold both the house and land to Laurent who added the vineyards to his own fields and renovated the house by updating the plumping, adding a new kitchen and installing a large garden under the plane trees.

He'd then presented the property to Grace to manage as a bed and breakfast. Newly divorced at the time, Grace saw the gesture as her last chance to get her life together after a series of nearly catastrophic life choices.

Dormir was born.

Maggie pulled into the gravel drive in front of the main house and parked. She'd called Grace to let her know she was coming and was now just hanging up from the Aix public defenders' office where she'd discovered the identity of the attorney who would defend Rochelle.

She felt a sense of heaviness in her limbs after her conversation with the law office.

"Yoo hoo, darling!" Grace called from the front door where she stood holding her grandson, Philippe. "Danielle's just pulled fresh *canelés* from the oven. We're in the garden."

Maggie grinned, feeling better already, and waved to the two of them before gathering up her purse and getting out of the car. She could smell the overripe scent of fallen apples from the two ancient trees in the southern corner of the flower garden. Laurent and Danielle had set out the bones of the garden of *Dormir* with a stronger emphasis on flowers than vegetables.

From where she sat in the garden, Maggie was looking at a wide swath of lavender and rosemary, both aromas competing for dominance in the hot summer air.

Grace leaned back into a wicker lounge chair, a teacup before her on the terrace and the plate of *canelés*. Behind her the au pair Adele ran across the lawn with little Philippe shrieking with joy as he chased her. Maggie remembered when Mila was that age.

Philippe was of mixed race although Grace's daughter Taylor had been very tight-lipped as to who the father was. Whoever he was, Maggie knew he was out of Taylor's life and had never shown any interest in Philippe.

She looked at the garden where the hammock swayed gently in the summer breeze. Aside from Phillipe's laughter, the scene was so peaceful that it was hard to believe anyone else lived here.

"I thought you'd be going crazy about now," Maggie said. "Didn't you say you were totally slammed?"

"I am, darling," Grace said. "And the guests are *relentless*. Especially the Germans. They're such a fastidious people. *More ice, more butter, why is there no air conditioning? The swimming pool is too cold.*"

"Where are they today?"

"They're all out looking at lavender and sunflower fields, thank God."

"Aren't most of the lavender fields picked? There can't be much to see."

"Yes, well, I told them when they booked that June or July would be a much more optimum viewing time, but God forbid the flower harvests should interfere with their vacation schedules. Besides, I think there's a few lavender bushes left to look at, aren't there? I thought I saw some driving over toward the Luberon."

Maggie waved to Danielle who she spotted coming out of the house to join them. The older woman wore a sleeveless shift. Her hair was cut short and casual waves framed her face.

"Hello, *chérie*," Danielle said as she leaned over to kiss Maggie. "Where are the children? I thought we were baking today?"

"I haven't even been home yet," Maggie said.

"Oh, that's right!" Danielle said settling herself at the table and reaching for a *canelé*. "You must tell me all about it. Is it true that Madame Rochelle killed the girl?"

"It wasn't a girl who was killed," Maggie said. "Your gossip mills got that part wrong, Danielle. The victim was in her early twenties."

"Who was she?" Grace asked.

"Someone who was working at the lavender farm, *La Lavandin,*" Maggie said. "That's all I know."

"Rochelle was working there too, wasn't she?" Grace asked.

"She was."

"And that is literally all you know?" Grace asked.

"Yes and no. I found out that Rochelle's public defender is Gilbert Segal," Maggie said. "So I'll be able to get more specific info on the case from him."

"Why does that name sound familiar?" Danielle asked.

"He was nearly disbarred last year," Maggie said, "for drunk and disorderly conduct at a music festival in Nîmes."

"That surprises me in France," Grace said. "Not that he got drunk but that anyone would care."

"I think there was some question of a sexual assault too."

"Ah, that would do it. Is he any good?"

"I don't know. But Laurent wants us to do everything we can to help exonerate Rochelle, so good, bad or indifferent I'll need to work with him."

"Laurent sounds very committed to helping her," Danielle said, raising an eyebrow.

"Rochelle is a friend of Laurent's," Maggie said. "And until we know for sure that she killed this woman, I agree with Laurent that we need to do what we can to see if she's being unfairly accused."

"Well, it wouldn't be the first time the police got it wrong," Grace said with a sigh.

"Exactly."

"Is the good detective LaBelle being helpful?" Grace asked sweetly.

"What do you think?" Maggie said.

"You need to throw Laurent in her path," Grace said. "That'll distract her."

"Very funny."

"Who's joking?"

It didn't surprise Maggie that Grace had picked up on Detective LaBelle's attraction to Laurent. He and she had met under extremely unpleasant circumstances a year and a half ago when a woman had been stabbed in Maggie and Laurent's vineyard during a scavenger hunt.

"Anyway," Maggie said with a sigh, "I told Laurent I'd do whatever I could."

"That is very magnanimous of you, darling."

Maggie gave Grace a baleful look. "We don't know for a fact that Rochelle is guilty. You said so yourself—the cops get it wrong half the time. If for no other reason than that Rochelle is American I need to do what I can for her."

"I believe you, darling. Millions wouldn't."

"And you really know nothing more about why she is in France?" Danielle asked with exasperation. "I have never understood that."

"Laurent said she's going through a bad divorce," Maggie said. "Plus she lost her job at the winery in California and needed a new start."

"And there was the fact that she met Laurent at her lowest point," Grace said as she sipped her coffee. "Not that I blame her but you can see she's in love with him."

"Oh, don't start," Maggie said, but she said it with no heat.

"But *whatever* her story is," Grace said, "and regardless of whether she's guilty or not, she deserves better than a has-been alcoholic public defender."

"Well, it might not come to that," Maggie said. "If I can find evidence clearing her before she's arraigned, the cops will be forced to look elsewhere for their suspect."

"If it turns out she is in fact innocent, *chérie*," Danielle pointed out.

Even Laurent would not insist they work to free a woman who had committed murder, Maggie thought.

Right?

"So what do you know about the murder?" Grace asked.

Maggie sighed.

"Her name is Chantal Lambert. Segal said she'd been stabbed last night around eight or nine in the evening."

"Stabbed," Grace said and shivered.

"Where?" Danielle asked. "At the lavender field?"

"Yes. Or on the perimeter of it. Segal said the spot was nearer to some high-end spa on the other side of the farm. Called Chantilly Lace or something."

"*Chatoyer*," Grace said.

"Do you know it?"

"I've not been to it, darling," Grace said. "But I've heard of it. Do they think this Chantal was somehow connected to the spa?"

"I didn't get that idea," Maggie said. "But it's close to where she was killed so it gets a look."

"It's a pretty name, Grace said. "What does it mean?"

"Chatoyer?" Danielle said. "To shimmer. I too have heard of the spa. It hasn't been there very long."

"Is that all?" Grace asked.

"So far," Maggie said. "Oh, and the fact that supposedly someone overheard Rochelle say something threatening about the victim near the time she was killed."

"That's never good," Grace said. "But never fear, darling. You'll get to the bottom of it. You always do."

Maggie smiled at her friend and eased back in her chair allowing herself a moment of relaxation before heading home.

The fact was no matter what her own motivations were for helping to find the truth about who killed the girl in the lavender field, the sooner she was able to free Rochelle—*if she was in fact innocent*—the sooner Maggie could get Laurent's naturally protective instincts back in the box.

And their family back on track.

10

That night ratatouille bubbled in a large pot on the stove, evidence of a surfeit of Laurent's garden tomatoes.

School would start in a few weeks as the last gasps of summer petered out. Jemmy was upstairs in his bedroom, probably on his computer or on the phone talking to his friends. Mila was also in her bedroom where she'd been sent earlier in the afternoon when Laurent came home and she'd repeatedly failed to water the *potager* after he'd asked numerous times.

Maggie maneuvered around Laurent in the kitchen in order to pull white ceramic bowls from the open shelving to serve the ratatouille in.

"Did you find out anything at the monastery?" Maggie asked.

"*Non.*"

Maggie turned to glance at her husband. He was taciturn most of the time but particularly so tonight. In fact, now that she thought about it, he'd been more closed up than usual all summer.

There was no doubt that the issues they were grappling

with both Mila and Jemmy were weighing on him. Typically this time of year, so close to when he would call for the harvest—he would normally be tense, yes, but in an expectant, nearly exuberant way. Not so this summer where if Maggie had to put a name to what she was sensing from him, amazingly she would have to say it was dread.

Did that make sense?

Of course this business with Rochelle Lando made it all worse. Laurent took his responsibilities for the world's downtrodden seriously, particularly when they were women. Grace was a perfect example of that.

Maggie pulled a baguette out of its paper sleeve and cut it into a dozen slices before sliding them into a napkin-lined basket for the table.

If Laurent hadn't contrived a job and a way of life for Grace here in Provence, Maggie had no idea where her friend would be now. The direction she'd started down was not one that could be sustained happily or for long.

"Did anyone at the monastery know Chantal?" Maggie asked. "I thought she lived at *La Lavandin*."

Laurent ladled up the first bowl of ratatouille, its luscious fragrance seeming to envelop the room.

"*She worked at the lavender farm b*ut she was staying at the monastery."

Maggie stopped what she was doing.

"Seriously? Laurent, that's information I didn't have before. You said you didn't find out anything new."

He shrugged and moved to the oven where he pulled out a small lamb roast encrusted in rosemary and set it on the counter.

"It means we should talk to the people at the monastery in addition to the lavender farm," Maggie said. "If they knew Chantal they'll know how close her relationship was to Rochelle."

"That will only confirm the police's view," Laurent said.

"How?"

"I talked to only a few people," he said as he tossed the dish towel that had been over his shoulder onto the counter. "But they all said Rochelle had no friends."

Maggie frowned. "Because of the language thing?"

Laurent scraped a hand through his hair in a show of exasperation.

"Probably," he said. "She should have been taking French lessons months ago."

"Any idea why she wasn't?"

He glanced at her. Maggie knew she would have to tread carefully on the subject of criticizing Rochelle to him. He was clearly defensive and Maggie had already given him plenty of evidence over the last few months of her burgeoning animosity for Rochelle.

Besides, it didn't matter. For whatever reason—probably because she hadn't bothered to learn the language—the main takeaway was the fact that Rochelle wasn't liked at the monastery.

That appeared to be the key.

Thirty minutes later, the family was seated around the table. Both Jemmy and Mila had mulish expressions on their faces as they ate their dinner and then carried their plates to the kitchen. Maggie knew she should make them wash the dishes but she was tired and didn't feel like facing the fight that would entail.

Laurent clearly felt the same because after he left the table with all three of the dogs to take a walk in the garden, he came back and filled the kitchen sink with hot suds and began to wash the dishes.

Actually Mila had been a little better tonight than usual.

Maggie wouldn't go so far as to call her behavior sweet but she ate her dinner without complaint and didn't bait her brother as she'd been lately in the habit of doing. Before retreating to her room, she even thanked Laurent for dinner which she hadn't done in months.

Jemmy unfortunately was still pouting about the iron-clad *no* he'd been dealt with regarding his hopes to attend the Avignon acting school over school break next year. Whereas Maggie would be open to at least touring the facility and talking with the teachers she knew it was a nonstarter with Laurent.

When it came to other more important battles to fight, this one was far down her list.

While Laurent was in the kitchen with his own thoughts and both children were upstairs, Maggie stole away to her office on the other side of the living room.

She loved her office, made more special by the many mementoes and treasures that she'd gathered over the years from Atlanta where she was from and also from her years of living in France. The room was not large but it featured a set of French doors that led to the back terrace and a hand carved oak door that had been a gift from Laurent for one of their anniversaries.

Every time Maggie saw the door she felt Laurent's support and respect for the work she did and it filled her with affection and tenderness for her husband.

Tonight, she went right to her desktop computer and opened up a browser window to google Chantal Lambert. All she could find was a brief news story referencing Chantal's recent death and a few social media links. She hesitated clicking on the links and decided she needed some real facts before she tried to deduce who Chantal had been from her social media presence. She'd learned long ago that what she saw on Facebook didn't tell nearly the whole truth about a person.

She picked up her cell phone and called Gilbert Segal.

"*Allo?*" a guttural voice answered, thick with either sleep or drink.

Neither situation was ideal for Maggie's purposes.

"Monsieur Segal?" she said. "This is Maggie Dernier. Is this a bad time?"

There was a pause on the line as Segal obviously tried to remember who she was. Maggie fought back a pinch of impatience.

How is this man going to represent Rochelle if he can't even remember me from a phone call we had six hours earlier?

"Ah, yes, Madame Dernier," Segal said tiredly. "I was just going over the case notes."

That surprised Maggie but she was pleased to hear it. Unless he was lying. The thing about alcoholics and drug addicts is that they get used to trying to tell people what they think they want to hear.

"Great," she said, deciding to err on the side of optimism. "Because I have some questions."

"I don't know if I will know the answers."

"You know more than I do. First, is it true Rochelle found the body?"

"*Oui*. She claims she stumbled over it at roughly zero seven hours this morning."

Maggie noted his use of the word *claims*. If Rochelle's own lawyer didn't believe her, she was in trouble from the start.

"What was she doing at the lavender farm at that hour?"

"She did not say."

Maggie felt a wave of frustration. It really did seem like a basic sort of question.

It is certainly the kind of question a prosecuting attorney will ask.

"I heard the victim was stabbed," Maggie said. "Has the murder weapon been found?"

"*Non.* But they have a good idea of the kind of knife because of the wound it was."

"What kind of knife was it?"

Maggie heard a rustling of papers and again felt a flinch of concern in her throat. These were not complicated questions. Surely he could remember without having to look up what kind of knife it was?

"Not a knife," he said. "A scythe."

Maggie blanched as an image of the wicked-sounding weapon came to her mind.

"It was probably used in hand cutting the lavender," Segal said. "They estimate it was fourteen-inches long, serrated, and curved."

Maggie cleared her throat. That was a brutal weapon. She could imagine the damage it must have inflicted.

"Where was she...cut?" she asked, half afraid to hear the answer.

"Across the throat," he said matter of factly.

11

Maggie swallowed hard. A scythe's blade across the throat was vicious. Did the fact that it was a lavender farm tool mean it wasn't premeditated? Except there was nobody cutting lavender at seven o'clock at night when Chantal was killed. So why did the killer have a scythe?

"Is there anything else?" Maggie asked, feeling a little warm. Looking up she saw that her ceiling fan wasn't on. She moved to the wall to start it. Domaine Saint-Buvard had no central air and while the summers seemed to get hotter every year up until recently she hadn't missed not having AC.

"Well, I'm looking at the photos taken of the body," Segal said and then burped loudly. "She appears to have been arranged on the ground."

"Arranged how?"

"Her arms were folded across her chest and her hair was pushed off her face."

"Strange," Maggie said.

Why would the killer take the time to arrange Chantal's body? Especially if the murder wasn't premeditated?

"Even stranger," Segal said, "is the fact that her clothes were stuffed with lavender blossoms and stems."

Maggie tried to get an image in her mind of what this looked like.

"Can you send me a picture?" she asked, texting him her phone number.

When the photos came through on her computer, she stared hard at the sight. There had to be at least fifty pieces of lavender tucked into the front of Chantal's dress, even in her hair.

"So strange," Maggie murmured, still on the phone with Segal. "What did the police make of it?"

"Well, this is Aix," Segal said with a snort, "so there was very little thinking going on. But if I had to guess, I'd say the killer was known to the victim."

Again Maggie felt a flutter of discouragement. So far nothing about this killing appeared random. Segal's observation was obvious and unhelpful.

Stuffing the corpse with lavender—which was always so fragrant—could be seen as a need to "sweeten up" the victim whom the killer believed to be foul or rotten in some way or possibly to pay sweet homage to her.

As a rejected lover might.

Maggie turned away from the photos on her screen.

"Have you had a chance to meet with Rochelle yet?" she asked.

"*Non.* As you know I was just informed it was my case this morning."

Alcoholics and addicts also tended to be primed with excuses.

There didn't seem to be anything more that Segal knew. Maggie asked him if Chantal had been drugged but he hadn't seen the toxicology report yet. She asked if Chantal was alive *before* having her neck cut and he didn't know and hadn't thought to ask.

Segal assured Maggie he would meet with Rochelle tomorrow and would call her if there was anything to report. Then he hung up.

Frustrated but not totally discouraged, Maggie turned to her computer and typed in *La Lavandin* in the search window. The farm's web page was basic but not amateurish. It showed a few pictures of lavender fields and then the equipment they used to harvest the lavender and what some of the finished products looked like.

The farm had been in operation for ten years which was not long considering that most Provençal lavender farms had been around for generations. It was owned and managed by Annette Toussaint. There was a picture of her standing in the middle of a lavender field but it was impossible to tell how recent the photo was.

Toussaint was in her seventies, her silver hair pulled back into a tight bun at the nape of her neck, her eyes small but uncompromising. In the website photo, taken in the middle of a vibrantly blooming lavender field, she looked stoic and tired, a tremulous smile on her lips.

Someone talked her into doing that photo, Maggie thought. Madame Toussaint didn't look like the kind of person who was comfortable in the limelight.

And now she had the limelight in spades.

From there Maggie finally went to Facebook and typed in Chantal's name. Instantly she discovered that Chantal was younger than Maggie had thought, maybe not even out of her teens. Plus, she didn't look like the typical homeless girl or refugee. She was blonde with blue eyes and was actually quite pretty.

How did she end up homeless? Maggie wondered.

And then a thought came to her. If Chantal was on Facebook, where was the laptop or cellphone she would've used to do that? Had LaBelle found a phone?

At that moment Maggie heard Laurent's voice. It was not a come-to-dinner voice, it was a voice that appeared to have edged way past judicious tolerance and was settling in comfortably into full-on parental fury.

She knew her respite was coming to a close. Whatever was going on in the kitchen would need her intervention if a full-scale battle was not to break out. Maggie picked up her phone and texted LaBelle asking for the name of the person who claimed to have overheard Rochelle and also if the detective had found Chantal's cellphone.

She stared at her phone screen and waited for a moment. It showed that her text had been received and then read. For a moment bubbles formed to indicate that LaBelle was forming a response. After a few seconds the bubbles stopped.

Maggie wasn't surprised. She'd only worked with LaBelle once over a year ago and that had been a largely unpleasant experience.

Suddenly she heard the sound of crockery breaking in the kitchen and jumped to her feet. She knew she should have gone in before this—before more crockery got broken or Laurent finally reached his limit and made good on his promise to throttle their only daughter.

12

The next morning Maggie was up after everyone else. The little dog Fleur had taken to sleeping with her in bed, something that Laurent didn't usually allow with their dogs—except for Petit Four of course—but lately hadn't seemed to care about. That was never a good sign but Maggie decided she had her hands full these days and would triage her skirmishes in order of seriousness.

It bothered her that Mila seemed so disinterested in the dog. With its dark floppy ears and big soulful eyes, it was hard not to love her. Fleur had a sweet personality too but perhaps she could sense that Mila wasn't to be trusted right now.

She sat for a moment in the kitchen reflecting and enjoying her coffee. She intended to visit the lavender farm today to see what she could find out. Everyone had somewhere else to be today it seemed. Laurent had dropped both kids off at *Dormir* this morning to work in the garden and help Danielle in the kitchen.

At least Mila would never dream of disrespecting Danielle who was as close to a beloved grandparent as she'd ever known. At least Maggie dearly hoped that was the case.

The air seemed to hold rain in it somehow—it felt heavier—even though the sun was out and what clouds there were seemed wispy and inconsequential.

Maggie drove for at least a mile with the carefully laid out purple fields rolling along side her before turning down the narrow dirt and gravel road that lead to *La Lavandin*. She put down her window as she drove and could detect the powerful scent of lavender filling the air.

The winding drive emptied out to a packed grassy area in front of a large two-story barn with a double garage access.

Maggie parked on the grass verge of the dirt road. Two police cars were parked near the barn and even from where Maggie sat in her car she could see the fluttering blue and white police cordon tape.

She pulled out her phone and snapped several pictures of the barn. There was a farmhouse off to the side. It didn't look falling down but neither did it look like anything Maggie would care to live in.

A tall woman, dressed in a pale blue *tablier* and leaning on a stout cane, stood at the front of the house speaking with three uniformed police. Maggie easily picked out LaBelle's rigid form in the group closest to Toussaint.

Maggie instantly recognized Annette Toussaint from the website photo she'd seen last night.

Sitting on the steps near the crowd of cops were two women. They were dressed in jeans and t-shirts, their hair pulled back and captured by brightly colored bandanas.

Maggie pulled out her phone and called up the camera function. She scanned the scene with her camera, shooting the group and then each of the people individually. A young man appeared from behind Annette Toussaint. He was handsome but rough looking. He had dark hair and a swarthy complexion making Maggie wonder if he had gypsy blood. He wore jeans and a torn t-shirt and when she zoomed in on his face she saw he had a hairlip that dragged down the bottom half of his mouth.

Suddenly she noticed that one of the policemen was pointing in her direction and talking to LaBelle. Maggie tucked her phone away and got out of the car.

She reminded herself that she had every right to be here. More than that, since she was working with Rochelle's lawyer, she had an obligation to be here.

She began to move toward the crowd at the same time she saw Detective LaBelle walking determinedly toward her. The detective's face was pinched into an angry visage of annoyance.

"Why are you here?" LaBelle said as she met Maggie halfway across the court in front of the barn. Behind her, Maggie saw one of the uniformed policemen taking notes and speaking to the girls on the steps.

"You know why I'm here," Maggie said, already tired of playing games with the woman. "I'm working with Monsieur Segal on Rochelle Lando's behalf."

Labelle's posture stiffened at the news.

"Where is your husband?" she asked.

"My...?" Maggie was taken off guard. "He...he's busy with the children."

Can't hurt to remind her he's a family man.

"This is an active crime scene," LaBelle said. "Remove yourself."

"I told you, I'm working with Rochelle's attorney and as such I'm authorized to question the people she worked with. I need to talk to the one who said he or she overheard Rochelle threaten Chantal Lambert the night she was killed."

"You don't need anything except to stay out of my way if you don't want to share a jail cell with her."

With irrefutable possession of the last word, LaBelle turned to see Annette Toussaint approaching them.

"Madame," LaBelle said to her loudly, "I would warn you against talking to this American. She works on behalf of the State's prime suspect."

Wow. Bias much? Maggie thought with irritation.

"I just want to ask you a few questions, Madame Toussaint," Maggie said over LaBelle's shoulder.

As Toussaint continued to walk toward her Maggie could tell that LaBelle wanted to push the issue. But after a slight hesitation, the detective headed back to where her men were talking to the two girls at the barn.

Maggie nodded at Annette Toussaint and stuck out her hand.

"*Bonjour* Madame Toussaint. My name is Maggie Dernier."

"You are married to Laurent Dernier?" Toussaint said, her eyes narrowing as she studied Maggie.

Maggie wasn't surprised that Toussaint knew Laurent. The work he did with the monastery—not to mention the seven mini houses he'd built for the refugees who worked the area's farms—was well known to most people in the vicinity.

"I am," Maggie said with a small smile.

French people didn't believe in a lot of unnecessary smiling and while a meeting over a suspicious death probably ranked even higher in the department of no-smiles-needed, Maggie knew that Toussaint would expect some show on Maggie's part to register her pride in her husband.

Toussaint nodded and motioned for Maggie to walk with her away from the police cars and their flashing lights.

"I am no friend to the police," Toussaint said as they walked. "But I would not deliberately make them my enemy."

Maggie was gratified to see that the woman appeared down to earth and open to talking to her.

They walked a hundred yards down the driveway where Toussaint turned to look at her farm, her eyes following the police as they stepped around her farm's perimeter.

"What did you want to ask me?" she asked without turning to look at Maggie.

"As Detective LaBelle indicated," Maggie said, "a friend of my family is being held by the police for Chantal's murder."

"You mean Rochelle Lando." Toussaint's lips twisted into a frown but otherwise she gave nothing away.

"That's right. I know Rochelle was working your fields this summer."

"As I told the police, Rochelle was a capable worker and did not complain which is more than I can say about many of my provisional workers."

Maggie watched the CSI team—at least four people in white overalls—as they processed a patch of land east of the barn which presumably was where the body was found. The crackle of police radios constantly broke the serene picture of waving purple lavender in the distance.

"Did Rochelle work with Chantal?" Maggie asked.

"Yes, of course. I have only a handful of employees and the fields are not that large."

"I guess what I really want to know is if they got along," Maggie said pointedly.

Toussaint hesitated. "Not really. Chantal had trouble with many people and an American who knows her own mind would not be someone she would bond with."

"So Chantal had problems with your other employees too?"

"She showed up and did as she was told. I had no complaints on that score."

"Was there another score that you *did* have complaints on?"

Toussaint looked uncomfortable.

"I did not mean to insinuate that," Toussaint said. "Please do not put words in my mouth."

Maggie could tell the woman was seconds from ending the conversation.

"How long had Chantal been working for you?" Maggie asked.

"A month."

"How did she get the job?"

Toussaint shrugged. "She showed up one morning and asked if there was work. It is how they all come. Except for Rochelle. Your husband brought Rochelle to me."

Maggie knew that.

"I have work to do, Madame Dernier," Toussaint said abruptly. "You will have to excuse me."

"I appreciate you talking to me, Madame Toussaint," Maggie said. "I only want to get to the truth of what happened to Chantal."

Toussaint stopped walking and turned to look at Maggie.

"Even if the truth is that your friend killed her?"

"Yes. Even then," Maggie said. "Can you tell me who found the body?"

Toussaint's eyebrows shot up.

"You don't know?"

Maggie shook her head.

"It was Rochelle," Toussaint said before turning and leaving Maggie where she stood.

13

As Laurent stood in the front drive of Domaine St-Buvard washing the Peugeot, it seemed as if the whole world around him was nothing but discordant noise: the sounds of bad music blaring, feet running up and down the stairs, door slamming and—the harshest most impossible noise to ignore of all—the blatant disrespect flung at him from every turn.

He sudsed the car's windshield and used the sponge to rake away the excess water, feeling a fleeting but satisfying feeling as if by cleaning his car he was doing something to fix what was wrong.

And not just wrong but egregiously wrong, wrong on every level, wrong to the whole world.

The dogs started barking on the far side of the house and Laurent paused for a moment. Then he turned and picked up the hose to rinse off the hood of his car.

Jemmy should be doing this, he thought. He should be doing *something*.

Nowadays demands or requests for unpaid chores were met

with defiance and unspoken hostility that spoke louder than words or even tantrums could.

Yet as much as he'd like to give Jemmy a good clout around the ears, he knew it wasn't Jemmy who was the problem. If anything he'd felt a flicker of relief this summer to see his son push back a little.

For years, Jemmy seemed to be so passive that Laurent worried about him ever taking a stand.

Mila of course was another story. He hated to make Maggie do all the heavy lifting as far as disciplining the girl. But he had no earthly idea what to do about her. He felt a fleeting chill scrape across his arms and he thought of the Mistral, that punishing Provençal wind that blew down into the Rhone Valley from the French Alps or Bavaria.

Perhaps a school in Switzerland?

He found himself wishing he could talk to Roger Bennett about it and then smiled ruefully. Roger never had any children of his own. He had a solid head on his shoulders but he was hardly the one you'd go to for childrearing advice.

Perhaps Frère Jean. An infinitely kind man with a no-nonsense, even blunt perspective, Frère Jean might have something to offer on the subject of angry teenage girls.

Thinking of Frère Jean made Laurent think of the monastery and then of the niggling feeling that festered painfully in the back of his brain—*Rochelle*.

His jaw clenched painfully. How could this have happened? Worse, how could he have let this happen? The woman was more indecisive than Grace, more muddled than Maggie's eighty-five-year old mother back in Atlanta. She seemed to default, unerringly, for the wrong solution *every time*.

How had he thought even for an instant that she could start over in a country where she didn't speak the language and had no job?

Hubris, he thought as he dropped the hose, letting the stream of water douse his pant legs in the process.

He should have seen her inability to help herself. Or had that been what had clinched the deal for him?

He felt a sudden and overwhelming weariness as he walked to the side of the house and turned off the faucet to the hose. It was uncanny how much Rochelle looked like Dauphine but even more, there was that unmistakable thread of remorse. It was as if Dauphine had risen from the grave.

Second chances? Isn't that why Rochelle came to France?

Isn't that my specialty? he thought in disgust.

The dogs began to bark frenetically again and Laurent stood and stared at his now glistening car.

Why was it he felt these days that he was all out of answers?

Right when it seemed there were more questions than ever...

14

Maggie hurriedly stepped in front of Annette Toussaint, blocking her attempt to return to the barn. It was clear to her now that the fact that Rochelle had found Chantal's body was the reason the police arrested her, over and above whomever had claimed to have heard her threaten Chantal.

"But Rochelle was arrested at the monastery," Maggie said to Toussaint, rubbing her forehead in confusion. "The day *after* the murder."

"I believe that is one of things the police find hard to reconcile," Toussaint said. "As I understand it, they found evidence at the scene linking Rochelle."

"You're saying Rochelle found the body but didn't report it?" Maggie shook her head in disbelief. "But Rochelle wasn't arrested until midmorning the next day. Did no one wonder why Chantal hadn't shown up for work?"

"We had just finished the hand cutting," Toussaint said, wiping a line of sweat from her forehead. Maggie noticed that the woman didn't look well. It was already a hot morning and Toussaint looked like she was feeling too warm.

"I wouldn't need any help in the fields until today," Toussaint said. "But of course now *that* isn't happening." She nodded in the direction of the police who were just leaving.

"So Chantal had Saturday off?" Maggie pressed.

"Yes. I'm sorry, Madame Dernier, I am feeling very tired."

"Oh, sure. Again thank you for your help. I just have one more quick question."

"Yes?" Toussaint said sharply.

"That guy standing over there by the girls?" Maggie gestured to the young man with the harelip.

"Enzo Corbin," Toussaint said. "He is my tractor driver although he was training Rochelle to take over for him."

"Why? Was he going somewhere?"

"I hadn't made up my mind," Toussaint said, watching him now as the man moved away from the barn to disappear inside. "But his work is sloppy and he is too rough on the equipment. He destroys as many lavender plants as he harvests."

"Did he just show up one day too?"

"With Chantal. He is her boyfriend. Now, if you'll excuse me." Toussaint turned and limped slowly back to the barn.

∼

The man arranged himself carefully in the juniper bushes that bordered the farm, noting not for the first time that the very air surrounding him was perfumed. But this time, he didn't enjoy it at all.

He brought the binoculars up to his face and settled on his stomach in the dirt, feeling foolish and uncomfortable but knowing he needed to see what was happening. He watched the American woman talking to the old woman.

At first they just seemed to be talking. But then the old woman started to wave her arms as if angry.

What is she saying? What is the American saying to upset her?

He adjusted the focus on the binoculars and looked over at the group of policemen as they began to climb into their police cars before he turned back to watch the American again.

Why is she doing this? Why does she care? Does she think she's smarter than the flic?

He lowered the binoculars and watched as Madame Toussaint walked away from the American. Her strides were slow but stiff with anger. She stabbed the ground with her cane as she walked.

He brought the binoculars back up to his face and tried to zoom in on the American. He had a sour taste in his mouth as he examined her face.

Americans always think they're smarter than everyone else, he thought.

Especially me. Everyone thinks they're smarter than me.

He watched the old woman disappear into her house and slam the door.

Except this time.

15

Maggie watched Annette Toussaint disappear into her house and then turned her attention to Enzo Corbin who was seated on a bench at the front of the barn with two other farm workers, watching as the police pulled out of the parking lot.

Maggie began to walk toward the group. She was trying to give LaBelle and her men enough time to clear out. The two girls saw her coming and both jumped up and disappeared through the barn door behind them. But Enzo watched her come with undisguised curiosity.

Maggie stuck out her hand when she reached him.

"Monsieur Corbin?" she said. "I am Maggie Dernier. May I ask you a few questions?"

"You're American," he said shaking her hand. "*La Lavandin* will be getting a reputation soon."

Maggie wasn't sure what that meant but she let it go for now.

"I'm a friend of Rochelle Lando's," Maggie said. "I'm sure you heard she's in some trouble."

"*Oui.* For killing Chantal."

Maggie sat down next to him on the steps. It seemed an insensitive thing to say if he was indeed Chantal's boyfriend. Maggie searched his face for any sign of emotional distress.

Or the lack of it.

"Madame Toussaint told me you came to work here with Chantal," Maggie said. "She was your girlfriend?"

"*Oui.*"

His expression gave nothing away.

"I am sorry for your loss. Had you been together long?"

"Long enough," he said with a shrug.

There were times when the French insistence on insouciance and world-weariness definitely got in the way of Maggie's ability to determine someone's emotional investment. She knew this firsthand from Laurent whom she had every reason to believe adored her but who rarely demonstrated the fact in ways Maggie had grown up believing were manifestations of the emotion—sending flowers, buying jewelry, saying *I love you* frequently.

She would try to give Enzo the benefit of the doubt on this but she couldn't help but think that the typical Frenchman might logically be expected to mine some normally hidden reservoir of emotion after violently losing a girlfriend just hours earlier.

"You must have been shocked," Maggie said, fishing for the right tone to hit for her questions.

"*Bien sûr,*" he said and examined his hands.

"Were you also shocked to see that Rochelle was arrested for her death?"

He looked at Maggie and frowned.

"You are asking if I thought Rochelle killed Chantal."

"Well, you knew them both," Maggie said. "You knew their relationship, presumably."

He shrugged again and looked out across the clearing at the

front of the barn. The weather had gotten even hotter in just the hour that Maggie had been at the farm.

"I didn't think Rochelle would kill her," he said finally.

"But you did see tension between them?"

"*Oui.*"

"Madame Toussaint hinted that Chantal had trouble getting along with everyone. Not just Rochelle."

He flexed his fingers in agitation.

"Madame Toussaint is not to be trusted," he said.

"Oh? In what way?"

"Her word," he said, nearly spitting the words out. "Did she tell you she'd fired Chantal the afternoon before she died?"

Maggie was surprised to hear this.

"Why did she do that?"

He snorted and rubbed his hands against his workman's trousers. It was the first time Maggie had seen his agitation and it looked very much as if it was triggered by his affection or regard for Chantal. He was defending her. His eyes glistened as he spoke.

"She wouldn't say," Enzo said. "She just said for Chantal to gather her things and get out."

"That sounds pretty severe."

"Toussaint is a racist," he said, his face flushed with heat.

Since Chantal was blonde and blue-eyed, this made no sense at first, but then Maggie realized he was talking about himself. The harelip was bad, something that should've been repaired when Enzo was a child.

Maggie didn't know why someone might be born with this kind of deformity. She didn't know if it might be the result of inbreeding which gypsies were traditionally accused of.

"Did the police talk to you?" she asked.

"Of course," he said, curling his lip. "I'm the boyfriend and I'm a gypsy. I am the logical suspect, *non?*"

Enzo stood up abruptly then turned and stalked off toward the lavender fields.

16

Usually a visit to Pâtisserie Béchard in Aix was the start of a good day. Laurent had found a parking spot down one of the side streets leading up to Cours Mirabeau where the famous *pâtisserie* was located. That in itself was unusual since parking in Aix was long considered nearly impossible.

As he walked away from the bakery, carrying a shopping bag full of *calissons, biscotins* and a dozen *pains aux chocolat*, he realized this errand was notable because for the first time he was feeling worse than when he entered the bakery.

The Aix police station was only a couple of blocks away but already the day's heat was pounding down on all living things foolish enough to be outside. By the time he reached its front doors, he'd sweated through his thin cotton t-shirt—*never a good look when you're visiting a police station*—and felt a headache coming on. He stepped inside, ignoring the waiting room to his right, and going straight to the receptionist's desk where a uniformed woman sat flipping through a fashion magazine.

"Excuse me," Laurent said to get her attention since a six

foot five man standing before her didn't seem to accomplish the job. "I have an appointment."

The woman looked up at Laurent and closed her magazine.

"Name?" she said turning to her computer.

"Laurent Dernier. To see Rochelle Lando."

He waited while she typed on her computer. Finally she looked over and glanced at his bag of pastries, the scent of which had already begun to fill the room.

"Your request has been denied," she said, her eyes on the bag.

"Look again," he said, forcing himself to keep his voice calm.

"I don't have to look again. It's not going to update. Your request is denied."

"Let me see Detective Capitaine LaBelle," he said, putting his sack on the counter.

"She's not here."

"Please check."

"There is no point. Detective Capitaine LaBelle is not here."

It had been a gamble, Laurent knew. He'd only had the possibility of a meeting with Rochelle today and none at all with LaBelle. But even the possibility had felt like he was doing *something*.

"*D'accord*," he said, and was about to turn away when the receptionist glanced at her computer screen and held up a finger to him.

"Wait. I think Detective Capitaine LaBelle has just returned," she said. "I will see if she will see you. I promise nothing."

"Of course," he said as she made a phone call.

The sergeant spoke into the phone before turning back to Laurent and nodding toward the waiting room.

"She will be out when she can," she said.

"*Merci*," Laurent said, leaving the pastries on the counter and walking to the waiting room to sit in one of the middle rows to wait.

Fifteen minutes later LaBelle strode into the waiting room and indicated for him to follow her. As they walked through a door behind the receptionist's desk and down a long uncarpeted hallway, Laurent could smell lavender on the detective.

"I cannot allow you to see the suspect," LaBelle said. "But you may speak with her. In my presence."

"*Merci*," Laurent said.

Her office was a barebones room with a desk and an empty shelf. Laurent knew the office had once been Roger Bedard's. It had been furnished with two comfortable visitors' chairs, a thick rug, a credenza of awards and photos of Bedard's daughter.

LaBelle went to sit behind her desk, and gestured to the metal chair opposite the desk.

Laurent sat and LaBelle picked up her phone and spoke into it. After a moment she handed him the phone.

"*Allo*, Rochelle," he said into the phone. "How are you doing?"

"Oh, Laurent," Rochelle said, her voice full of tears. "I knew you would call! Can you come see me? Can you help me? I feel so alone."

"I know, *chérie*," Laurent said. "I am working on that." He glanced at LaBelle who arched an eyebrow at him.

"You promised you would help me, Laurent," Rochelle said, her voice shrill. "I don't know what to do if you don't."

"Of course I will do everything I can," Laurent said.

"I think I've done something, Laurent," Rochelle said, dropping her voice.

"Mind what you say," Laurent warned her, deliberately not glancing at LaBelle.

"Why? I know I can tell you, Laurent."

"*Non*," Laurent said sternly. "You must mind your words."

"Enough," LaBelle said impatiently and held her hand out for the phone.

Laurent hesitated and then spoke again into the phone ignoring LaBelle's hand.

"Be strong, *chérie*," he said and handed the phone to the detective.

LaBelle hung up the phone and folded her arms across her chest.

"What is your relationship with the suspect?" she asked.

"She is a friend."

"A friend," LaBelle said, raising an eyebrow.

Laurent's face gave nothing away. He could see the different emotional factors warring in the detective—jealousy, insecurity, longing—and he would give her nothing more to arm her.

He wasn't as naïve as Maggie seemed to think when it came to his effect on women. He knew that LaBelle was infatuated with him and while normally he didn't like to take advantage of that, this time, he would use it to his advantage.

"What can you tell me about her case?" he asked.

He watched her react to him, her shoulders soften, her lips part. He didn't like to manipulate people. But LaBelle was his adversary. He would do what was necessary—use whatever weapons he had at his disposal—to achieve his ends.

"I can't tell you anything," she said, but her voice was not firm.

Laurent knew this game. He invented this game. She would tell him. She just wouldn't do it the first time he asked. "I need to see the forensic report," he said.

She shifted in her seat. "Don't be ridiculous," she said. "No," she said, alerting him to the fact that her no was not at all final. She would need to be asked again.

"What can you tell me?" he repeated.

She stood up with a sharp intake of breath and then, as if embarrassed about revealing herself, sat down again.

"I can't tell you anything," she said, licking her lips. "Nothing. Rochelle Lando is my prime suspect in a capital murder case."

"Have you found the murder weapon?"

She shook her head. Laurent had seen this evasion tactic before. Many times before. Mila and Jemmy had in fact done the very thing as children when they wanted to admit the truth but couldn't bring themselves to speak it out loud.

LaBelle hadn't spoken but she *had* answered him.

"She said she'd done something bad," LaBelle said.

"*Non*," Laurent said. "She only said she'd done something."

"She's sitting in a jail cell charged with murder. It is implied that it was bad."

Laurent didn't answer. The police didn't have the murder weapon which was good. He knew if they found it, it would suddenly be very bad. For everyone.

Himself included.

"But she did do something," LaBelle said nailing Laurent with her most direct gaze so far. "And what she did was not good. Not for her."

Laurent frowned. LaBelle was again trying to tell him something without saying it. This time he didn't have the patience to decipher her message.

"What did she do?" he asked.

LaBelle shrugged as if to say that whatever it was, she herself was not responsible for what would happen next. Laurent had seen this too in his past life of crime. Many atrocities could be committed and confessed to if only absolution might be promised.

As it happened, Laurent was in a position to offer a promise of absolution.

But a promise only, and therefore worse than useless. But

not to the guilty. He'd seen it time and time again. To the guilty one, even a baseless promise of amnesty was worth something.

"You have no evidence of her guilt," Laurent said, fishing, prodding, his eyes drilling the detective.

"I know," she said, surprising him. "But now I don't need it."

"And why is that?" he asked, bracing for her words.

"Because, this morning at zero eight hundred hours," LaBelle said formally, dramatically proving beyond a shadow of doubt that she'd intended to tell him all along, "Rochelle Lando confessed to murdering Chantal Lambert."

17

Dinner that night at Domaine St-Buvard was a classic hot-weather dish—*Salade Niçoise*. They ate it on the back terrace under the plane trees. The heat, still prevalent in the air, combined with Mila's nonstop complaining about the fact that they didn't have a swimming pool and Jemmy's sulking made the meal a trial.

Maggie had arrived home too late to help compile the salad but she could tell by Laurent's quiet affect that the process of assembling the dish was just what he needed—a lot of dicing and mincing to occupy his mind without going too deep into any real thinking.

He'd been quiet ever since he returned from Aix. Except for the surprising mention of a brief meeting he'd had with LaBelle and an even briefer phone conversation with Rochelle, he had been exceptionally non forthcoming about his day.

He'd arrived with a baguette and a *tarte framboise* from Béchard so it was possible he'd just done the family shopping after his visit to the Aix police station and nothing more. But regardless of where he'd gone today, it was pretty clear that *something* was on his mind.

Once dinner was over Maggie knew her best opportunity to feel him out was once the children had been released to their rooms and she and Laurent could wash the dishes together. It was a domestic scene they'd performed together hundreds of times.

Laurent washed, and she dried. But before she could plan her approach with him, he surprised her and went first.

"You went to *La Lavandin* today?" he asked.

"I did but I'm not sure how helpful it was," she said wondering how he knew where she'd been today.

"Tell me."

Maggie couldn't help but note that Laurent was much more interested than he'd ever been in discussing any of the cases she'd ever been involved with—even one that had involved him as the possible suspect.

"I talked to Madame Toussaint, the manager of the farm," she said. "She told me that Chantal didn't get along with anyone but neither did Rochelle, which is basically what you told me about Rochelle at the monastery."

Maggie watched Laurent for a reaction to the possibility that *Rochelle* might be the problem, but his face was impassive, revealing nothing. She sighed.

"Chantal's boyfriend Enzo Corbin told me that Madame Toussaint fired Chantal the day she was killed."

"And you believe him?"

"Not necessarily, but he claims to have an alibi so if he *didn't* kill her, why bother throwing Madame Toussaint under the bus?"

"Under the—?" Laurent frowned.

"Never mind. Anyway I also found out that Chantal was killed with a scythe of some kind, which is one of the tools used at the lavender farm to cut lavender."

Laurent seemed to flinch at the news. Maggie knew he wasn't so sensitive as to be reacting to the thought of someone running into the business end of a hand-held harvesting scythe. But as usual, Laurent wasn't forthcoming.

"At least they know what they're looking for as far as the murder weapon," she said. "So that's good. But of course they still have to find it."

Laurent stared fixedly over the sinkful of dishes into the darkness through the kitchen window as if lost in his own thoughts.

"When you talked to Rochelle today," Maggie said, "did she tell you her alibi?"

Laurent turned to look at her. It was not a friendly look.

"We did not talk about that," he said.

"Because that would've been really helpful if you had," Maggie said. "I have a nagging fear that she's told the cops she couldn't have killed Chantal because she was busy watching a high school production of *A Midsummer Night's Dream*."

Laurent turned to look at her.

"You think she came to Jemmy's play to create an alibi?" he said, his eyes hard as he regarded her.

"I don't know. Is that what she told the cops?"

"I told you, Maggie. I don't know what she told them."

This was the second time he'd called her by her first name instead of *chérie*. A thought crossed Maggie's mind. *Had Laurent asked Rochelle what her alibi was? And had she told him that she'd used Jemmy's play?*

It would be easy enough to find out. Gilbert Segal was a mere phone call away.

After the dishes were done, Laurent opened the back door to let the dogs out and he stepped outside too. This was a habit from years of walking in the vineyard after dinner and smoking.

He'd given up smoking but Maggie knew from experience that walking in his beloved vineyard was a good opportunity to get him to talk when he might not normally be inclined.

"I'm coming too," she called to him as she grabbed a cotton cardigan off a chair in the dining room. Even with the hot Provençal summer days, the evenings tended to be cool.

She hurried down the garden path, spotting the two hunting dogs loping off into the vineyard ahead of Laurent. Fleur had stopped and was waiting for Maggie.

"I texted LaBelle and asked for the autopsy results," Maggie said when she caught up with Laurent. "And also to ask her if she found Chantal's cellphone, but she didn't respond. Maybe I should have gotten *you* to call her."

They walked in silence for a few moments before Maggie spoke again.

"Okay," she said brightly. "So you didn't talk about her alibi today. Can I ask you what you did talk about?"

"Her mood mostly."

Maggie felt a flicker of annoyance. Naturally she understood that Rochelle needed someone to confide in but it would be a whole lot more helpful to her case if she would actually start helping them by giving information, like where she was during the time of the murder and if she knew of anyone who might want to make it appear she was guilty or even why she'd been walking around the lavender field at seven in the morning.

"I can imagine," Maggie said, tamping down her burgeoning irritation. "I'm sure she must be fairly despondent at the moment."

"*Oui.* So much so that she has confessed to the murder," Laurent said.

Maggie stopped walking. "Wait. What?"

Laurent stopped too. He looked at her and then back out at the vineyard.

"She *confessed*?" Maggie said as if trying to wrap her mind around the concept. "So she killed Chantal. Why didn't you tell me this not unimportant bit of news and what are we still doing talking about trying to prove her innocence?"

"If you don't want to help just say so," he said, cracking his knuckles.

Maggie felt a fluttering feeling in her chest as a flush of adrenaline tingled through her.

"What kind of help does she need?" she asked. "A better lawyer? A prayer chain? She *confessed*, Laurent."

"Even LaBelle said the confession didn't sound genuine."

"So LaBelle released her?" Maggie asked.

Laurent gave her a baleful look

"What possible reason would Rochelle have for confessing then?" she asked.

"Perhaps she feels she is being a burden," Laurent said.

"You mean to you?"

He snorted.

Maggie's mind was in a whirl. *Rochelle confessed to killing Chantal. Open and shut. Slam dunk.* And yet it didn't matter. Laurent still expected Maggie to try to find Rochelle innocent.

At least it explained why Rochelle didn't have an alibi.

Guilty people often don't.

She glanced at Laurent's profile, looking so intractable and stubborn in the moonlight as he surveyed his vineyard. Somehow she would have to operate with the information of Rochelle's confession as if it were irrelevant or hadn't happened.

"Look, I'll do what I can," she said, "but you have to know that her confessing makes things way harder."

"*Je sais.*" *I know.*

"Why did they even arrest Rochelle? I got the impression that it was on the basis of one person badmouthing her. One person who could be lying. What do the cops know that we don't?"

"LaBelle said there was physical evidence of Rochelle at the crime scene," Laurent said.

That made sense. Rochelle found the body so of course there would be physical evidence of her at the scene. Still, even if you discounted her confession it was starting to sound like the police had the right person for the crime.

"Hear me out, Laurent," Maggie said. "Rochelle found the body *and* she was overheard threatening the victim *and* she confessed to killing her. I'm not sure I understand why you're resisting this. Sometimes the things we want just don't turn out as we'd hoped."

"As I said, *chérie*, if you want to walk away, that is fine."

Except it wasn't at all fine. Just one look at his mulish expression told Maggie that.

"How am I supposed to find evidence of her innocence," Maggie asked trying to demonstrate calmness, "if she doesn't claim to be innocent?"

"What was her motive?" Laurent asked. "Why would she kill the girl?"

"They were roommates at the monastery. Maybe there was an issue with somebody using someone else's hairbrush."

"*Comment?*"

"I'm not being facetious, Laurent. You know very well that the motivation to kill could be anything. It could be something mundane and trivial and in Rochelle's case that's probably true. Rochelle is under a lot of pressure right now with the divorce and being virtually homeless and all. Maybe she just snapped."

"So you think Rochelle, annoyed that Chantal used her hairbrush without asking, took the scythe, followed the girl into the field—"

"Okay, that was just an example," Maggie said in frustration. "I'm only saying people have killed for a lot less provocation."

They were quiet for a moment.

"Do you have anything else besides Rochelle's confession that you want to share?" She worked to keep the resentment out of her voice.

"Not at the moment," he said. "Except…"

"Yes?"

"Are we safely past the point where you are going to stop working to help Rochelle?"

Maggie sighed dramatically.

"Yes, Laurent. I've signed on to the bitter end. I won't quit now. Even if Rochelle does. I promise."

"*Bon.* Then I can tell you that before Rochelle went to work at the lavender farm, I attempted to ease her way a bit."

Maggie narrowed her eyes.

"Ease her way how?" she said holding her breath and fairly sure she did not want to hear whatever it was he was about to tell her.

"I loaned her one of our scythes."

18

The next morning was even hotter than the day before. As Maggie drove down the country road outside of Aix with Mila and Jemmy in the backseat, both hooked up to their separate electronic devices, she passed vineyard after vineyard—most of them in some stage of harvest.

Maggie knew that Laurent was on the verge of calling for the harvest to begin. If the forecast could nominally guarantee a lack of rain for the next few days, he would call it. Usually this was Laurent's favorite time of the year—just before the harvest.

It was the culmination of a year-long effort of the cultivation of his grapes—including all the hours of tending, staking, feeding, watering and weeding them. Like every year, he had spent uncountable hours in various village cafés with the other vintners in the area talking and arguing about the status of this year's grapes and comparing them to past years.

Maggie dropped Mila off at Marie-Fleur's house first. They'd known each other since *jardin d'enfants* and had managed to stay friends through *école intermédiaire* even though their mutual interests had largely disappeared. Marie-Fleur was interested in science and scholastic achievement.

Aside from her fantasy of walking a catwalk in nine-inch heels and not much else, Mila's future career interests had yet to be determined.

Next, Maggie dropped Jemmy off at a girl's house from his school whom Maggie and Laurent had met several times. At fifteen, Jemmy was dating a little—as much as one can without a car—but Bethane seemed to be more friend than girlfriend which suited Maggie just fine. There was plenty of time for serious dating down the road.

After she dropped Jemmy off, Maggie headed down the road in the direction of the Ponte l'Abbe and the monastery on the other side of it. Her intention was to talk to Brother Luis and anyone else who'd spent time with Rochelle. Maggie knew that some of the people at the monastery, the temporary residents especially, would tend to tell her what they thought she wanted to hear about a fellow American so she was prepared to take what they gave her with a grain of salt.

Maggie also knew that Laurent would be furious she was doing this. He would see her coming to the monastery as proof that Maggie didn't believe in Rochelle's innocence. The truth was her efforts today truly were all a part of her investigation.

But the other truth, of course, was that she wasn't at all sure about Rochelle's innocence.

Why would Rochelle confess to a murder she hadn't committed?

Maggie had left several voice messages for Segal asking for the details of the forensics report on Chantal's body. Maggie expected the report to reveal Rochelle's DNA all over the crime scene. Naturally it would since she discovered the body. But who else's was there?

Had the cops fingerprinted everyone from Rochelle's dorm at the monastery? And what about the workers at the lavender farm?

Surely the cops would've already done this, she reasoned, if for no other reason than to eliminate people from consideration.

Unless you are a lazy detective who is very happy with her prime suspect and doesn't want to do any more work to find somebody else.

Is that who Margaux LaBelle was? Unlike a few other detectives Maggie had worked with over the years, LaBelle had struck Maggie as conscientious, someone who didn't want to just close cases but who wanted to get it right.

But regardless of all that, there was still the question of what Rochelle had been doing in that part of the lavender field when she discovered the body.

And then there was the murder weapon which sounded very much like it used to reside in the tool shed at Domaine St-Buvard.

Maggie made a mental note to ask Segal to ask Rochelle where she put the scythe. If she didn't have it anymore—if she'd lost it—that would be very bad. Of course if it were found and shown that it had been used to kill Chantal, that would be worse.

How would the killer get his or her hands on the scythe that Laurent gave Rochelle? What was the likelihood? Had *La Lavandin* confirmed that the scythe wasn't one of theirs?

And then there was the matter of the mud Maggie had seen on Rochelle's shoes that night. Just the thought of that sent a chill across her heart. Muddy shoes were out of place if you were going to a theater or performing arts event.

But they made total sense if you'd just come back from dumping a body.

19

Maggie walked from the gravel parking lot of *l'Abbaye de Sainte-Trinité* to its imposing front gate. The structure, easily sixty feet high and visible from a mile away, always made her think of a medieval castle with its cylindrical turrets and stone towers.

She seemed to remember somebody telling her that most monasteries in France had been destroyed or decommissioned after the French Revolution.

East of here was another monastery—this one a ruin until it had been renovated to become a high-end spa complete with tennis court and swimming pool. And of course there was Abbaye de Montmajour near Arles, a popular tourist destination. Maggie shivered at the memory of a terrifying night she'd spent there the year before Mila was born.

Upon reaching the front door of the monastery she grabbed its heavy wrought iron door handle and pushed hard to open the door which led to a small foyer that opened up into the main dining area. This room featured a high arched ceiling of rock over stone floors and walls inset with tall narrow windows. Metal and wooden tables had been set up in no particular order where at least two dozen people sat eating their midday meal.

The metal dining tables jarred with the image of the façade of the ancient abbey as they lined the center of the long hall. Children ran laughing and screeching across the stone floor and groups of men and women sat at the tables with bowls of steaming soup before them. Laughter welled up in the hall, echoing and doubling in volume as it reverberated off the stone walls.

Maggie entered the main hall, moving past a row of narrow tables and nodding at anyone who made eye contact with her. The first person she recognized was Madame Grier who worked at the monastery as a housekeeper and dining hall manager. Unlike everyone else who came and went from the monastery, Madame Grier had lived in the monastery for nearly ten years, longer even than most of the monks.

Madame Grier was seated alone eating her soup. She saw Maggie coming and put down her soup spoon in anticipation of their greeting.

"*Bonjour* Madame Grier," Maggie said. "May I join you?"

Madame Grier shrugged and Maggie sat opposite her.

All around them Maggie heard the sound of table and chair legs scraping loudly on the stone floor which echoed throughout the bare-walled dining hall.

"This is about Chantal, isn't it?" Madame Grier said.

"It is," Maggie said.

"Your husband already talked to me."

"I know. I thought I might ask different questions."

Madame Grier raised an eyebrow, but she nodded slightly as if intrigued.

"Why didn't anyone notice that Chantal hadn't come to bed the night she was killed?" Maggie asked.

"There is only a curfew for the young ones. Chantal was nearly twenty."

"So nobody knew she wasn't in her bed?"

"I do not know what anyone else knew. I go to bed at twenty-two hundred hours. I did not know she wasn't there."

"Who did she room with?"

"Four other women. Two who have already left, Madame Lando, and a gypsy girl named Bèbè." Madame Grier scanned the room. "I don't see Bèbè but I know she is here somewhere."

"Why did the other two leave? Most vineyard owners have yet to begin their harvests."

"Not everyone is here because of a harvest," Madame Grier pointed out. "They had relatives in Dijon."

"They were related?"

"Sisters I believe. They were only here a few days."

Maggie made a mental note to ask LaBelle if she'd tracked them down and questioned them. It seemed like a lot of effort to expect from the detective, but Maggie was hopeful.

"Laurent seems to think that Rochelle and Chantal had few friends here," Maggie said.

"I do not know who is friends with whom."

"Then how did he get that impression?"

Madame Grier shrugged. "I might have mentioned that they were unfriendly. I never saw them interact with anyone here."

"What about you? Did you like them?"

"*Non.*"

Maggie looked around the sea of faces in the dining room, most of whom were watching them with open curiosity. One in particular, a young man with a fierce expression, was watching Maggie with unabashed loathing. His neck was corded with tension as he stared at her.

He wore his patched and stained jeans low on his skinny hips and a dilapidated pair of binoculars hung from a rope around his neck. It made Maggie's flesh crawl to see what felt like unadulterated hatred directed against her.

"Who is that?" she asked.

Madame Grier turned to see who Maggie was talking about and then grunted.

"That's Erté," she said. "He is not right in the head."

Knowing that helped somewhat. Just as Maggie was about to ask for a description of Bèbè, Frère Luis approached the table. He clasped his hands together and Maggie noticed nicotine stains on his fingers.

"Is everything all right, Madame Dernier?" he asked, looking from Maggie to Madame Grier.

"*Oui, mon frère,*" Maggie said. "I just wanted to talk to a few people about Madame Lando. You know she is being held for Chantal Lambert's murder."

"Yes," he said. "I was here when she was arrested."

"Right, of course. I was wondering if I might see her room? The one she shared with Chantal?"

"Yes, of course," Luis said. "But the police have taken her things and we have two other women in that room now."

"I'd still like to see it. Thank you for your help, Madame Grier."

Maggie followed Frère Luis to the women's dormitory which was on the second floor of the dining hall. It was now late morning and there were few people in the halls.

"I guess most people are already gone to their offsite jobs?" Maggie asked the tall monk as they climbed the stairs to the second floor.

"Yes, only the elders like Madame Grier are still eating breakfast." He smiled affectionately as if to indicate that this was their due.

Frère Luis stopped outside the first door they came to and rapped loudly.

A small voice answered from inside. "*Entrez.*"

Frère Luis swung open the door but did not step inside. He waved for Maggie to go in.

A dark-skinned girl in her late teens was sitting on one of the beds. She stood up when Maggie entered, a look of concern on her face. She looked past Maggie to Frère Luis.

Maggie knew that many of the women who came to the monastery had been sexually assaulted and came to *Abbaye de Sainte-Trinité* with considerable distrust of men. Laurent had told her on more than one occasion that Frère Jean and the other monks worked hard to allay their fears but in most cases it amounted to making themselves scarce in these women's presence.

The placid expression on this girl's face made Maggie think she was not one of those women.

"Why are you still here, Bèbè?" Frère Luis asked. "Are you not working in the garden today?"

"*Oui, mon frère,*" Bèbè said, standing up. "I just came upstairs to get something."

Maggie's eye went to the bed that Bèbè had just stood up from. A bulge under the pillow told her the girl had just hidden something.

Maggie turned to the monk.

"Frère Luis," she said. "Do you mind if I talk to Bèbè privately?"

Luis's eyebrows shot up at the request but he quickly complied.

"Of course not," he said. "Take your time." He nodded and then turned away, closing the door behind him as he did.

Maggie went to the girl and stuck out her hand to shake.

"My name is Maggie Dernier. And you are Bèbè?"

Bèbè shook Maggie's hand and nodded.

Maggie sat down on the bed. She saw the corner of a grease-stained napkin sticking out from under the pillow. Bèbè saw her glance and turned to it and pulled out the package of breakfast rolls.

"It's not stealing," she said. "I just wasn't hungry at breakfast."

"Of course," Maggie said. "Very practical."

Bèbè seemed to relax somewhat and she tucked the bundle of biscuits back under her pillow.

"Do you mind if I ask you a few questions?" Maggie said.

Instantly the distrust was back in the girl's eyes.

"About what?"

"Nothing specific to you," Maggie assured her. "But you shared a room with Chantal Lambert, right?"

Bèbè set her jaw but nodded.

"Were the two of you friends?"

"I didn't know her long."

I guess that's a no, Maggie thought.

"How about the American? Rochelle Lando? Was she nice?"

"I guess."

"Do you remember the night Chantal died?"

Bèbè was definitely not looking at Maggie now. Maggie could only assume the girl was fearful that Maggie was accusing her of something.

"I wonder if you remember when Rochelle came in that night," Maggie pressed.

Bèbè looked up as if trying to think and then frowned. "Not too late," she said.

"So, maybe twenty-two hundred hours?" Maggie prompted.

"I don't have a watch."

"What time do you normally go to bed?"

"When everyone else does."

This is getting ridiculous.

"And when is that?"

"About two hours after dinner."

That was a little more helpful. Maggie knew that the evening dinner hour at the monastery dining hall was at eight o'clock.

"So you were awake when Rochelle came in that night?"

Bèbè nodded her head.

"Did you think it strange that Chantal never came to bed?"

"No."

"Had she ever stayed out all night before?"

"A couple of times. The Brothers only mind if you're under twenty."

"I see."

Maggie didn't bother asking her why she didn't report the fact that Chantal wasn't in her bed. The code of the refugees seemed to be *Keep your head down and don't make trouble.* Come to think of it, not a bad philosophy for most people, Maggie thought. But not at all helpful in piecing together a murder investigation.

"Okay, Bèbè," Maggie said, standing up. "Thank you for your time. Can you tell me which bed was Rochelle's?"

She pointed to a cot by the window identical to hers.

"Someone else is sleeping in it now," Bèbè said.

Maggie walked over to the bed and glanced out the window. There was an expansive view of the monastery gardens. A chestnut tree grew by the window but it was too far away to be used as an access of any kind.

"Did Chantal have a cellphone?" Maggie asked.

"She slept with it under her pillow," Bèbè said. "But the police took all her things."

"Okay. Well, thanks for your help," Maggie said, smiling at Bèbè as she turned to leave.

"Madame?" Bèbè asked, stopping Maggie before she could leave.

"Yes, Bèbè?"

"Do you think Chantal was killed because she was bad?"

. . .

A few minutes later Maggie left the dining hall on the first floor. Bèbè's question surprised her but it shouldn't have. There was a lot of fear and superstition in these places. In Maggie's experience shame was a close partner to guilt and sometimes it was hard to know which was which.

As she stepped outside the dining hall she saw the young man Erté seated on a bench across from the entrance. Maggie smiled and waved and Erté jumped to his feet.

"*Bonjour*," Maggie called to him.

Erté threw down the stick he had been whittling and turned and ran off down the gravel path leading toward the back garden.

"Leave me alone! I didn't see nothing!"

Maggie watched him disappear into the garden. There was no reason to think he had any useable information about Rochelle or Chantal. She looked around the courtyard but it was now deserted. Anyone who had a job was at it and everyone else was either washing dishes or working in the garden.

The muffled sounds of melodic chanting coming to her from the chapel indicated where the brothers were this morning. Discouraged with what she considered her lack of results from her visit, Maggie turned and headed to the parking lot.

As she got into the driver's seat of her car, she felt her phone vibrate and she pulled it out of her purse to see she'd received a text.

She read the text with astonishment. It was from Detective LaBelle announcing that she'd just emailed Maggie a copy of Chantal's forensic report.

Maggie felt lightheaded at the news and hurriedly put the car into gear and headed back to Domaine Saint-Buvard. Perhaps the day wasn't a total waste after all.

Was this Segal's doing? she wondered.

Or had Laurent worked his magic?

In spite of her excitement only seconds before, the thought that Laurent was the reason LaBelle had capitulated gave her a queasy feeling in the pit of her stomach. She knew it shouldn't matter as long as she got the information she needed.

But somehow it did.

20

Laurent stood on his back terrace in the heat of the late afternoon, his vineyard splayed out before him, and stared into the mid-distance.

The Domaine St-Buvard fields were sectioned into quadrants by two tractor roads that carved rutted tire tracks into the dirt. One road stretched a kilometer from the side of the *mas* across the width of the vineyard to the dividing wall. Across that wall, which was now also Laurent's land, was an apple orchard that so far they had not harvested. The other road, also dirt and choked with weeds, scored the vineyard down its center.

Laurent walked to the first line of grape vines and plucked a grape and popped it in his mouth. It was bursting with juice, perfectly ripe. He turned back to the *mas* and wiped the sweat from his forehead. With both children gone for the day, the house seemed bigger, emptier.

He would make a simple supper tonight of steak and a green salad. They would eat out on the terrace if it was not too hot. Just the two of them, as it used to be.

He registered that he felt a weighed-down feeling in his legs at the thought.

They are only gone for the night, he scolded himself. *I am getting as bad as Maggie.*

Why does this year feel so different? Was it because up until now he'd had the hope that Jemmy and Mila would become interested in the vineyard? Or because he'd had Luc on hand to mirror his own passion for it?

Even with Luc gone this summer, Laurent had been encouraged by Rochelle's enthusiasm. Like most vintners she was obsessively interested in all aspects of the fields. Hadn't she taken the sting out of Luc's departure this spring with their frequent walks through the rows? Had he truly been using her as a sop against the disappointment of not having Luc here?

And now they were both gone. The harvest would go on as it had every year, only this time it was empty and uninspiring.

What's missing?

He walked back to the house and then turned on the terrace and looked out over the thick tall rows of vines.

Is it no longer enough?

A decade ago it had been enough. Learning what he needed to know—and when he started he knew nothing about growing grapes—had demanded all his time and focus. And when the children began to grow and play among the vines, he realized as so many generations of vintners before him must have realized that the *domaine* wasn't for him at all but for *them.*

The miracle of that realization had captivated him. In some ways it made him feel as if he'd joined the human race. And never would he have thought that having children would have given him that. He smiled to himself.

I have Maggie to thank for that.

Her intention to be a mother might have been instinctual—something that Laurent and most men did not have—but it was nonetheless directed toward growth, something that had only been a concept for Laurent until then.

Having a son had taught him that. Holding Jemmy in his arms as a newborn had given Laurent the first vestiges of a belief that he was doing all of this for someone other than himself.

I thought I was creating this for me. But actually it was for him. For my son.

He felt his vision blur for a moment.

And he wants no part of it.

Fortunately there was Luc who actually *was* interested in the family business.

Laurent's side pocket vibrated which startled him. He didn't often carry his phone—much to Maggie's annoyance when she was trying to reach him. He pulled it out now and saw a text from Luc. Even before reading it, his mind did a fast calculation. Sixteen hundred hours here meant it was seven in the morning in California.

Laurent scanned the text, his eyebrows drawn together.

<Dad—good time to call?>

Knowing how most of Luc's generation preferred communicating by text, a vein of trepidation coursed through Laurent. He called Luc.

"Hey, Dad," Luc said, answering.

"Is everything all right?"

"Oh, yeah, I just wanted to talk."

Again, not a good sign. Laurent unconsciously patted his top shirt pocket for the packet of cigarettes he used to keep there—before he gave them up two years ago.

"What's up?" Laurent asked, keeping his voice neutral.

"I was wondering how you'd feel if I stayed here over the August break," Luc said. "Until fall semester begins. It's only two weeks. Seems like a big expense to fly me home and then back again."

Laurent felt his stomach twist.

Luc was asking permission to miss the harvest.

"Would you have a place to stay during the break?" Laurent asked.

"I've got a couple of friends whose families live in the valley," Luc said. "And they've invited me to stay. We were going to hike the Yosemite Falls Trail. Have you started the harvest yet?"

"Not yet," Laurent said, feeling the sadness seep into his voice but fighting to keep Luc from hearing it. "I will talk with Maggie but I'm sure it's fine."

"Are you okay with me missing the harvest?"

"Of course. There will be other harvests. I'm glad you are making friends." He paused and then, perhaps because he was feeling vulnerable, he did something he would never have imagined he might do.

"Is there a girl?" he asked.

Luc laughed nervously. "Kind of. Maybe."

And then the sadness in Laurent's chest gave way to another bigger feeling. A feeling of pride.

This boy, who didn't even know he was the son of Laurent's brother, had been given a building stone experience in his life that if not for Laurent and Maggie would have been denied him.

Orphaned eight years earlier, Luc had been destined to live hand to mouth before heading unerringly toward a life of constant defiance of authority and eventual incarceration.

And yet here he was, a boy who'd dropped out of school and who'd only spoken French just three years ago, excelling at an American university, dating a California girl and being invited to spend his break hiking with her and her family.

Laurent and Maggie had taken Luc's trajectory and forced it onto a track he'd never been destined to travel. Because of them Luc's future was big and endlessly promising.

It was of course completely to Luc's credit that he'd been able to make the necessary pivot—and all the work that that entailed—to make the most of the opportunity that was handed to him instead of feeling beaten by the world. But it was also thanks to Laurent's determination to give his brother's son the chance at a life that Gerard could never have managed.

And for that, Laurent realized he felt just fine about missing Luc this year for the harvest. Even more than that, he felt fine about the fact that Luc felt free to ask for it.

There was a selfless vein in Luc—a temptation to deny his own wants and desires in order to endlessly thank Laurent and Maggie for what they'd done for him. The fact that he'd allowed himself to make this request, knowing how much Laurent was looking forward to him coming home—as any natural born child would have felt comfortable doing—was the sign that Laurent had been looking for in Luc for the last three years.

He'd been willing to chance disappointing Laurent—his first and only father figure—in order to explore the world that had been opened up to him.

For Laurent, that fact alone made it all worth it.

21

Dinner was a quiet affair that evening. Laurent grilled the steaks and served them with potatoes sautéed in duck fat and a green salad from rocket lettuce he'd bought that day at the Aix produce market.

Both Mila and Jemmy were sleeping over with friends leaving just Laurent and Maggie eating alone for a change.

The large stone terrace stretched from the back door in three tiers to the curving gravel path that led to the vineyards beyond. Dogwoods and towering Italian cypress gave spotty to nonexistent shade. It was normally too hot to eat outdoors but they'd pushed dinner back until eight—something not usually workable when the kids were there—and the air had cooled enough to allow for a pleasant meal under the stars.

Throughout the meal Laurent kept his eye on the silhouette of the vineyard beyond the garden. There was enough of a moon so that even in the dark, the outline of the thick uniform lines was visible.

"Have you picked a date yet?" Maggie asked as she cut into her steak, done exactly the way she liked it.

Laurent didn't answer at first. Rarely had she seen him so

phlegmatic this close to harvest time. Whatever was wrong with him was seriously wrong. Even in years past when they'd grappled with significant problems—debt, the loss of loved ones, betrayals and health scares—he'd always managed to be buoyed by the anticipation of the coming harvest.

Not this year.

"We will start in two days," he said.

"Oh! That's exciting."

"I have a meeting with the new pickers at the monastery tomorrow," he said. "I was thinking of having Mila and Jemmy work the fields this year."

"Oh, Laurent, is that a good idea? They'll both see it as punishment."

Laurent only grunted.

It was quite possible, Maggie realized, that Laurent meant it as punishment.

"Is everything okay?" she asked. "I mean, aside from Rochelle and the kids driving us both crazy? Are things okay at the monastery?"

"You tell me, *chérie*," he said flatly. "Since you were there today."

Maggie felt a thickness in her throat. She knew she should've expected someone to tell Laurent she'd been there. She reminded herself she had nothing to feel guilty for. She'd done nothing wrong. On the contrary.

"I needed to talk to a few people who knew Chantal," Maggie said, clenching her jaw, annoyed that he had her on the defensive like this. The only thing she was doing was everything she could to find out the truth of what happened to Chantal.

If that wasn't the same as freeing Rochelle, then maybe Laurent needed to come to grips with that sooner rather than later.

"And did you learn anything?"

Maggie sighed. She knew the reason he was unhappy she went there was because he thought she was trying to find dirt on Rochelle.

"Sometimes the things you learn aren't immediately evident," she said slowly. "I didn't learn anything new."

Laurent turned his gaze back to the vineyard. Izzy, one of the hunting dogs, whined. All three dogs were seated nearby. Maggie knew they weren't fed table scraps—unless Luc was home—so they were probably just impatient for their after-dinner walk.

"You're in a funk, Laurent," Maggie said. "I wish you'd talk about it."

"I don't know this word," he said, not looking at her.

"Funk. It means bad mood, lethargy, depressed," Maggie said.

"I am fine." He stood up and the dogs began jumping around him. He picked up his plate and reached for hers but she put her hand out to take his plate from him.

"I'll do it," she said. "Go on. Take your walk."

He hesitated and then handed her his plate.

"It's not you, *chérie*."

"I know," Maggie said. "But it's something."

"It's not important," he said as he turned to head out into the vineyard, the dogs at his heels.

But that, as Maggie knew only too well, was not at all true.

22

Maggie cleared the table while Laurent disappeared into the vineyard, the two big hunting dogs loping easily at his side and the little scruffy dog racing madly to keep up with the longer strides of the others.

She was glad Laurent had decided on the start date for the harvest. It would keep him engaged. Whatever was on his mind and eating at him would be eased with the demands of the upcoming harvest.

As she watched him vanish into the gloom of the darkened vineyard she had to admit that the evening had been so much less tense with the children gone. The realization depressed her, but she reminded herself that this was just a phase. They wouldn't always be like this.

The family just needs to get through it in one piece, Maggie thought as she carried their plates inside.

She stacked the dishes in the kitchen and debated putting them in the dishwasher, but she knew that Laurent didn't mind washing up and she had work to do in her office. She had glanced at the attachment that LaBelle had sent earlier in the evening but hadn't had a chance to examine it in depth.

She made her way through the quiet house to her office and had just settled in her chair when she heard a scratching sound at one of the French doors of her office that led to the terrace. Her heart caught in her throat at the sound. It reminded her of Petit Four who would often demand to be let into the house by scratching at that door.

She went to the door and looked out one of the mullioned windows. Fleur stood there waiting patiently to be let in, one ear crooked. Maggie opened the door and the dog came in and looked up at Maggie with soulful, sad eyes.

"Get left behind, did you?" Maggie said, reaching down to pick up the dog and settle with her into her office chair. The animal immediately lay its head on Maggie's arm and sighed contentedly.

Maggie turned back to her computer but before she had a chance to open up the email attachment from LaBelle her phone rang. She saw it was Grace calling.

"Hey, you," Maggie said picking up.

"Hello, darling, is this a bad time?"

"No, it's good. LaBelle sent me Chantal's forensic report and I've got a quiet house and all evening to go over it."

"Oooh, sounds like a fun evening," Grace said with a laugh. "I just heard from Zouzou."

"How's she doing?"

"Loving Paris, not sure she wants to come home, happier than I've ever heard her."

"Oh, I'm glad. So the course is working out?"

"In spades. It's confirmed for her that making pastries is what she wants to do for a living."

"I wish Mila would get some kind of confirmation for what she wants to do."

"Well, Mila's five years younger than Zouzou. Plenty of time for her to find her thing. How about Luc? Have you heard from him recently?"

"We did. Turns out he wants to stay in California until the next term starts instead of coming home."

"What about the harvest? Laurent needs him, doesn't he?"

"Laurent doesn't want to hold him back from getting the most out of his experience in California."

"And this from the man who said a college education was over-rated," Grace said.

"I know. Turns out Laurent wants for Luc what he never had the option for himself."

"Hardly surprising. But what will he do about the upcoming harvest?"

"I imagine he'll do what he did before Luc landed in our lives."

Maggie thought back to the first time Laurent had brought Luc to their house. She herself had been right in the middle of a serious family event and later regretted that she hadn't reached out to him in a way that made him feel more welcome. But that was before she realized that Laurent intended to make Luc a permanent fixture in their family.

Now she couldn't imagine their lives without him.

"Well, I'm sure it'll all work out," Grace said. "Gotta go. Philippe's bath time."

"Give him a kiss for me."

"Will do."

Maggie hung up and then shifting the dog in her lap, found the email from LaBelle on her computer and clicked on the attachment.

Right away she saw that two paragraphs toward the end of the report had been heavily blacked out.

What's the point of giving me the forensic report if you're going to redact half of it?

She scanned the report before going back to look at it in detail. The ME's findings at the end said that the victim had been killed by a slash to the throat at approximately nineteen hundred hours on the sixteenth of August.

Maggie put the dog down on the floor before going into the kitchen to pour herself a glass of wine. She went to the French doors off the dining room to try and see the light from Laurent's flashlight out in the field.

She marveled at how many years she'd done exactly this—watch her husband roam his beloved vineyard—and she found herself remembering her first harvest at Domaine St-Buvard which at the time she'd thought and hoped would be her last.

She caught sight of Laurent coming down the garden path toward the kitchen and so turned and took her wine back to her office where Fleur was waiting for her.

She sat back down at her computer and the dog curled up at her feet. Maggie scrolled to the beginning of the forensics report, noting the case investigator was listed as Margaux LaBelle. A brief overview was followed by a description of how the evidence in the case was acquired included scrapings of dirt and grass surrounding the body as well as the lavender stems that had been found placed in Chantal's clothing.

A description of the likely murder weapon was also given. A photograph of a generic scythe was attached. *Fourteen-inches long, serrated, curved with either a wooden or stainless steel handle.* The report suggested that this sort of blade would match the gash in the victim's throat.

Maggie would have to show the picture to Laurent to see if he could confirm it looked like the one he'd given Rochelle. Had Rochelle told LaBelle that Laurent gave her a scythe?

She must not have or the detective would be pounding on our door ready to haul Laurent off in cuffs.

Under *Steps Taken* in the report, the medical examiner had also included the results of a toxicology panel done on Chantal which revealed what she'd eaten for dinner that night—very little food, no alcohol or drugs.

The report went on to say the victim hadn't been sexually assaulted, and finished by saying that aside from the presentation of the body and the lavender buds in her clothing, the only other thing of mild interest was the fact that a sheen of perfumed salve had been detected on her cheek.

Written under the subhead entitled *Analysis* was:

Victim was killed as a result of a single sharp-force injury to the throat. Death was not instantaneous. Cause of death was massive loss of blood from the slash to the throat—which created an incised wound as opposed to a stab wound—which has been determined to be the killing injury.

Due to the position of the slash on the victim's neck—high on one side and then down and across the front—it is further concluded that the victim was attacked from behind.

There were no defensive wounds.

Maggie closed her eyes as she saw the assault on Chantal in her head. She could see the girl walking through the lavender field. Was she running or was she oblivious to the fact that she wasn't alone?

Feeling a sudden coldness in her extremities, Maggie shook the image out of her head. She leaned down and scooped up the dog, feeling a need to hug something warm and alive.

She didn't know if it was good or bad that Chantal hadn't been facing her killer when she was attacked.

Probably good.

Especially if she knew her killer.

23

Laurent tapped on her office door and opened it. "It is getting late, *chérie*," he said. "Come to bed."

Maggie looked at the clock and was astonished to see it was after eleven o'clock already.

"I will in a minute," she said. "I just want to finish up something."

"You have made a friend."

Maggie glanced down at the little dog curled up in her arms.

"I can't believe Mila lost interest in her," she said. "She's so sweet."

"Mila has lost interest in many things lately," Laurent said ominously.

"It's just a stage, Laurent. Be patient."

He grunted and left the room.

Maggie turned back to the document on her screen and re-read the list of ingredients for the trace emollient that was found on Chantal's cheek.

Linalool, linalyl acetate, lavandulol, geraniol, bornyl acetate, borneol, terpineol, and *eucalyptol* or *lavandulyl acetate.*

Was this a sunscreen or some other kind of makeup?

Did it make sense that Chantal was wearing sunscreen? Most of the refugees didn't have enough money for soap let alone sun protection, particularly an expensive one with lavender additives.

Taking each of the components one by one Maggie looked them up online. She discovered that a high concentration of the *lavandulol* and its acetate which appeared in the ME's notes resulted in a rosaceous, sharp floral aroma.

She frowned.

So was it primarily a fragrance or a medicinal treatment of some kind with fragrance added as a secondary feature?

And whatever it is, was it on Chantal or her killer?

It occurred to Maggie that if it was a fragrance it might mean the killer was more likely a woman.

Maggie felt her pulse quicken. Not that men don't wear cologne but it seemed unlikely. Maggie flashed to the memory of Enzo. The man didn't look he bathed, let alone wore cologne. Maybe he used cologne instead of bathing?

She opened another browser window on her computer and called up a map of the lavender farm field. It was approximately twenty hectares and featured three structures: the processing barn, the storage shed, and the house where Madame Toussaint lived.

What about her employees? Where did they live? Did anyone besides Chantal live at the monastery?

She opened up Google Earth to look at the three structures on the farm to get a better idea of the sizes of them but couldn't tell if there was any kind of sleeping facilities for Toussaint's temporary workers.

She went back to the map of the property and zoomed in, tracing a line with her finger on the screen to see how close the property was to the spa, *Chatoyer*.

Under a mile. Easily walking distance.

Maggie eased back into her chair and stared at the screen. Was that relevant?

The facts stated that the perfume or trace unguent that had been found on Chantal's cheek had been made from a derivative of lavender. That did not in any way restrict the possible source of the substance to the lavender farm. In fact, from what Maggie had seen from the farm's website *La Lavandin* only produced flowers for potpourri and for culinary use. This salve or whatever it was on Chantal's cheek was an amalgamated product.

It had been made in a laboratory, not in a barn by unskilled transient workers.

Maggie heard Laurent close the back door off the dining room. The dogs were safely in and he was locking up the house for the night. She herself had a full day tomorrow. But she had every intention of connecting with Laurent before he fell asleep tonight. It didn't have to be words, in fact, she could probably reach him better without words.

She made a mental point to check out the *Chatoyer* website in the morning. Being in Provence they undoubtedly had lavender products—cosmetics, aromatic oils and moisturizers—for their clients' use. If *Chatoyer* was the source of the mystery salve, that would be the first major clue toward moving the evidence of culpability away from Rochelle.

As Maggie closed down her computer, her eye fell on a line in the report which gave the time of death as between six and eight o'clock. That was a wide enough window to have allowed Rochelle to kill Chantal and make it to the theater in Aix with no one the wiser.

Maggie shivered at the cold bloodedness that that would have entailed—to sit in an audience and applaud like a normal person while your hands were still stained from the murder you'd just committed? Only a true sociopath could pull that off.

As she turned off her desk lamp, she realized she was thinking of Rochelle as the killer again.

Either I'm incapable of being impartial about her, or I'm just trying to be open-minded in order to see what the cops are seeing.

Pushing away her annoying bias, she willed herself to believe the latter.

As she left her office, the little dog trotting at her feet, Maggie saw Laurent standing at the foot of the stairs with two glasses of brandy in one hand. That was a good sign.

Because regardless of how evasive he was or how resistant to verbally sharing his feelings, the fact that he was waiting to be with her tonight meant that even he knew it was time to start communicating.

24

The next morning the sun shone hot and staggering. Maggie could practically smell the grapes on the vine as she sat in the back terrace and drank her morning coffee.

She and Laurent had connected last night and while it was largely wordless, Maggie felt the intimate connection had helped sand off the rough edges to their anxiety over Rochelle, the children and life in general.

It was a start anyway.

Laurent made her coffee, his movements fluid and light, he was humming, and took off in the car to run a few errands in Aix before heading to the monastery where he would meet with his new batch of pickers.

Normally Laurent would have housing for them while they worked his fields, but this year the residents of his houses had stayed on from last year in order to pick up area work. While he'd built the houses to accommodate the people picking his fields, he didn't discourage the ones who'd decided to stay in the area.

He still checked on the maintenance of the houses, gave day

work to those who wanted it, and helped them access the various social services available to them. Much like he'd done for Rochelle, Maggie realized.

Maggie was glad that the harvest was poised to begin. Even if it didn't appear to be the magical time of achievement for Laurent that it had been in the past, it would certainly demand all his attention at least for a few days.

The dogs Izzy and Buddy were inside the house but Fleur had opted to curl up on the end of Maggie's chaise lounge while she enjoyed her coffee. They'd rescued the dog four weeks ago but this was the first time that Maggie realized that Fleur—regardless of how much Mila had begged and pitched a fit to own her—apparently belonged to her now.

"Is that okay with you, little girl?" she said to the dog.

Fleur perked her floppy ears and cocked her head in Maggie's direction. Her spindly little tail wagged tentatively.

Maggie's phone chimed indicating she'd received a text and she picked it up to see that it was from Jemmy.

<Dads here. Do we really have to leave yet?>

Maggie was surprised Jemmy had the nerve to attempt to go over Laurent's head by asking her to intervene. It wasn't too long ago that Jemmy would never have considered doing that. But he was fifteen now. It was probably time he started standing up to the authority figure in his life.

She texted him back.

<If he's there to pick you up then yes. Sounds like you had a good time?>

Maggie put the phone down but Jemmy didn't text her back.

She was surprised to hear that Laurent was ready to collect the children. She assumed he was on his way to pick up Mila too. While the respite from their demands was restorative, she found it curious that Laurent was ready to jump back into the fray with them.

She debated texting him to ask why he was picking them up but decided enough people were questioning his motives.

If he was truly thinking of recruiting them for the harvest, it would make sense that he'd bring them to the monastery so that they could listen to his spiel to the pickers.

She leaned over and ruffled the little dog's ears.

"I can't imagine *that's* not going to go well," she said to the dog who responded by wagging her tail appreciatively. Maggie took her coffee cup into the house and rinsed it out, placing it in the sink drainer.

Whatever was going on with Laurent he clearly had a plan and as per usual he wasn't ready to share with her. She would trust he knew what he was doing.

She grabbed her purse and cell phone, double checked that all the burners were off in the kitchen, and left the house.

∼

Laurent was about at the limit of his ability to block out the bickering of his children in the back seat of the Peugeot as he drove to the monastery. Twice he'd caught himself accelerating down the narrow village road in an unconscious desire to get there and get rid of them as fast as possible.

"Put your headphones on," he said to both of them.

I'm sick of listening to you.

Last night had been pleasant. The lack of tension due to the kids' absence at one point made Laurent wonder if he even loved his children anymore.

He found himself thinking of his own father and how complicated that relationship had always been. And while he knew for a fact his father had never felt the depth of emotion that Laurent felt for Mila and Jemmy—and Luc, too—it niggled at his brain in an uncomfortable way that there was a possibility he was allowing a difficult time to affect his affection for them.

Maggie had actually insisted it was okay to like their children less during this time. She felt that the love was always there but just buried under resentment, outrage and frustration. In time, those things would fall away and the love would be the only thing still standing.

Be that as it may, Laurent would not give up or allow himself to become discouraged about this so-called stage.

Which was why last night he'd devised a plan.

A plan that gave him back control and a sense that things were moving forward. One that helped underscore the idea that this was a temporary situation. And most importantly one that focused his troublesome progeny on matter of their family. Laurent had decided that he and Maggie had been too lenient with the children.

They needed to be reminded that they were part of a unit.

And that there were consequences to behaving against that unit.

25

Twenty minutes later Maggie pulled into the driveway of *La Lavandin*. She waited in her car for a moment and watched the two young women enter the barn, followed a few minutes later by Enzo.

She glanced at her watch. Four days after the murder and not an ounce of evidence that the police had even been here. Were they really finished processing the crime scene?

She left her purse in the car, tucking her phone in her slacks pocket and walked toward the barn. As she neared she heard the voices from inside. She pushed open the double door but didn't enter.

In front of her was a tractor and beside it a large machine that was difficult to tell the front from the back. It looked like a monster lawn mower but featured a hydraulic ladder, two giant rakes in front, and a rusting platform.

Maggie looked from it to the long tables of lavender, some piled, others tied in bundles and stacked, some tied and hanging upside down.

The fragrance of lavender was so intense in the closed area that for a moment Maggie thought she might throw up.

"May I help you?" one of the young women jumped up from the table where she'd been tying twine around stalks of lavender.

"My name is Maggie Dernier," Maggie said, smiling and rubbing her forehead, behind which she felt a throbbing headache emerging. "I'm Rochelle Lando's friend."

"We don't have to answer your questions," Enzo said, suddenly materializing from behind a giant metal container of lavender buds.

The other woman, clearly not a teenager like the first one now that Maggie was closer to her, stood up and walked to where Enzo was. She put her fists on her hips and glared at Maggie. She was attractive but rough looking, a scar on her cheek and her hair braided in one long plait down her back.

"That's true," Maggie said, moving further into the barn. "And if you have nothing to tell me about what happened here last Friday night then you may choose not to talk to me."

"Exactly."

"But you should know that I own a tourist newsletter with over ten thousand subscribers and should I mention anything about how unhelpful this operation was to me when I toured the facility, I'm sure Madame Toussaint might be less than pleased with you."

There was a pause as if the air in the room had been sucked out. Maggie waited to see which way the coin would fall.

"You want a tour?" the teen girl asked.

"Absolutely," Maggie said with a shrug. "I might do a feature on this place."

"She's lying," Enzo said.

Maggie turned to him. She held up her cellphone and snapped his photo.

"Hey! What are you doing?" he said, his face reddening.

Maggie turned and photographed the table full of lavender fronds and then turned to the teenager.

"What's your name?" she asked.

"Brigitte."

"What are you doing here?" Maggie indicated the table where the girl had been working.

Brigitte pointed to the giant metal basket of lavender.

"I take the flowers from there, sort and batch them," she said.

Maggie looked at the metal basket and then the mower that it was still attached to.

"So the mower—" she started.

"It's called a harvester," Brigitte said, giggling and looking over at Enzo and the other woman to see if they were amused too.

"Okay, the harvester," Maggie said, moving closer to the machine. "Wow. That's impressive."

"Enzo drives the tractor," Brigitte said as she walked around the harvester, clearly encouraged by Maggie's interest. "As he drives, the harvester cuts the flowers with that two-drum disk mower." She pointed into the machine but to Maggie all the blades and rakes looked the same. "And then it just rakes everything into the trapper where the head of the lavender is cut off."

"So you don't have to cut the lavender by hand?" Maggie asked.

"Oh, no we do," Brigitte said, the color suddenly leaving her face. Maggie could see the moment that Brigitte remembered how Chantal was killed.

"But we only do one section of the field by hand," she said, now subdued and looking down at her feet. "The harvester is used for the big batches of lavender."

"This is a lot of lavender," Maggie said, trying to help the girl feel at ease again. "Does it ever give you a headache to smell it all day long?"

The girl nodded her head and then smiled shyly. "Every day!"

"I can imagine. So what do you make with the lavender?"

"We make pillows, potpourri, and hanging decorative stalks. Plus we sell the buds to different places to make soaps, medicines and for use in cooking."

"But you don't make those kinds of things here?"

Brigitte glanced back at the table as if the very sight of the rough hewn sorting table was answer enough.

"Not really."

"What about cosmetics?" Maggie asked.

"No, nothing like that. But I think Madame sells some to people who do."

"Like the *Chatoyer* spa?" Maggie asked.

"I think so," Brigitte said.

"Hello? Can I help you?"

Maggie turned to see Annette Toussaint enter the barn. She looked disheveled as if she'd just awakened from a nap.

"*Bonjour*, Madame Toussaint," Maggie said brightly. "I was just asking some questions about your operation here. The kinds of lavender products you make."

Madame Toussaint smiled but it was strained and looked artificial.

"As you see," she said tightly, "we make no products except for the lavender itself. Enzo, Brigitte, Gené, please get back to work."

"She interrupted us!" Enzo said.

"I understand that," Madame Toussaint said, not looking at him. She turned to Maggie and held out an arm as if to guide her back out the door.

"So Brigitte was saying how you sell some of your lavender to the spa down the street?" Maggie asked.

Maggie followed Toussaint outside into the heat, the light immediately highlighting the deep lines in the older woman's face. Maggie couldn't help but think that Toussaint must have spent most of her life working under the hot Provençal sun.

"We sell a fourth of what we grow to area hotels and to two spas in the region," Madame Toussaint said smoothly.

"A fourth seems like a lot," Maggie said.

"It is what it is."

"So it's a lucrative business for you?"

"May I ask the point of these questions?" Madame Toussaint said.

"You know I'm still working with the police about Chantal's murder," Maggie said pleasantly. "And she was killed on your property."

"Yes, of course I could hardly have forgotten that," Madame Toussaint said tartly. "But the police have questioned us and have now left us alone."

"I see that," Maggie said. "But they are happy with the prime suspect they have for Chantal's murder. And I feel as if there are still a few questions that haven't been answered."

"Like what?" Madame Toussaint asked, folding her arms across her chest.

"Like where do your employees sleep?" Maggie asked.

Toussaint appeared surprised at the question.

"Brigitte and Gené sleep in the back of the storage shed," she said. "It's perfectly comfortable."

Says the woman who sleeps in a bed in the house.

"Why didn't Chantal sleep there too?"

"She did sleep there until she proved too disruptive, at which point I insisted she move to the monastery."

"Where does Enzo sleep?"

"I have no idea."

"How long have Brigitte and Gené been working for you?"

Toussaint let out a loud breath of impatience.

"Brigitte began at the beginning of summer. She'd been living at the monastery. Gené has been with me for three years now."

"Is she a mute?"

"I beg your pardon?"

"Does she speak? I've seen her twice now and—"

"Yes, of course she can speak. She is from Montpellier though and I would imagine her accent might be difficult for an American—even one who speaks French as well as you do, Madame Dernier—to understand."

Maggie looked out over the field.

"So when will your harvest be done?"

"We'll harvest the last of the lavender later this week," she said.

"And then is everyone out of a job?"

"The girls will have another two weeks of work processing the lavender."

"What about Enzo?"

"He knows I will not need him after this week. If Rochelle hadn't gotten arrested, I would have let him go today."

"Any idea what he intends to do?"

"He is a transient worker, Madame Dernier," Toussaint said tartly. "I do not expect your husband gathers employment history or personnel details from his harvest pickers when they are finished. And now if you will excuse me, I should be inside overseeing the processing of the lavender."

"Sure," Maggie said. "Thanks for your time."

As she watched Toussaint disappear back into the barn, Maggie couldn't help but think the woman was a lot less friendly today than she'd been when Maggie had first visited her.

Did that mean she had something to hide?

Maggie pulled out her phone as she walked back to her car. First she scanned the photos she'd taken inside the processing barn. There was nothing that jumped out at her in any of them. She studied the picture of Enzo and wondered if he had a record and if LaBelle had a file on him.

Then she located the number for *Chatoyer* and called the

spa using a strident American southern accent to make an appointment for the following day for a full day's spa treatment. She disconnected, waited a few seconds and then called back, this time using her most careful textbook Parisienne French.

"*Allo,*" she said when the receptionist answered again. "I am Bonnie Caldwell from *Fashionista* magazine. I am calling to confirm my appointment with Étoile Monet for tomorrow morning?"

The receptionist, flustered, put Maggie on hold for a moment.

Maggie leaned against her car and stared out over the purple fields. The fragrance of the lavender from the barn still clung to her clothing and hair but out here in the sunshine the effect was bearable, not cloying or oppressive.

"Madame Caldwell?" the receptionist said, coming back on the line.

"*Oui?*"

"Madame Monet is looking forward to seeing you tomorrow at eleven o'clock."

"Very good," Maggie said. "*Merci et au revoir.*"

She hung up and turned in the direction where she imagined the spa was located. Just a few hundred feet a head of her between the farm and the spa was the spot where Chantal's body had been found. Maggie imagined the girl standing in the lavender fields last Friday on what had been a dark, moonless night.

She closed her eyes and saw the violence, the struggle, the final kiss. And then she saw in her head as Chantal's killer began gently, systematically stuffing Chantal's clothing with the lavender fronds before finally arranging her arms as if to be seen hugging herself.

What had that meant to the killer? What was the purpose of that?

With a sad sigh, Maggie opened her eyes and began to turn toward her car door when she felt the hairs on the back of her neck ignite in a wordless warning seconds before a terrible pain erupted at the base of her head—sending her plummeting into a star-filled abyss.

26

"You can't be serious!" Mila said, trailing Laurent and Jemmy as they entered the monastery compound walls. "Does Mom know you're doing this?"

Laurent ignored her but glanced at Jemmy who although less willing to verbally complain appeared no happier about the situation than Mila.

Frère Luis appeared in the courtyard, his eyes registering surprise at the sight of the two children with Laurent.

"*Bonjour*, Monsieur Dernier," he said. "You have brought us more workers, I see."

"*Exactement*," Laurent said. "You are still needing help in the garden?"

"Always," Luis said.

"Dad, no!" Mila said under her breath but Laurent was sure she wouldn't complain further in front of the monk. Probably not.

"I am just here for a few hours," Laurent said to Luis. "But my children would help if you need them."

Luis turned to both children with a broad smile.

"That is wonderful," he said. "Yes, of course. It is a hot day today and we will be able to allow the older ones to do indoor work. It is much appreciated."

Laurent was tempted to see if the monk's praise was having any effect on his fractious children but it wasn't worth the effort. Especially since he had every reason to believe he would be disappointed. With Mila at least.

"*Bon*," Laurent said before turning to walk toward the dining hall. "I will be back in a few hours."

Again, the presence of the monk meant Laurent was able to retreat without any audible grumblings that he was sure he would otherwise have had to endure.

When did Mila and Jemmy become comfortable being insolent with him? When had they stopped caring for his good opinion?

Was it him? Had he and Maggie caused this? It was true that Laurent and his brother Gerard had been treated harshly by most of the adults in charge of them but to have been openly contemptuous with those adults? It would have been unthinkable.

Perhaps he should not use himself—with a ten-year history as a con man—or Gerard—a man who went on to be a murdering, thieving degenerate—as examples of anything.

Maggie had been unreservedly loved and pampered by her parents. Had she gone through a "difficult" stage like Mila?

Laurent entered the dining hall. It was well past lunch time and the only people visible in the hall were the ones wiping down tables and stacking dinner trays. At the far end of the hall he saw a half dozen people lounging at a long wooden dining table.

His pickers for this year's harvest.

As he approached, the individuals at the table straightened up and turned in his direction. He could tell that most of them were young, late teens. Harvesting was a hard job. A full day in the brutal heat starting at a little after dawn with only an hour's break for lunch and then on until it was too dark to see.

Almost all the grapes grown on Domaine St-Buvard—now enlarged by an additional one hundred and sixty hectares—were fermented and aged in the cellars of *l'Abbaye de Sainte-Trinité* which had a medieval wine cellar. Laurent had invested in stainless steel fermentation vessels and oak barrels for the monastery and had hired several of the formerly homeless refugees living there to learn the art and skill of making wine.

This was his fifteenth harvest. The first had been poor due to his lack of experience. In the second year, arson had destroyed most of his crop a week before it was due to be harvested. After that came the recovery years. Years of learning, to be sure, but bit by bit the wine had improved.

One year the rains had bleached the sweetness from the grapes. And then there were years the *Mistral* dismantled all his hard work in one evening of wind. That kind of bad luck, combined with an ill-timed delay in picking, could turn a year's hard work and effort into hectare after hectare of destroyed or drowned vines. While always a hit or miss proposition regardless of the care he took, the last few years had been decent.

This year promised to be a good year.

The life of a *vigneron*, he thought ruefully. *Always thinking that the next harvest will be the one.*

Laurent seated himself at the table among the pickers. There were four men and two young women. In Laurent's experience, the men were too rough with the grapes but year to year there were never enough women interested in doing the job.

"How many of you have picked grapes before?" Laurent asked the group.

Most of them merely shrugged. One boy raised a hand.

"*Oui?*" Laurent asked. "Where?"

"Not grapes," the boy said. "Corn."

The others laughed. Laurent sighed. Of course it would be

easier if they'd had some experience, he told himself but it was probably better this way. He wouldn't have to correct their bad habits. He could show them exactly how he wanted it done.

The girls were looking at their nails. One of the boys had a cellphone, which in itself surprised Laurent. But just because these people were homeless didn't mean they were without personal possessions. Laurent wondered how the boy paid his bill without a steady job or address.

"How much are we paid?" one of the girls asked.

At that question, everyone's head seemed to swivel toward Laurent.

They didn't care, he realized. They didn't care if they picked more bushels or managed not to bruise the grapes. They didn't care if Laurent was happy at the end of the harvest or if the wine was any good.

Is the whole world just putting one foot in front of the other without any focus or commitment or desire?

Could he blame them for only caring about the money? Most of the people living at the monastery have had the very worst of hard times. They've lost their homes, their countries, their loved ones. And whether that was from bad personal decisions or bad luck, whether they deserved to be where they were today or not, they would do whatever they had to survive.

He couldn't blame them for not enjoying the process along the way.

"You are paid by the day," he said. "Not the hour."

"That's slave labor!" one of the girls said.

"You are being *paid*," Laurent reminded her. "You are not forced to do the work." He gestured toward the door.

"You have us over a barrel, Monsieur," one of the boys said. "You know we are desperate."

"I pay the going rate," Laurent said. "You are free not to accept it."

"You know we have to accept it," one of the girls said with a frown, her arms crossed.

They have gotten used to charity, Laurent thought. They have gotten used to receiving without doing anything to earn it.

He looked at their faces and tried to imagine the self-respect and commitment he'd once seen in his pickers ten years earlier. They had been grateful to have the work so that they didn't need to accept charity.

Charity was no longer considered shameful.

He felt a powerful urge to tell them all to go sign up for government handouts—except he knew they wouldn't qualify—and then to go elsewhere for his workers.

But where? He needed to start tomorrow. The weather would not hold forever. And once it rained past the time the grapes should've been picked, the bushels would sink into mold and rot.

"I can't do all day," one of the girls said. "I have stuff to do."

That was when Laurent saw Mila in their faces. That's when he saw his own children—uninterested, privileged, bored—staring back at him. He felt the overwhelming urge to walk away.

From all of it. From the disinterested masks of the people looking at him now, from the grapes waiting in the two hundred hectares of his fields, from the assumptions of the area's vintners and the wine co-op expecting a certain amount of product from him—not to mention the vendors in Aix and Arles who had already paid him for the wine from this harvest.

Even Luc, the only one interested in the vineyard, was more interested in living in the States. Why would he want to come back to the family farm? A family he doesn't even know is really his, a family he'd only joined less than three years ago? A family farm tucked away in the backside of rural France?

"I pay sixty euros a day," Laurent said.

"At the end of each day?"

Laurent felt his body temperature rising.

"No," he said. "When the harvest is complete."

"I don't know if I can stay the whole time," the boy with the phone said. "How many days is it?"

"Depends on how well you work," Laurent said, his face stony, discouragement fluttering through him. "Typically five days."

"How many bushels would one person we expected to pick in a day?" one of the other men, a swarthy middle-eastern man with a nasty scar across his cheek, asked.

"Between one and eight," Laurent said.

They stared at him as if considering what he said.

Laurent was wondering if it was too late to rent one of the automated picking machines. If there wasn't another one available in the area—which was unlikely since most of the area vintners had already begun harvesting since *they* were not doing it by hand. The sound of the heavy dining hall door opening and slamming shut again made him turn in that direction.

A young novice wearing a heavy shirt over his tunic ran toward them, his sandals slapping against the stone floors.

The boy was gasping when he reached them, his chest heaving with his breathlessness, his eyes wide with the urgency of his mission.

"Monsieur Dernier," he said, stuttering in his attempt to get his breath back. "Fr-frère Jean says to come qu-quickly."

"What is it?" Laurent asked before noticing the streaks of blood on the boy's sleeve.

"Hurry, Monsieur!" the boy said, his face flushed with fear.

27

The blow to the back of her head drove Maggie against her car door. But she instinctively scrambled away from her attacker. Leaning against her car, she turned to see the woman Gené standing in front of her with a cricket bat in her hands.

Enzo ran up to her and snatched the weapon from her.

"Gené, *non!*" he said, the veins in his neck standing out in his agitation. "Are you mad?"

Brigitte hurried over to them and took a tentative step toward Maggie. Her eyes were wide with fear.

"Are you all right, Madame?" she asked timidly.

Maggie put her hand to her head which was now throbbing.

"Give me one good reason why I shouldn't call the police," Maggie said to Gené.

"You mustn't!" Enzo said desperately to Maggie. "Gené has been very upset about Chantal's death."

Brigitte turned and ran back to the barn.

"That's a lie," Maggie said to Enzo. "Chantal had no friends except for *possibly* you."

Gené turned and spat at Maggie's feet.

Maggie pulled her cellphone out of her purse. "Suits me," she said.

"Wait!" Enzo said before turning to Gené and speaking to her in rushed Provençal French.

Maggie put a hand to the back of her head. She could feel a lump forming but she could tell it wasn't serious. In the distance at the front of the house Maggie saw Brigitte standing on the porch with Annette Toussaint.

"Better hurry," Maggie said to Gené, "before you have to tell it in front of your boss and the police."

Gené spoke in rapid, complicated French, her eyes flashing at Maggie. Enzo's face paled and his shoulders slumped.

"What's she saying?" Maggie asked. After more than twenty years living here, her French was very good. But she could still only understand one or two words from the woman's tirade.

Maggie saw Toussaint hurrying toward them, her cane clutched in her hand, with Brigitte keeping pace beside her.

"She said she thought you were trying to get me in trouble," Enzo said, putting an arm around the woman. "This is my fault. I complained about you yesterday after you were here."

"Is that because she thought you'd killed Chantal?" Maggie asked.

"No, she is just being protective."

"Because she's your new girlfriend?" Maggie turned to Gené. "Ask her where she was last Friday night during the time Chantal was killed."

"*D'accord!*" Enzo said in frustration. "Gené and I are each other's alibis. She was with me."

"Convenient," Maggie said, her eyes narrowing at Gené. There was no doubt that Gené could understand her. *The question was, why is she refusing to speak for herself? And why did she see Maggie as a threat?*

Was it because Gené killed Chantal and was afraid Maggie might stumble onto the truth?

"What is going on here?" Toussaint said when she reached them, her eyes going from Enzo and Gené to Maggie. "Brigitte said you were attacked?"

Enzo gave Maggie a pleading look and she decided he was more useful as an ally than an enemy.

"No," Maggie said. "I caught my foot in a pothole and stumbled is all."

Annette narrowed her eyes, clearly not believing Maggie's explanation. She turned to look at Gené, her gaze hardening.

"Seriously, Madame Toussaint," Maggie said. "It's not a problem."

Annette nodded. "*Okay*," she said. "So everyone back to work."

She tucked her cane under her arm and clapped her hands sharply and both Enzo and Gené turned and walked back to the barn.

Annette turned to look at Maggie. "You are sure?"

"Completely," Maggie said. "Sorry to make a fuss."

"*Pas du tout*," Annette said. "When Brigitte told me that Gené had hit you I was afraid it was because you discovered the time she set Chantal's bed on fire."

∽

An hour later, Maggie stood at the bar of a village café a few miles from the lavender farm eating a day-old sweet roll and drinking a very strong espresso to try to stop her head from hurting.

She would have loved to have talked more to Toussaint about the whole bed-burning incident but the lavender farm manager had clearly realized she'd revealed more than she should have and quickly returned to her house. Maggie had been left to either walk the crime scene—which seemed pointless since it had already rained twice since the murder—or go find some caffeine to help dull the clanging in her skull.

Outside the café was a small fountain, long without any actual cascading font of water. Pigeons pecked at the stonework and waited for crumbs from anyone who would throw them.

Was Gené the one who overheard Rochelle threaten Chantal? Since she is sleeping with Chantal's boyfriend, isn't that motive? Even in France?

Did Maggie really believe that Toussaint had accidentally let slip the information about Gené burning Chantal's bed?

Had Chantal been in it at the time?

Was that the reason Toussaint had moved Chantal to the monastery?

If Gené was as violent as she appeared—bashing people over the head and setting their beds on fire—why didn't the cops look at *her* more closely?

If Maggie had anything to say about it, they soon would.

Maggie glanced at her watch. It was past four o'clock. Laurent would be home by now and she was curious to find out how his day went with the kids and what his intention had been.

Her phone vibrated on the counter where she'd placed it and she saw his photo appear on her screen.

Speak of the devil.

"Hey," she said. "Are you home?"

"This is Frère Albert," a squeaky voice said into the phone. "Monsieur Dernier cannot come to the phone right now."

"Why not?"

"He is at the Aix emergency room," the boy said, hiccoughing.

Maggie felt a sudden tenseness in her stomach.

"Is he hurt?" she asked, throwing down a five-euro note onto the counter and snatching up her purse as she hurried toward the door.

"No, Madame. I'm afraid it is the children."

28

Maggie ran through the entrance of the Aix Emergency Room fighting the terror that had ridden with her all the way from the café.

The smells of the room permeated her numbness as she looked around. Doctors in white coats bustled past her and a woman worked hunched over in a glassed-in reception area.

Maggie walked down the main corridor and spotted Laurent and Mila seated on chairs there. She hurried over to them. Laurent stood up but Mila didn't move.

"Mila," Maggie said and reached for her but Laurent pulled her back.

"She is fine," he said, his face bland except for one tic over his left eye.

Maggie looked around and the fear stabbed deep into her gut. Her brain tried to form the words when she realized Jemmy wasn't there. Before she could manage to get the words out, Laurent turned to her and held her by the shoulders.

"Jemmy will be fine," he said.

"*Will be* fine?" she asked, her voice rising in hysteria.

"Where is he?" She looked in the direction of the line of treatment rooms.

At that moment a young man with a stethoscope around his neck emerged from a curtained room.

"Is this the mother?" he asked Laurent.

Maggie pushed past him to enter the interior of the curtained room where she saw Jemmy on the treatment table, his face white, nervously biting his lips. When he saw her, his eyes filled with tears.

"Mom," he said.

Maggie ran to him and saw the thick white bandage a nurse was finishing putting in place across his chest.

"Jemmy, darling," Maggie said, her tears welling up.

"It's no big deal," Jemmy said. "The doc said it was just a scratch."

"How...how did you...? What happened?"

She saw Jemmy's attention shift to something over her shoulder and she turned to see Laurent entering the room.

"What happened?" she asked him, her tone thick with accusation.

Before Laurent could answer, the nurse turned from Jemmy and pointed at the curtain.

"Please wait outside," she said. "We will release him shortly and you may pick up his prescriptions at the front desk."

Maggie hesitated.

"Mom, I'm fine," Jemmy said and then sagged back against the pillows.

"Come, *chérie*," Laurent said, his hand on her elbow. "We will see him in a moment."

Maggie allowed him to maneuver her from the room.

She stood in the hallway, seeing nothing, not Mila sitting in the hall watching her or the other doctors and nurses bustling past her, nor did she hear the sounds of the public address system with its constant and monotonous messaging. From somewhere she heard moaning.

Maggie felt overcome with exhaustion as if the drive to the hospital and the last few minutes had taxed her beyond what she had strength for. She wanted to sit down, to lie down. But whatever had happened, Jemmy was alive and he looked as if he would recover.

She turned to Laurent but his face was set in a determined grimace of purpose.

"Later," he said as he signaled for Mila to join them in walking down the hallway toward the hospital pharmacy.

Fifteen minutes later, after collecting Jemmy's pain medication, they stood waiting for him to be brought out in a wheelchair. During that whole time Mila stood silently, refusing to look at her mother, confirming to Maggie that she had played a major role in today's drama.

"What happened?" she said to Laurent.

Keeping his voice neutral as if to downplay his words, Laurent briefly outlined the events that had brought them to the hospital. Maggie listened, her fury growing with every word.

"So let me get this straight," she said when he'd finished. "You took the kids to the monastery to weed their garden as some sort of character trial?"

Laurent didn't answer.

Heat flushed through her body in mounting anger. She turned to Mila. "And then you did *something* which provoked one of the refugees to attack your brother with a *knife*. Is that about the gist of it?"

Mila's eyes filled with tears.

"It wasn't my fault," she muttered.

"Then why is Jemmy in the ER getting six stitches across his ribcage?" Maggie asked sharply, taking Mila's chin and forcing her to look at her.

"The doctor said it was only a shallow cut," Mila said, looking at Laurent as if for support.

Maggie tried to tamp down her growing fury. She knew it was mostly the result of her fear mixed with relief but she felt out of control of her emotions. She closed her eyes and massaged the back of her head. Her brain felt like it was going to explode inside her skull.

"You keep rubbing your head," Laurent said, his eyes narrowing. "Did you hit your head?"

Last spring Maggie had sustained a concussion in a risky undertaking that in the ensuing months Laurent had found several opportunities to be vocally and relentlessly furious about. The last thing she needed today was to remind him of that incident or to hint in any way that she might have gotten herself hit on the head again.

"Please don't change the subject," she said arching an eyebrow at him before turning back to Mila. "If I have to hear the reason Jemmy was attacked from Jemmy instead of you, I swear I will send you to a German boarding school and we'll see if *they* can hammer some sense of personal accountability into you."

"*Maman, non!*" Mila said, her mouth gaping in horror.

Maggie glanced over to see that even Laurent was mildly shocked at her words and while she couldn't be sure how much of her threat was real, borne from the terror she'd experienced in the last hour, a part of her knew that if Mila couldn't take responsibility for having gotten Jemmy hurt, then they were no longer qualified to finish parenting her.

It made her sick to believe it, but she'd faced harsher truths in the past.

"I was kissing Bernard," Mila said in a whispered voice.

"What?" Laurent roared, making nurses and lab techs turn their heads to look at them where they stood.

"I'm sorry, Papa," Mila said, her lips trembling as she looked at him. "I don't know why I did it. We were just playing around."

"And Jemmy saw this?" Maggie said, trying to defuse whatever head of steam Laurent looked determined to detonate.

Mila nodded. "Jemmy came rushing over and punched Bernard! I tried to stop them. But Bernard pulled out a knife! I thought he was going to…I was so scared!"

Maggie felt faint as she envisioned the scene and realized how lucky they all were that Jemmy had only ended up with a shallow cut.

It could have been so much worse.

Maggie licked her lips and took a breath. Laurent was literally pacing in the narrow emergency department hallway. Any moment, Maggie expected him to drive his fist through one of the corridor walls.

"I am sorry," Mila said, tears rolling down her face. "I need to tell Jemmy how sorry I am! I didn't mean for it to happen."

Maggie put an arm around her daughter just as Laurent turned away from the two of them. Mila broke away from Maggie and watched Laurent's retreating back.

"Daddy?" Her voice broke.

Laurent turned to look at Mila, his face a thundercloud of fury which suddenly softened when he saw his daughter's face. He hesitated and then held out his arms. Mila rushed into them.

Laurent lowered himself to one knee and held her. He looked up at Maggie over Mila's shoulder, his face a picture of complete and utter confusion.

29

Maggie thought back to all the years of harvests at Domaine Saint-Buvard.

It seemed that always before on the eve of the harvest the very air would sing with excitement. Maggie would be tasked with buying and laying out the outdoor midday meals for the workers, Mila and Jemmy would help decorate the long tables, their delighted babbling serving as background music to the anticipation of the event.

In many ways it was as exciting as Christmas. Maggie had always thought it was the very epitome of anticipation. To work so hard to create something and then finally realize the fruit of your labor in just a few frenetic, exhausting but exhilarating days.

But tonight the mood was like nothing she could have imagined the day before a harvest. It felt heavy, oppressive and spoiled. Mila begged to be allowed to skip dinner and while Laurent initially refused her, when Jemmy asked to take his dinner in his room Laurent finally agreed. It was just as well.

Mila's contrition seemed to have worn off on the drive home and her usual manner of sass and contrariness was back front and center. Jemmy was quiet from his pain pills and his natural reticence. Maggie had been mildly concerned he'd not be able to keep his head up at dinner.

Both children took their dinner plates to their separate bedrooms and once more Maggie and Laurent dined alone on the terrace where the fading summer light was just enough to allow them a muted view of the vineyards.

Maggie had had time to recover from the shock of the emergency room visit—every mother's worst nightmare—and to process that Laurent's intention had been a desperate attempt to try anything he could think of to engage the children and reach them. She couldn't fault him for that. A lot of fathers would have just signed off in the face of their children's bad behavior.

Laurent's own father in fact.

After a quiet meal, Laurent stood up to take his evening walk through the vineyards with the dogs and hesitated as Maggie began to clear the table.

"Join me," he said, holding out a hand to her.

The moment reminded her of how it had been when it had just been the two of them all those years ago when they'd decided to make a go of it in Provence. And even though at the time she'd been less than eager to live abroad, there was excitement and adventure every morning she woke up in those days —even if they were also tinged with insecurity and misgiving.

She set the plates back down and went inside to get a sweater since now that the heat of the day had dissipated, a relentless coolness had set in.

She walked down the garden path to where it met the vineyard where Laurent waited. They entered the vineyard together, the three dogs romping at their heels.

They walked silently for a few moments, Laurent's eyes seeming to scan his vineyards as if even now he were searching for something in them.

"Do you like your pickers?" Maggie asked as she looped her hand through his arm to prevent the possibility of stumbling in the growing dark and the uneven paths through the field.

"Not very much," he said.

Maggie frowned. "Aren't any of the ones from past years available? The ones living in the mini houses?"

"Most of them have found permanent employment since last summer," he said.

"That's good."

"It is, of course." He stopped at the crest of a gentle hill past the ancient shed with its abandoned well. "I find I don't care."

At first Maggie didn't think she'd heard him correctly. She looked at him but as usual his face was impossible to read, especially in the gloom of the half moon.

"What do you mean?" she asked. The idea of Laurent not caring about any facet of his vineyard was just not a concept that was immediately comprehendible.

"I don't find this work...fulfilling anymore."

At first Maggie thought he might be joking except this was nothing like the kind of *bon mot* she'd ever heard from him. Matched with his mood of late, she had the terrible realization that he was finally sharing with her what his problem was.

"But you've done so much with the label!" she said. "When we first came here, we didn't get even four bushels, hardly enough to make three bottles of wine. Remember? Now you're constantly being asked to chair wine committees all over Provence and you're the head of the co-op and everyone comes to you for advice—"

"None of that means anything!"

Laurent raising his voice chilled Maggie. If he wasn't proud of what he'd built here then what had it all been for?

"Why doesn't it mean anything?" she asked. "I don't understand."

"I know you don't but I don't want to talk about it."

"Laurent, you need to talk about it. I'm your wife."

"So American."

"Be that as it may, you need to tell me why your *joie de vivre* seems to have gone right out of you."

He clenched his jaw but wouldn't speak.

"Don't make me guess," she said. "I'm sure I'll guess wrong. I need you to tell me."

"Where were you when you got the call to come to the emergency room?"

She looked at him in surprise and then narrowed her eyes at him.

"I was in a café near St-Cannat."

"Where else did you go?"

She knew he wasn't just attempting to distract her from grilling him about his thoughts but also because at some level he wanted—needed—to get his teeth into another project, maybe even a project he could fix.

"I was at *La Lavandin* again," she said.

"How is your head?" he asked, his eyes still searching, still scanning the darkened vineyard.

Now why would he ask that? It was uncanny how he knew the very thing she might be trying to hide from him.

"Fine, thank you," she said.

"Did something happen there?"

"If you mean did everyone act way more suspicious than they had when I talked to them before, then yes. How astute of you to figure that out."

He turned to regard her. "Suspicious how?"

Maggie hadn't really had time to sort out her impressions from her visit and she found that now was as good a time as any to do it.

"Well, nobody gets along for one thing," she said. "Nobody liked the victim at all. *Or* Rochelle." She glanced at him to see how he might take this news but not surprisingly, his expression didn't change.

"Plus I discovered from the forensic report that LaBelle sent me—by the way, that was your doing, wasn't it? Getting her to share that with me?"

When Laurent merely grunted in response, she went on.

"I discovered from the report that there was a kind of emollient or salve found on Chantal's cheek that doesn't look like it could've been made at the lavender farm. It might've been sourced there—"

"What does that mean?" Laurent frowned.

"It means I might have found a connection between the lavender farm and the spa that's about a mile down the road. As far as I know, Detective LaBelle hasn't even talked to anyone there. I made an appointment to visit there tomorrow."

Laurent stopped walking and Maggie turned to him and crossed her arms.

"So far I have a gypsy boyfriend who may or may not have a record of violence—"

"Why do you say that?" Laurent asked.

Maggie shrugged. "Let's just say he strikes me as the type to fly off the handle. And then there's a woman there who worked with Chantal who definitely has a history of violence."

And I should know since she walloped me with a cricket bat today.

"How do you know this?"

"I'm a detective, remember?" Maggie said with a smile, hoping he would let it go.

He narrowed his eyes as if he would ask more along those lines but then turned to head back home. He called the dogs. The two bigger dogs had raced away deep into the vineyard. Only Fleur still trotted beside them.

"Did you discover anything that might prove Rochelle's innocence?" he asked.

Maggie sighed.

"Not really. I've been trying to find evidence that someone else killed Chantal."

It was then that Maggie realized she'd steered away from investigating Rochelle too closely for fear that she would find what a part of her was sure she *would* find—proof that she'd killed Chantal.

The two of them stopped and leaned against the stone wall that enclosed Laurent's kitchen garden at the end of the vineyard. The heat from the direct sunlight earlier in the day was still palpable in the stones as Maggie leaned into them.

"Can I ask you something?" she asked.

He turned to her and frowned.

"Why are you so protective of Rochelle? Why is she special?"

"You are not jealous, *chérie*?"

"No. Just confused."

He nodded and took her hand in his. It was big and warm and Maggie felt instantly safe and loved. He pulled her to him and held her. Her face against his chest, she smelled the scent of lemons and soap. In the old days there would have been tobacco too. She was surprised to realize she missed it.

"She reminds me of the wife of a friend I once had," he said in a low voice. "Many years ago."

"Did something bad happen?"

"*Oui*."

"Is she still alive?"

"I cannot imagine that she is."

"What about your friend?"

"*Non*."

Maggie was quiet for a moment. Over the vineyard, she could see the stars in the sky slowly growing brighter by the moment. The night air felt thick as a blanket.

"Was she someone you wished you'd helped?"

Laurent leaned down and kissed Maggie.

"*Oui, chérie.* I know it was not my place but..." He lifted his shoulders in frustration. "My friend was not...capable."

"Drugs?"

He sighed. "That and other bad choices."

"You know you can't save everyone, Laurent. Some people just won't let you."

"I could have tried harder."

So there it was, Maggie thought. Rochelle was his chance at redemption. His do-over. A way to put the ghosts to rest. Maybe even to atone for the fact that his life turned out so wonderfully —a loving marriage and family, a thriving business—when everyone he'd known in the old days was either dead or in prison.

As they turned to make their way back to the house, Maggie found herself wondering if clearing Rochelle would even matter. Even if Maggie were able to somehow absolve her of all charges, Rochelle seemed to Maggie to be the classic case of the person who was her own worst enemy.

She could well imagine Rochelle wriggling out of this mess only to create a brand new one down the line.

But that was not something she could say to Laurent.

And then of course it would all happen over and over again with Laurent failing to get the amnesty he sought and the process just sending him deeper and deeper into the regrets and guilt of the life he enjoyed but felt he had not earned.

Later that night, Maggie checked on both kids in their rooms and made sure that Jemmy wasn't hurting, then began to get ready for bed herself.

. . .

On the one hand her conversation with Laurent had been discouraging but also hopeful in the fact that he was at least talking about what was bothering him.

She might not have any answers—and it had been mildly discouraging to realize that proving Rochelle's innocence might well not be the end of it for him—but at least Laurent was talking and she knew from experience that the simple act of putting his fears into words could help frame the problem for him.

Except if he's feeling guilty about how much he has that's just one more thing to add to his growing pile of remorse.

After showering she braided her long damp hair and went to the antique dresser she and Grace had found at a *brocante* in Arles a few years ago. She opened a drawer with many lavender and rose sachets in it and took out her favorite night gown. The scent of flowers tickled her nose as she pulled it on over her head.

Fleur had already positioned herself at the end of the bed. Maggie could hear Laurent downstairs securing their home, letting the big dogs out one last time, locking the doors and windows, checking that the burners were off in the kitchen.

In the old days he would then step outside for one last cigarette, maybe even take a walk around the perimeter of the *mas* as if on patrol, protecting all they had inside. She wondered what he did now in lieu of that routine.

She climbed into bed and reached for the tube of lavender cream on her bedside table and began to massage it onto her knees and elbows. The scent itself started to make her sleepy and she could feel the kinks in her shoulders ease. This particular tube she'd gotten from the Aix L'Occitane store a few months ago. She looked at the tube label and read its ingredients.

Water, glycerin, butyrospermum park, cetearyl alcohol, grape seed oil, *Lavandula angustifolia, cera alba corn starch, xanthan gum, ethylhexylglycerin, linalool-limonene.*

As she held the tube and enjoyed its light familiar scent, she found herself feeling a lingering sadness for Chantal, the girl she'd never met. She felt sad at the thought of her brutal death, of course, but also at the image of the malevolent entity who'd arranged the girl's arms and legs and tucked lavender flowers into her clothing before gently kissing her cheek.

The more she thought about it, the more Maggie was sure it had to be a kiss. It was the only explanation.

She looked at the tube in her hand. The copy written on the tube suggested it could be used as a salve, a perfume or a moisturizer. The killer could've been wearing some kind of face moisturizer. It didn't have to be lipstick.

But whatever had been transferred to Chantal's face—assuming it hadn't originated on Chantal's face to begin with—must have been on the killer's face, lips or hands. Maggie got another image of the killer touching Chantal's cheek with a hand—almost kindly or even lovingly.

She sighed. Of course it was impossible to determine *how* the residue had come to be on Chantal's face, whether it was from a kiss or a gentle stroke of the killer's hand.

Laurent came into the bedroom, glanced at the little dog but except for a subtle grimace made no reaction. He went into the bathroom to shower and Maggie turned to see her phone light up on the nightstand with an incoming text.

She picked it up, half expecting it to be Luc but the number was not one she recognized.

The message read,

<*You should know that Chantal and Rochelle had a big fight the night C was killed*>

Maggie instantly typed a response back.

<*who is this?*>

When there was no answer, she called the number. It rang but the call didn't go to voicemail.

Maggie chewed a nail as she studied the text wondering who'd sent it and what it meant.

Clearly, someone was trying to implicate Rochelle. The killer?

Then remembering what the emergency room visit had kicked out of her brain, Maggie put in a call to Grace.

"Hello, darling," Grace answered. "I'm surprised you're still up. Big day tomorrow."

"I know, listen, Grace I need you to do something for me. It's a big ask and I'm sorry it's so last minute. Can you get away tomorrow?"

Because of her work at the *gîte* the likelihood of that wasn't always a given.

"I might be able to," Grace said. "The Germans left today and the Americans are all doing a day trip to Paris. We've got no new guests coming in until the weekend. What's up?"

Twenty minutes later, after hanging up with Grace, Laurent came into the bedroom toweling his wet hair when his phone on the nightstand chimed. Maggie watched him go over to it and pick it up.

"Who is it?" she asked.

"Luc," he said. "Wishing me luck on the harvest tomorrow."

As she watched Laurent drop his phone onto the bed and turn to his dresser to find a clean cotton t-shirt, Maggie was torn between the urge to try to somehow cheer him up or give credence to the reality of what they were both feeling—wistful that the one child who even remotely cared about tomorrow's harvest was six thousand miles away.

30

A heavy scent of wisteria dragged Maggie out of sleep. Sunlight was already filtering through the east-facing window making dark rectangles on the bedroom carpet. The cream-colored draperies fluttered in the breeze and she could hear the sounds of voices as if coming from a long way away.

She glanced at her nightstand and saw the cup of coffee, now cold, that Laurent had placed there at least two hours earlier.

Well, it's the thought that counts, she thought as she swung her legs out of bed.

The house was quiet but her open window let the vineyard voices carry into the room where she lay in bed.

Today was the first day of the harvest.

She reached for her robe and stepped to the large bedroom window that faced the garden at the back of the house. A platoon of olive and fig trees lined the pebbled path from the terrace leading to the fields that she and Laurent had walked the night before.

From where she stood, the truffle oaks, thyme bushes and

cypresses seemed to create a virtual park, demarcating the property and framing the entrance to the two hundred hectares of grape fields where Maggie could see a handful of moving figures.

Two tractors inched slowly down the parallel paths of the hillside, each loaded with empty crates that would soon fill with the grapes of *Domaine St-Buvard*. The pickers moved slowly in front of the tractors, combing the vineyard, methodically stripping the vines as they went.

In the midst of them Maggie saw Laurent's familiar form—always the tallest—moving steadily around the knot of workers.

She noticed that he'd set up outdoor lighting along one side of the outer perimeter of the vineyard. Often the pickers worked into the evening, as it was cooler and more pleasant to pick at night. Maggie knew Laurent—like all the vintners in the area—was hoping to finish before the rains came. That meant picking as much as humanly possible each day.

Which meant creating his own lighting system and picking into the night.

Turning away from the window, Maggie went to the large closet she'd had Laurent build for her years ago when they'd first moved to Domaine St-Buvard to select her outfit for the day. It was important that she get her look right since she was going to pose as a writer for a luxury magazine.

She selected a Jil Sander belted taffeta dress to wear with her best Prada pumps and pulled her long hair back into a messy bun at the nape of her neck. She applied her makeup carefully—not too much but enough to cover the freckles and lines from fifteen years of living under the hot Provençal sun.

When she finished dressing, she inspected the result in her bedroom mirror and decided it would do. By the time she got her foot in the door of Étoile's office, she probably would have only about fifteen minutes before the woman figured out she'd been tricked and that Maggie had about as much to do with couture as a turkey does with the Tour de France.

But as far as Maggie was concerned, fifteen minutes should do it.

After spritzing on a healthy blast of *La Vie est Belle*, Maggie checked on both Mila and Jemmy—both of whom were grounded for the foreseeable future. Jemmy had pulled his desk chair to the window in his bedroom which faced the back terrace in order to watch the pickers.

She thought about telling Laurent later this evening about Jemmy's interest but decided it would only serve to get his hopes up. Jemmy would be just as interested in what was going on outside his window if there was a crew of workmen taking down a plane tree.

Mila on the other hand was a few seconds too slow in hiding the iPad that she'd been watching a TV show on when Maggie opened her bedroom door. Maggie had been forced to take the device from her and bear the immediate knee-jerk wrath of her only daughter.

"You have a whole bookcase full of books," Maggie said as she stood in the doorway of Mila's bedroom with the iPad under her arm.

When Mila glowered at her, Maggie simply shrugged, her voice cheerful and unaffected.

"Your father is expecting both you and Jemmy to help lay out the lunch for the workers at midday," she said. "You'll find everything you need—"

"But you normally do that!" Mila protested.

"Yes, but today I have something else to do. You're thirteen years old, Mila. That's plenty old enough to—"

"Oh, stop!" Mila said, rolling her eyes. "Fine. Whatever."

"Great," Maggie said and closed the bedroom door as she left.

An hour later, Maggie was driving down a winding country

road to *Chatoyer* spa. As she drove, mindful of oncoming cars, she put a call in to Grace.

"Ready for today?" Maggie asked.

"Are you kidding?" Grace said with a laugh. "This is the kind of undercover work I was born to do."

"Now remember, talk some but not too much. The main point is to get your quarry—whoever that turns out to be—talking."

"Yes, darling, I do know what I'm doing," Grace said. "Remember Grenoble?"

Maggie felt her stomach tighten at Grace's words. The memory of Grenoble was not a happy one, regardless of how it had all turned out. The point of the trip, now eight years ago, had been for her and Grace to reconnect after an unfortunate two-year gap in their friendship. When the trip started, Maggie had been adamantly uninterested in salvaging her relationship with Grace. But by the time it ended not only had she and Grace rescued their friendship but they were able to begin again stronger than before.

"Don't be a hero," Maggie warned Grace now. "You can use the audio recording function on your phone."

"How am I supposed to do that when I'm naked under a sheet on a massage table?"

"Set it up in your clothes beforehand," Maggie said.

"Do you seriously think my masseuse is going to tell me something worth knowing?"

"I don't know but I think it's worth the effort. *Chatoyer* is less than a mile from where Chantal was killed. As far as I'm concerned the lavender salve found on her cheek puts them in the frame."

"Uh oh. Does that mean that as far as the *police* are concerned, the spa isn't suspicious?"

"Yes, but that means nothing," Maggie said. "Just be a little bit gabby, throw in some chit-chat about the murder and see what happens."

"And am I to chit-chat about death and gore with everyone I meet? Won't that look suspicious?"

"Not a bit. Just lay it on like you're a clueless, insensitive American tourist," Maggie said. "They'll happily think the worst of you and never suspect a thing because you're a foreigner."

"Hmmm. I must say that's a lot easier than trying to charm them," Grace noted. "I'll do my best, darling. And thanks again for the opportunity to get a free deep-tissue massage. It's been ages."

31

For some reason Maggie had expected to see a castle or some kind of ancient edifice set in the middle of Provence but the building she drove up to looked like it had been built in the seventies. A truncated lawn framed with boxwoods fronted the entrance walk that led to the double doors.

In spite of the long winding drive to reach the building, the final destination looked remarkably bland and characterless to her.

It was a Wednesday and for no reason that Maggie could discern, the spa appeared remarkably vacant. There were a few cars parked in the gravel parking lot but those could belong to employees of *Chatoyer*.

For a moment a niggling thought flitted across Maggie's brain.

Could this place be a front for something else?

Once inside she saw the lobby was a glamour magazine picture of sleek wood, low lamp lighting and giant crystal vases of fresh flowers that must have come from the Aix flower market. There were also bundles of lavender stems in large ceramic vases which were set on marble top tables.

Maggie walked to the front desk where a young woman sat, her face heavily made up; and her painted nails were at least two inches long.

"Do you have an appointment?" the woman asked with a frozen smile before Maggie could speak.

"I am Bonnie Caldwell here to see Madame Monet," Maggie said briskly.

The receptionist gave Maggie's outfit a baleful glance before turning away.

I guess that answers the question of whether or not midcalf length is still vogue, Maggie thought.

"Take a seat," the receptionist said with undisguised contempt. "I will tell Madame Monet you are here."

Maggie went to the waiting room and sat in one of the color coordinated plush armchairs. A rack of brochures next to her touted cosmetic procedures and products. She picked up one but didn't see anything that specifically mentioned lavender.

After flipping through a recent copy of *Marie-Claire* that she'd picked up from the coffee table, Maggie looked at her watch and saw that she'd been kept waiting for over fifteen minutes. As far as her cover was concerned she wondered if she should respond as if arrogantly annoyed at being kept waiting —*what would a reporter from a snobby Paris magazine do?*—or pretend to be oblivious as if she were above such pettiness as keeping score?

In the end, she decided that working to fool the receptionist seemed like a lot of effort for very little return. She would save whatever guile she had in her for her actual interview with Étoile Monet.

Besides, trying to impress the receptionist was probably futile,

I could be the prime minister's wife and she would still condescend to me.

"Madame Caldwell?" the receptionist said, standing. "Madame Monet will see you now."

Maggie gave the girl as patronizing a smile as she could manage and followed the girl down a narrow carpeted hall. Even in the administration section, the spa felt hushed and muted.

The girl, who Maggie was sure was wearing Valentino—and not last season's either—led the way down the hallway tottering on six-inch Blahniks.

How does a receptionist afford a pair of thousand euro shoes?

They passed a line of doors with plaques on them labeled as treatment rooms and stopped in front of a set of double doors. The receptionist opened the door dramatically and ushered Maggie inside.

The office was every bit as relaxing and calming as the waiting room with a bowl of potpourri in one corner and three flickering, scented candles on the credenza by the window.

A statuesque blonde was standing in the room by a large light wood desk in the center of the room. She walked over to Maggie, her hand outstretched.

"Thank you, Bijou," Étoile Monet said to the receptionist who turned and promptly closed the office door behind her.

"I am Étoile Monet," Étoile said as she and Maggie shook hands.

"Bonnie Caldwell from *Fashionista*," Maggie said, prepared to explain that her magazine was new if Monet questioned her. "Thank you for seeing me."

"Of course." Étoile gestured to a thickly padded velour chair in front of her desk.

Maggie sat and pulled out her phone.

"Do you mind if I record our interview? My French isn't as good as I'd like."

Étoile hesitated for just a moment.

"No, of course not," she said as she slowly seated herself.

Maggie set the phone on the desk between them. She was sure Madame Monet was not at all comfortable with the idea of a recorder which in itself indicated something.

"First," Maggie said. "I have a few boiler-plate questions. Just basic stuff about your operation here."

"Operation," Monet said with a condescending smile. "*Mon Dieu.*"

Maggie's research last night had revealed that there were no other spa facilities within a fifty mile radius. Most were situated on the east side of Aix or clustered around Arles.

"How many people do you have working here?" Maggie asked.

"We have a staff of twelve," Étoile said. "But because it's August we have reduced bookings so we are on a reduced staff."

"What can I tell our readers about *Chatoyer*?" Maggie asked.

Monet leaned back in her chair and steepled her fingers as if composing her thoughts.

"We have all the usual services, of course," she said. "But unlike some of the older spas in the area, we also offer yoga instruction, lifestyle retreats, meditation, Tai Chi, aromatherapeutic practices as well as smoking cessation and weight loss."

"So you're more of a high-end fat clinic than an actual spa?" Maggie asked.

"Weight reduction is only one of the many services we provide," Étoile said with annoyance.

"In my pre-meeting research," Maggie said pleasantly, "I didn't find any feature stories on *Chatoyer*. So are you new to the area?"

Étoile frowned lightly as if giving serious consideration to the question.

"Yes," she said. "New enough by Provençal standards. We opened our doors less than two years ago."

"Why did you choose this area?"

Étoile flushed, which surprised Maggie. She'd hardly thought that a very challenging question but Étoile acted as if she needed to choose her words carefully.

"I lived and worked in Paris for many years. I worked at *Picot* there."

Maggie nodded, very aware that the woman had not answered her question.

"How is it that you were familiar with this area?" Maggie repeated. "Are you from here?"

Étoile tugged at her jacket for a moment and cleared her throat.

"Not really, no," she said, staring fixedly at a Lladro figurine on her desk.

Either you're from here or you're not. Pretty easy question I would've thought.

"But you know the area," Maggie pressed.

"My...family is...was from around here."

"Oh? What's their name?"

Étoile licked her lips but didn't answer.

"I assumed Monet was your married name," Maggie said, trying to ease the way for the woman and wondering why the simplest questions seemed to be throwing Étoile into a panic.

"It was," Étoile said. "I mean, it is." Her hand fingered the pearl choker at her throat. "I'm sorry, I don't mean to be rude but could you show me some identification from your magazine?"

"Of course, Madame Monet," Maggie said smoothly, reaching into her purse for her fake press identification. Unfortunately, she'd told Étoile she was from *Fashionista* Magazine and her fake ID had her as an *International Tribune* reporter. Either Étoile wouldn't look too closely at the identification or the jig was about to be royally up.

"I just wondered if the lavender farm down the road had

any bearing on your choice of setting for your spa," Maggie said, pretending to root around in the bottom of her bag for her ID.

Étoile's mouth fell open and she began to blink rapidly.

"Why would you say that? What has *La Lavandin* got to do with anything?"

"Oh! So you know the name of the farm. I'm impressed because most people in the area just call it the lavender farm."

"Your identification, please, Madame," Étoile said, her eyes now glued to Maggie's purse.

Maggie stopped pretending to search in her bag.

"I suppose you heard about the murder that happened there last Friday?" Maggie asked.

"Who are you?" Étoile turned and reached for the intercom switch on her desk. "Bijou, come in here," she said into the intercom.

"I'm wondering if you knew the woman who was killed," Maggie said. "I think the police believe she had some connection to *Chatoyer*."

That was of course a complete lie.

But it seemed to do the trick.

Étoile sat up straight in her chair, her voice rising in pitch and volume.

"How...why would anyone imagine that that unfortunate woman had anything to do with *Chatoyer*?"

"Well, as I understand it, there was forensic trace evidence that connected her death to *Chatoyer*."

"That...that's preposterous." Étoile said, her eyes darting around the room frantically. "Unless my mother—"

Étoile clamped her mouth shut just as the receptionist swung open the door.

"Your mother?" Maggie prompted.

"Bijou, will you please escort Madame Caldwell—if that's

even your name—off the premises. If she resists, ask Beau to assist you."

"*Oui,* Madame Monet," Bijou said obsequiously.

"You're not saying that Annette Toussaint is your mother?" Maggie said in astonishment. "The manager of the lavender farm down the street?"

"How dare you?" Étoile said, her face flushed with fury. "I am not here to...to satisfy your disgusting American prurience."

"Madame," Bijou said from behind Maggie. "You will come with me."

"Do the police know about this connection?" Maggie asked as she stood up, picking up her phone from the desk.

"There is no connection!" Étoile said, raising her voice. "Get out now! Bijou!"

The receptionist put a hard hand on Maggie's shoulder and pinched. Maggie jerked away from her.

"I'm leaving," Maggie said, maneuvering away from Bijou's grip and turning toward the door.

She felt a lightness in her chest as she left the spa matched by a spring in her step.

While it was true her meeting with Étoile Monet would have to qualify as the shortest interview she'd ever done before being thrown out, it was quite possibly one of her most productive.

32

Grace saw Maggie's car in the car park and felt a flush of pleasure.

Nancy and Bess at it again, she thought, referencing the detective partnership of Nancy Drew and her best friend Bess. In years past she'd always loved to think about how she and Maggie worked so well together to solve a few cases in the area that for whatever reason the local detectives wouldn't or couldn't solve.

Admittedly, that partnership had happened a lot less in the past few years, mostly because unlike Maggie, Grace was not only raising a two-year old but had a full time job that kept her very pinned down. Not that she regretted that fact at all. Laurent had saved her life by giving her *Dormir* to run. Probably literally.

More than that, he'd given her a place to raise Zouzou and Philippe and a feeling of belonging. Even more, he'd given her the opportunity to experience a sense of accomplishment. It was true she'd had to do the hard work to make it happen, but he'd given her the chance.

But there were times when she desperately missed the

freedom she'd once enjoyed. She thought back to her marriage to Windsor. Their relationship was a shambles now but there had been a time when they'd been insanely happy.

And so rich.

She shook the memory from her mind.

Don't go there.

Today's visit to the spa would be a lovely reminder of the life she'd once had, a life of privilege and affluence.

Today, after her facial and deep-tissue massage, she would go home and strip five beds, launder the sheets, clean and chop vegetables for a *tian* before scrubbing the bathrooms in Apricot and Prune cottages in preparation for the incoming weekend guests.

Yes, life was very different these days.

As she sat in the parking lot she realized with surprise that she wasn't really sad about that. She had Danielle—a dear friend who helped her shoulder the workload not to mention gave her sage advice and a willing ear—and she had darling little Philippe and also Zouzou who not only didn't hate her as she so easily might have after everything that had happened but was a happy, loving member of their little family of three.

Well, four if I count Danielle which of course I do.

A large late model Citroën pulled up not far from where Grace sat. She watched a young woman with a vintage Chanel bag get out of the car and walk into the building. The woman was young and beautiful but the icy expression on her face was one of perpetual disdain.

Grace shook her head in bemusement.

A spa was the only place Grace knew of where the people who worked there were even snobbier than the clientele.

Time to go to work, she thought with a smile.

An hour later, Grace lay naked under a warm blanket on a heated table. The sounds of a gentle forest rain permeated the room from three speakers set in the walls.

In order to encourage the people she interacted with in the spa to believe she was exactly who she was pretending to be—just a typical spa client—she'd allowed herself to act the part. And luxuriate in every minute of it.

She decided the young man working on her neck and shoulders had magic hands, and she fought to stay awake.

"You've worked here long?" she asked casually.

The man, who Grace guessed was in his late twenties, had told her to call him *Beau*. He was handsome—nearly uncomfortably so given the fact that Grace was naked and he had his hands on her—and seemed single-mindedly focused on the task in front of him.

"*Oui, Madame,*" he said. "Two years."

"How do you like living in Provence?"

"Very nice, Madame."

"Do you live in the village?"

The closest village to *Chatoyer* was La Barben. It was small with only a *boulangerie* and a combination café and bar but Grace had noticed a few older apartments above the shops.

"*Non, Madame.* In Aix. It is not a far commute."

That wasn't at all true. Aix was easily forty minutes away—and then if you were speeding. Beau must really love his job to do a ninety-minute commute each day to work here. Unless they were paying him more than the going rate.

Because if the present lack of clientele was any indication of their success, he was hardly raking in the tips.

"You are from Paris?" she asked.

"*Non, Madame.* Normandy."

"Oh, that's a lovely area."

"*Oui.*"

Grace wondered if any of Beau's other clients were this chatty.

Probably just the ones trying to seduce him.

The thought made her wonder if he thought that was *her*

intention with all the questions. Oh well. There was nothing for that. She had a job to do.

"Terrible thing what happened to that girl on the lavender farm," she said as he began to slather a fragrant emollient on her arms.

She could have sworn he hesitated when she said that. But he didn't respond.

Is that odd? Wouldn't a normal person have agreed that it was a terrible thing?

"Have you ever taken a tour of the lavender farm?" Grace asked. "They're really fascinating operations, lavender farms. If you haven't gone on one—a tour, I mean—you really should. I wonder if the girl who was killed at the farm ever came here for a massage? I mean, I'm sure picking lavender is backbreaking work. She could probably have used a good deep-tissue workover."

Grace took a breath but she only heard breathing from her masseuse as he continued to work on her arms.

She wondered if he often had people prattle on endlessly without feeling the need to throw in the occasional comment or grunt? Was he even listening or had he tuned her out?

She realized that the scent of the lotion he was massaging into her was lavender. That in itself wasn't a surprise given the fact that the spa was located in Provence. It reminded her that Maggie said the sheen of lavender lotion found on Chantal had been too sophisticated to have come from the farm.

"Mm-mmm. That smells lovely," she said. "Where do you get the lavender products you use?" she asked innocently.

"I am not sure, Madame."

"Would it be possible for you to find the name of the product for me so I could buy some to bring home with me?"

"Of course, Madame," Beau said quickly wiping his hands on a towel. "I will be right back."

As soon as he left, Grace sat up and wrapped the sheet

around her. She looked around the room but not surprisingly there were no personal effects in the room except for her own.

Just as she was about to lie back down, she heard whispering that made her slide off the table and step closer to the door to listen.

Most people think whispering was the best way to hide their voices, she thought but actually the opposite was true. A low voice was harder to detect than whispering which not only is more audible but calls more attention to itself because whispering heralds the desire to be secretive.

Grace put her ear against the door. The whispering instantly became audibly clearer. It was definitely Beau's voice and a woman's. They were speaking outside in the hallway.

"Don't be so paranoid!" the woman's voice hissed. "She's just a typical American. Talking about nothing for no reason."

"But why did she even mention it? In the middle of a massage? You don't think that's strange?"

"I think you're feeling guilty and so you hear accusations everywhere."

"What do I have to feel guilty about?!"

"Lower your voice! You know very well what you have to feel guilty about! You might fool Étoile but I know you!"

This is great! Grace thought giddily. These two knew the victim! Had they conspired to do away with her? Why else would they be huddled in guilty confab discussing guilt and blame?

Maggie will be so thrilled!

Suddenly, the treatment table that Grace had been leaning on gave way, its casters moving to hit the wall, rattling the bottles of unguent and oils on its shelves.

Grace held her breath, hoping they hadn't heard. But the whispering stopped.

Torn between the desire to stay quiet and hope they would continue talking and hurry back to the massage table to pretend she hadn't been eavesdropping, Grace froze in position with her ear still pressed to the door.

She thought she could hear breathing.

Suddenly the door swung open. Grace grabbed for support against the door jamb but tripped over the hem of her sheet and fell straight into Beau's arms.

With her sheet now pooled on the floor.

33

The woman with Beau was no more than twenty-five and Grace instantly recognized her as the cold-faced young woman who'd parked beside her in the parking lot. She wore a white lab coat that had been fitted to her form.

"You were listening to our private conversation!" the young woman said hotly, her face twisted into an expression of outrage.

Beau gaped at Grace as she snatched up the sheet from the floor and wrapped herself back up in it.

"I was looking for the loo," Grace said imperiously. "How dare you insinuate otherwise?"

She looked from one to the other and played back their conversation in her head. They were definitely guilty about something related to Chantal's death. Even now, Beau stood facing her, with horror and shame etched across his face.

"You were eavesdropping!" the girl said.

Grace leaned over and read the name off a badge on the woman's lab coat.

Harlequin.

Beau, his ears bright red, shuffled backward until he disappeared from the hallway.

"I don't care how much money you have," Harlequin said angrily, taking a step toward Grace, her hands bunched into fists at her sides. That was a private conversation!"

"It certainly was," Grace said archly, "and I can see why you'd want to keep it private."

Harlequin was breathing shallowly, her eyes wide now with nervousness as she appeared to be replaying her conversation with Beau in her head. She stared at Grace with clearly oscillating emotions of fear and obstinance crossing her carefully made-up face.

"Are you the police?" she asked.

"I am affiliated with the police," Grace said haughtily. "And after what I just heard between you and Beau, I'd say you have a few things to say to me."

Harlequin bit her lip.

"I'll lose my job," she said, the perfectly manicured nails of one hand finding their way to her mouth.

"I can ensure that doesn't happen," Grace said evenly. "But you will need to tell me everything you know about the girl who died at the lavender farm."

Twenty minutes later, Grace sat fully clothed in one of the facial treatment rooms sipping a glass of mineral water with a lemon slice floating in it. Harlequin sat across from her, a tissue twisted in her hands, her makeup seemingly unaffected by the lone tear that had found its way down her chiseled cheek.

"So did you know Chantal?" Grace asked.

Harlequin shook her head.

"I never heard of her until I saw her picture in the papers after the murder," she said.

"Then what were you and Beau talking about? Did Beau know her?"

"No, of course not! Chantal was a filthy refugee!"

Grace flicked away nonexistent flecks of lint in her Stella McCartney French Terry sweatpants.

"Perhaps it would save both of us time," she said, "if you would just tell me what you *do* know."

"I know almost nothing."

"I'm sure that's not true. But if I can say this," Grace said with an encouraging smile, "talking to me now will be much more comfortable than talking to the detective on the case at the police station in Aix."

Harlequin looked immediately stricken.

"Yes, okay. But what I know is mostly just..." she struggled to find the words.

"Supposition?" Grace supplied.

Harlequin nodded. "*Oui.* Supposition."

"So let's hear it."

Harlequin took in a breath before plunging in.

"I'm not the only one who thinks this but there is talk that Madame Toussaint at the lavender farm is a witch."

When Grace made a face, Harlequin continued.

"Not a magical witch," she clarified. "But definitely evil."

"How did you come up with this assessment?"

"Madame Monet hinted as much to me."

"Madame Monet, the owner of *Chatoyer*?"

"*Oui.* She talks about Madame Toussaint frequently and it's never good."

"Do they know each other?"

"Perhaps. Some things that Madame Monet says makes it sound as if she knew Madame Toussaint when she was a child."

"Is Madame Monet from this area?"

"I don't know."

"What sorts of things does Madame Monet say about Madame Toussaint?"

"She says Madame Toussaint is trying to ruin our business and that she should close down or move her farm away from us."

"How is the lavender farm ruining your business?"

"I have no idea. But I heard her say that Madame Toussaint probably killed the girl."

"Really?"

Harlequin nodded. "She said the girl was probably stealing from Madame Toussaint."

"And she thinks Madame Toussaint might kill someone for stealing from her?" Grace asked.

"*Évidemment.*"

"But you have no idea how Madame Monet knows Madame Toussaint?"

"No, but Jaeger, the man who trims our oleander bushes claims they are related."

"Related how?"

"He didn't say."

"You mean like mother and daughter?"

"Well, that would be ridiculous," Harlequin said with a laugh. "Madame Monet is elegant and refined. I've only seen Madame Toussaint once but she looked like a peasant working in the fields. There is no way they could be closely related."

"Why would Madame Monet believe that Madame Toussaint killed Chantal?" Grace asked.

"I don't know except one time she told me that Madame Toussaint was ruthless."

"Ruthless in what way?"

Harlequin shrugged. "I just remember her saying it."

Harlequin glanced at her watch.

"Do you have to be somewhere?" Grace asked.

"I have to give a pedicure in five minutes. And you are

signed up for a facial at the same time with Genèvieve."

Grace felt pretty good about the information she'd gathered although she would definitely need to track down Beau to see if he could add anything to the picture that Harlequin had created.

"Well, thank you for your assistance," Grace said. "I'll be sure and tell the police how helpful you've been."

"Thank you, Madame," Harlequin said, an expression of relief on her face. "Shall I show you to your treatment room?"

"That would be lovely," Grace said as she collected her things by her chair.

She followed Harlequin down the quiet hallway of closed doors, her shoulders back and her chin high. She couldn't wait to tell Maggie what she'd learned.

A possible blood connection between the owner of the lavender farm and the nearby spa, plus enmity between them? Combine that with the fact of the lavender salve found on the body, and—while Grace wouldn't go so far as to say she'd necessarily cracked the case—she was pretty sure she'd uncovered essential evidence.

"It is through here, Madame," Harlequin said quietly as she opened a door. "And thank you again for your discretion."

"Of course," Grace said as she stepped through the door.

The shock of the heat from the sun overhead slammed into her at the same time the door behind her clicked shut.

Grace was on the building rooftop, her foot slipping off the sharp cant of the pitched roof. She whirled around, dropping her purse and the shoes in her hand. They both plummeted to the ground forty feet below forcing a stifled scream from her. She gripped a cement ledge on either side of the closed door with both hands.

Her heart raced as she pressed her body against the side of the building, her toes curled around a narrow stone parapet meant only to accommodate pigeons.

34

That night at Domaine St-Buvard, Laurent and Jemmy worked together in the kitchen making *moules marinières*. Mila was watching TV in the living room with Fleur curled up beside her. Maggie was glad to see it.

She'd hoped to get on the Internet before dinner to try to determine if she could find definitive confirmation that Étoile Monet was indeed Annette Toussaint's daughter but it was clear there were other things—family things—that needed to be attended to first.

As they worked together in the kitchen making the garlic and onions that would go in the broth, both Laurent and Jemmy were unnaturally quiet and subdued—even for them. Maggie imagined that Jemmy was attempting to ingratiate himself with Laurent to make amends for his part in yesterday's drama at the emergency department.

But she also knew that no matter what Jemmy did or how contrite he was, Laurent would never accept his trying to make a living as an actor.

She paused in the living room where Mila was engrossed in her television program.

"How did lunch go?" Maggie asked, hoping Mila wouldn't take her question as a heavy-handed intrusion.

Without taking her eyes off the screen, Mila shrugged.

"Dad canceled it," she said.

Maggie stared at her daughter for a moment and felt the surprise jolt her.

It was true she hadn't been in touch with Laurent today which was unusual, especially on such an important day. She felt a tremble of guilt. This was the first time in fifteen years that she had not put on the lunch for the pickers. Both she and Laurent had agreed it would do Mila good to do it and she was old enough.

Why had he canceled it?

Now that she thought about it, when she'd gotten home today at a little after five, she had been surprised to see that there were no workers in the fields.

That, of course, was not a good sign.

She made her way into the kitchen just as Jemmy left it to set the table in the garden. Going up to Laurent, who was taking a baguette from a paper sack, she raised up on tiptoe to kiss him.

"How was the picking today?" she asked.

"The alternator belt broke," Laurent said.

Maggie assumed he was talking about one of their tractors.

"When did it happen?"

"Mid-morning."

That explained why Laurent had sent the pickers home without lunch.

"Were they able to pick very much?"

Laurent turned and focused on spooning up bowls full of the fragrant broth and mussels.

"Not enough," he said. "The parts place in Aix doesn't have the size I need. I will go to Marseille tomorrow."

"I wish you'd texted me," Maggie said. "I could've run to Marseille."

"You would not have known what to ask for," he said.

Maggie knew that any delay in the picking, especially after they'd started, was dangerous. The more the just-picked grapes sat in baskets, the greater chance of mold.

And then there was the weather forecast which Maggie had heard on the way home from *Chatoyer*.

Rain was predicted in three days.

She watched as Laurent opened a bottle of wine and poured himself a glass. That was highly unusual. Laurent only drank wine with food—which meant only at the table.

Maggie took down a wineglass and poured a glass for herself. Her intention was to talk to him more about his worries for the harvest but he turned his back and said only, "Dinner in fifteen minutes."

Dinner that night was solemn. Both children were quiet and seemed to have no appetite. They begged to be released from the table early and both retreated to their rooms for the rest of the night.

Maggie felt like her whole family was disintegrating before her eyes.

Later, as Maggie carried the platter of empty mussel shells into the kitchen, she saw her phone vibrating on the counter from an incoming call. She picked it up and saw Grace's photo on the screen.

"Hey, Grace. I'm sorry I haven't called. Things were—"

"You are not going to believe what happened to me today," Grace said excitedly.

Maggie settled down on the couch with her phone. From where she sat, she could see Laurent through the French doors walking the vineyard with the two larger dogs. She wished Jemmy could have made the effort to go with him.

"What happened?" she asked.

"I was nearly killed today, that's what happened!" Grace said.

"Seriously? At a spa?"

"Yes!" Grace said indignantly. "Those people are vicious! The girl who does the mani-pedis practically threw me off the roof! I had to get one of the groundskeepers to get me down."

Maggie frowned.

"Why?" she asked. "Did they suspect you were something other than a client?"

There was a slight pause on the phone.

"Okay, darling, I admit I had to pivot when certain things happened which may have forced me to reveal my true purpose."

"Ergo you got shoved onto a rooftop."

"Yes, okay, but not before I got some very interesting information. For example, would it surprise you to learn that Étoile Monet and the manager of the lavender farm are in some way related?'

"I think Annette Toussaint is Étoile's mother," Maggie said.

There was another pause on the line and Maggie found herself sorry she'd stepped on Grace's big moment.

"It would have been helpful," Grace said with a sniff, "if I'd known that going in."

"I didn't know it before today," Maggie said. "What else?"

"Well, that was my big news," Grace said. "Unless you want to consider the fact that attempting to kill me is in itself a very suspicious action for someone who supposedly has nothing to hide."

"You're talking about the mani-pedi girl?"

"She is a very strong girl and quite capable I should think of overpowering a slighter girl. She literally pushed me out onto the roof!"

"So you said. And that's terrible. Anything else?"

Grace released an exasperated sigh.

"I heard her say—her name is Harlequin Martin by the way—when she was talking to one of the masseuses, Beau Dubois, something to the effect that they knew Chantal and were feeling guilty about what happened to her."

Maggie sat up straighter on the couch.

"Guilty how?"

"Well, Beau said he was worried about all my questions about Chantal and Harlequin told him he had every reason to feel guilty and that he might be able to fool Étoile but he couldn't fool her."

"You're right. That does sound suspicious."

Maggie felt her pulse begin to quicken. She would need to follow up with both Beau and Harlequin. Somehow. Which might be difficult seeing how she had been essentially thrown off the grounds today.

Unless she could get LaBelle to go to Chatoyer?

"More suspicious than pushing someone out on a roof top to plummet to her death?" Grace asked, incredulously.

"It certainly doesn't seem the action of an innocent person. Good work, Grace."

"I'm pretty sure you now have a direct avenue to your most likely prime suspect," Grace said.

"You mean Harlequin?"

"She tried to push me to my death! *Of course* I mean Harlequin!"

"Well, it's a thought," Maggie said.

After talking for a few more minutes—and in spite of the fact that Harlequin pushed Grace out onto the spa's roof—Maggie still didn't feel as if she were any closer to finding a viable suspect to take Rochelle's place.

She and Grace made plans to get together the next morning and after disconnecting, Maggie went into the kitchen, her mind swirling with everything that Grace had told her combined with her own experience today at *Chatoyer*.

Laurent was still in the field, which was unusual for him, but she found the process of washing the dinner dishes mildly therapeutic as she tried to piece together what she'd learned today at the spa along with what Grace had just told her.

Why would the mani-pedi girl act so aggressively when Grace questioned her about Chantal? What did it mean that there was animosity toward Madame Toussaint on Étoile's part —especially given the possibility that they were mother and daughter?

Suddenly Fleur who had been keeping Maggie company in the kitchen barked sharply and ran through the dining room toward the front door.

Maggie dried her hands and peered out the kitchen window. A car she had never seen before pulled silently up the gravel drive and parked.

Wishing Laurent would return from his walk, Maggie went to the front door at the same time she heard the knock.

Maggie pulled open the door and blinked in surprise.

"Well? Are you going to let me in?"

Detective LaBelle peered into the house before pushing past Maggie to step inside.

"We need to talk," she said.

35

Detective LaBelle stepped into the foyer at Domaine St-Buvard, an entrance tiled with an intricate Moroccan mosaic laid decades before Maggie and Laurent inherited the property. Maggie always thought it made a magical first impression.

She was pretty sure the effect was lost on LaBelle.

LaBelle moved directly into the living room and sat at one end of the couch, moving the colorful and tasseled pillows that Maggie had found in shops from Arles to Paris. She waited for Maggie and Laurent, who had just come into the house to join her.

Maggie sat down opposite the detective and the two waited while Laurent went into the kitchen. Detective or not, there was no way he was going to be able to endure having a guest in his house without offering something to drink.

"Have you got something to tell us?" Maggie asked LaBelle.

The detective grimaced and moved one more pillow away from her.

"We will wait," she said as she gazed around the living room, clearly trying to determine what the side tables, the upholstery and drapes, the coffee table full of squat vases full of flowers and stacks of home decorating magazines told her about Maggie—and possibly Laurent.

Finally, Laurent brought a tray of drinks in and set it down on the coffee table in front of LaBelle.

"This is an official visit," LaBelle said as she nonetheless reached for a glass of Amontillado.

"Has something happened?" Maggie asked.

"No," LaBelle said. "And in a way that is the point of my visit." She looked at Laurent and nodded. "Very good sherry," she said.

He nodded his acknowledgment.

"As you know," LaBelle said, leaning back into the couch as she held her drink, "Madame Lando remains my prime suspect. I wanted to inform you both that she will be moved to a holding facility in Nice before the weekend."

"That's fast," Maggie said with a frown.

"Whether it is or isn't," LaBelle said, "she is in Aix now and is asking to see Monsieur Dernier which I have decided to allow."

Maggie gave her a pinched expression. She was sure Rochelle only wanted some sort of emotional support from Laurent but what she *needed* was to work with her lawyer—or Maggie—to find *something* they could mount a working defense on.

Besides, Laurent only knew the basics of Rochelle's case. Wondering if she should say something that might allow her to visit Rochelle instead of Laurent, Maggie caught LaBelle's eye and was shocked by what she saw.

The look LaBelle gave her appeared to be an invitation to share a commiseration with her. In that moment Maggie realized two astonishing things.

One, based on their mutual love and admiration for Laurent but more specifically for their mutual frustration with his magnetism to a certain kind of woman, it appeared that LaBelle was open to a sort of relationship with Maggie. That in itself was a startling revelation although admittedly not an unwelcome one. But it was the second realization that was the most revealing and the most shocking to Maggie.

LaBelle wanted to please Laurent.

Absurd as it sounded, she knew it was true. LaBelle appeared willing to compromise her case in order to please him. Not just by dropping by to give him a heads-up that Rochelle was going to be moved but by allowing him to visit her prime suspect.

Both of which led Maggie to her third realization of the night which was the fact that while LaBelle's hands were clearly tied as far as her being able to help Rochelle, *it didn't mean she didn't want to.*

Maggie allowed herself a moment to reel from these revelations and when she took in a breath and looked at the new situation before her, she saw that as a result of LaBelle's interest in Laurent, there was a possibility now of a partnership between them.

Between LaBelle and Maggie.

"Yes, of course I will see her," Laurent said.

"*Bon*," LaBelle said, draining her glass and standing up. "I will call you tomorrow with the specifics."

"Can I ask you a question, Detective?" Maggie asked, also standing. "I've uncovered some recent information that hints at the possibility that some people at the spa *Chatoyer*, might have known the victim. I was wondering if you'd interviewed anyone there."

LaBelle snorted. "Next question."

"I'm told that Chantal had a cellphone," Maggie said. "Did you find it?"

LaBelle waved away the question. "There was no cellphone."

The woman's dismissive arrogance was beginning to grate on Maggie.

There clearly *had* been a cellphone. Just because LaBelle hadn't found it, didn't mean it didn't exist!

"Okay. How about the other two women who shared Chantal and Rochelle's dorm at the monastery?" Maggie asked. "Have you located them?"

"There was no point," LaBelle said, standing up. "They left the monastery the morning of the murder. They were therefore irrelevant to my investigation."

She nodded at Laurent. "Goodnight."

Maggie followed her to the front door.

"I wonder if you'd heard that one of the lavender farm workers once set Chantal's bed on fire," Maggie said, "which was probably the reason Chantal was sleeping at the monastery."

LaBelle looked at Maggie for a moment.

"I had not heard that," she admitted.

"I have a few other things that I've heard here and there," Maggie said.

"Here and there?"

"I was thinking if you had time to go over them with me, sometime at your convenience, perhaps we could meet?"

LaBelle glanced at Laurent before answering.

"*D'accord*," she said to Maggie. "I'll text you."

∼

An hour later, the children were asleep, and Maggie and Laurent sat on the back terrace drinking another glass of sherry.

Maggie wasn't sure if Laurent was in the mood to talk about his concerns on how poorly the first day of the harvest had gone. Knowing him, he wouldn't see the merit in talking about it.

His view tended to be: *talking can't reverse the day and make the tractor belt to not have broken, so what's the point?*

Maggie took a moment to appreciate the beauty of the vineyard at this time of evening. She and Laurent often enjoyed walking it after dinner when the final rays of sunlight appeared to drape the fields in a soft glow.

"Jemmy seemed to enjoy working in the kitchen tonight," Maggie said.

Laurent shifted in his seat but didn't answer. Maggie turned to look at him.

"It doesn't need to be related to the vineyard," Laurent said. "I would be satisfied if he was interested in working with food. Does he not know that?"

Maggie turned her attention back to the vineyard.

"As far as deciding on his life's direction," she said, "surely you see that making *you* happy is not his primary goal."

She wrapped her cashmere wrap around her as a surprising breeze lifted her hair.

"Or at least it shouldn't be," she added.

"So American," he growled. But he lifted a tendril of hair away from her face.

She smiled at him and debated reminding him that life was long and wonky harvests and difficult children were fleabites in the general scheme of things. But then she tried to think whether a single time that sort of Pollyanna-type thinking had ever made *her* feel better during a bleak moment. She decided to hold her tongue.

Laurent patted his jeans pocket for his phone, making Maggie realize that it must have vibrated, alerting him that he was getting a call or text. She watched him as he read the text and then shut off the screen and put the phone away.

"Anything important?" she asked.

"Probably not," he said. "It is late. I'll lock up."

He stood and whistled for the two hunting dogs before turning to go into the house. Maggie watched him go and then got up, Fleur at her feet, and followed him.

She was sorry the mysterious text message had derailed what had been up until then a very intimate moment between them—better than that, an honest moment where she felt they were shoulder to shoulder in facing their current problems.

As brief as the moment had been it had given her comfort and support and she hoped Laurent felt the same.

But he was male and French so there was no telling.

And then there was the text message from a sender Maggie had in fact glimpsed before Laurent put away his phone.

It was encouraging on some level that Laurent considered an urgent text message from Rochelle as *probably not* important.

But it had still been enough to disrupt an intimate moment between them.

So it was definitely something.

36

The next morning, Maggie was sitting at one of her favorite cafés in Aix and watched as a clot of dead leaves scuttled across the café's sunlit terrace.

She'd told Grace not to be late and now as she looked down Cours Mirabeau she realized that—miracles of miracles—her friend had actually listened for once.

Grace arrived in a flurry of designer silks and a cloud of *Joy* perfume. She kissed Maggie in greeting and signaled to the waiter before taking her seat at the café table opposite Maggie.

"I can't stay long. Being gone most of yesterday, you'd be surprised how quickly things fall apart when you're running a bed and breakfast," Grace said smoothing out the wrinkles in her pale green Fendi silk blouse.

"Is everything okay?" Maggie asked.

She was glad Grace was on time for their date this morning. She wanted a moment to debrief with her before their surprise guest arrived.

"You mean aside from nearly getting killed yesterday?" Grace asked.

"Well, if it's any consolation," Maggie said. "You're right, doing that definitely tipped her hand. The good news is I think we can have the police question her and that should shake something loose."

"So did you tell LaBelle what happened?"

"Not yet," Maggie said as she spotted the detective's form striding toward them.

Grace turned just as LaBelle pulled out a chair and seated herself.

"I don't have long," LaBelle said, signaling to the waiter to bring her a coffee. "What did you have to tell me?"

"Detective LaBelle," Maggie said. "Do you remember Madame VanSant?"

LaBelle looked at Grace and frowned.

"From the stabbing death in the vineyard last year," LaBelle said before turning back to Maggie. "So what did you want to tell me?"

"Right, fine," Maggie said with a tinge of exasperation. "One of the reasons I think the spa *Chatoyer* is something you should investigate in relation to Chantal's murder is because of a recent visit that Madame VanSant made there."

LaBelle's frown intensified but she turned to look at Grace.

"Let's hear it," she said.

Maggie could tell Grace wasn't pleased to be telling her story to such an unreceptive audience. She straightened the folds of her napkin and then brushed invisible crumbs from the café tabletop.

"I was assaulted at *Chatoyer* yesterday," Grace said bluntly. "After questioning one of the attendants about Chantal's murder I was shoved out onto the roof and left there."

LaBelle barked out a rude laugh and looked at Maggie as if expecting her to admit this was a joke. When Maggie maintained her serious expression, LaBelle turned back to Grace.

"You're serious?"

"The spa attendant was Harlequin Martin," Grace began.

"I thought she was the mani-pedi girl?" Maggie interrupted.

"What difference does it make what her specific job is?" Grace said in annoyance.

"You are making an official complaint?" LaBelle asked impatiently.

"You know what?" Grace said, tossing down her napkin. "Maybe I am!" She turned to Maggie. "Both Harlequin and Beau know something about Chantal's murder. And from the way he was talking about her, I'm pretty sure my masseuse knew Chantal in *that* way if you get my drift."

The waiter delivered LaBelle's coffee to her.

"What do you mean?" she asked reaching for two packets of sugar on the table.

"I overheard Beau and Harlequin in the hallway talking about Chantal," Grace said. "And they both sounded extremely guilty. Not to mention, and I didn't tell you this last night, darling," she said to Maggie, "because it took me awhile to figure it out myself but the two of them—Beau and Harlequin—are definitely together."

"How can you tell?" LaBelle asked, unconvinced.

"Trust me," Grace said to the detective. "They're an item. I'm thinking that if Harlequin thought Beau had been with Chantal—which was what she seemed to be insinuating when I heard them talking—well, that's motive."

LaBelle snorted. "In France?"

Maggie turned to LaBelle. "What's Harlequin's alibi for Chantal's death?"

"What are you talking about?" LaBelle said, stirring her coffee and giving Maggie an incredulous expression. "Why would we interview anyone at the spa?"

"After what you've just heard?" Maggie said patiently. "Don't you think there's reason to? On top of which both Grace and I found out separately that the owner of the spa, Étoile Monet and the owner of the lavender farm are possibly related. Maybe even mother and daughter."

"That's ridiculous," LaBelle said.

"Why? Because one wears Gucci and one wears gum boots?" Grace said. "Harlequin told me Étoile hates Madame Toussaint."

"Did she say why?" Maggie asked.

"No, but she said that Étoile thought Madame Toussaint was the one who killed Chantal."

"This is all speculation," LaBelle said, rolling her eyes. "Worse, it's gossip and hearsay."

"All witness testimony is hearsay," Maggie said through gritted teeth, "until it shows up in court. You need to find out where Harlequin was during the murder. And also Étoile Monet."

"You might throw in Beau while you're at it," Grace said.

"Good point," Maggie said.

"I'm not asking anyone at *Chatoyer* for their alibis," LaBelle said firmly.

"It's a likely place for the killer to have come from!" Maggie protested.

"Says who?"

"Your own medical examiner! In the forensic report the ME pointed out that there was a sheen of some kind of fragrant emollient on the victim's cheek."

"It was the victim's perfume."

"It was found on her *cheek*!"

LaBelle frowned at Maggie in confusion.

"People don't put perfume on their cheeks," Maggie said patiently. "It's not a pulse point."

"What are you talking about?"

"Wrist, behind the knee, earlobe or against the throat are all typical places you add perfume. Nobody puts perfume on their cheeks."

LaBelle frowned. "Really?"

"But maybe it's not perfume," Maggie said. "I looked up the chemical makeup of what was found on Chantal and it seems more likely to be moisturizer or lipstick in which case it explains why it might have ended end up on her cheek."

"So now you are a chemist?"

Maggie ground her teeth in fury.

"I think the killer stabbed Chantal," Maggie said, "arranged the lavender around her, and then kissed her on the cheek or caressed her with a hand. The chemical properties sound closer to lipstick or gloss than they do moisturizer."

"Does this mean the killer is a woman?" Grace asked.

"Not necessarily," Maggie said, taking a breath to calm down. "It could be a man who works with emollients and fragrant salves."

"Someone like a masseuse who's up to his arm pits in the stuff all day long," Grace said.

"*Voila*," Maggie said, nodding.

Activity in the little café had begun to pick up as the midmorning doldrums gave way to the before-lunch crowd. The waiter passed them twice without asking if they wanted more coffee.

It was just as well, Maggie thought. Grace had to get back to *Dormir* and the detective surely had other things to do.

As she studied the detective it occurred to Maggie that LaBelle, with her masculine pants and short unstyled hair, might be insecure about stepping foot in a spa.

"Look, Detective LaBelle," Maggie said. "I know you shared important case notes with me and I appreciate it but I can't help but think there is something you're holding back."

Specifically the redacted lines in the forensics report.

"I have no idea what you are talking about," LaBelle said.

"I'm talking about the three paragraphs blacked out in the document you gave me."

"That information is not pertinent to the case."

"Are you serious? In a murder case? Everything's *pertinent*. You know that. I shared with you the fact that it appears that the owners of *Chatoyer* and *La Lavandin* are related. Are in, fact mother and daughter—"

"And I will confirm that in due course."

"Great. Now if you would be so kind as to share with *me* the information that only you and the medical examiner know about the body, we'll call it even."

"That information has nothing to do with the manner in which she was killed."

Maggie shook her head in bewilderment.

"*What* has nothing to do with the manner of how she was killed?" she asked in exasperation.

LaBelle stood up and hovered by the table as if not sure what she would do next.

"I could be sidelined," she said finally, "even fired, for giving you the document I gave you."

You did it for Laurent, Maggie thought. *And so that's the button I need to push.*

"I know that," Maggie said, "and *Laurent and I* both appreciate the risk you took. It was brave and you didn't have to do it. But I need to know what was left out."

LaBelle sat back down as if suddenly too tired to stand. She ran her hands through her hair to the end of her ponytail and then turned to Maggie and dropped her voice.

"I'm sure it has nothing to do with why she was murdered."

"You're probably right," Maggie said. "What is it?"

LaBelle sighed and then gave a helpless shrug.

"She was pregnant," she said.

37

The room where Laurent was scheduled to meet with Rochelle was cold and unwelcoming. As it would be, he thought as he took in the IKEA couch with three flat cushions, since it was inside a detention unit in the police station. Next to the couch was a side table with a pitcher of water, one glass and a box of tissues.

Laurent had no sooner stepped into the room than the door on the opposite side of the room opened and Rochelle stepped inside. She was not handcuffed but a policewoman walked behind her.

She wore a yellow jumpsuit and her long hair was scraped back into a low-hanging ponytail. Her face instantly animated into a wide grin that she seemed unable to contain.

Rochelle threw herself into his arms and clung to him. Laurent was struck by how much taller than Maggie Rochelle was. His hands fell to her waist and he gently disengaged from her.

"No touching!" the policewoman snarled and banged a truncheon against the metal table in the room. Rochelle flinched.

"Let us sit," Laurent said, indicating the couch by the wall.

They sat, she nearly on top of him, her hands resting on his knee, her face so close to his so that he could see the tears glittering in her eyes. But she was smiling. With hope and expectation.

"How are you, *chérie*?" he asked stiffly.

"I'm good," she said. "This has been a nightmare but I'm good now."

He nodded, reminding himself that he was here to comfort her and if possible get any information that might help in freeing her. He searched her face, his heart pounding with the sinking feeling of knowing that he should be in his field right now.

What had he seen in this woman that had so drawn him in? She was a vintner too! She knew what she was asking of him to be here instead of in the field today.

But he knew very well what he'd seen in her and it made his stomach hurt when he saw it again in her face, flickering in and out of her expression like a cloud of moths obliterating what was really there.

"Were you aware that you confessed?" Laurent said, looking into her eyes.

"Confessed?" Rochelle said leaning back into the couch, her hands slipping from his knees. "Yes. I knew. I meant to confess."

"Why?"

"Would you think me mad if I told you I don't even know?"

There are some people in this life who are their own worst enemies. And those people need all the help the rest of us can give.

"Did the police coerce you?"

"Oh, Laurent, no. Not like that." Rochelle hunched her shoulders in shame. "I just…I had a bad night. You know?"

He nodded encouragingly for her to go on. But he didn't at all know. He really needed to understand how a bad night would prompt behavior that could only make all her following nights much, much worse.

"I think I thought I just wanted it all to be over, you know?"

She looked beseechingly at him as if it were important that he believe her.

"It won't count," he said to her. "Your lawyer can find ways to make it not count."

"How?"

"You weren't in your right mind, you felt you were being coerced, you felt you were being threatened. You can recant."

"Okay."

"I have another question."

"Anything, Laurent. But, wait, shouldn't you be at your harvest? It's soon isn't it? Have you started?"

"Yesterday."

"Why are you here? Oh, Laurent. You shouldn't have come."

"You asked me to come. Of course I should have come."

"But I wasn't thinking. You need to go. Please. I'll never forgive myself."

"Rochelle, stop. It's fine. I have people I trust running it in my absence."

That wasn't true. When Laurent had brought Rochelle to France nine months ago it was supposed to have been the two of them managing the harvest. With Luc.

There was only a handful of disgruntled refugees who didn't want to be picking grapes in his field today. He'd be lucky if they didn't end up setting it on fire or stealing his tools while he was gone.

"Why are you so kind to me?" she asked, cocking her head and looking at him with sadness. "I've only brought problems into your life."

"That's not true."

If this were anybody else, Laurent would not have answered. He was not in the habit of putting up with self-indulgent behavior. But Rochelle needed him. And if he couldn't immediately free her, then he needed to at least be here for her.

"No really," she said. There's something there, isn't there?" She put her hand on his where it rested on his knee. "Something you're not telling me?"

Because he was forcing himself to speak when normally that would not have been his default response, he told her.

"You remind me of someone," he said.

She removed her hand, her smile suddenly stiff.

"Someone special I hope," she said.

"She was the wife of a friend."

"Oh, that's always complicated."

"It wasn't like that."

"If you say so," she said, watching him carefully. "But she meant something to you?"

"As do you," he said. "In your own right. For who you are."

"Of course. I know."

A moment of awkward silence came between them. Finally Laurent couldn't wait any longer. He glanced at the police woman and then back at Rochelle and then dropped his voice.

"Where is the scythe I loaned you?" he asked.

"The what?" She frowned. "Oh, the scythe. I'm sorry, I think I misplaced it. I know you love everyone at the monastery, Laurent, but most of them steal like crazy. You can't put your lunch tray down without someone trying to make off with it."

Laurent listened to her and nodded. It was what he expected she would say. What he expected had likely even happened.

"Do they think that's the murder weapon?" she asked, her lips whitening slightly.

"I don't know," he said. "But if you lost it, you lost it."

"I did. You believe me, right?"

"Of course," he said. And then he reached out and took her hand and squeezed it. A part of him knew that Maggie would be horrified at the gesture. Not because it would make her jealous but because he was normally so resistant to any kind of public display of affection.

But he also knew he had very little to give Rochelle in the way of real help or hope in her situation. A bit of human warmth seemed the least he could give.

When he did, he saw a flash of Dauphine in her face and his insides seemed to grind painfully as he thought once more of how he was sure he could've saved her.

If only he'd tried.

38

"Chantal was pregnant?" Maggie said in surprise. "Who knew about this?"

"Do you mean outside of my forensic team?" LaBelle asked.

"I mean did you do a DNA test on Enzo Corbin to see if he was the father?"

"*Non.*"

"So if you didn't do a paternity test then you don't know if he's the father," Maggie said triumphantly. "I don't know how it is where you come from, Detective, but in my world a surprise pregnancy is what we call motive."

She snorted. "We French are not like you Americans."

"Praise the Lord for that," Maggie said and then nearly bit her tongue. It wouldn't help to antagonize the woman.

"An unwanted pregnancy is not worth killing over," LaBelle said.

"You don't know that," Maggie said in exasperation. "Maybe it was worth it to the father whoever he is."

"*C'est ridicule!*" LaBelle said her muscles rigid with exasperation. "If Enzo Corbin was the father and did not want the responsibility, he did not need to kill Chantal! All he had to do was walk away. He is a vagrant. Nobody will be docking his paycheck for child support."

She had a point. But Maggie knew Chantal's pregnancy had to mean something. It was too coincidental that she was killed *and* pregnant too.

"You have to test him," Maggie said. "Enzo was Chantal's boyfriend. You need to rule him out."

LaBelle stood up.

"I don't have to do anything," she said, baring her teeth. "And I certainly do not have to sit here and listen to you telling me how to do my job. Perhaps you should learn to do *your* job better, Madame Dernier."

"What is that supposed to mean?"

"Did you know your husband is downtown right now meeting with Rochelle Lando?"

Maggie felt a sickening thud in her stomach. Not because Laurent was meeting with Rochelle. She'd expected that after LaBelle's visit last night. Not even because when he left this morning he never mentioned he was seeing Rochelle today.

She felt sick to her stomach because as a vintner this was arguably the single most important day of Laurent's year. He was in the middle of a troublesome harvest. Of all the days to be missing in action, this was one day that was simply not negotiable.

Maggie would have thought.

~

Maggie and Grace left the café together a few minutes after the detective did. Grace had dropped her car off at a body shop in town and needed Maggie to give her a lift back to *Dormir*.

"Did you know Laurent was going to see Rochelle today?"

Grace asked as they walked to the underground parking deck at the end of the Cours Mirabeau.

"No," Maggie said. "I knew he would see her some time."

And there was that "not important" text message last night.

"I thought there was a problem with this year's harvest," Grace said.

"Yes, Grace, there is," Maggie said with irritation. "I'm sure Laurent thought he could multitask picking up the tractor part in Marseille and popping in to see Rochelle."

"Not really very practical since they're nearly twenty kilometers apart," Grace pointed out. Maggie didn't respond.

"He put the harvest off much later this year, didn't he?" Grace asked.

Maggie stopped as she was unlocking the car and looked at Grace, realizing that she was right. The harvest *was* much later this year. She wondered if there was a reason for that.

Had Laurent delayed, hoping that Luc would come back for it if he pushed the date back? Surely he wasn't consciously thinking of that. The timing of any harvest was crucial. Even being off by a few days could be catastrophic to a whole year's work.

"I don't know what his thinking was," Maggie said as she got in the car. "But you know Laurent."

"I do," Grace said, straightening out the crease in her slacks as she fastened her seatbelt. "Danielle and I were talking just the other day that he seems to have a lot on his mind these days."

"Well, naturally, the harvest—" Maggie said.

"More than that, we thought," Grace said.

"The kids have been horrid," Maggie said as she maneuvered out of the parking lot.

"Jemmy too?"

"No, but he's leaning in a direction that Laurent feels the need to fight him on."

"That's never good. And Mila?"

"Let's just say we'll both be glad when this stage of her development is over."

Maggie and Grace were silent for a few moments. Maggie knew Grace was thinking of Taylor—her own problem daughter who never did outgrow her difficult stage.

Maggie merged onto the A8, her eye on her phone. She still couldn't believe Laurent wasn't home right this minute directing the pickers. She was tempted to text him but knew not receiving a reply from him would just make her more upset.

And going home, while giving her the answer, would do nothing toward moving them all forward.

"Do you mind if we swing by *La Lavandin* on the way to your place?" Maggie asked.

"Not at all," Grace said. "I only have a clogged drain and six quiches to make when I get back."

Maggie glanced at her.

"Bad attempt at levity, darling," Grace said with a smile. "I'm not complaining."

"It's hard work what you do," Maggie said.

"Work I'm grateful for every day," Grace said firmly. "I wouldn't change my life for anything I ever had in the past."

Maggie nodded. She believed her too. She'd never before seen the bloom of satisfaction and deep-set happiness that she'd seen in Grace the last few years. It was a hard life but one that suited her.

Thirty minutes later Maggie turned off the highway onto a village road and drove through the closest village to the lavender farm. They'd passed a few fields that still had sunflowers in them but none with lavender.

It looks like Laurent isn't the only one who had a late harvest this year, Maggie thought.

She turned down the dirt and gravel drive that led to the farm and parked in the grass before turning off the engine. There was nobody outside and no one in the fields.

"So you do know that Beau, the *Chatoyer* masseuse, could also be the father," Grace said.

"That thought did cross my mind."

"Why do you think LaBelle didn't want you to know about the pregnancy?"

"I don't think she was holding back the news of the pregnancy specifically. I think she felt insecure about giving us police documents and redacting some pieces of it made her feel better about what she was doing."

Maggie watched as the door to the barn opened. She saw Enzo Corbin walk out carrying a large flat basket of lavender buds.

As she watched him, she found herself thinking of Laurent sitting in the Aix jail, talking to Rochelle instead of attending to the harvest of Domaine St-Buvard.

"Is that the boyfriend?" Grace asked, snapping Maggie back to the present.

Maggie unbuckled her seatbelt but put a hand on Grace's knee.

"Stay in the car," she said. "I don't expect trouble but desperate people tend to do desperate things."

39

The wafting cloud of lavender scent felt like a physical impasse to Maggie—thick and impenetrable—as she walked across the grass and gravel expanse toward Enzo. The man had clearly seen her drive up but was making a production of pretending she wasn't there.

"Excuse me, Enzo?" she called to him.

Finally he turned around and watched her approach.

"I'm surprised to find you here," Maggie said. "Madame Toussaint said your job was finished."

"Clearly she found something else for me to do," he said with a curl of his lip.

Maggie pulled out her phone and scrolled to the text she'd received two days ago.

"Did you send me this?" she asked as she showed him the text message on her phone. He glanced at it and then drew closer to read it and frowned.

"*Oui*," he said, finally.

"Okay. Why?"

"Why what?"

"Well, first why didn't you tell me this when we talked

before? You sent me this text the same day we talked. And secondly, *why* did Chantal and Rochelle fight?"

He licked his lips and looked at the basket he'd been sorting before turning and jutting out his chin in Maggie's direction.

"How would I know why women fight? But I heard Rochelle threaten Chantal several times."

So was *Enzo* the eyewitness the cops were using as their main evidence against Rochelle? Enzo? A vagrant? Someone who probably had a record? Was that remotely possible?

"Okay," Maggie said, putting her phone away. "So why didn't you mention this before?"

"It slipped my mind."

Maggie stood facing him.

"A woman is murdered," she said locking his gaze with her own, "and someone has a violent altercation with that woman the day she dies and you just forgot about it?"

"It is the truth."

Maggie was pretty sure that was the last thing it was.

"Did you tell the police?"

"No."

"Why not?"

"I didn't want to get anyone in trouble."

His evasive answers were starting to get on her nerves. It was time for a little questioning blunt force trauma style.

"Why didn't you tell me about the baby?"

His mouth fell open. "What?"

"As if you didn't know. Chantal was pregnant."

His face instantly whitened and he looked off into the distance. His eyes looked suddenly wet.

It looked real. *Can he be faking this?*

"You didn't know?" Maggie asked.

"*Non*," he said, shaking his head. "I didn't know."

Maggie wasn't sure what else to ask him at this point. LaBelle needed to get down here and swab him up to rule him out as the father. Although if Enzo *thought* he was the father, did it really matter if he was? And if he *wasn't* the father, wasn't that an even bigger motive for killing Chantal?

In any case, after her coffee with LaBelle this morning, Maggie thought the chances of the detective doing anything along the lines of conducting paternity tests seemed fairly remote.

"Is Madame Toussaint in?" she asked glancing over at the house.

"Probably," Enzo said, turning back to his basket. Maggie noticed his hands shook.

Maggie glanced at her car and saw that Grace was still inside, her head bent, probably on her cellphone. She walked to the farmhouse around the back of where the barn was and knocked on the door.

She waited only a moment before Madame Toussaint appeared in the doorway.

"Am I going to have to ask the police to remove you?" Madame Toussaint asked through the screen door.

"I went to talk to Madame Monet at the spa next door," Maggie said. "She said you two are related."

Toussaint seemed to sag against the door jamb for a moment. The hand that went to her throat was trembling.

"Is it possible you did you not know you were related?" Maggie asked. "Or are you just surprised she'd admit to it?"

Whatever shock Toussaint had sustained from Maggie's words, she recovered quickly.

"I'm afraid we French are not as comfortable as you Americans when it comes to broadcasting our family secrets," she said primly.

"So it's true?"

"What's true is that it is none of your business."

Maggie could see that Madame Toussaint was not in the mood to answer any more questions. In her experience a little shock was in order if she wanted to get the floodgates moving again.

"I also found out," Maggie said casually, "that Chantal was with child when she was killed."

Like Enzo, Toussaint's face paled but Maggie couldn't tell if it was because the information came as a shock or because she was discomfited that this fact would now become widely known.

"I need an answer, Madame Toussaint," Maggie said, "as to why you gave Chantal notice the day she died."

"You think *I* had something to do with her death?"

Her face reddened and a vein jumped over her left eye.

"I just need an answer as to why you were firing her."

"I'll tell you," Toussaint said, her breathing coming in short shallow bursts, her hand on the door as if ready to slam it in Maggie's face at any moment.

"I was reliably informed that Mademoiselle Lambert was selling her services to the other workers in the field," Toussaint said.

For a moment Maggie didn't understand what Toussaint was saying. Her face must have revealed her confusion because Toussaint burst out, "Chantal was a whore! She was selling her body in my lavender field!"

The older woman slammed the front door.

As Maggie slowly turned away to make her way off the porch she realized that for Madame Toussaint the thought of Chantal prostituting herself in itself might not be as shocking as the fact that she was doing it in her lavender field.

And *that* was something she might well consider a killing offense.

40

Maggie turned slowly and made her way down the steps, wondering how what she'd just learned might fit into the puzzle that was forming in her head. She was so jarred by the news that Chantal was selling her body in the lavender field that she didn't see Gené until she stepped directly into her path.

Maggie stopped abruptly and tensed, remembering all too well her last run-in with the woman.

"Did you get my text?" Gené asked.

Maggie blinked in surprise.

"*You* sent the text?" she said.

"About Rochelle threatening Chantal? *Oui.*"

Maggie frowned, momentarily confused.

Why had Enzo said *he* sent the message?

Her mind did a fast calculation. If Gené was the eyewitness who'd come to the police to point the finger at Rochelle, the cops might well have found her word a little more credible than Enzo's.

The operative phrase being "a little more."

Maggie made a mental note to ask LaBelle if Gené had a

record of any kind. Not that she'd tell her. But she could always ask.

"Did anyone else hear this fight?"

"You don't believe me?" Gené asked.

"I just need corroboration. One person's word is just hearsay."

"Chantal was a bitch. Rochelle wasn't the only one she fought with."

"Like you for instance?"

"We had words from time to time." Her face was unreadable as she spoke but Maggie thought she detected a slight tremor around her eyes as if she were forcing herself to remain calm.

"Did you tell the police any of this?"

"I don't speak to the police if I can help it."

If she was telling the truth, then it meant Maggie still hadn't found the one who'd incriminated Rochelle.

"When I first met you," Maggie said, "I didn't realize you spoke English."

Truth be told she hadn't been sure the woman spoke at all. But the conversation they were having now was in English, not French, and that in itself was highly unusual.

It made Maggie wonder where Gené had learned English. Most immigrants and refugees had been forced to leave school very early on and were lucky to get the basics of their own language, let alone a foreign one.

"I had an Australian lover when I was younger," Gené said with a shrug.

"They say that's the best way to learn a language," Maggie said, feeling a sudden and unexpected kinship with this woman who'd attacked her with a bat the last time she'd seen her.

As if reading her mind, Gené gestured at Maggie's head.

"I didn't want to hurt you," she said. "I held back."

"I appreciate it."

Gené smiled vaguely as if sharing in some kind of joke and then turned and walked away. Maggie made her way back to the car. She climbed in, not sure what her visit had provided in the way of useable information.

"Any luck, darling?" Grace asked as she put away the lipstick she'd been using to freshen her face in the car visor mirror.

"Yes and no. I found out that the reason Madame Toussaint fired Chantal was because she believed that Chantal was engaging in prostitution here at the farm."

"Goodness."

"And I also found out who sent me a mysterious text two nights ago about a big knock-down drag-out that Chantal and Rochelle had."

"Good work," Grace said as she blotted excess lipstick from her lips with a tissue.

"But I still haven't found out who told the cops that Rochelle threatened Chantal with her life. Supposedly that was the reason they arrested her in the first place."

"Oh! Well, maybe I can help," Grace said as Maggie started the car.

"Really?"

"I went for a walk over by the sorting shed," Grace said, "while I was waiting for you. The whole place really does smell incredible, doesn't it? Anyway I was talking with a girl who works here, dark hair, braids—"

"Brigitte?" Maggie prompted.

"The very one. Sweet girl. And she told me that the whole farm knows that the person who told the police about Rochelle threatening to kill Chantal was Madame Toussaint herself."

41

That night Maggie came home and after cheerfully asking Laurent about his day and receiving no indication that he was going to tell her that he'd seen Rochelle, felt her mood dip dangerously.

Turning her back on the palpable tension that seemed to exist everywhere in their home, she escaped to her home office while Laurent made dinner. As she settled in at her desk with Fleur curled up at her feet, Maggie reviewed the information that Grace had found out at the lavender farm and tried to make sense of it.

First, why would Toussaint accuse Rochelle of killing Chantal? Was she trying to distract attention away from herself? After all, she'd fired Chantal the very day she was killed. And while there was reason to believe that if you fired someone presumably you didn't need to kill them, firing was usually a rancorous operation in most employment situations.

What if Chantal wasn't about to go away easily? What if she had some way of making trouble for Toussaint? The fact that Toussaint had thrown Rochelle under the bus was curious on several levels. Of course, there was always the possibility that what Toussaint said was true. Possibly she *had* heard Rochelle threaten Chantal. But Toussaint had not shown any sense of wanting to be helpful to the police, had in fact indicated she didn't like the police, so why did she volunteer the information about Rochelle?

With Rochelle in jail and Chantal dead why was this sounding more and more like a two birds with one stone sort of deal?

Maggie heard raised voices through her office door—the rumble of Laurent's deeper one and Mila's shriller one—and realized her break was over.

"Come on, girl," she said to the dog who got to her feet when Maggie did. "Play time's over."

She walked through the living room, spotting Jemmy lounging on the couch watching television. There'd been a time when he would no sooner watch television when it was time to get dinner on the table than roller blade naked down the Cours Mirabeau.

But Laurent had his hands full right now and Jemmy was obviously taking advantage of the fact. Maggie was about to say something to him when she heard Mila's voice again.

"It's not fair!" she said, her voice piercing like it might shatter glass.

Maggie entered the dining room where Mila was sullenly setting the dinner table, slamming down the silverware at each place setting.

How much of this are we supposed to tolerate? Maggie thought as she felt a familiar headache coming on. *If she's doing it for attention and we don't give it to her, won't that just make it worse?*

She could see Laurent in the kitchen, his back turned to the dining room. She tried to imagine what he was thinking, how he was managing to block out Mila's whines and complaints. Or if he was.

On the one hand she felt an urge to go to him, to put a hand on his back and remind him that he wasn't alone in this. Instead, surprising herself, she turned and walked through the dining room to the French doors that led to the back garden. She stepped outside.

Instantly she felt the tension in the room behind her evaporate with the closing of the French doors.

It wasn't just Mila doing her best to make everyone miserable, Maggie thought as she took in the vista of sweeping undulating grape vines beyond the back garden. Laurent was tied up in some sort of internal midlife struggle of his own.

From the few monosyllabic answers she'd elicited from him, she knew that the pickers had generated an adequate number of baskets but for reasons that were not immediately forthcoming, they'd again left before it was dark.

Was the work they'd done enough to make up for the bad start with the broken alternator belt? It was hard to tell just by looking at the field. And Laurent wasn't sharing his view on the status of the harvest.

She turned back to the house but before she put her hand on the door handle Maggie felt an overwhelming urge to tell everyone—all her loved ones currently raging or sulking inside the *mas* walls—that she was done. They could either snap out of it or continue on without the willing audience she'd always provided.

She opened the door and went inside, not entirely sure she wasn't going to tell them exactly that, when she saw Laurent standing at the stove, his eyes directed on a spot in the mid-distance, unfocused and indeterminate, the pot on the stove boiling madly.

Her heart went out to him.

"Laurent?" she said as she entered the kitchen. Both children were nowhere to be seen.

He turned to her and smiled but she'd seen that smile before and his heart wasn't in it.

"How did the picking go today?" she asked. "Are we all caught up?"

He turned back to the pot which he quickly snatched the lid off of and then shook his hand since he'd failed to reach for a potholder first.

"*Oui, chérie.* We're good."

Maggie knew he was referring to the commitments they had to the various restaurants and retailers in the area. The Domaine St-Buvard label needed to produce so many bushels to fulfill those commitments.

"So would you say we'll have a decent harvest this year?" she pressed.

He smiled at her. Again, *that* smile.

"*Oui, chérie.* We are doing well. The broken tractor part did not deter us."

He turned from her and called to Mila who Maggie now saw was sitting and glowering, in one of the dining room armchairs, her iPad in her hands.

"Feed the dogs," Laurent said.

Mila made a noise of disgust at this request but she stood up as if to belie her sign of rebellion.

There was a time when that snort alone would have had her sent to her room without dinner.

But we are picking our battles now, Maggie thought as she watched Mila move into the kitchen and wrench the lid off the dog's plastic kibble container.

Don't look, Maggie chided herself. *She's going to do what she's going to do.*

However she turned too late not to miss Mila tossing a scoop of dry food into one of the dog bowls, spilling most of it on the floor.

Before Maggie could witness Laurent's any-minute-now explosion—if he was even present enough to do that—she walked away and into the living room where she again noted Jemmy in front of the TV.

He was glued to a show that Maggie was sure he'd watched at least a half dozen times before.

"Jemmy?"

"Yeah?" He kept his eyes on the screen.

"Walk with me," she said and turned toward the front door.

Even though it was dinner time, Fleur hurried to accompany her. After a brief hesitation, Maggie pulled a leash off the hook in the foyer, attached it to the dog's collar and stepped outside to wait for her son.

42

Maggie walked to the end of the long curving front drive and paused to glance over her shoulder at the kitchen window where she glimpsed Laurent inside.

He stood with his head down, looking at something on the stove. But just the sight of him backlit in a one-dimensional silhouette made her sad.

She turned back to walk down the driveway.

It didn't get dark until much later these long summer days which Maggie had always enjoyed. She glanced down at the dog at the end of the leash. Fleur was prancing excitedly beside her, sniffing at the oleander bushes that bordered the driveway, her tail wagging happily.

It was so much easier then, she thought. When they were little.

"Mom?"

Maggie turned to see Jemmy step outside. In an instant she saw him as a little boy, his eyes bright, a smile always on his face. He seemed to always run everywhere even if it was only a few feet.

"Dad says it's nearly time to sit down at the table," he said.

"We won't be long," Maggie said turning back toward the village road that fronted their house.

She waited as Jemmy hurried to catch up with her.

"Man, Mila and Dad are really getting into it," he said. "What is her deal these days?"

"I don't know," Maggie said. "I wish I did."

"Dana said Mila asked her if she'd ever smoked pot."

Suddenly Maggie felt clammy as a needle-sharp sensation of fear jabbed her.

Dana was the American girl who'd lived in Aix for the summer with her parents. She'd gone home to Atlanta a few weeks earlier. She and Mila had met in an art class in Aix earlier in the summer.

Jemmy knelt to pet Fleur. "Hey, girl. You like being away from the others, don't you?"

"Do you think Mila is…experimenting?" Maggie asked, nearly afraid to form the words.

"Nah, she was just trying to impress Dana. Trust me, Mom. Mila isn't doing anything like that."

Maggie nodded but she wasn't convinced. She was glad that Jemmy had told her and she would make every effort not to over-react—or tell Laurent—but she would keep an even sharper eye on the girl.

"What about you, Jemmy?" Maggie said lightly. "Is everything okay in your world?"

He snorted. "Whatever that means."

He was right. It was an idiotic thing to say. Especially to a teenager.

"You know how proud your father and I are of your performance in the play last weekend, don't you?"

The last thing Maggie wanted was for Laurent and Jemmy's clash over his interest in acting to drown out the positive points of Jemmy's achievement.

"But not so proud you'd actually encourage me," Jemmy said, his mouth pinched and angry.

Maggie wasn't sure what to say to that. She could see how Jemmy would view their reaction—well, really Laurent's reaction—as an overall assessment about him. But it was more complicated and nuanced than that.

Wasn't it?

"My acting teacher said she thought I'd be a natural for the drama school in Avignon next summer."

Maggie bit her tongue. First of all, the acting teacher was a dental hygienist who worked with the kids part-time and was hardly a judge of any kind. But on the other hand, next summer was a long way away. Not that she'd ask Laurent to agree to it now with the hopes that Jemmy would lose interest by then—they probably weren't that lucky—but they might be able to stall him without making a definite promise.

"I'm not surprised," she said. "You were so good in the play."

"I'm serious, Mom," Jemmy said quickly. "I come *alive* when I'm on stage. It's the most amazing feeling!"

Maggie smiled at her firstborn. She loved seeing his excitement and passion, loved seeing him so energized and happy. She would give anything to be able to tell him to follow his heart and that she and his dad would support him. But he wasn't twelve years old. He would be sixteen by next summer. He wasn't a child anymore.

"Will you at least talk to Dad?" Jemmy said, tugging the leash out of her hand as they turned back to the house. "You know, pick your time or whatever?"

He thinks I'm on his side, Maggie realized. *He thinks his best chance to get what he wants is for me to handle Laurent.*

She really didn't want him to think this was how her relationship with his father was. She didn't want him to think this was how you worked out problems with people you loved—going around them, waiting for the right time, setting the stage.

It all seemed so less honest than what she'd wanted to portray to him. Was that the picture she'd given him growing up?

"We'll discuss it, darling," she said, patting his shoulder. "But I'd ask you not to get your hopes up. A lot can happen in a year."

"If you're hoping I'll stop wanting to be who I think I was born to be," he said with a scowl, "maybe you shouldn't get *your* hopes up."

That seriously hurt. Right in the gut. It hurt to know that he might think even for a moment that his own mother would want him to be anything less than everything he wanted to be.

"I just want you to be happy," Maggie said as they walked toward the house.

"Yeah, right," Jemmy said. "That's what people always say when what they really care about is making *themselves* happy."

43

Laurent tossed the lardons and diced onions into the hot glazed pan, listening for the satisfying sizzle as he did.

In the back of his mind he heard Mila drop the scoop of dog food on the floor. He felt a flicker of annoyance but forced himself not to respond.

Instead he turned to the cut up chicken and seasoned it, his mind jumping from his meeting with Rochelle today to the debacle that his harvest appeared headed for.

By the time he'd gotten back from Marseille where he'd gone to get the tractor belt, the pickers were lounging around smoking, having long stopped working. Two of the girls had left.

Down two workers—since he'd have to fire the girls now—and at least thirty bushels of grapes in danger of molding.

And rain forecast for tomorrow.

He wondered if instead of going to see Rochelle in Aix he'd raced to Marseille and gotten the belt for the tractor and raced straight back to the vineyard if it would've made a difference.

Just thinking about Rochelle tore into his emotions. How

could he have been so wrong about her? Most people when they were struggling were not at their best. He accepted that.

Grace had slapped Laurent on a public street and tried to get her lawyer to give custody of Zouzou to Windsor in exchange for money. Luc had broken into Danielle's house and given access to it to his thug friends. And there were others, many others. Each time, Laurent had seen the good, seen what could be saved, who just needed a hand to climb back to some semblance of a normal life.

Rochelle had been in trouble but she'd once had a full and rich life. She'd had kids and a marriage. She'd run a vineyard. She just needed a hand, some encouragement.

And that of course was the problem. She'd been so like Dauphine, who also on the face of it appeared salvageable, that Laurent had been determined to give her what she needed to make things right for her.

Like he hadn't done for Dauphine.

He placed the chicken skin side down in the skillet to brown, and he thought of how he'd wasted a day of grape-picking—maybe even a critical one to the overall success of the harvest—for no Intel that would benefit anyone, least of all Rochelle.

Nor had he given her much emotional comfort either which he could tell was what she had been lobbying hardest for.

But on the other hand, as much as he'd paid a high price for it, he did discover something that he hadn't known before.

Rochelle wasn't like Dauphine. Except possibly in the way that she was already beyond helping. It was at least something but it pained him to know he'd probably sacrificed his harvest to discover it.

He rubbed a hand across his face and his eye caught movement through the kitchen window in the front drive. He watched Maggie and Jemmy as they walked back to the house and he felt his heart squeeze at the sight of them.

Maggie didn't need to know about his visit with Rochelle today. She tried to hide her dislike of Rochelle from him—afraid he'd see it as jealousy—but it was there. She was doing everything she could to help Rochelle—at his request. He wouldn't make it harder for her. He had nothing positive or substantive to tell her so he'd say nothing.

The sound of the dish shattering snapped him out of his thoughts and he turned to see Mila standing in the kitchen, her hands on her hips, her chin raised to him as if daring him to reprimand her.

He threw down the dishtowel as he felt his hopelessness ignite into a full-blown fury.

He stared at his daughter, feeling his peripheral vision go red as he did. Somewhere in the background of his mind he heard the dogs begin to bark.

44

Both hunting dogs were barking when Maggie and Jemmy opened the front door. That was a rarity with Laurent in the house but even more unusual than that was the distinct scent of burning onions.

"Uh oh," Jemmy said as he undid Fleur's leash.

Maggie hurried into the kitchen to see one of her favorite Moustiers faience plates in pieces on the floor at the very moment that Laurent turned off all the stove burners and advanced on Mila.

Mila stood facing him, her hands on her hips, defiant.

"Enough," Laurent said in a low growl.

Maggie wasn't sure if he was talking to Mila or himself.

He didn't seem to register Maggie's presence when he turned and walked past her. Jemmy flattened himself against the hall wall to avoid contact with the pulsating whirlwind of fury that her husband had become.

She heard the front door slam and within seconds heard the sound of their car starting up.

"This is not my fault!" Mila shouted at Maggie.

"Stop shouting," Maggie said to her. She pointed to the

broken dish on the floor. "And clean that up. Jemmy, wash your hands and let's see what part of dinner can be salvaged."

Maggie turned her back on Mila. She didn't want to hear the grumbling and the endless denying of responsibility. In her heart she couldn't imagine how anyone could be unaffected by the sight of her father storming out of the house knowing she was at least partly responsible.

The futility and weariness of that thought was enough to keep Maggie from confronting Mila.

Jemmy scraped the pot with the burnt onions into the trash.

"Finish frying up the chicken," Maggie said. "Don't worry about making *coq au vin*. Just get it cooked."

"I can make a risotto," he said dubiously. "If you want."

"I do," Maggie said. "Unless pasta is easier?"

Jemmy pulled out a saucepan.

"No, I'll do the risotto. It won't be as good as Dad's."

"It will be delicious," Maggie said, turning to Mila who had just finished sweeping up the broken shards. "Did the dogs get fed?" she asked.

"All except that one," Mila said, nodding at Fleur.

Maggie felt a swell of fury at the girl and she knew that was irrational. The fact that Mila had insisted on their adopting Fleur and now referred to her as *that one* made it worse.

"I'll make you a plate," Maggie said to her, "which you can eat in the dining room with me and your brother or take it up to your room."

And I honestly do not care which.

Mila's eyes widened when she realized she wasn't going to be punished for her behavior—far from it, she was going to be spared the family table.

"I'll feed Fleur," Maggie said to Mila. "But I can bring her upstairs to you afterward."

Mila screwed up her face. "What for?"

"For company?"

"She smells."

"She doesn't," Maggie said patiently. "But if you want you could give her a bath."

Mila snorted as if Maggie had made a joke.

"As if," she said, turning to throw the broken ceramic pieces into the kitchen trash can, making what Maggie was sure was as much noise as possible in the process.

Later Mila went upstairs with her dinner and Jemmy took his into the living room to finish watching his show. When they did—and with Laurent gone—Maggie again felt the startling absence of tension and stress. She hated that Laurent had left the way he did. She tried to remember another time in their marriage when he'd stomped out in a fury.

But he'd never had an adored daughter in her teen years before.

She poured herself a glass of Pinot Noir and took her dinner plate into her home office, wondering if the only thing that kept her entire family from splintering into separate eating routines was Laurent and his determination to keep them all at the family table.

Routines and rituals were all very good, she decided.

But sometimes you just need a break from them.

She turned on her computer and googled *Étoile Monet*. As she ate her dinner, she drilled deeper into the Internet, clicking on every underscored hyperlink until she came to a scanned document that led her to a jpeg of Étoile as a teenager in a school picture from Éguilles.

Maggie squinted at the picture. Except for the glasses, the unruly hair and the cheap *tablier*, it was clearly Étoile.

The caption on the picture listed her as Edithe Toussaint.

So that's that.

Maggie leaned back in her chair and sipped her wine, a shimmer of triumph rippling through her.

Étoile *née* Edithe was Madame Toussaint's daughter. Short

of a DNA test, this school photo was as close as Maggie was going to get to definitively making that connection.

Maggie made a mental note to go to the Éguilles city hall tomorrow to look at the records. They weren't online in the little villages, but she should be able to verify the connection between the two women.

If Annette Toussaint really was Étoile's biological mother, it had to mean there was some reason they were both trying to keep it a secret. She'd have to find out why and then how their relationship was connected with Chantal.

Maggie pushed her half-finished dinner away and gazed out the French doors in her office to the darkened view of the garden.

The two facts she now had from her visit to the lavender farm were that Étoile's mother Annette Toussaint had pointed the finger at Rochelle—*and Toussaint never mentioned that to me* —and Enzo lied when he said *he* was the one who'd texted Maggie.

She leaned back over her desk and picked up a pen to jot down the note: *ask LaBelle to check if Enzo has a record. Also Gené.*

She'd probably refuse to do it, but it was worth a try.

Why do people lie?

That's easy. To hide things.

On the tail end of that thought came the image of Laurent and how he'd been all evening before leaving in a rage— incommunicative, evasive, angry.

All evening she waited for him to bring up the fact that he'd seen Rochelle today.

Why wouldn't he mention that to me?

It was possible that nothing fruitful had come from his meeting. Perhaps Laurent was only thinking of it in terms of concrete Intel that might aid the case?

But if that was true and nothing helpful came from the

meeting, then what *had* come from it? And what part of the meeting was contributing to his foul mood?

Did something get said between them he doesn't want me to know?

Maggie stood up in frustration, sorry that her earlier discovery that Étoile was Annette Toussaint's daughter was now blotted out by Laurent's secrecy and bad mood.

She opened the door to her office and saw that Fleur was sitting patiently outside.

"She's been waiting for you for like an hour," Jemmy said from the couch, his focus still on his television show.

Fleur began to wag her tail as Maggie opened her office door wider to allow her in and then returned to her desk where she picked up her phone and called Rochelle's lawyer.

Segal finally answered after letting it ring.

"*Allo?*" he said.

"Monsieur Segal? This is Maggie Dernier."

"I know," he said and belched. "I have caller ID."

"I was wondering if you had any initial impressions after talking to Rochelle Lando."

If he acts like he doesn't know who she is, Maggie thought in mounting frustration and impatience, *I swear I'll report him for being drunk on the job.*

"No initial impressions," he said, slurring the word.

"Okay," she said patiently as Fleur jumped on her couch and curled up on the cashmere throw Maggie kept there. "Can you tell me if her explanation of events matched what the cops are saying?"

"I am a very busy man," Segal said huffily.

Maggie hesitated.

"Have you not gotten in to see her?" she asked, feeling—hoping—she might actually be offending him by even suggesting such a thing.

"I am a very busy man!"

"She's been in custody for nearly a week! You haven't talked to her yet?"

"*Non*, and I do not like your tone, Madame," he said haughtily before slamming down the phone receiver.

Maggie stood holding her phone to her ear for several long seconds after Segal had hung up before taking in a long breath and pushing in the number for Detective LaBelle.

"What?" LaBelle said, answering. "I'm busy."

"So am I," Maggie said firmly, her voice brooking no denial. "And I need to see Rochelle Lando."

45

The next morning it rained.
By the time Maggie drove away from the house, the pickers still hadn't shown up and as far as Maggie knew they might have even been told to stay home.

Laurent returned home late last night and had been even quieter than usual. She knew he'd probably gone to Le Canard —the café bar in Saint-Buvard—and she found herself glad he had a place to go.

Since he clearly wasn't anywhere near solving his problem with Mila it was probably for the best for all that he remove himself from the playing field.

Or in his case, the battlefield.

Thinking of this as she drove into Aix made Maggie decide that instead of insisting that Laurent help partner with her in dealing with Mila, perhaps she needed to do a better job of insulating him from the relentless day to day aggravations that Mila seemed hell bent on putting him through.

She'd had no opportunity to speak to him this morning since he was up and gone before her. Whether he was going to tell the pickers not to come or head back to Le Canard, she had no idea. She wished he would share with her what he was thinking and what he was going through, but that wasn't his way.

She went downstairs to see that he'd made a pot of coffee for her that was still hot. Both children were still asleep.

She knew Laurent would have let all three dogs out before he left so she wrote a quick note to Jemmy to feed them when he got up. She didn't want to take the chance of Mila ignoring the note and felt an immediate stab of anger that she was allowing the girl to evade her responsibilities as part of the family.

Thirty minutes later, Maggie found a parking spot in front of the Aix police station.

I should have done this as soon as I heard Laurent promised we would help, she thought. *Why didn't I?*

It didn't matter. What did matter was that Rochelle's lawyer was useless and Maggie had gone as far as she could with uncovering evidence and supporting testimony without registering Rochelle's side of things.

It was past time.

The room that LaBelle had set up for Maggie to meet Rochelle in was not quite an interrogation room—there were no handcuffs hanging from a chain on a table—but it was decidedly skimpy on creature comforts. A simple couch and a side table were the only pieces of furniture in the room.

Maggie had asked to see Rochelle alone and had been surprised when LaBelle agreed.

When Maggie came into the room Rochelle was already there. She was dressed in a dark jumpsuit with her hair pulled back in a ponytail. Maggie even thought she detected a hint of lip gloss.

She came in and sat down opposite her. Rochelle glanced at Maggie's hands as if she were expecting something.

A note from Laurent perhaps?

"Laurent doesn't know I'm seeing you today," Maggie said.

Rochelle's eyebrows arched and a faint smile etched across her lips.

"I see."

"I'm here because I don't feel like your attorney is doing his best job by you."

"If he would ever contact me," Rochelle said, "I'd fire him."

Maggie nodded.

"And I don't blame you. But he's appointed by the court. Unless you want to defend yourself—something I don't recommend—you can't fire him."

Rochelle shrugged. "It doesn't matter."

Maggie found herself wondering why it didn't matter. In fact, the more she watched Rochelle, the more she was amazed by the fact that Rochelle did not look very worried. Not even a little bit.

I know the food's better than an American jail, but it's still jail. Is something going on I don't know about?

"In any case," Maggie said. "I'm here to hear your side of things, Rochelle. Afterward, I can interface with your attorney since he seems to be very...pressed for time."

"Whatever you want."

There it was again. That insouciance or unconcern.

"Your husband is amazing as I'm sure you know," Rochelle said. "I can't imagine enduring any of this without him by my side."

Effectively discounting the *by my side* comment Maggie was about to confirm that Laurent was indeed a very caring man but she was pretty sure that wasn't the message Rochelle had intended to deliver. She found herself biting the inside of her mouth.

"He reminds me of my first husband," Rochelle said. "Before things went bad. In fact I told him recently if I'd met him instead of Danny, I wouldn't be getting a divorce."

Rochelle leaned across the metal table and put her hand on Maggie's wrist.

"Want to know a secret?" she said in a hushed voice. "When I first met Laurent last summer in Calistoga I did everything in my power to get him into bed. Hand to God."

Who says this to a man's wife?

Maggie knew there was a certain brand of Californian who prided themselves on an almost perverse kind of honesty and would think a declaration like this was a positive character feature.

"Yeah, well, get in line," Maggie said with a strained smile. "Now, if you don't mind. I don't have a lot of time and I need your take on a few things to help me fill in the gaps."

She was mildly appeased by the look on Rochelle's face at her confident indifference to the bait that Rochelle had dangled.

"First off," Maggie said. "Can you tell me why you confessed to a crime you didn't commit?"

"Are you sure I didn't do it?"

"Don't play games with me, Rochelle," Maggie said. "Laurent believes you're innocent so that's enough for me. Why did you confess?"

Rochelle looked at her with a steady gaze.

"I thought it would be easier on everyone."

That is literally the stupidest answer I ever heard.

"How about your kids?" Maggie asked. "Would it be easier on them?"

Rochelle's eyes filled with tears.

"Please don't talk about my children," she said.

"Are you in touch with them?"

"No. Dan has seen to that."

"Do they know what's happening to you?"

"What *is* happening to me?" Rochelle gave a dismissive laugh. "You mean, do they know I'm in a French jail under suspicion of murder? No, they don't know."

"How did you think confessing would be a good thing for your kids to hear?"

"Can you just stop?" Rochelle said, crossing her arms. "I'm sorry I did it, okay? Laurent already verbally spanked me for doing it. I tried to retract it with that lady cop. Anyway Laurent said it wouldn't count since I was recanting."

Maggie couldn't help but think that Laurent had said an awful lot of things in his meeting with Rochelle. She fought down the stab of jealousy, angry at herself for having it at all.

"All right," Maggie said. "Let's move forward. What do you know about Annette Toussaint?"

Rochelle leaned back in her chair, tapping her foot.

"Nothing. She's the manager of the farm."

"Did you get along with her?"

"Well enough. We weren't friends but she didn't hate me."

"Would it surprise you to know that Madame Toussaint was the one who said she overheard you threaten Chantal?"

"Not at all. She was civil to me but nothing more."

"When would she have heard you threaten Chantal?"

"Well, since I never threatened her, I don't know." Rochelle narrowed her eyes. "You think I killed her, don't you? Does Laurent know that's what you think?"

"It doesn't matter what I think," Maggie said blandly. "If you're innocent, I'll do everything I can to get you free."

"Because Laurent told you to."

"Because it's the right thing to do."

"So you would do it for anyone?"

"We don't have to be best buds for me to want to help you, Rochelle. Did you see Chantal the evening she was killed?"

Rochelle narrowed her eyes at her.

"Briefly," she said.

"Some people said they heard you arguing with her."

Rochelle looked away.

"She was teasing a friend of mine," she said.

"Teasing?"

"Look, what difference does all this make? Chantal was a piece of work and nobody liked her. She was taking advantage of someone who...who couldn't look after himself and I told her to back off."

Maggie realized that Rochelle must be talking about Erté, the mentally handicapped man at the monastery.

"Did anybody hear this part of the argument where you were defending Erté?" Maggie asked.

Rochelle made a face and folded her arms across her chest.

"I don't know who heard what," she said.

It's almost like she doesn't care, Maggie thought in bewilderment.

"What about Enzo?" Maggie asked. "Any thoughts on him?"

"None except he and Chantal deserved each other."

"And Gené?"

"I didn't know her well. I don't think she speaks English."

Or she didn't want you to know she did, Maggie thought.

"And you and Chantal didn't get along, right? That's what everyone says," Maggie prompted.

"Look, Chantal didn't get along with anyone. For someone who was turning tricks to buy lipstick, she was pretty arrogant."

"Would it surprise you to learn she was pregnant when she died?" Maggie asked.

"Not at all. She slept with anyone who looked her way. Anyone except Laurent of course."

Why would she even say that? Was she saying Laurent knew Chantal?

"Laurent never met Chantal," Maggie said, her jaw tense.

"Are you sure about that, darling?" Rochelle said with a smile.

46

"Laurent is a man of many secrets," Rochelle said. "He told me a little of how he used to make his living in the old days."

Maggie was shocked that Laurent had shared any of his past with Rochelle, especially his time as a conman on the Côte d'Azur. That was a time he wasn't particularly proud of and he rarely brought it up.

Maggie wasn't sure what game Rochelle was playing but she was quickly wearying of it. It was clear that for whatever reason Rochelle was hoping to discombobulate Maggie.

"I'm pretty sure Chantal and Laurent never met," Maggie said, knowing she was taking the bait but not able to stop herself.

"Well, I don't want to speak out of turn," Rochelle said, smiling condescendingly at Maggie. "But in any case, I'm sure you don't have a thing to worry about with Laurent."

And now she's reassuring me that I can trust my own husband?

"Walk me through where you were the night Chantal was killed, " Maggie said. She felt her body tensing. "Ending with your finding the body."

"I've been through this a million times already."

"Yes, but you're going through it this time with someone who wants to help you."

What is with her? It's too much trouble to try to save her own skin?

"Fine. Well, I knew I had the play that night," Rochelle said with a heavy sigh.

It was all Maggie could do to say that Rochelle needn't have put herself out. Nobody was waiting anxiously for her arrival at Jemmy's play.

Except possibly for Laurent.

"There was a line for the showers in the women's dorm at the monastery by the time I got back from the lavender farm—"

"What time was this?"

"Around seven. Anyway, there was a line so I washed my face and hands in the sink and brushed off the worst crud and dirt on my pants."

The play started at eight o'clock. For Rochelle to have killed Chantal she would've had to go straight to the field, stabbed her, and then hitched a ride to Aix, still covered in blood, in order to get there before the curtain went up.

Certainly doable. But likely?

"I walked to Ponte l'Abbe to catch the bus but I'd just missed the last one."

"What time was it then?"

Rochelle sighed as if all of this was way too much trouble.

"Around seven thirty, I guess?"

"So you didn't take the bus. How did you get to Aix?"

"I flagged down a car and asked for a ride to the D7N. I figured I could hitch from there. But the guy was going to Aix so I got lucky."

"What kind of car was it?"

"The police already asked me this. I don't know. I'm not good with car makes and models. It was blue."

Maggie nodded to indicate that Rochelle should continue. So far there was nothing in what she was saying that could help her. Tracking down a blue car pulling out of Ponte l'Abbe village wasn't exactly impossible but the village was east of the highway and, unlike other more rural villages, it wasn't unusual for travelers to stop there for gas and a meal before continuing on.

Maggie already knew without asking that there were no CCTV cameras anywhere in the village.

"And the rest you know," Rochelle said. "I arrived just before the curtain went up, stayed for the after-show party, and got a ride back to the monastery around eleven o'clock."

Rochelle had gotten a ride back the monastery with Laurent.

"And the next morning?"

It irritated Maggie that she had to prompt the woman like this!

Doesn't she know I'm trying to help her? Can she not tell the difference between me and LaBelle?

"I got up at the usual time around eight o'clock..."

"That seems late to be the usual time," Maggie interjected with a frown. She knew from talking to Laurent that most of the refugee workers at the monastery were up at dawn cleaning, weeding, or boarding the buses to take them to whatever neighboring fields they were scheduled to work that day.

Rochelle smiled.

"I think they cut me some slack because I'm an American," she said.

"Why does that matter?"

"I don't know. Maybe because we helped them out in the war?"

Is this woman for real?

Maggie made a mental note to ask Frère Luis about Rochelle's work schedule.

"Please continue," she said.

"You don't like me, do you, Maggie?"

"I'm sorry not to be all best chums friendly," Maggie said. "But what I'm doing is not a game. And neither is your situation. Do you not know how dangerous it is?"

"I'm pretty sure the American government isn't going to let me go to a French prison."

"Based on what?" Maggie asked in bewilderment. "What in the world makes you think that?"

Rochelle wrinkled her forehead and shrugged as if suddenly unsure.

"Because I'm an American citizen," she said.

"You think Americans can just do what they want and there are no consequences when they visit a foreign country?"

"I...but I'm not a...the rules here..."

"Are you seriously that stupid?" Maggie blurted out and then blushed. "I'm sorry. Forgive me. But honestly this explains a lot." She took in a long breath and reminded herself to be kind. This woman was in a bad spot even if she didn't know it.

"Look, Rochelle, if you're found guilty of murder here in France the US State Department will not swoop in and whisk you away. You will be sent to a French prison where I guarantee you will finally learn the language—along, I might add, with a few other things."

"No," Rochelle said, shaking her head. "*No.* You're just saying that because you're jealous of my relationship with Laurent."

Maggie felt like laughing, her earlier spike of jealousy totally gone.

"I can't talk you into taking this seriously if you don't think it is," Maggie said. "But for your own sake, Rochelle, I'm asking you to walk me through how you found Chantal's body."

Rochelle seemed to be considering Maggie's response for a moment before she finally spoke.

"As I said, I was up at eight o'clock. I ate breakfast in the hall and there are lots of people who can vouch for the fact that they saw me."

If only having an alibi for the time eighteen hours *after* a murder counted for anything, Maggie thought.

"I thought I was supposed to be working in tandem with Enzo that day, walking alongside the tractors, so I went back to my room and got my gum boots and a sun hat. I walked to the farm—"

"What time was it then?"

"Probably closer to nine by then. It took me twenty minutes to walk to *La Lavandin* because I took the shortcut across the lower field."

"How did you discover this shortcut?"

Rochelle frowned.

"I walked it in the beginning with Chantal. She was living at the monastery too, so at least at first—until we got to know each other—we'd walk to the lavender farm together."

"So this was *Chantal's* shortcut?"

"Yeah, I guess so."

"Go on."

"Well, I hopped over the big stone wall and right away I saw her. Laid out with lavender fronds sticking out of her clothes. At first I thought she was playing some kind of weird joke."

"And then? When you realized it wasn't a joke?"

"I left. It really freaked me out. And then I remembered that Toussaint didn't need me that day. So I just came back to the monastery."

"You literally didn't remember you weren't expected to work that day? Because that's not something most hourly workers forget."

It wasn't even a shot across the bow. More like a series of cluster shots aimed at dead center but Maggie didn't feel a bit sorry about it.

Rochelle blushed angrily.

"I'm just telling you what happened," Rochelle said, biting off every word.

"So you came back to the monastery," Maggie prompted patiently, "at which point you went on with your day as if nothing had happened?"

"Okay, I hear the judgment in your voice," Rochelle said. "So yeah, I guess I should've told someone."

"You think?"

"I'd like to see *you* find a dead body and see how clearheaded *you* are!"

Maggie let that one go. She knew seeing death, especially in one so young, wasn't easy to shrug off. She tried to allow for that with Rochelle.

"So you're saying you were so upset about seeing a dead body that you just pretended it hadn't happened?"

Rochelle was chewing her lip now and wiping her damp palms on her prison jumpsuit.

"That's exactly what I'm saying."

"Well, I have to say I'm not surprised Detective LaBelle doesn't believe you."

"I can't help what she does or doesn't believe," Rochelle said, jutting out her chin in sudden anger. "All I can say is that when I told Laurent, he took me in his arms and comforted me. Because that's what friends do. They accept and support you."

Maggie registered the self-satisfied look on Rochelle's face. And it was all she could do not to shake her head in pity.

Because it was pretty clear that the fact that Rochelle believed she had Laurent to lean on was giving her the freedom to ignore the reality of her situation.

Which meant she was going to hang herself.

47

The harvest was an unmitigated disaster.

Laurent stood in front of twenty half-filled baskets of grapes. He'd counted them twice, testimony to his mounting disbelief. But no matter how many times he counted, the number wasn't going to change.

The field looked stripped, not harvested, but there was still plenty of fruit on the vine.

It had finally stopped raining a little after lunch but it hardly mattered at this point. The grapes he'd harvested were already molding in the shed, the ones still on the vine were dropping on their own accord. Still worth picking but he would never have enough for his commitments.

He turned, no longer able to block out Mila's whining as she sat on the ground a few feet away from him. Maggie had gone to Aix for an errand and Laurent had insisted that both children put down their electronics and come outside with him.

As usual, he didn't know why he bothered.

Jemmy looked bored but compliant—a trait Laurent had noticed in the last few years and hated. He'd rather the boy openly defy him than bow his shoulders and soldier through. It wasn't just dishonest, Laurent thought, it was disrespectful.

"I'm serious!" Mila said from the ground where she was picking a grape branch apart in the epitome of agonized boredom. "Why do I have to be here? Why don't you just kill me and get it over with?"

He looked at her and felt something stir deep inside him. Attempting to tamp down his anger only made it worse. He felt like walking away from this creature. Walking away and never having to listen to her again.

"Be quiet, Mila," he said quietly as he stared into the distance, seeing nothing.

His harvest was ruined. His children were a disappointment.

"I hate you!" Mila shouted at him. "You're the worst! I can't wait to leave home!"

He turned to look at her and felt a similar version of how he'd felt two nights ago when he'd left before dinner to spend the evening at the bar in the village and felt grateful he hadn't strangled his only daughter before leaving.

"Why are you looking at me like that?" Mila said with no fear or trepidation in her voice, only indignation and irritation.

She trusts me. As horrible as she's behaving. She can't imagine I don't love her.

The thought rocked him. And he blinked, staring at her as if unable to fully comprehend what he'd just discovered.

As a child Laurent had never felt what Mila so intrinsically felt. He'd never had a template or been trained to believe something like that feeling even existed.

And yet even without experiencing it himself as a child, he'd given it to his daughter.

As big a monster as you are, he thought, as he stared at his petulant child with a grin beginning to etch across his face, *I will love you no matter what.*

And you know it.

He felt like laughing and then in the middle of what both Jemmy and Mila clearly had to think was a nascent madness overtaking their father, Laurent realized the solution to his problem, in fact to all their problems.

It was so obvious, so perfectly clear, that he did not know why he hadn't seen it before. And not only was the solution obvious to him, for the first time in his life, he didn't need to even think about it.

He was *sure*.

Just recognizing that he'd already made the decision to act felt like a leaden weight had been lifted from his shoulders.

He wanted to throw back his head and laugh for the sheer idiot relief of it. Instead he turned and strode back toward the house leaving both children to scramble to their feet and run after him in bafflement.

He would tell Maggie tonight. He would set the stage, light the candles, shoo the kids off to bed early, and reveal to his loving, adorable wife the answer to all their problems.

They would sell Domaine St-Buvard and leave France.

48

That night Mila had a stomachache which pulled her out of the family line up for the night—the result of which changed the course and tenor of the entire evening.

After putting Mila to bed for the night, she and Laurent and Jemmy sat down to a simple dinner of *pan bagnat* and a miraculous evening of blessedly tension-free conversation.

If only Mila could come down with some mild, nonlethal condition that kept her indisposed and in bed for weeks at a time.

I'm a terrible mother to even think it.

Maggie was amazed that Laurent, who was relaxed and content for the first time in weeks, also seemed almost completely uninterested in talking about the harvest. The pickers had been in the field most of the day but it was hard to imagine that the paltry number of baskets filled with grapes—clearly visible from the back garden—would be able to meet many of their commitments.

After dinner, Maggie begged off on taking a walk with Laurent and Jemmy so that she could call Detective LaBelle.

A part of her hated not to be a part of the family moment

and without her there she was a little worried that Jemmy might push his luck with Laurent and ruin what up to now had been such a pleasant respite from their recent family squabbles.

But it had been a part of the deal she'd made with the detective when she'd asked to be allowed to visit with Rochelle that she tell her what they talked about.

"Hey," Maggie said when she connected with the detective. "Is this a good time?"

"Are you calling to tell me what the suspect said to you today?" LaBelle asked.

"As agreed."

"You know I had the interview recorded."

"Then why did you bother to have me call you? Are you just bored?" Maggie asked with a strong hint of frustration in her voice. "With nothing else to do?"

"*Au contraire.* I am extremely busy. But yes, also a little bored."

"Well, then you heard it. I imagine she told me pretty much the same thing she told you in your interviews."

"That is correct."

"But what you *don't* know," Maggie said, "is that I caught someone lying about their behavior at the lavender field."

"Who?"

"Enzo Corbin."

"The boyfriend."

"Exactly. You know, in the real world the boyfriend is always the first suspect."

"He has an alibi."

"But he's the *boyfriend!*" Maggie said, throwing her hands up in exasperation. "And probably the father of her child. Why isn't he the first person you would look at?"

"Um, let me see. Because I have a confession from Rochelle Lando?"

"You heard what Rochelle said about that. It won't stand up in court now that she's recanted."

"You never know."

"What about Brigitte?"

"Who?"

"She's one of the workers at the lavender farm. Not the one sleeping with Enzo. Does *she* have an alibi?"

Maggie hated to even ask. Brigitte seemed like such a sweet girl. But desperate times called for desperate measures."

"As it happens she does," LaBelle said. "She went home that night to her parents' home in St-Cannat—a good twenty kilometers away—and we have confirmed it. Is there anyone else you want to blame this on? How about the mail carrier? I believe there is a boy who occasionally delivers bread to the farm. I could see where he was on the night in question."

Maggie refused to allow the detective to fluster her.

"Are you still determined not to question anyone at *Chatoyer*?" Maggie asked. "Because I have now confirmed a connection between the lavender field and the salon."

"You already told me this."

"Yes, but now I've come up with conclusive evidence that proves Madame Toussaint and Madame Monet are in fact mother and daughter."

Actually Maggie had yet to dot the i's on that but she felt justified in the white lie if it would prompt LaBelle to go out to the spa and interview the people there.

It didn't.

"Half the people in this area are related," LaBelle said. "How does that fit with a homicide? My boss knows I have a prime suspect and that's that. I can't use any more departmental expenditures toward a case that is already solved."

"It's not solved," Maggie said between gritted teeth. "And you know it."

"Who says I do?"

"I do! I could be way off base here but I think you want the right person to go to prison for this murder. I think it matters to you who gets proven guilty—not just case clearance rates in your department or pleasing your boss."

"You know nothing."

But Maggie had heard the hesitation in the detective's voice and she suddenly was gripped by a really great, possibly mad idea.

"When's your next day off?" Maggie asked impulsively.

"Who gets a day off? But I am possibly free tomorrow."

"Good. Meet me at Lido's on rue Banc."

49

The next morning was still drizzly and steam seemed to rise up from the sidewalk surrounding the bistro where Maggie and LaBelle sat in Aix. They both ordered coffees and croissants.

Maggie had had the feeling all night long that Laurent wanted to tell her something last night. When he and Jemmy returned from their walk, he acted more attentive than usual as if on the cusp of sharing something with her but every time she asked what was on his mind, he shook his head.

Laurent had left before dawn to collect his pickers and bring them back to Domaine St-Buvard to finish the harvest. The rain had slowed to a sprinkle and he clearly had hopes of picking the rest of the grapes. Maggie was astonished that he was able to fool himself to that degree. It was obvious that the harvest was a disaster—the worst they'd ever had.

Even worse than the year someone lit a match to the fields.

But for whatever reason, Laurent seemed at peace about it. And since Maggie had her hands full trying to free Rochelle and keeping Mila—who was feeling better now and back to her old mouthy self—out of Laurent's direct reach, she wouldn't question why.

Yet.

Maggie sipped her coffee.

"Do you know the guy that Rochelle was talking about?" Maggie asked. "The one she said the fight was about?"

LaBelle frowned. "She probably just made him up."

"There's a guy at the monastery who's mentally challenged," Maggie said.

LaBelle snorted.

"What is that supposed to mean?" Maggie asked, feeling her exasperation ratchet up.

"*C'est ridicule.*"

"It's not ridiculous. I've seen him myself so that part is true. If this guy doesn't have all the mental faculties that a non-handicapped man would have, he would be totally vulnerable to someone like Chantal."

"You mean like being forced into making love to her?" LaBelle said sarcastically.

"No," Maggie said patiently, "I mean being fleeced. Everything I've heard about Chantal tells me she was not a particularly nice person. Okay, maybe she had troubles and she was doing the best she could, but she was definitely an opportunist. I think we need to find out where Erté was during the time of the crime."

"We? Do you think I am playing for your team now? Have you forgotten who I am?"

"All I'm asking is for you to spend a little bit longer on the case," Maggie said through gritted teeth. "That's all. Ask a few more questions before you hand Rochelle over to the prosecutors."

LaBelle didn't respond. Two teens flew by the front of the café on skateboards forcing a businessman to jump out of the way. He cursed them as they sailed by.

"Okay," LaBelle said finally. "Why are we here?"

Maggie rubbed her hands together.

"You generously agreed to walk through a series of other possible suspects one at a time."

LaBelle signaled to the waiter to bring her another coffee.

"Let's start with Étoile Monet," Maggie said.

LaBelle snorted again.

"You're not being at all open minded about this," Maggie said.

"What possible reason would someone like Madame Monet have for traipsing through a muddy field to kill a homeless prostitute? The thought is absurd."

"Maybe on the face of it, but we can't just dismiss the possibility out of hand!"

"Fine. Motive? None. Next!"

LaBelle glared at Maggie as if challenging her to disagree.

"Okay," Maggie said reluctantly. *No motive that we know of*, she wanted to say but knew there was little point.

"Who's next?" LaBelle said with a curl of her lip. "The elderly and somewhat infirm Madame Toussaint? You do remember she uses a cane, yes? Motive?"

Maggie shook her head. "Okay, no motive. *That we know of*," she said. "By the way, what was her alibi? You did ask her, right?"

"Do not be offensive," Labelle said. "She was at home."

"Alone?"

"*Oui.*"

"So no alibi," Maggie said.

"But also no motive," Labelle pointed out.

"Fine," Maggie said, conceding. "What about Beau Dubois?"

"Who?"

"The masseuse at *Chatoyer*. He knew Chantal *and* he acted guilty when he was questioned about her."

"That is not a crime."

"Yeah, okay, but it's a reason to look at him."

"He has no motive," Labelle said.

"Not unless he's the father of Chantal's unborn child."

"How is that a motive for murder?" LaBelle said with a heavy sigh. "Besides, in order to prove it I'd have to get a warrant for a DNA test. Why would he agree to that?"

"To prove himself innocent?"

"Except he's not accused of anything. And before you say it, the same goes for Enzo Corbin."

"Enzo, the victim's boyfriend who was sleeping with someone else and who I assume has a rap sheet?"

"You know I'm not going to tell you that."

"As the boyfriend, he has the most motive!"

"And also an alibi! Do you see a pattern here?" LaBelle said tossing down her napkin. "*None* of these so-called suspects are remotely suspicious. No motives, and in most cases no opportunity."

"We just haven't uncovered the evidence, that's all!" Maggie said. "What about Harlequin Martin? She's the one who pushed Grace out on the roof! Are you saying *she's* not suspicious?"

"Perhaps she found Madame VanSant as annoying as I do," LaBelle said. "What would her motive for murder be?"

"Jealousy? Chantal might've been trying to steal her boyfriend or—"

"Harlequin is a beautiful self-possessed woman with her own apartment, clothes and money. Chantal was a penniless fieldworker."

Maggie looked at the detective in surprise.

"So you looked into Harlequin's background?"

LaBelle shrugged. "Madame VanSant didn't want to press charges, but if her allegation was true it was worth a few minutes of my time on the SIS data base."

Maggie knew LaBelle was referring to the European police database.

"Does she have a record?" Maggie asked.

"None of your business." LaBelle paused and took a sip of her coffee. "But no, she doesn't."

Maggie leaned back in her chair. She could see how LaBelle would come to the conclusion that nobody was as suspicious as Rochelle for Chantal's murder.

Honestly, she was halfway there herself.

"But if nobody has a motive *that we know of*," Maggie said, "you have to admit that neither does Rochelle."

"That we know of."

"Yes, okay, but you're not holding anyone else for the same reason—a lack of evidence. How can you hold Rochelle?"

"Because we have forensics which does connect to Madame Lando," LaBelle said. "And which is even better than motive. Plus she found the body and didn't report it which is very damning, *non*? On top of that she was overheard threatening to kill the victim."

"But she has an alibi," Maggie said. "She was at a play in Aix during the time of the murder."

LaBelle looked at Maggie pityingly and shook her head.

"It would have been close but she could have done it," LaBelle said.

"You know what I think?" Maggie said, leaning conspiratorially across the table toward LaBelle.

"There is no telling," LaBelle said with the nearest thing to a smile Maggie had yet seen on her.

"I think we need to take a field trip."

"Field trip?" LaBelle frowned.

"Yep. You and me. We need to go to a few of the places Chantal went."

"I have already talked to everyone at the lavender farm,"

Labelle said. "And I am not going to embarrass myself by questioning anyone at *Chatoyer*."

"Actually, I was thinking we should visit the place where Chantal spent most of her time when she wasn't cutting lavender."

"Do you mean the monastery?"

"Have you talked to anyone there?"

"Besides my prime suspect and her roommates? *Non*. As I said, my boss does not encourage my wasting valuable time and resources."

"Look, if you're not willing to investigate the spa, then the monastery is our next best source. Both the victim and your would-be killer were living there. If nothing else we can confirm Rochelle's story that she was trying to defend Erté."

"What good would that do? So she is a good person who defended a helpless simpleton. It doesn't mean she wasn't capable of killing someone."

"What have we got to lose by at least asking?" Maggie said raising her voice.

"Only a valuable hour in my rare day off," LaBelle said as she picked up the bill and squinted at it.

"I told Laurent we would," Maggie said and held her breath.

LaBelle looked up slowly from the bill and in that moment Maggie knew that LaBelle knew that Maggie knew the truth about her feelings for Laurent. It was one split second when LaBelle stood naked before her.

It had been a gamble, invoking Laurent's name, and if LaBelle reacted badly, it would ruin any chance of an amicable relationship between the two of them in the future.

But it was a risk Maggie felt she needed to take to move the detective forward. She lifted her chin to meet LaBelle's gaze and narrowed her eyes hoping to transmit her message as silently but succinctly as possible.

Let's put our cards on the table, shall we?

"Well," LaBelle said after a long pause, her face impassive and unreadable as she raised her hand to call the waiter.

"If you told Laurent we would go," for the first time not referring to Laurent as *your husband* or *Monsieur Dernier*, "then I suppose we need to go."

50

Maggie was fairly optimistic about their visit to the monastery.

First, since LaBelle wasn't on duty, Maggie was sure she would be more open to talking to people than she would be within the confines of a formal police investigation.

Second, it was clear that she and the detective had begun a connection. Unless Maggie was wrong, she'd detected a begrudging respect from LaBelle that Maggie felt would further open the detective's reception to her ideas.

As they pulled into the parking lot of the monastery Maggie turned to LaBelle.

"We should talk to Erté first and see how well he knew Chantal."

"Fine," LaBelle said. "As this is my day off I will leave it in your hands."

Maggie led the way through the stone archway toward the monastery dining hall. It was too early for lunch but the last time she'd noticed Erté hanging around the dining hall before was right around this time.

They entered the hall, their footsteps echoing loudly on the stone flooring. At the far end of the room, Maggie saw Madame Grier again, this time with another woman Maggie didn't recognize.

LaBelle followed behind as Maggie led the way to the two women who were now warily watching them approach.

"*Bonjour* Madame Grier," Maggie said. "Do you remember me?"

"Of course," the old woman said. "Since I don't have dementia. You were only here last week."

Maggie turned to introduce LaBelle. "This is—"

"We know who she is," Madame Grier said. "What can we help you with?"

The woman who had been standing with Madame Grier—a hard-looking woman in her fifties—started to step away.

"Excuse me, Madame?" Maggie said to her. "Would you mind staying?"

The woman looked startled and instantly cagey.

"I don't know anything," she said.

"How do you know what we will ask you?" LaBelle asked.

Maggie wished LaBelle hadn't said anything. It was clear the woman was nervous and LaBelle's words seem to thicken the layer of distrust that the woman openly wore.

"We just want to know anything you might know about Chantal," Maggie said hurriedly.

"Or Rochelle Lando," LaBelle added to Maggie's annoyance.

Ignoring her, Maggie turned to the second woman.

"My name is Maggie Dernier."

The woman's face softened and her eyes flickered over to LaBelle for a moment.

"I know your husband," she said.

"I'm not surprised," Maggie said. "He comes here a lot. Will you answer a few questions?"

The woman hesitated and then stuck out her hand to Maggie.

"I am Madame Bantu," she said.

"Thank you, Madame Bantu. I wanted to know if you knew if Rochelle Lando ever hung out with Erté at all."

"Hung out?"

"Were they friends?"

"Of course not."

"Okay. How about Chantal? Were Chantal and Erté friends?"

Both Madame Grier and Madame Bantu glanced at each other and then after a pause, burst out laughing.

"*Non,*" Madame Bantu said, still laughing. "But Erté thought he was in love with her. He followed her everywhere."

Maggie turned to LaBelle to see how she was taking this news. The fact that a mentally handicapped man was stalking the murder victim was extremely relevant.

"Is that all?" Maggie asked the two women. "Did it ever go beyond that?"

"Oh, remember, Cecile?" Madame Bantu said to Madame Grier. "The day he tried to drag her into the bushes?"

They both made disgusted clucking noises.

"The monks had to pull him off her," Madame Grier said. "But not before Chantal slapped him."

"Until then I did not think she could be offended," Madame Bantu said with a sniff.

"Marie, for shame!" Madame Grier said. "He had no money!"

The two burst out laughing again at which point Maggie thanked them and led LaBelle out of the dining hall.

"Well?" she said to the detective when they were outside. "What do you think?"

"What do I think of what?"

"Erté stalked her. And Chantal hit him. Maybe the slap ignited something in him. Pushed him over the edge."

"You think he overreacted to being slapped by killing her?"

"I don't know him. I've never even spoken to him. I don't know if he's violent."

"He is *not* violent," Frère Luis said walking up to them, his face serious and troubled. He nodded at LaBelle and then turned to Maggie. "Erté is a gentle, good soul."

"Would he have tried to rape someone?" LaBelle asked.

"Absolutely not. I cannot imagine it. No."

Madame Bantu and Grier came out of the dining hall together and caught the last part of the conversation.

"I am telling you, *mon frère*," Madame Bantu said firmly. "I saw it with my own eyes."

"We both did," Madame Grier said.

Luis shrugged helplessly.

"Erté is gentle," he insisted. "And respectful of women."

"With all due respect, *mon frère*," LaBelle said, "sometimes sex can make a man do crazy things."

Luis didn't speak but Maggie thought she saw a refusal in his manner to accept or believe what LaBelle was suggesting. At least where Erté was concerned.

"Why don't I bring him in for questioning?" Labelle said.

"What? No! Why?" Maggie said taking a step back in shock. "He's literally your weakest suspect!"

"In your opinion. Besides, you should be thrilled I'm thinking of someone besides Lando for this murder. There is no pleasing some people."

This so-called partnership is the worst! Maggie thought in frustration.

All of their ping-ponging back and forth about possible suspects wasn't any sort of Socratic method to enable them to drill down into more intense questioning or open up new avenues to consider other suspects.

It was just sending them in circles!

Circles that ended up doing exactly what LaBelle had intended to do all along.

Maggie hurried behind LaBelle as she moved down the brick pathway back toward the dining hall again where Frère Luis was holding the door open for a trickle of people coming in for lunch.

"Detective LaBelle," Maggie said, running along beside her. "You can't do this! You have no evidence against Erté except hearsay."

"Where are the men's dormitories?" LaBelle asked Luis who looked even less happy than Maggie did.

"I must first inform Frère Jean," he said.

"What you need to do is tell me where the men's dormitories are," LaBelle said sternly, "before I start thinking obstruction charges."

Luis shoulders slumped in defeat. "Follow me," he said with resignation. He opened the door to the dining hall and then hesitated at the foot of the interior stairs immediately to the right of the entrance.

"Please allow me to see if anyone is upstairs in a stage of... undress," he mumbled but LaBelle wasn't having it. She pushed past him.

"Not necessary, *mon frère*. I've seen it all, believe me," she said. "*Pas de problème*."

Maggie stayed at the foot of the stairs while Luis and LaBelle went upstairs. She heard Luis calling for anyone upstairs to cover up because a woman was about to be present.

Maggie waited and when she turned to glance in the direction of the rows of dining tables she saw no fewer than ten people seated in the dining hall, all turned and staring in her direction.

"We are looking for Erté," she said to them. "Has anyone seen him?"

No one answered and Maggie heard the unmistakable sounds of LaBelle and Luis beginning their descent down the stairs.

"I saw him by the garden shed," a little girl called out.

"When?" LaBelle barked as she came to stand by Maggie. "When was this?"

The little girl ran to the arms of her mother who sat at a back table and glared at LaBelle.

Luis quickly approached the two and knelt in front of them. Maggie saw the little girl smile shyly at him. He was obviously in the right business, Maggie thought. He'd either built a trust among these people or just had a natural way with them.

"Heloise," Luis said to the child. "When did you see Erté in the garden? This morning?"

The little girl nodded.

"He was crying," she said.

Maggie felt her stomach turn at the child's words. Luis patted Heloise's shoulder and smiled at her mother but when he turned to face LaBelle, Maggie saw his face was stricken.

Maggie wanted to ask Heloise if she knew why Erté had been crying but LaBelle was already moving out the door in the direction of the back garden.

Maggie hurried to catch up with LaBelle.

"Look, is this really necessary?" Maggie asked, breathlessly. "Erté is obviously upset and I'm not sure being interrogated by the police is going to improve things."

"Of course he's upset," LaBelle said. "He's probably dealing with the guilt of having brutally killed the girl who rejected him."

"That's a pretty big leap," Maggie said in agitation. "We don't know he had anything to do with Chantal's murder."

"Then why has he run off?"

Maggie wanted to say it was just as likely that he'd wandered off but she could see LaBelle wasn't in any mood to hear it.

Up ahead was the garden shed, its paint peeling and faded in the harsh Provençal sun.

Maggie turned to see that Frère Jean had joined Luis behind her and nearly a third of the people in the dining hall were following too.

This is a disaster.

Maggie had only wanted to talk to Erté to see what he knew. That was all! And maybe talk to a few people at the monastery who might have heard or seen Rochelle being protective of Erté. But now LaBelle had it in her head that Erté was a possible suspect!

And it is all my fault.

LaBelle hesitated outside the shed just long enough for Frère Jean to catch up. He reached out and grabbed her by the arm which LaBelle quickly shook off.

"Madame Detective," Frère Jean said, panting from his exertion. "I must protest. Erté is under the shelter of the monastery."

"He's a person of interest," LaBelle said. "And possibly a dangerous one, too."

"Erté is not dangerous!" Luis protested. "And he has not run off! All of his things are still next to his bed!"

"Which is exactly where they would be if he needed to leave in a hurry," LaBelle said as she pulled out her phone. "You want to keep those people back?" she said gesturing to the small group that had gathered in the garden.

"Luis," Frère Jean said, nodding at the crowd. "Please."

Luis hurriedly turned to the crowd and held up his hands in a futile effort to get them to pay attention to him.

LaBelle was on her phone asking for back up. Maggie moved away from the detective. LaBelle wasn't going to listen to her anyway. This whole disaster was going to play out however it would and nothing Maggie could do would alter that.

Her stomach roiled painfully as she thought that she was the one who had brought this disaster down on poor Erté. She walked to the edge of the garden and watched from there, a ball of anxiety in the pit of her stomach growing larger.

"This is all my fault," a voice said, making Maggie turn to see a young novice monk with his hands shoved into the sleeves of his tunic.

"How so?" she asked gently.

His eyes were moist as he watched the scene before him: the crowd, curious and insistent, Luis trying to get them to disperse or at least stay calm, Frère Jean trying to talk to LaBelle who now had her ear to the door of the shed.

"I was supposed to watch him," the novice said. "He was my responsibility today."

Maggie felt a glimmer of hope at his words.

"Do all of you take turns looking out for Erté?" she asked.

He nodded.

This was good news. Being constantly monitored would make it very difficult for Erté not to have an alibi during the time in question. Maggie looked at the crowd by the shed. Someone had gone off to fetch a crowbar and was just returning with it. Maggie watched Jean gesture for Luis to break the lock.

"Is that shed usually kept locked?" Maggie asked.

"I don't know," the novice said. "We rarely use it. But I can't imagine Erté is inside. Unless someone locked him in there."

The sudden sound of wood splintering made both Maggie and the young monk turn to see Luis step back and wrench open the door. LaBelle was the first one inside.

It seemed as if the entire gathered congregation held its collective breath. Within seconds, LaBelle was back outside conferring with Luis and Jean.

"It's empty," Maggie said. "He's not in there."

"Thank God."

"What is your name?" Maggie asked.

"Albert. Fr-rère Albert."

"You were the one who called me on my husband's phone last week," Maggie said. "When my son got hurt."

"*Oui*, Madame," Albert said, rubbing his nose and staring at his feet.

"Do you have any idea where Erté might have gone?"

Albert looked around helplessly.

"He is always with one of us," he said.

"Doing what?"

"Weeding the garden, washing dishes, feeding the horses."

Maggie didn't want to make things worse for the novice monk but she had to ask.

"Why weren't you with him today?"

"One of the new refugees got hurt," he mumbled, his eyes still focused on his feet.

"Surely that's an acceptable reason?" she said but she saw his eyes dart to the crowd. When she followed his gaze she saw a teenage girl standing at the back of the crowd. She was watching Maggie and Albert. Even from here Maggie could see the bandage on the girl's knee.

Suddenly Maggie saw what must have happened and why Albert was feeling guilty.

"This isn't your fault," Maggie said firmly to Albert.

"But Erté is not responsible for himself," he said.

Maggie saw LaBelle striding toward her. She was on her phone again. This time it sounded like she was issuing an all-points bulletin for the whereabouts of one Erté Moulin. She quickly described him and then disconnected.

"Rochelle Lando said she got into an argument with Chantal," Maggie said to Albert. "She said the argument was because she thought Chantal was taking advantage of Erté."

Albert blushed crimson which told Maggie he understood what she was talking about.

"Do you think that's what happened?" she asked.

He shrugged. "Maybe," he said. "We are all protective of him."

"Even Madame Lando?"

"I do not...did not know her very well," he said.

Maggie studied him for a moment before deciding there was nothing more to learn. It was just as likely that Rochelle saw how everyone took care of Erté and realized she would be better believed if she claimed to be doing the same thing.

The Erté connection for Rochelle was a dead end. Plus, Maggie thought, feeling a tingling of dread comb through her, it was just as LaBelle said.

Even if Rochelle *had* been defending Erté, it didn't mean she didn't kill Chantal.

51

LaBelle spoke on the phone, her face animated and alive, barking orders to the monks at the same time she was strutting around the courtyard, directing people to get out of her way.

She's enjoying this, Maggie thought.

"The man is mentally deficient so that will prioritize the fact that he is missing," LaBelle said as she joined Maggie. She turned to look at the young monk. "Who is this?"

Albert looked startled to be suddenly under LaBelle's critical gaze.

"Just one of the monks," Maggie said, turning to walk back toward the monastery. "He doesn't know where Erté is."

As she and LaBelle walked back toward the dining hall Maggie saw Laurent's car through the curved stone entrance arch as it pulled up outside the monastery. She watched as the passenger car doors opened and four people got out.

"The harvest is over at Domaine St-Buvard?" LaBelle asked as she watched too.

"I guess so," Maggie said.

A part of her wanted to call out to Laurent but another part of her saw no point. The fact that he was dropping off his pickers at three o'clock in the afternoon told the story better than words could. The Domaine St-Buvard harvest, such as it was, was over.

"You are not going to talk to your husband?" LaBelle asked, glancing at Maggie through her tangle of uncombed fringe.

"Why?" Maggie said to her, peevishly. "*He* doesn't know where Erté is."

LaBelle shrugged but stayed to watch as Laurent's car drove off.

Maggie waited until she was sure Laurent was nearly home before texting him to tell him she would be home late. Whatever had happened with the harvest, she would hear about it when she got home and good or bad she could do nothing about it now one way or the other.

She went to the dining hall where Luis and Jean were standing at the front of the room on a small stage instructing the group gathered to search the stables, the furthest reaches of the garden and the orchard and vineyards on the far side of the monastery. LaBelle was now joined by two officers in uniform and she was briefing them.

Maggie saw Albert standing by the stage, his head hanging. Luis was talking to him and Maggie saw him put a hand on his shoulder as if to console or reassure him. Albert was nodding.

It was a very tight community and she knew that all the monks took very seriously the safety and shelter of the people who came there for refuge and who depended on them for help.

Losing Erté—regardless of what he might have done—was like losing a child. Everyone in this room felt that loss keenly.

Maggie walked to the stage where Frère Jean was giving the last instructions to the crowd of searchers.

"When it gets dark," he said to them, "you will be provided

with flashlights. We will not stop until Erté is found. Does everyone understand?"

Several people nodded.

"All right, then split up into three groups, please. Frère Luis will lead one group to the orchard on the other side of the southern stone wall, Frère Thomas to the vineyard and Albert at the lower garden."

Maggie followed the crowd as they shuffled out the door. She decided to join Albert's group. She felt an immediate sense of relief leaving LaBelle behind, LaBelle who only wanted to find poor Erté so she could clap him in handcuffs.

How has he gone from a total nobody this morning to LaBelle's number one suspect after Rochelle?

In any case, Maggie knew that the fact that Erté had run off was not a good sign. She didn't need LaBelle to point that out to her.

An hour later, Maggie was hot, scratched by a hedge of rose bushes and her bare legs were welting up with insect bites.

She hated the fact that she seemed to be in such bad physical shape compared to the refugees that she had to continually stop and catch her breath. It was true she hadn't gone to yoga or Jazzercize classes in months and because Grace was so busy with the bed and breakfast they hadn't played tennis in forever either.

She was thankful for the long summer day which would allow them to search in daylight for several more hours. She leaned against one of the tidy waist-high stone walls that enclosed the monastery garden and fanned herself and watched her group surge on ahead. She was embarrassed that she was having to stop and rest yet again.

"Water, Madame?" a voice called out to her.

Maggie turned to see the girl Bèbè walking up to her. She

was carrying several bottles of water and two canteens crisscrossed around her chest.

"Thank you," Maggie said gratefully as she reached for one of the water bottles.

Bèbè leaned against the wall and pulled out a cigarette pack. Maggie recognized it as the same brand that Frère Luis smoked. The first thing that came to Maggie's mind was that the cigarette brand was not a common one. The second was wondering where Bèbè had gotten the money to buy cigarettes.

"The whole place has gone mental," Bèbè said as she lit a cigarette. "More cops have shown up. And Frère Jean is having a coronary."

"Well, it's a scary thing for Erté," Maggie said.

Bèbè snorted. "The cops don't think he's missing. They think he ran off because he killed Chantal."

Maggie turned to Bèbè.

"Does that sound likely to you?" she asked.

"That Erté killed Chantal?" Bèbè shrugged and blew out a puff of smoke. "Maybe."

"I thought Erté was supposed to be super gentle," Maggie said.

"He is. But he was crazy about Chantal." Bèbè looked at Maggie and said emphatically, "*Crazy*."

Maggie nodded, feeling a pulse of frustration that she wouldn't be able to talk to Erté before LaBelle did. She could only imagine how counterproductive a police interrogation would be to them getting any useable Intel from the poor man.

I should have come back here on my own. Why did I think working with LaBelle was going to be an advantage?

"Well, I'd better get going," Bèbè said, grinding out her cigarette against the wall. "People need water."

"Thanks again," Maggie said, lifting her bottle of water.

She watched Bèbè hurry down a mild slope toward the gate that led to the vineyards and then pushed off the stone wall and took a few steps. She stopped and scanned her immediate environment. Her group was long gone but she supposed it didn't really matter which group she was searching with—or even if she searched with any group at all.

For that matter she could probably just go home. One more person in a crowd of twenty wouldn't make much of a difference. But something made her feel as if she had to stay.

Maybe because it was me who brought the police to Erté's door, she thought guiltily.

The least I can do is stay and make sure he's okay.

She trudged up the slope.

Hearing excited voices made her quicken her pace.

Have they found him?

She squinted in the direction of the vineyard where she thought the voices were coming from and forced herself to move faster, keeping her eyes on the horizon, waiting and watching for the moment when she would catch a blur of movement and form that told her she was going in the right direction.

Will he be hurt? Afraid?

She prayed that it was Frère Luis's group who found him. As much as it would make Albert feel better to be the one, it was what was best for Erté that mattered at this point.

A sudden exclamation erupted from the horizon and without thinking, it spurred Maggie to run toward the sound. She hadn't gone two steps when her foot slammed into something solid and hidden in a low depression in the uneven ground. She cried out as the ground rushed up to slam into her face, knocking the air out of her.

She lay trembling on her stomach, her eyes clenched shut as she fought for breath, her muscles quivering and convulsive. The soundtrack of her mind still heard the voices she'd been following but now they sounded like they were coming from a very far distance.

She opened her eyes and saw her water bottle a few feet away from her, its contents spilling out on the ground.

She told herself to move slowly. If she'd broken something, she'd only make it worse if she tried to—

That was the second when she realized her leg was resting on something soft. Her brain ignited trying to fill in possible answers.

A bag of garbage.

A stuffed pillow.

A dead animal.

Clawing at the dirt in front of her, she pulled herself forward until her leg eased off whatever it was that had tripped her.

Sweat popped out on her forehead and she tasted salt in her mouth. She'd bitten her tongue when she'd fallen. Slowly, she turned over, her heart pounding in her throat, the sound of it obliterating all other noise around her.

Her leg wasn't broken. Her hands, skinned and embedded with dirt, were only bruised. Blood droplets from where she'd bitten her tongue dribbled down the front of her shirt. She looked down the length of her body at what she'd tripped over.

Knowing before she looked exactly what it was.

Covered in lavender fronds, half buried in a shallow ditch.

The obscene smile of his neck wound, crimson and final.

Erté.

52

Maggie was so physically and mentally drained by the time the uniformed policewoman pulled up to her house that she wasn't sure she had the energy to make it up the porch and into the house on her own.

She'd spoken to Laurent twice in the last few hours and now she saw him appear on the front steps, his hands on his hips, watching, waiting for her.

After her horrific discovery in the gorse, time seemed to have telescoped for Maggie, rushing forward through a cacophony of crackling police radios and a steady murmur of people's aghast voices and reactions as if all the sensations were rippling through her.

LaBelle had instructed her men to take Maggie to the monastery office where she waited alone for nearly an hour before LaBelle came to take her statement.

There hadn't been much to stay.

No, she hadn't touched him. Except for falling over him.

That was it. That was all.

By the time Maggie crossed the monastery courtyard to the waiting police cruiser, she felt as if her legs were made of concrete. Just barely visible in the distance, she could see the sky illuminated by the outdoor lights that LaBelle's team was erecting in the garden where Maggie had found the body.

Maggie remembered seeing Frère Luis and Frère Jean, both stricken and pale. She felt an irrepressible urge to apologize to them as though, if it hadn't been for her, somehow Erté would still be alive.

She'd asked LaBelle a few questions about the body, none of which the detective had been willing to answer. And by the time LaBelle assigned an officer to drive her home to Domaine St-Buvard, Maggie was almost too tired to care.

She reached the doorstep of the *mas* and Laurent stepped out and put an arm around her to draw her inside. Just the feel of his strength and warmth nearly made her knees give out.

It was all she could do not to let him carry her inside.

"*Chérie*," he murmured to her as he helped her inside. "Have you eaten?"

Maggie couldn't help but smile. No matter what tragedy befell any of them, Laurent would always look to food as a way to comfort if not outright fix the problem.

"I'm not hungry," Maggie said as she moved toward the living room, knowing it wasn't an answer Laurent would accept.

"Go sit," he said, giving her a gentle push toward the couch. "I will bring you a drink."

"Where are the kids?" she asked as she sat down heavily on the couch feeling her weariness intensify as soon as she stopped trying to be strong.

"Upstairs," he said as he left her.

Maggie glanced at her watch. It was only a little after eight o'clock which was inconceivable to her. She felt like she'd been up for days.

Fleur jumped up on the couch and gave her a concerned look before curling up by her hip. Instantly Maggie reached for the dog, taking comfort in running her fingers through its curly pelt and floppy ears.

Laurent came back with a glass of brandy just as Maggie's phone began to ring. She pulled it out of her purse which she was still wearing crosswise across her body. It was Grace.

Maggie answered it and took a sip of the brandy at the same time.

"Darling, are you home?" Grace said breathlessly into the phone. "I can't believe this happened!"

"I know," Maggie said, taking another sip of the liqueur and feeling it vibrate and burn all the way down her throat.

Laurent studied her for a moment and then left the room. When he did, Maggie realized she was smelling sauteed onions and peppers coming from the kitchen.

"Was it an accident?" Grace asked.

Maggie put her drink down and rubbed the area between her eyes as a slight headache began to form. The image of what she'd seen slowly re-materialized in her brain.

"No," Maggie said feeling mildly better from the restorative. "His throat was slashed."

"Heavens! And *you* found him? That's wretched, darling. How?"

"I heard a shout that made me think he'd been found so I started to run—"

"Bad idea, darling."

"I know. I wasn't thinking. I tripped over him. It was horrible."

"I can't even imagine."

"Whoever killed him," Maggie said, "had obviously tried to hide the body."

"But why would anyone want to hurt him? I thought he was cognitively compromised."

This very thought was something that, as tired as she was,

Maggie had spent a good deal of time mulling over in her mind on the ride back home.

"He was," she said. "But he still had eyes. Everyone I talked to at the monastery said Erté basically hounded Chantal, stalked her everywhere she went. So it occurred to me—what if he was following her the night she was killed? What if he saw something?"

"Oooh, darling. I just got chills when you said that."

"It's the only explanation for why he was killed in basically the same way that Chantal was. Down to the lavender flowers in his shirt."

"So clearly it was the same killer as Chantal," Grace said. "Does this mean Rochelle is in the clear?"

"What do you mean?"

"Well, she could hardly have killed Erté since she was in police custody. If you're right and the poor man was killed because he saw who killed Chantal—"

Maggie couldn't believe she hadn't thought of this herself.

"You're right!" she said, slapping her hand against her thigh. "Look, Grace. I need to call LaBelle. But thanks for calling. I'm fine."

"Are you sure?"

"Positive. Laurent is feeding me and I think Rochelle just found her lucky break."

"All right, darling. Call me if anything changes, okay?"

"I will," Maggie said and then disconnected.

Hurriedly she dialed LaBelle's cellphone. At first the line rang so many times Maggie thought it would go to voice mail and then LaBelle answered.

"Do you have any idea how busy I am?" the detective said when she answered.

"What is the medical examiner saying about the throat wound?" Maggie asked, feeling her pulse race. "Is it similar to Chantal's?"

Maggie heard background noises on LaBelle's end that made it sound as if she were in a warehouse or large echoing room, definitely not outdoors any longer at the crime scene. She was either in the police morgue or at the monastery still interviewing people.

"The same weapon, he believes," LaBelle said.

"So either someone found the murder weapon that was used on Chantal," Maggie said breathlessly, "and used it on Erté—"

"Or the killer had the weapon all along and used it again."

"Have you found the weapon?"

"My men are looking for it now."

"Will you let me know if you find it?"

"*When* we find it and I will have to see."

"If it's the same one that killed Chantal," Maggie said, "will you release Rochelle?"

"It is too early to say at this point."

Maggie forced herself not to respond. Keeping her comments to herself when it was obviously time to release Rochelle was like trying to hold a helium balloon down with both hands. She comforted herself with the thought that it didn't have to be tonight. But sooner or later LaBelle would have to release her.

"I saw the lavender blossoms stuffed into his shirt," Maggie said.

"Which the killer could have done to throw us off the scent," Labelle said.

"When do you decide it's not a copycat killing but a serial killing?" Maggie asked, feeling her impatience beginning to evaporate .

"I will decide that when the forensics speak to me," LaBelle said. "If I do release Lando she will not be allowed to leave the area. What we know at this point is not conclusive! And it might not be when we find the weapon. Someone could have found Lando's weapon which she might have hidden after she killed Chantal—in which case we have two killers on our hands."

Maggie's mind was racing. She still hadn't mentioned to LaBelle the fact that the murder weapon might very well be one that Laurent had loaned to Rochelle. She knew she should've said something before now. It was going to come out and when it did it would be a whole lot worse if LaBelle found out on her own.

But aside from that potentially disastrous little detail and regardless of how it sounded like LaBelle didn't want to totally give up Rochelle, Maggie knew that once the detective made that leap—especially now that Erté was in the clear—it didn't leave too many other possibilities in the way of suspects.

"You need to go to *Chatoyer* and swab Beau Dubois," Maggie said. "If he's a match for Chantal's baby, that's motive."

"We've had this conversation," LaBelle said dryly. "There are easier ways of getting rid of a baby than killing its mother."

"You know I'm right," Maggie said.

"I know nothing of the sort. Right now I have a dead body and no murder weapon. Trying to connect Chantal's unborn child to her murderer is...is...ludicrous." LaBelle was sputtering.

"Maybe, but doesn't it make sense to get as much evidence as possible? Tell me if you have a single solitary suspect at this point!"

"I don't have the money or lab personnel for testing random people who are not suspects!"

"Give me the damn swab!" Maggie said. "*I'll* do it. Or I'll send Laurent to the spa to collect it from the guy."

LaBelle laughed breaking the tension between them.

"I think I would like to see that," she said. "But even if the masseuse was a match for paternity, it wouldn't be admissible.

Besides which we need probable cause to get a warrant and he would never agree to it on his own."

"The same person who killed Chantal killed Erté," Maggie said firmly, "probably because Erté saw something he shouldn't have."

"And probably you have seen too many detective dramas on TV."

"You know I'm right."

"I know I don't have time for this tonight," LaBelle said and disconnected.

Maggie sat on the couch, her phone in her hand and felt the exhaustion of her emotionally wrought day cascade over her. She turned to Fleur who had cocked her head at her in a questioning sign.

"I know I'm right," Maggie said softly to her before closing her eyes and leaning back into the couch. "The baby's paternity is the key. Find the father and we'll find the killer."

53

"Mom! Mom!" Mila screamed.

Maggie was on her feet before she knew she was even awake. Her eyes were glassy as she stared around the living room where she'd dozed off, looking for the fire or pit of poisonous snakes or other natural catastrophe that could possibly have provoked Mila's hysteria.

Mila stood before her, her hands on her naked hips wearing a crop top and skintight pants that began just above her pubic bone.

Fleur began barking frantically at Mila. Maggie blinked and stared at her daughter.

"Tell him!" Mila said indignantly pointing in the direction of the kitchen. "Tell him he doesn't own me! I'm the owner of my own body!"

"Are...are you wearing false eyelashes?" Maggie asked, rubbing her own eyes.

"Dinner is ready!" Laurent called from the other room.

Maggie felt a dull headache form behind her eyes as she walked to the dining room where Jemmy was setting down plates of *pot au feu*.

Dear heaven, Maggie thought. *Is it really only dinner time?*

"Mom!" Mila said.

"Be quiet, Mila," Maggie said going to her place at the table and picking up her water glass. She drank thirstily, feeling as if she might never hydrate enough.

Jemmy stood and folded his arms across his chest.

"I have an announcement to make," he said, turning toward the kitchen and raising his voice. "Dad! I have an announcement!"

Laurent slowly appeared in the doorway between the dining room and the kitchen, his face, as usual, unreadable.

"I've talked to Luc," Jemmy said, turning his back on Laurent to speak to Maggie. "And I've bought a ticket with my own money to go see him in California for the two weeks before school starts." He took a breath and maintained eye contact with her. "I'm leaving next week."

"Why are you still here?" Laurent boomed out.

For one insane minute, Maggie thought he was talking to her. Or perhaps even Jemmy.

"You're not the boss of me!" Mila screeched back at him.

"I am the boss of this house and all who are in it," Laurent said threateningly, his eyes dark and hooded as Maggie had never seen before in a family situation. "You will go upstairs and change into something that does not make you look like a whore or you will sleep in the garden tonight."

"Mom!" Mila said, her voice an unholy whine. "Did you hear what he said to me?"

"Okay, stop!" Maggie shouted, holding a hand up to Laurent, Mila and Jemmy. It seemed as if the very air had extinguished on the end of that word—as if her whole family were holding their breath to hear what she would say.

And what would she say? That she had seen a poor man brutally murdered today? That she had seen his life oozed out onto the ground in an ultimate act of unfairness?

She turned to Laurent and saw he was the embodiment of fury. And that's when she saw the problem.

Like a sudden illumination, she saw the situation they were in and the problem which, if not created by Laurent, was made absolutely worse by him.

It was amazing to her that Laurent had always hit the exact right tone with everyone else—so many other troubled youths, Zouzou and Luc, to name two, even Taylor come to that. And yet with his own children, he continually missed what was right in front of him.

Maggie turned to Mila and realized as she watched her daughter's face that on some level Mila was aware of this. She knew that the more she bedeviled Laurent, the more ineffectual and helpless he became.

Which was why, unlike most families where the daughter and the mother clashed, Mila had always gone for her father.

Maggie held up a finger to Laurent insisting on quiet.

"Wait a moment," she said. She wasn't sure how much energy she had for this tonight but she knew they'd come to the tipping point. And it had to be tonight.

She turned to Jemmy first. "I think you could have presented that information a little less confrontationally. But your father and I are fine with you traveling to California."

Jemmy's eyes widened at Maggie's words and a startled smile edged his lips. Laurent's roar of rage seemed to rattle the dishes in the china cabinet but Maggie didn't look at him. She turned to Mila and forced a smile.

"As for how you look, darling," she said. "I think it's adorbs and I am now thinking of getting exactly those cute pants for myself." Maggie patted her tummy as if just imagining how the low-hung hip-huggers would fit on her decidedly more plump frame.

Mila's mouth fell open in horror.

"You're not serious!" she said.

"What size are they?" Maggie asked innocently. "We might even be able to share. I'm a ten but I think I could squeeze into an eight if you—"

Mila turned and stomped up the stairs. "I hate you!" she screamed.

Maggie turned back to Jemmy.

"Jemmy, take your plate upstairs. Your father and I need to talk."

Jemmy didn't wait for her to finish her sentence before he snatched up his dinner plate and was on his way out of the room and up the stairs.

The humming in the room which was Laurent's fury seemed to be a palpable strumming. Maggie moved on uncertain legs to her chair and sat down reaching for her wine glass.

"Sit down," she said quietly, not sure she had any more decibels left in her volume.

Laurent walked to the head of the table but did not sit. Out of the corner of her eye, she saw him as a vibrating tower of outrage.

"I cannot believe you would allow our son to tell us what he will do," he said, jabbing his finger at her, his nostrils flaring. "Without consulting me."

Maggie looked at him and felt a sudden rush of love for this man who tried so hard, worked so hard to keep them all safe. She knew Laurent's overreaction to both his children was born from his need to protect them at all costs, as well as his frustration at not being able to control them anymore.

And of course his fear of losing them.

"He is not getting on an airplane," Laurent said. "I will enroll him in military school first."

"Please sit, Laurent."

He jerked out his chair and sat, crossing one ankle across his knee, his eyes flashing with anger riveted on her.

"You are making things worse," she said, gently.

He narrowed his eyes at her but said nothing.

"They know your buttons," Maggie said, "and they push them. At least Mila does. And you, without fail, react."

"I am supposed to allow my son to leave the country when he informs me he is?"

"This isn't the nineteen fifties," Maggie said, smiling at him and praying he could feel her surge of love in his direction. "Jemmy is fifteen and old enough to handle a transatlantic trip on his own. And he'll have Luc on the other side to watch out for him."

"That is irrelevant!"

"No, it's very relevant. Jemmy has a good head on his shoulders. You don't want him to go because he didn't ask you first."

Laurent glowered but didn't respond.

"And he didn't ask," Maggie said, "because he's tired of hearing the word *no* and is trying to stand up for himself."

"He is not yet in control of his life. That is still my province."

"Yes, of course. Everyone knows that. Even Jemmy knows that. Here's what's going to happen now. Please stop glowering. We're going to allow Jemmy to spend the rest of the summer with Luc."

Laurent stood up and walked to the French doors, his back stiff with fury.

"It's only two weeks," Maggie said. "Luc will look out for him. And allowing him to go to the States will also send the message that we are listening to him."

"Is he stupid enough to think that matters when he doesn't get what he really wants in the end?" Laurent asked, turning to glare at Maggie.

"We are fighting *this* battle in increments, Laurent. And this is the first baby step."

Laurent waved a hand in feigned capitulation and turned back to stare out at the vineyard.

"And Mila?" he said. "Do you have an answer for Mila?"

"Whatever is going on with Mila sending her away will not fix," Maggie said. "In fact, I'm sure it would make it worse. No, you and I and Mila are locked in a life and death struggle that is her teen years and nobody is getting out alive until we emerge from the other side. Hopefully all of us mostly intact."

They were quiet for a moment as Maggie glanced at the view out the French doors.

"I didn't get a chance to ask you how today went," she said softly. "You let the pickers go early."

"The work was done."

"Can you be honest with me, please?"

He frowned and turned to glance at her.

"I am being honest."

"So the harvest was good this year?"

"It was decent. I will deliver the commitments as usual."

Maggie felt a wave of frustration that he was still trying to gloss the truth with her.

"Look," she said, standing up and going to where he stood in front of the French doors. "I *know* the harvest was a disaster this year, okay? I'm a vintner's wife, remember? I *know* what a good harvest looks like."

Laurent looked at her and his shoulders lost their rigidity. He turned away from her.

"I am sorry, *chérie*."

"For what? For doing your best and getting blindsided by life?"

"It was my fault. I left the harvest too late."

"So you're human. I'm actually relieved to hear it. It doesn't matter what you did or why you did it, Laurent. It doesn't even matter that the harvest was a failure. Okay? There's always next year."

"I have been wanting to talk to you about next year, *chérie*," Laurent said, turning to face her fully now. "I have called the estate agent."

"Whatever for?" Maggie asked with a frown.

"I want to put the *mas* and farm up for sale as soon as the harvest is over."

Maggie watched his face and tried to remember if she'd ever seen him so serious before.

"Okay," she said slowly. "Well, we'll talk about it when we've all calmed down a bit."

She was shocked to realize that a part of her reflexively felt like this suggestion was not a bad idea at all. But she was tired of rushing head first into situations she hadn't investigated.

"I won't change my mind," he said.

"Fine. And I'll support whatever you're determined to do. *After* we've given it enough thought and time."

Her phone vibrated and she realized with surprise that she was still holding it in her hand from when LaBelle had hung up on her.

It was a text message from the detective which Maggie quickly read. Twice.

"I have thought about it," he said.

"Okay," she said, looking up at him. "So now it's *my* turn to think about it. And I need some time."

"Fine. But no matter what we decide about the farm, I will never allow Jemmy to be an actor."

"What the hell is your deal, Laurent?" Maggie said in exasperation. "He's not asking to write bad checks for a living. He just wants to give acting a try."

"It is not any kind of career. We will be supporting him his whole life, or Luc will be."

"We don't have to solve this tonight," Maggie said tiredly. "But something we do have to sort out tonight is Rochelle. LaBelle is releasing her tomorrow."

His eyebrows shot up but that was the extent of his surprise. Maggie realized that he had already come to the assumption that with Erté's murder, Rochelle might be freed.

"I will go and get her in the morning," he said.

"If you want her to stay here for a couple of days..." Maggie said and her voice trailed off.

"I am surprised that you think that would be a favor to *me*," Laurent said, narrowing his eyes, "and not something anyone might do for someone who has had this kind of misfortune."

"Whatever," Maggie said wearily. "Do whatever you think is right. But I'm going to bed and I can't manage a bite. I'm sorry."

She turned and walked away from the table and wondered if she'd ever left the playing field with Laurent before. Always before she tried to talk and talk until the problem, whatever it was, was solved, or mitigated or at least reduced to a manageable level.

But not tonight. Tonight she was too exhausted to attempt to find a meeting point or wrangle a reconnection with him.

Tonight, she just needed a hot bath and to climb into bed with a compliant and content little dog and for one night to just let tomorrow and the world sort itself out without her.

54

The next morning Maggie stood in the kitchen at the window and watched Laurent head out in his Peugeot to pick up Rochelle in Aix. After their conversation last night she half expected him to say something about her edict.

But for all his noise and bluster, confrontation wasn't Laurent's style. At least not with her. If he agreed with her, he would say nothing and simply go along with it. His unspoken argument being *why did she need him to rubber stamp a perfectly logical solution?*

If he *didn't* agree with her, he'd just create his own plan and implement it without any further input from her.

But as she watched his taillights disappear, Maggie found herself trusting him in his silence. He was a good man who worked hard to do the right thing. Yes, he was passionate and even violent at times—although of course never with her or the children—but he was introspective too. And in the end, no matter the cost, he would do the right thing for all of them.

That much she knew was true.

And today, right now, the right thing was to allow Jemmy to

go to California and even to explore his interest in being an actor. As for Mila, Laurent needed to step back and allow Maggie to steer the vessel through the storm. At least for now.

She would take a moment at some point to impress upon him that she wasn't asking him to back off from his involvement in their daughter's life. Or if she was, it was just for a little bit. Just until they got through this phase.

Jemmy came downstairs and looked around the kitchen.

"Is Dad here?"

"He's running an errand," Maggie said. "Do you want breakfast?"

"Just coffee," Jemmy said.

"Try again."

He grinned. "Cocoa is fine."

Maggie turned and spooned up a bowl of oatmeal. She set it with a mug of cocoa, and separate bowls of chopped nuts and raisins in front of her son.

"I wanted to thank you, Mom. About last night."

"You can thank me by making sure we don't get a call in the middle of the night while you're in California," she said.

He laughed. "I promise."

Maggie wiped down the counter and put away breakfast items while she listened for the sounds that would tell her that Mila was up. She'd gotten used to Mila sleeping late.

As she tidied the kitchen she found herself wondering if Rochelle would throw herself into Laurent's arms when she was released into his care. She wondered if LaBelle would be there. She cringed to think she would witness the American woman's brazen possession of Laurent.

Maggie also wondered what it meant that they all seemed to be back to square one on who killed Chantal.

Just as she heard Mila coming down the stairs from her bedroom, Maggie's phone rang and she saw it was Grace.

She set out boxes of cereal and a glass of orange juice for

Mila and went into her office to take the call, little Fleur trotting at her heels.

"Hey," Maggie said answering the phone. "You seem to have a lot of time on your hands lately."

Grace laughed.

"The Americans decided to cut their time with me. They left for Paris this morning."

"Did they pay you first?"

"Oh hell, yes," Grace said. "So what's the latest? You know I'm just over here waiting to hear any news."

"Laurent's gone to Aix to pick up Rochelle."

"No way! So LaBelle released her?"

"Seems so."

"So does she have a replacement for who killed Chantal?"

"That is the million-dollar question, isn't it?" Maggie said settling in at her desk. "Except it seems that you and I are the only one asking it."

"Did she confirm that Erté's killer was the same as Chantal's?"

"Not in so many words. But she's released Rochelle on that assumption, so I'm going with *yes*."

Grace made a clucking sound with her tongue that Maggie recognized as the one she often made when she was thinking.

"The problem with that," Grace said, "is that I'm not sure I'm able to visualize Harlequin slinking around a muddy monastery field in search of Erté so she can stab him before tossing him in a ditch."

"I know," Maggie said with a sigh. "If we're leaning toward believing that Chantal's killer is the same as Erté's, then it might be time to take the women suspects off the list."

"Which basically leaves Beau and Enzo, right?"

"Right."

"Does LaBelle agree?"

"I have no idea. What I do know is that she currently has no prime suspect and I have no idea which way she's leaning."

"Well, she'd better lean fast. Tick tock."

"That's what worries me," Maggie said. "If LaBelle can't find someone to fit the bill for both Chantal and Erté's murders, she's going to reach back out for Rochelle for at least Chantal's murder."

"You're probably right. Is there anything you need me to do?"

"No, but thanks," Maggie said. "I think I need to go back over a few leads I found that didn't look promising before."

"Like what?"

"Chantal's pregnancy for one. I still think it's connected somehow. And the fact that Étoile and Madame Toussaint are related. I don't think that's a coincidence either."

"Are you going to work with LaBelle again?"

"I don't think so. Her idea of partnership is to chase down leads I suggest and then grill poor innocent witnesses under a naked bulb."

"Well, whatever you do, be careful," Grace said.

"Aren't I always?" Maggie said as she reached for Fleur to tousle the dog's ears.

"Ha ha," Grace said. "Oh! Did you hear? It looks like Erté's memorial service is going to be held tomorrow afternoon."

"Seriously? That's fast."

"I thought so too. But supposedly Frère Jean thinks the monastery needs closure as soon as possible. Will you go?"

"Definitely," Maggie said. "It might be something that Mila and Jemmy should experience too. They seem to think their lives are akin to concentration camp victims. A dose of the real world with real problems might do them good."

"What about Laurent? Is he happy now that Rochelle is free?"

"He's decided he wants to sell Domaine St-Buvard."

"Okay, so he's lost his mind."

Maggie laughed but she felt no real mirth. As exhausted as she'd been last night and with the image of Erté's mangled body in her head she'd had trouble sleeping mostly because she kept imagining dismantling their lives here in France. It depressed her that Laurent was so discouraged with his life that he wanted to rip it all up.

As many times as she'd imagined doing just that—*drive-through banking! people who understood you when you spoke! Fried chicken and barbecue!*—somehow it didn't feel right to draw a line under their lives here and call it done.

At least not in the way that Laurent was doing it. Not during a nadir when everything around them seemed to be falling apart. To leave on the cusp of their worst harvest ever felt reactionary and wrong.

If they were going to leave France, leaving on a high point—perhaps after Mila graduated high school—made much more emotional sense.

This way felt like giving up.

"Raising kids," Grace said with a sigh. "It takes every ounce of sanity you ever had and once you lose your mind I'm pretty sure you never get it back."

"It's not the kids so much as Mila," Maggie said. "She's frankly a little monster. Especially with him."

"She'll outgrow it."

"I know," Maggie said. "I'm betting on that too. The question is will she do it before Laurent kills her?"

55

Maggie spent the rest of the morning cleaning and making a *gratin* with the eggplant she found in the refrigerator. As she worked, every thirty minutes or so she found herself checking the front drive.

She'd resisted the temptation to call or text Laurent and imagined that the red tape of releasing a murder suspect was a tad more time intensive than getting a haircut.

She imagined he might take Rochelle to lunch before bringing her home. In Laurent's mind, few problems could not be solved by a nice *bouillabaisse*, a good bottle of wine and a simple *tarte tatin*. There were several restaurants in Aix he liked which would easily serve his purpose.

As Maggie carefully layered fried eggplant slices and fresh tomatoes in alternating, spiraling rows in a casserole pan her mind was on the image of Rochelle and Laurent at one of these cozy little restaurants, often only big enough for three tables. In her mind's eye she saw Rochelle gushing her thanks as if Laurent had single handedly rescued her and Laurent stolidly accepting her gratitude while focusing on his meal.

Maggie made ham and Gruyère sandwiches on bread she knew Laurent would feed to the birds but she considered still good enough. Jemmy was upstairs in his room on his computer probably doing some planning for his trip. Mila was outside on the terrace.

She went to the French doors and watched her daughter as she painted her toes and talked on the phone—probably to the American girl Dana. She remembered what Jemmy had said about Mila asking Dana about pot and she felt an uncomfortable stirring in her stomach.

Were they going about this all wrong? So far they were simply enduring the hits that Mila doled out, withstanding them like a bending tree in a cyclone. Were they doing that to show her that they loved her no matter what? Or because they had no idea of what else to do? Did Mila really need that kind of assurance? Or were they taking the easy way through the storm? Instead of their parentally stoic acquiescence, was the better approach to be more proactive? Should they instead restrict her? Confront her? Punish her?

Maggie pinched her lips together in frustration. She was pretty sure she could read fifty books on the teenage years and get fifty different takes. And depending on who the teenager was, they could all be right or disastrously wrong.

Fleur barked sharply behind Maggie, alerting her to the fact that a car was pulling into the driveway. Maggie turned to the kitchen, glancing at the wooden mantel clock over the dining room fireplace.

It was nearly three o'clock. She went to the kitchen window to see Laurent's car pulling up the front drive beside the dogwood tree. She watched as he got out and then came around the car to open Rochelle's car door. Then he gathered up several bags of groceries.

Maggie recognized some of the paper bags found at the

produce market on Place Richelme in Aix. She felt a quiver of annoyance as she imagined Laurent and Rochelle strolling around the market like lovers on a lazy Saturday afternoon.

Midlife crisis or not, I've about had it with this.

As if he could feel her eyes on him, Laurent looked up at the window and locked gazes with her. Maggie lifted a hand in greeting but didn't wave.

She went to the front door and opened it. Laurent's arms were full and Rochelle walked gingerly as if she were recovering from some debilitating illness. She smiled wanly at Maggie.

"Hello, there," Rochelle said.

Maggie nodded. "Rochelle."

"Is the guest room ready?" Laurent said to Maggie as he passed her in the foyer. "Rochelle needs to rest." He continued on to the kitchen.

"Of course," Maggie said, reaching for Rochelle's jacket and wondering how anyone could wear one in all this heat.

"Thank you so much for letting me stay," Rochelle said as she handed over her jacket.

"Of course," Maggie said again and bit the inside of her mouth. Rochelle was thanking her for the guest room and not the fact that Maggie had spent the last week doing everything she could to work for her release.

As she ushered Rochelle into the house, Maggie reminded herself that in all honesty she never quite believed that Rochelle was innocent—which Rochelle had already accurately detected—and so a thank you for rescuing her was probably inappropriate anyway.

Laurent came back into the living room where Maggie and Rochelle stood and clapped his hands together.

"*Bon,*" he said, eyeing Rochelle critically. "Go to bed. Do you need help? I will call you for dinner."

"I'm fine, darling Laurent," Rochelle said with a fond smile toward him. "I'm not crippled. Just a little tired."

"It's your old room," Maggie said, reminding Rochelle that she'd been a house guest at Domaine St-Buvard once before.

"Oh, good," Rochelle said, turning toward the stairs. "Although it will break my heart to look out at the vineyard. I feel so responsible." She turned to Laurent and smiled sadly. "Not that I could have done anything to change how things turned out. But I could hardly have made them worse." Then she turned to Maggie. "Would a bath be possible, do you think?"

Rochelle had lived at Domaine St-Buvard for three months. She knew very well how to work the upstairs tub.

"We don't haul water in from the well anymore," Maggie said and could have bitten her tongue at her sarcasm. She was letting the woman get to her.

Laurent cleared his throat—his not-so-subtle hint that he was becoming annoyed at what he perceived as Maggie's rudeness.

"Did you talk to your children when you were sprung?" Maggie asked as Rochelle turned to go up the stairs.

Rochelle stopped and her hand on the bannister seemed to twitch.

"I didn't want to wake them," she said over her shoulder. "The time difference always makes it so hard."

"Oh, sure," Maggie said, knowing that since France was six hours earlier than the States, unless Rochelle's children were moles or otherwise nocturnal, they would likely be awake and functioning.

"*Maggie*," Laurent said pointedly to her under his breath as Rochelle disappeared upstairs.

Maggie shrugged off his admonishment and walked to her office. She'd done what she'd promised him she'd do—

attempted to facilitate Rochelle's release—and a few things she hadn't signed on for—like giving the woman a room in her house and twenty-four-seven access to her husband.

She'd be damned if she pretended to like her on top of it.

56

While Rochelle napped and Laurent cooked, Maggie spent the afternoon in her office laying out and shuffling through the suspects over and over again.

She tried to sort out who could have done which one of the murders and which could have managed both. She ignored all possible alibis for the moment since she had no way of confirming them and so she opted not to trust them.

She also decided to ignore motive for now. As yesterday's café meeting with LaBelle had revealed, every single person Maggie had in mind who might have killed either Chantal or Erté had no obvious reason for doing it. That was the sort of thing she knew might only come out during a confession in police custody.

That just left opportunity.

She opened up a software spreadsheet program on her computer and listed all the names in a grid.

Étoile Monet
Annette Toussaint
Beau Dubois

Enzo Corbin

Harlequin Martin

Gené Demel

Maggie stared at the names going from one to the other and allowed her gut to have full rein—something she knew a real detective would never do. But she wasn't a real detective and sometimes, as she knew from experience, the things she knew about a suspect she only knew subliminally—as if she'd picked up the information and stored it away, not even realizing she'd done it.

It meant that a part of her brain was predisposed to preferring one suspect over the other and Maggie never really knew why.

And for now that was okay.

After looking at each name and letting whatever feeling wash over her that was triggered by each one, she hesitated and then added Rochelle's name to the list.

This was a private document and unless she was mowed down by a bus or in some other way disabled or killed in some untimely manner, no one would ever see it. She cringed at the thought of Laurent seeing it because she knew he would consider it a betrayal.

But she assured herself that it was hardly likely that he would ever see it. The fact was, as far as Maggie was concerned Rochelle belonged on the list.

She looked at all the lavender farm suspects first.

Toussaint

Enzo

Gené

Rochelle

All four had opportunity because they worked right there where the crime happened. Rochelle was doubly suspect since she not only spent time at the lavender farm but also at the monastery where Chantal lived. Maggie selected Rochelle's name and put it in boldface.

Just doing it gave her a pleasant feeling of guilty satisfaction.

Next of course was the monastery.

While technically there were nearly sixty people living in the monastery who could have had contact with Chantal and possibly even have wanted to kill her, Maggie narrowed her list to the dormitory where Chantal had lived. Excluding the two refugee girls who'd left the day before Chantal was killed gave Maggie two people on the list.

Rochelle

Bébé

Maggie tapped a pencil against her desk and stared at Bébé's name. She didn't know why she hadn't given Bébé any serious thought as a possible suspect before this moment. Unlike Étoile, Harlequin or Madame Toussaint, the young gypsy girl would have had no problem crawling through muddy fields.

She remembered Bébé said she went to bed early the night Chantal was killed. She also remembered Bébé saying that the brothers only cared about the underage refugees staying out past curfew.

Maggie pulled her cellphone out of her purse and called the monastery. Frère Jean himself answered which surprised her.

"I am so sorry to bother you," Maggie said, "especially during this terrible time for the monastery."

"How are *you*, Madame Dernier?" Frère Jean asked. "You have had a monstrous shock."

"I'm fine, *mon frère*. But I have an important question that I hope you can help me with. It's about one of the girls there. Named Bébé?"

Frère Jean made a noise and Maggie heard him talk to

someone in the room with him before he came back to the phone.

"If she has stolen something from you, Madame Dernier, the monastery will do everything in its power—"

"No," Maggie said. "Nothing like that. I just wanted to know if…the night Chantal died…if you knew whether Bébé had gone out."

"One moment," he said and turned away again.

Maggie watched as Fleur curled up on the couch. She could hear the ticking of the dining room clock through her door. Finally Frère Jean came back on the line.

"I am informed that Bébé was in her room all night," he said. "She was seen going to bed and was checked on at least twice by Madame Zimmerman who watches the young girls."

"Not just a lump in the blanket?" Maggie hated to ask but it was an old trick and needed to be asked.

"I am told Madame Zimmerman spoke with the girl both times."

"Okay, good," Maggie said, feeling a flicker of relief. "Thank you, *mon frère*."

"*Pas du tout*. You are coming to the service for Erté tomorrow?"

"Yes. The whole family will be there."

"*Bon*. I will see you then."

Maggie hung up and looked back at her suspects sheet and deleted Bébé's name from the list.

That just left Rochelle.

Maggie turned to the suspects she had from *Chatoyer*.

Étoile

Beau

Harlequin

Each of the three had opportunity in that they were just down the road from both the lavender farm and the monastery and could easily have managed the murders.

But, as she and Grace had already discussed, Erté's murder had been a particularly physical one, tracking the man out in the middle of a field and attacking him with a scythe. It was one thing to imagine someone like Bébé who was young and athletic, but neither Étoile or Harlequin could conceivably have managed it.

When she eliminated the women she was left with only Enzo and Beau. Maggie stared at her screen at the two names.

Enzo Corbin

Beau Dubois

Enzo had an alibi. It was possible Gené was lying but at this point he had an alibi so Maggie would cross him off the list.

That left Beau.

Like Enzo, Beau knew Chantal personally. Plus Beau had acted guilty in the face of Grace's questions about Chantal. It wasn't much but it was the hint of something.

Maggie selected Beau's name on the screen and put it in boldface.

She stared at his name and then at Rochelle's which was also in boldface.

She'd already tried the above-board approach to gathering Intel at the spa and now it was time for the under-the-table approach.

She'd find an opportunity to interview Beau—which she could do by simply ambushing him in the parking lot on his way to or from work—but what she needed now were answers that he might not readily provide.

Grace had mentioned that the employees at the spa had a locker room where they dressed for their various duties. A locker room, presumably, with lockers in it.

And lockers hold secrets.

Or in the case of murderers, trophies or other evidence of guilt.

Maggie turned off her computer and sat silently for a moment, allowing her thoughts to come together.

Finally she glanced over at the dog who was now watching her intently.

Maggie had come to the inevitable conclusion that to get to those secrets she would need to make a visit to the spa.

Tonight.

With nobody there.

57

Maggie checked her watch as she drove down the dark and winding country road and punched in the phone number on her cellphone.

"Hello?" Grace answered.

"Hi," Maggie said. "I need a favor."

"Of course, darling. Anything."

"I need you to cover for me tonight."

There was a blip of silence on the line.

"Cover for you?" Grace said. "As in you want me to lie to Laurent?"

"You know," Maggie said. "I could probably have just told him the truth but—"

"Don't tell me," Grace interrupted. "You think you're protecting him."

"No," Maggie admitted. "I have to run by *Chatoyer* tonight and I didn't want to have to spend an hour and a half convincing him first."

"He might have wanted to go with you."

"Trust me, he wouldn't. Now that Rochelle is free, he doesn't care who killed Chantal. Or Erté."

"Darling, I'm sure that's not true."

"Well, in any case, if he checks up on me—and I'm ninety-nine percent sure he won't—just say I'm with you or on my way home."

"Why wouldn't he just call your cellphone?"

"I'm pretty sure I'm going to have a battery issue."

Grace clucked her tongue. "You know what Thomas Jefferson said about lying? *He who permits himself to tell a lie once, finds it much easier to do a second and third time til it becomes a habit.*"

"Good to know," Maggie said. "Glad you're keeping busy reading American history on your slow days. I will literally only be gone an hour—"

"At *night*?"

"Grace, this is not a big deal so please don't go all Laurent on me. Okay? I need to get into Étoile Monet's office to get a look at her personnel records and maybe a little look-see in Beau's locker."

"You think the killer is Beau?"

"I think it's possible. So please. One hour."

"Will you call me when you're on your way home?"

"I will but I'll be fine."

"That's what they all say," Grace said grimly.

A few minutes later Maggie switched off her headlights and drove to the furthest corner of the parking lot at *Chatoyer*. A lone car was parked close to the front of the entrance, so battered and ancient it could only belong to the night security guard.

Seeing it parked there was actually encouraging since it lent credence to the idea that the spa had no modern security features like an alarm. Maggie had already decided that if an alarm did go off and she was caught, she would just throw herself on the mercy of her new pal Marguerite LaBelle and bandy Laurent's name about sufficiently to obtain her release.

It was a plan anyway.

But now seeing the security guard—an elderly and stooped-shouldered man who emerged from around the back of the building—made it clear that Étoile was hoping the crime rate in the middle of the bucolic countryside didn't merit any more expense beyond a part-time pensioner rattling doorknobs and later falling asleep in his car.

Maggie waited until the old fellow had once more disappeared around the back of the building and, snatching up the lock-picking tools she'd purchased years ago on Amazon, made her way to the front door of the darkened building.

She'd held her breath as she'd eased open the front door but as she'd suspected, there was no alarm triggered by the movement. Within minutes, she found herself inside the wide marble foyer. She went first to the receptionist's desk but found only gum, lipstick and a pack of cigarettes in her desk. There was no file cabinet in this room, confirming to her that she would have to go through Étoile's office for that.

Hurrying down the hall, she passed a door that said *les casiers* and slowed. *Lockers*. She glanced at Étoile's office door down the hall. She would still check it but there was every possibility that the files she wanted were on Étoile's computer and if it were password protected—which presumably it would be—that was going to be a dead end.

Patting the lock-picking tools she'd tucked back in her slacks pocket, she went to the locker room door and opened it.

Even the locker room here smelled nice, she thought as she stepped into the room. Floor to ceiling metal lockers lined the wall opposite the door. The other walls held shelving with pads, balls, weights and hoops, jump ropes and even small trampolines.

Maggie went first to the line of lockers without locks and quickly scanned inside each one before determining that they were all empty. Only one locker had a padlock on it.

Padlocks were trickier but she'd had some success with them. With the details of the You Tube video she'd studied earlier still fresh in her mind, she used her grip tool to pry off the bottom of the padlock and then, positioning her phone with its flashlight on a nearby shelf to give her the light she needed, eyed the lock and selected the correctly sized pick to wedge into the bottom.

She needed to feel some resistance as she wiggled the tool around and when she did she twisted the tool until she felt it catch.

One down. Only three more to go.

It took her longer than she'd expected. The padlocks that she'd practiced on at home from time to time had given her a steady and sure hand but the one on this locker—she hoped it was Beau's—was newer and it was harder to feel the tumblers catch.

Once she got the second number. She leaned her head against the locker and took in a breath. Then she reinserted her tool and quickly found the third and fourth numbers until she was able to tug the lock arm open.

Feeling lightheaded from her success, she jerked open the locker and grabbed her phone to shine its light on the interior. A white coat hung on a hanger with Beau's name on the pocket. A pack of gum. A pair of running shoes. A water bottle. A small leather Dobb kit with nail clippers, aspirin and hard candy inside.

Suddenly she noticed something shiny at the back of the bottom of the locker. She reached down and wrapped her fingers around a flip phone. She pulled it out and studied it. It was an old model—certainly not the kind of cellphone she would imagine Beau having.

She looked at the phone and found herself wondering why he would keep his cellphone in his locker? And then the answer hit her.

Because it isn't his.

Maggie opened the phone and was surprised to see it was charged up. She looked in Beau's locker and spotted an older looking charger she assumed belonged to the phone. She also saw the Amazon packaging that the charger came in.

She looked back at the phone and an image appeared on the tiny screen.

Her heart began to beat faster when she saw the picture of Beau with Chantal sitting on his lap.

This is Chantal's phone.

Maggie took a breath and tried to think what this meant. When the truth hit her so did a wave of nausea as she realized the problem she'd just created. Had she ruined the chain of evidence by touching the phone? Would her testimony be enough to prove that she had found it in Beau's locker?

Should she wipe her prints from the phone and put it back where she found it?

How was she going to prove to LaBelle—or anyone—that she hadn't planted the phone herself which Beau could now claim she had?

Suddenly the room seemed to explode in noise and light. Maggie turned and, startled, dropped the phone on the hard uncarpeted floor where it broke into pieces.

She blinked at the light and stared at the hulking figure poised in the doorway, his face a mask of surprise and fury.

"What the hell are you doing?" Beau snarled as he advanced on her.

58

Maggie staggered backward as Beau came at her, his eyes going to his open locker and the broken phone on the floor between them.

When he realized what he was seeing his face flushed and he seemed to bulk up in front of her, limbering his shoulder and neck and pulling back his lips with a guttural growl.

Maggie looked helplessly around the room, looking for a bat, a soccer cleat, anything she might use to defend herself with. But there was nothing in the room except the row of lockers, a long bench and a stack of yoga mats.

"I got lost," Maggie said, backing up against the wall.

Beau stood in front of his locker, alternating between staring at Maggie and the swinging door of his locker. He cracked his knuckles ominously.

"What did you take?" he asked jabbing a finger at the locker.

"Nothing," she said hastily. "I didn't take anything."

"You were going through my locker."

"Is that your locker?"

Maggie licked her lips. She figured she had one of two ways

to go with this situation and she knew that the longer she hesitated the less believable either of them would be.

Play dumb or play indignant.

While she'd never met Beau before, Grace said he had acted guilty when she asked him about Chantal.

Beau turned to her, his hands clenched into fists as he faced her, a vein jumping over one eye.

She made her decision.

"You are in a lot of trouble, buster," she said, forcing herself to take a step toward him and trying not to focus on the giant fists-like-hams he kept clenching by his thighs. She pointed to the debris on the floor between them.

"What are you doing with Chantal Lambert's cellphone?" she said in her best *you're in trouble now* voice as she pointed to the phone on the floor between them.

Beau took a step toward her and her stomach plummeted to her knees thinking her bluff had failed when suddenly the tension seemed to be sucked out of his shoulders. He sagged inward on himself, the very picture of shameful dejection.

"I can explain," he said.

Maggie allowed herself to let out the breath she'd been holding while she wondered which way the situation was going to go.

"I'm listening," Maggie said, feeling the nominal security of her own phone in her hand and wondering if she'd have time to use it in the event she needed to. "Tell me how you got her phone."

"I took it from her the last time I saw her," he said sadly staring at the debris of plastic on the floor.

That didn't sound good.

"When was that?" Maggie asked as gently as she could while she secretly activated the record function on her phone.

"A week ago."

Chantal was killed a week ago.

"Why did you take it from her?" Maggie asked, willing her heart rate to slow down.

"She had a picture of us," he said rubbing his hands down his pant legs. "I told her to delete it but she wouldn't. I grabbed it from her and then we heard someone in the hallway."

"This happened here? At the spa?"

He nodded. "We were in one of the massage rooms."

"Had you met her here before?"

He nodded again, this time with a sick look on his face.

"It's charged up," Maggie said, nodding at the plastic debris on the floor. "Why?"

He ran a hand through his hair. "I thought I'd give her a new charger as a gift."

"That's a lie. You wanted to see who might call her."

He shook his head. When he spoke his voice was flat and emotionless.

"The battery was nearly dead when I grabbed it from her. How was I supposed to delete the picture if I couldn't turn it on?"

That had a ring of truth to it.

"Then, after...after what happened to her," he said, his shoulders rounded "I didn't have the heart to delete it."

"Why was it so important that you delete the picture? Were there other pictures?"

"No, I don't know. I don't think so," he said, miserably. "She told me she was pregnant and the baby was mine." He looked anxiously at Maggie. "I'd lose my job if that got out."

"Okay, so you took her phone," Maggie prompted. "Then what?"

"Then nothing! When we heard the noise, she ran off. The next day I heard she got killed."

"So you just kept the phone."

"What was I supposed to do?"

Maggie believed him. She noted that he wasn't very smart

or maybe he was so smart that he was successfully pretending not to be. In any case, he seemed genuinely sorry that Chantal was dead.

Which of course, in Maggie's experience, didn't mean he didn't kill her.

"I didn't kill her," he said touching the broken phone with the toe of his rubber clog.

"Do you have any idea who might have?"

He glanced behind him and then shook his head. Maggie couldn't help but wonder if he'd been looking in the direction of Étoile's office?

"Are you sure?" she pressed.

"I'm sure," he said.

But there was definitely something about his expression that told Maggie he wasn't telling the whole truth. Some people were natural born liars. Maggie would bet the family farm that Beau was not.

"There's something you're not telling me," she said folding her arms across her chest. "You should know that not divulging information is as bad as lying. It qualifies as being an accessory to murder."

"Seriously?" he said, his face naked with vulnerability and dismay.

He licked his lips and it was all Maggie could do not to push him further. She knew she'd get more out of him if she let him get there on his own.

"Chantal told me she had a secret about Madame Monet," he said finally, looking at his feet in total dejection.

"What kind of secret?"

"She wouldn't say. But she said it was going to make her rich."

Chantal was blackmailing Étoile?

"Who else did you tell this to?" Maggie asked.

"Nobody! I swear!"

"And you didn't think this was information the police should have?"

"How could I tell them? That would have gotten Madame Monet in trouble if it was a bad secret. Maybe she committed a crime! If she went to jail I'd lose my job for sure!"

"Does your pal Harlequin know about this?"

"Harlequin? No."

"Do you know where Harlequin was the night Chantal died?"

"There's no way Harlequin would have done anything to Chantal."

"Good friends, were they?"

"No, but Harlequin is super squeamish about blood. She's fainted twice when a pedicure went wrong."

Maggie would need to confirm that but she had to admit that if Harlequin couldn't stand the sight of blood she was not likely to try to kill anyone with a scythe.

"What about you?" Maggie said. "Where were you the night Chantal died?"

Beau shifted uncomfortably and glanced at the door as if debating rushing through it.

"Home watching television."

"Alone?"

"No. With a friend."

"This friend have a name?"

He made a face. "Maybe I was alone after all," he said.

"Whoever you're trying to protect, Beau, I'm sure they would not want you to go to jail on their account."

"I was alone," he mumbled unhappily.

Maggie sighed. "What about yesterday?" she asked. "About midday?"

He ran a hand over his face. "I was home sick," he said.

"Anybody going to be able to confirm that?"

He hung his head. "No."

Maggie nodded, feeling sorry for him and she didn't know why. He had no alibi. He had motive—especially if he was the baby's father. And he had opportunity—for both murders.

The sick realization that came over her as she watched him fidget and clutch his hands in front of her was that regardless of how much she liked him, when it came to viable murder suspects, Beau Dubois just jumped to the head of the list.

59

The next morning Maggie stood in the dining room and watched the morning sun creep across the carpeted floor. Laurent had let her sleep in this morning and she decided she probably needed it.

When she came downstairs she saw Rochelle through the French doors sitting in one of the old Adirondack chairs, a cup of coffee in her hand, with Mila, Jemmy and Laurent in chairs around her.

Even from this distance Maggie could see the tension gone from Laurent's shoulders, his face relaxed and calm. She watched the group for a few moments and tried to remember the last time her family had spent a moment as carefree and drama-free as what she was witnessing.

Rochelle laughed and appeared not to let a single opportunity go by where she could rest her hand on Laurent's arm—or for that matter, Mila or Jemmy's.

Maybe that's what this family needs, Maggie thought in bemusement. A little California chilling.

She turned back to the kitchen to get herself a cup of coffee from the French press on the counter.

She'd not been late in getting home last night but she easily could have been. Rochelle and Laurent had been sitting outside on the terrace drinking brandy when she got home. When she stepped outside to tell Laurent she was back she got the distinct impression he'd forgotten she'd even gone out.

Whatever had happened with Laurent's friend and his wife all those years ago Laurent obviously still felt responsible. It was annoying but on the other hand, Maggie was well aware that it was also a part of her husband's character that she was intensely proud of.

People mattered to Laurent.

Especially damaged or weak people. Worthy or not. People like his brother, Gerard. And in some ways, Grace. If it hadn't been for Laurent refusing to give up on her, Grace never would've been able to manage the do-over she'd pulled off with *Dormir* and with Zouzou.

Maggie poured herself a cup of coffee and sat at the kitchen counter, grateful for a few moments to herself.

Today would be a long day, starting with another visit to *Chatoyer*—this time in the daylight—and what Maggie fully expected to be an extremely uncomfortable conversation with Étoile and ending with the memorial service for Erté at the monastery.

Maggie had debated calling LaBelle last night to tell her what she'd learned about a possible blackmail attempt with Étoile. But knowing LaBelle she'd probably rush over to *Chatoyer* and arrest the spa owner without getting any other confirmation.

Worse, once LaBelle got around to ripping the scab off her hesitancy to interview the spa's workers, she would likely discover more than a few clues that would lead her straight to Beau's door.

Not that Maggie didn't want the person responsible to pay

for these murders, but she registered that she no longer had complete faith in LaBelle's judgment.

The fact that LaBelle had recently given up her prime suspect meant she was strongly motivated to replace Rochelle with *someone*.

And while it was true that on the face of it, things didn't look good for Beau, Maggie's gut told her he wasn't Chantal's killer. But if he *was* her killer, the least Maggie could do was see what Étoile had to say first

The sound of the French doors opening made Maggie turn to see Laurent coming in from the terrace. He was rubbing his hands together in a pictorial indication that he had nothing more on his mind today than what to whip up for lunch.

Just the sight of him so happy and unconcerned about anything made her want to slap him. Now that Rochelle was in the clear, he really did seem to have washed his hands of the murders of both Chantal and Erté.

"There you are, *chérie*," he said, his mien one of placidity and ease. "There are still croissants if you are hungry."

"Nope," Maggie said. "I'm good. Everyone seems to be getting along pretty well out there."

"Mila thinks Rochelle is a movie star," Laurent said as he came into the kitchen and began opening cabinet doors.

Maggie wondered if it was the California connection or the fact that Rochelle had been arrested for murder that had Mila so enamored.

"I'm heading out for a bit," Maggie said.

Laurent turned to regard her. "Where?"

"Back to the spa. I have a lead I want to follow up on."

He pulled a coffee mug out of the cabinet and placed it on the counter.

"The memorial service is right after lunch," he said.

"I know. I'll be there."

"Maggie," he said, his voice strained. "Why are you doing this? Rochelle is free."

"That was never the only reason I was trying so hard to find out the truth," Maggie said, trying to force down her growing anger at his complacency.

"That is Detective LaBelle's job," he said, his face expressionless.

"You weren't saying that when Rochelle was still being held for it."

"Yes, but now she is not. So there is no point. Let LaBelle do her job."

She and Laurent held each other's gaze for a moment and it was then that Maggie realized it wasn't just the murders that Laurent had signed off on. Even though Maggie had not agreed to it, he'd already made up his mind about selling Domaine St-Buvard. That was the thing that didn't feel right to her. Laurent, out there on the terrace, smiling and laughing in full view of his vineyard and the recent botched harvest only hours old.

In his mind, Domaine St-Buvard was already over.

Maggie drained the last of her coffee into the sink and turned to collect her purse and car keys.

"I'll meet you at the monastery," she said, hoping she could make it all the way out the door before the tears came.

60

As Maggie pulled into the parking lot of the spa she congratulated herself on not crying on her drive to the spa, convincing herself that just because Laurent was acting like they were moving back to the States, didn't mean they were.

As she sat in the parking lot watching as Harlequin stepped outside to smoke a cigarette, Maggie realized that a part of her felt a little better after witnessing Rochelle's magic with Mila. It told her, as she hoped it showed Laurent, that there were good times ahead with Mila.

The older she got, the better things would be.

Even with the car's air conditioning on, Maggie felt the promise of the unrelenting heat of the day beginning to bear down on her.

She had already noticed Beau's car parked by another car that she assumed was a customer's. At a little before eleven she saw Étoile arrive and park her Peugeot RCZ—a gorgeous car that Maggie knew had to cost forty thousand euros. Wearing a floral tiered miniskirt and oversized blouse, Étoile got out of her car looking cool and collected.

What had Chantal known about Étoile that she could use to blackmail the spa manager? And while blackmail was always an excellent motive for murder, Maggie reminded herself that physically, Étoile still wasn't a natural candidate for doing the job herself.

But Beau was.

Could Étoile have hired Beau to do her dirty work?

Maggie checked her phone for any messages from home but there were none. On impulse, she called Laurent. He didn't often carry his phone so she was surprised when he answered.

"I thought you would have left by now for the monastery," she said.

"We are waiting for Danielle," Laurent said. "She is giving us a ride."

"What's the matter with the Peugeot?"

"Nothing," he said, not offering any more information.

"Then why are you getting a ride with Danielle?" Maggie asked patiently.

"Rochelle and Mila went into the village. They are not back yet. I have left a message for them to join us at the monastery."

"I see. I guess it's pretty nice that the two of them are getting along so well."

"Rochelle is doing with Mila what you and I have failed to do," he said. "I see Danielle pulling up. Do not be late, *chérie*."

He disconnected.

Maggie took a few quick moments to confirm that whatever feelings she was experiencing, jealousy was not one of them. If anyone could get through to Mila, then that was all to the good. Maggie didn't care if that person was Idi Amin.

Firmly believing what she was telling herself, Maggie got out of the car to go ask Étoile Monet about why she was being blackmailed.

· · ·

One thing Maggie knew was that to hesitate was to allow herself to be thrown out of the spa before she had a chance to do what she'd come to do.

Even knowing that it would be Beau whom Étoile would summon to do the actual throwing out—and that, considering what Maggie knew about him, Beau would possibly be hesitant to actually eject her—she wanted to make this interview as clean and swift as possible.

She walked purposefully through the front door and bypassed the receptionist who immediately looked up and began squawking.

"You cannot come in here!" Bijou said stridently. "I will call security!"

Maggie made a mental note to find out where Bijou had been during the two critical times of the two murders, but even as she did she knew that Bijou with her talon-like acrylic nails and sky-high designer heels could no more be Chantal or Erté's killer than Étoile herself.

Walking quickly down the hall, Maggie didn't hesitate when she reached Étoile's office. She pushed open the doors, turned and locked them behind her, and then faced Étoile who was in the process of hanging up her white leather Prada bucket bag on the coat rack by her desk.

"How dare you!" Étoile said, reaching for the intercom.

"I'll be fast," Maggie said, figuring that if Bijou or Étoile called the police she'd have at least thirty minutes before they arrived. And with two active murder cases in the area, possibly more than that.

"Get out!" Étoile screeched.

"Why was Chantal Lambert blackmailing you?" Maggie said, marching over to Étoile's desk.

Her words had the effect of a punch to the midriff. Étoile gasped and fell back into her chair, her mouth opening and closing like a guppy panting for air.

Bijou began pounding on the double doors.

"Open the door!"

"Tell her to go away," Maggie said. "Or my next step is a *Yelp* review where I give *Chatoyer* a review and mention its manager was being blackmailed by a girl who was murdered at a lavender farm last week."

Étoile's face blanched and she held a shaking hand to her mouth.

"Bijou, leave us!" Étoile panted weakly. "Go! I am fine!"

The abrupt silence on the other side of the door was immediate. Maggie walked across the cushioning carpet and at about the level where she imagined Bijou's ear was positioned against the door and rapped loudly.

"Ow!" Bijou said.

"Go away, you creature!" Étoile shrieked and when Maggie turned around she realized the spa manager was speaking to her employee.

Satisfied, Maggie went back to the desk and sat down in a chair in front of Étoile.

"I already know that Chantal was trying to blackmail you," Maggie said. "Before I go public with it I need to know why."

Étoile stared at Maggie and then slowly lifted her hands to her face and buried it in them. Maggie waited to hear sobbing or whimpering but Étoile made no sound at all. Finally Étoile turned and with small careful movements opened a drawer in her desk and brought out a small knife and laid it on the desk.

It hadn't occurred to Maggie to be concerned about being attacked by Étoile in broad daylight. But before she could warn Étoile not to try anything, the spa manager brought out a long green cucumber and a small cutting board.

"Did you hear what I said, Madame Monet?" Maggie asked as she watched Étoile carefully slice two thin discs off the cucumber.

"I cannot tell you why," Étoile said meekly as she placed

one cucumber slice over each of her eyes and leaned her head back.

Maggi shook her head in disbelief that Étoile was more concerned that her tears might give her puffy eyes than the fact that she was being accused of having the ultimate in murder motives.

"Then let's try something a little easier," Maggie said reasonably. "Where were you the night Chantal was killed?"

Étoile took in a breath and lifting one of the cucumber slices from an eye, she opened another desk drawer and took out a piece of paper which she pushed across the desk to Maggie. Maggie reached out to take the paper which appeared to be a receipt for services rendered by a spa in Aix.

"What am I looking at?" Maggie asked.

"I was getting a skin-lightening treatment in Aix," Étoile said softly. "I brought Harlequin with me to learn how to do it."

Maggie stared at the receipt and saw the date and time matched with Chantal's time of death.

"You took Harlequin with you?" Maggie said.

"As I have just said," Étoile said. "It is a complicated treatment and she needed to learn how to do it properly."

Damn. That meant both Étoile and Harlequin had alibis for Chantal's murder.

But, as Maggie reminded herself, she hadn't expected a woman to be capable of the murder anyway. She still could have hired the job out. Maggie put the receipt down on the desk.

"What about two days ago? Midday?" Maggie asked.

"You are referring to the time of death for the boy at the monastery?"

"That's correct."

"I was with Beau."

"He said he was out sick."

"He lied. I told him to. He was with me." Étoile pulled the

cucumber slices off her eyes and Maggie had to admit they'd helped. "I can prove it."

"How?"

"We made a video. A very tasteful video," she said defensively. "It's time and date stamped."

On the one hand, Maggie was glad that Beau had an alibi and she was impressed that he wouldn't tell on Étoile but Maggie wondered if Harlequin knew that her boyfriend was sleeping with the boss.

"Okay," Maggie said. "I'm convinced. Or I will be when I see the video. Meanwhile we still have the question of the blackmail."

"It is nobody's business but my own!"

"I'm sure that's true, Madame Monet," Maggie said. "But when your blackmailer ends up dead, you can see how all bets are off on the question of privacy, right?"

Étoile stared at Maggie, her chin quivering.

"Must I say?" Étoile said softly.

"I'm afraid so. If the secret is not related to the murders, it won't have to become public."

That was a lie. A blackmailer had died brutally. The secret, whatever it was, was germane and the whole of Provence would know about it in graphic detail before everything was said and done.

"My own daughter," Étoile said, bitterly, her eyes filling again with tears.

Maggie frowned, not understanding.

"What about your own daughter?" she said softly. "Did Chantal know her?"

Étoile shook her head in misery. "I was so young," she said, her tears streaking down her cheeks. "He...was much older than I."

Maggie's mind did a fast calculation.

"You were...you had an illegitimate child?"

Was that the information Chantal was blackmailing Étoile with? Maggie frowned. She'd been in France long enough to know that as embarrassing as something like that could be, it was hardly worth killing over.

Unless...

"Wait a minute," Maggie said as a bright light began to illuminate in her brain. "Are you saying *Chantal* was your daughter?"

61

Maggie could tell by the look on Étoile's face that she'd guessed correctly. Chantal was her illegitimate child.

"Did she have proof?" Maggie asked.

But as she spoke Maggie realized that there *was* a resemblance between Chantal and Étoile. Both had refined facial features, with small, sculpted noses, full lips and honey blonde hair.

"People won't need proof," Étoile said bitterly. "If I were to deny it and it turned out not to be true, it wouldn't take long before someone found out where my real child was. The damage to my reputation—my business—would be done."

"How did Chantal know?"

Étoile shrugged helplessly. "My mother chose the orphanage sixteen years ago. Chantal grew up there. Someone there must have told her."

"They're not supposed to do that."

She laughed sourly. "I believe the one who told her was a sweet elderly nun who now has dementia. It seems the legal system cannot always allow for the human variable."

"So you don't know if Chantal really was your child, only that she could reveal to the world that you had an illegitimate child."

"She was mine, I'm sure," Étoile said.

"How?"

"I know," Étoile said in a flat, emotionless voice, "because I have never had a single ounce of good fortune that didn't involve a terrible price for me at some point down the line."

An hour later Maggie was on the road driving to the monastery. After assuring Étoile that she would do everything in her power to keep her secret safe, she left the spa as if on auto pilot, blind to a single landmark along her way, passing without seeing the many village war memorials, fountains, statues.

Even Bijou who escorted her out the door with a steady stream of vitriol and threats was nothing more than a mildly annoying fly buzzing about her head.

Before she'd talked to Étoile, Maggie had planned to talk to Beau again but now she didn't see the point. Regardless of what she'd told Étoile she knew she had to give this information to LaBelle and let the pieces fall where they may.

And she was pretty sure they were all going to fall really ugly.

As she drove, her mind buzzed with the fact that Chantal—dirty, whoring, blackmailing, homeless, lavender-picking Chantal—was the illegitimate daughter of the elegant and stylish Étoile Monet.

That fact in anybody's eyes was definitely something worth killing for.

Or was it? Yes, it was horrible information to disseminate and if it did get out it would probably ruin Étoile. The French don't mind scandals, but throw in a little healthy doubt about someone having killed their own child and they were less forgiving.

Could Étoile have killed her own child?

Maggie shook the question from her mind. All of that would be for LaBelle and her team of investigators to figure out. The only thing Maggie needed to do at this point was lay the facts at the detective's feet. It was up to LaBelle to make them fit the crime.

Even so, Maggie found herself feeling discouraged.

If Étoile was the mastermind of the murder and Beau was the muscle, then nothing about this case was anything other than cold-blooded and abhorrent. Is that the way it happened?

Maggie pulled into the parking lot of the monastery. It was full of cars which she should have expected. She scanned the lot for Laurent's Peugeot before remembering he hadn't driven it. She spotted Danielle's car, a Citroën SUV, so she knew Laurent and Jemmy were here. Through the soaring stone archway she saw a crowd of people standing outside the chapel, waiting for the service to begin.

As she got out of the car she thought of how Chantal's body —how both bodies—had been discovered with lavender tucked into the folds of their clothing. Was that something Beau would think to do? He might be sweet—if he wasn't a murderer—but that touch with the lavender blossoms was a level of sensitivity Maggie hadn't really seen in him.

Unless Étoile told him to do it when she ordered the hit?

Maggie grimaced at the thought. That made even less sense.

Maggie clenched her jaw in frustration.
None of this feels right!

If Erté truly did see the killing as Maggie theorized, did Beau then go after him? Except Étoile said she had a time and date stamped video that proved that Beau couldn't have killed Erté.

Were there two killers?

Maggie's mind began to swim and she told herself to leave it all at the gate—at least for the length of the service for poor Erté. As she stepped through the arch, she saw LaBelle and another plain clothes detective talking to two of the monks who had their backs to Maggie.

Her stomach clenched at the sight of the detective. She didn't doubt that the killer might show up at the service. That wasn't unheard of. Maggie scanned the group waiting outside the chapel. But how could you possibly tell who they were in this crowd of villagers and well-wishers?

Craning her neck to look for Laurent, Maggie moved in a wide arc around the group in order to avoid having to talk to LaBelle. She wasn't ready for that just yet. As she moved, she saw a lone figure leaning against the stone wall surrounding the monastery garden. A curl of cigarette smoke lingered above her head. It was Bébé. And she was crying.

Maggie's immediate assumption was that Bébé was crying over poor Erté. But the young gypsy girl hadn't seemed very upset about Erté two days ago when she was handing out water to the searchers.

Curious, Maggie walked over to the girl.

"Hey, Bébé," Maggie said. "It's time to go in."

Bébé looked up from the ground where she'd been unhappily staring. She shook her head as Maggie joined her.

"I'm not going in," she said.

Maggie saw the cloth bag at Bébé's feet.

"What the matter?" Maggie asked.

"Frère Jean is going to kick me out," Bébé said, a tear streaking down her cheek.

"That doesn't sound like him."

"I know. But he is." Bébé wiped the tears from her face with a grubby hand. "I've done things. Bad things."

Maggie leaned against the wall and realized she was in no hurry to get inside the chapel. She already felt hemmed in and confused and a little bit hopeless.

"What did you do? Steal stuff?"

Bébé snapped her head around to give Maggie an incredulous stare.

"How did you know?"

The idea had come to Maggie when she put together the memory of Bébé stealing food when Maggie first met her, smoking cigarettes she couldn't afford, and finally Frère Jean's query if Bébé had stolen from Maggie when she had asked him about her.

"I don't know why I do it!" Bébé wailed. "I'm a bad person!"

"You have enough to eat here, right?" Maggie asked.

"That's what Frère Luis asked me," Bébé said miserably. "It's not about food. I don't know why I do it."

Maggie nudged the bag at Bébé's feet. "What's all this?"

Suddenly Bébé stood up and faced Maggie.

"Will you help me, Madame?" she asked urgently.

"If I can."

Bébé snatched up her bag and shoved it into Maggie's arms.

"Give it back for me. Don't say where you got it. You can tell Frère Jean you found it."

Maggie opened the bag and looked inside. A leather notebook, a souvenir keychain from the Arles amphitheater, a plastic dish from the dining hall, a stained bandana, a pack of cigarettes. Bébé took the cigarettes and stuffed them into her pocket.

"Just tell him you found them in the garden," Bébé said pleadingly. "Please?"

Maggie cocked her head at the girl.

"I'll do it on one condition."

"Anything!"

Maggie took the items out of the sack and put them in her handbag.

"If more things go missing I'll need to tell him who the thief is."

"I promise I'll never do it again."

"I mean it, Bébé. You only get one chance."

"I only need one chance. I'm happy here. Everyone's kind to me. I don't want to leave."

"Okay. I'll do it. Now we'd better get inside."

As they turned toward the chapel, Maggie saw Madame Toussaint talking with Brigitte and Gené. It suddenly occurred to her that if Chantal *was* Étoile's daughter, that meant she was also the granddaughter of Annette Toussaint, who had been about to fire her own granddaughter for prostitution.

Maggie didn't think any woman could have easily wrestled Erté to the ground and killed him, but she'd seen a lot of things in her life that she'd never imagined were possible.

As she watched Madame Toussaint, her arms muscled and toned after a lifetime of working a farm, the older woman suddenly appeared much stronger than Maggie had originally noticed. And exactly how lame was she? At all?

"Madame?" Bébé said.

Maggie turned to the girl.

"There's one more thing I took but I need your help in giving it back."

"What is it?"

"Please don't make me feel any worse about it but I took a little girl's doll."

Bébé pinched her lips together and looked at the ground.

"Okay, well, go get it. But hurry."

"That's just it, Madame. I can't," Bébé said, licking her lips and watching as the monks Jean, Luis, Mateus, Thomas and the novice Albert stood at the door to the chapel greeting the crowd.

"Why not?"

"I gave it to Chantal."

Maggie frowned. "How could you—?"

"Not alive. I went to her...to where it happened, you know?

At the lavender farm? People have been bringing flowers and things there and I thought—she told me about the baby so I thought the doll would be good to leave for her."

"You left the doll at...where Chantal died at the lavender farm?"

Bébé nodded dejectedly. "But every day I see the little girl crying for her doll and I feel so bad. I don't know why I do these things!"

"Okay, Bébé," Maggie said patting her arm. "Calm down. I'll go and get the doll."

"Oh, bless you, Madame! I promise I'll never steal another thing ever!"

Maggie was less than optimistic about that, but she would do what she could for the girl.

As Bébé turned and hurried toward the waiting crowd, Maggie caught a glimpse of Enzo standing back from the group but poised to enter the chapel.

And right there it occurred to her that there was nobody at the lavender farm at the moment.

62

As Maggie drove from the monastery to the lavender farm a fine haze seemed to have bleached the blue sky white and the scent of new-mown grass was thick in the air.

She felt a definite quickening in her pulse at the thought of exploring the farm while everyone was gone. She imagined there would be a sort of reception in the monastery dining hall after the memorial. And while she couldn't count on Toussaint and the others staying for it, there was a good chance they would.

Ponte l'Abbe was like any other provincial village in the area. It was committed to its rituals and parades of saints, weddings, and funerals. Annette Toussaint had lived in the area most of her life. She'd definitely stay for the reception. Maggie guessed that Enzo, Gené and Brigitte would stay if for no other reason than the free food.

It still didn't give her much time.

As she drove onto the property her eye went first to knoll where Chantal's murder had taken place. Even at a distance she could see that people had placed items there, turning the site into a shrine or memorial on its own.

It seemed strange to be at the farm with everyone gone. Even with four people, there had been a level of busyness and activity evident from the moment one drove down the driveway when the barn and house revealed themselves.

Maggie was tempted to go to the site immediately and grab the stolen doll. But she decided she couldn't waste the precious moments she had to go through the house while nobody was home.

She was grateful she hadn't seen Laurent at the monastery after all. She could always tell him she'd gotten held up and hadn't been able to make the service. But explaining how she'd been there and then left would be trickier.

Unless I find the one clue that will point me unerringly in the direction of the person or persons who killed Chantal and Erté, she thought.

Would he care? Maybe not, but he'd at least understand.

Maggie parked nearer to the closest path that led to the now-shorn lavender fields. She didn't know when everyone would come back, but she knew she could always say she'd come to look at Chantal's shrine.

Somebody might even believe her.

From her car, she could see more clearly the items that people had set out on Chantal's murder site. Flowers still wrapped in clear or colored plastic, a basket with slowly rotting apples in it, even a few balloons bobbing sadly in the afternoon breeze. She couldn't see the doll, but if it was there, she'd grab it on her way out.

She left the car unlocked in case she needed to get into it in a hurry, then patted her pockets for her cellphone, lock pick and her car keys, and hurried toward the house.

Maggie knew that getting caught roaming through the lavender processing barn was nowhere near as serious as getting caught inside someone's home. Especially if she had to break in to get inside.

Besides, any secrets or evidence worth keeping would be in the house. She was sure of it. She skirted the house and saw a first floor back window that would allow her to exit in a hurry without being seen if she needed to.

Her heart pounding at what she was about to do, she climbed on the front porch and with shaking hands rattled the front door handle. Working quickly, she jammed the lock pick into the old-fashioned house door lock and it quickly opened. Then she turned and dropped the pick into the tangle of weeds and wild yarrow in the bed at the foot of the porch. She could always get another one on Amazon, but if she were caught trespassing with the pick on her, her actions today would escalate from a misdemeanor to a felony in the blink of an eye.

Once inside, she locked the door behind her. She'd go out a window when she left and with the front door locked, there'd be no reason for Toussaint to suspect anyone had been in her house.

Maggie turned around to get her bearings and was instantly greeted by the sight of a tabby cat as big as a bulldog. The cat twisted its head to look at Maggie as if mildly curious. Maggie took in a series of steadying breaths to attempt to calm her pounding heart, then went to Toussaint's bedroom.

She'd debated bringing disposable gloves for this—she had a pair in the glove box of her car—but decided the chance of her doing anything that might prompt the cops to come with fingerprint kits was pretty low. She hoped.

As she stepped into the old woman's bedroom, Maggie reminded herself that what she was looking for—at its most basic—was simply proof that Toussaint knew that Chantal was her granddaughter.

Although bloody gloves and a scythe would work too, she thought grimly.

In the back of her mind she knew that Chantal's blackmail claim still had to be proved. While she would have loved to have completed that step before breaking into Madame Toussaint's house, she just hadn't had the time.

It was a matter of, if she was right and didn't break in, she'd have lost her one chance to confirm what she thought she knew. But if she was wrong, she'd be no worse off than she was right now.

Maggie stood for a moment to get a sense of the room and her bearings. The decor was incredibly old-fashioned with a wooden dresser and mirror, a nightstand and a narrow bed with an ancient quilt on it.

Secrets tended to be kept in jewelry boxes. And unless they were hidden under a loose board under the carpet—which Maggie hoped very much was not the case—her best chance of discovering a treasure lay close to the bed.

She went to the bedside table that seemed to be the side where Toussaint slept. On top she saw a water glass, a clock, a figurine of the Madonna that looked like hand-painted ceramic. Maggie resisted the urge to handle any of the items.

When Maggie saw the Madonna figurine, she felt a flinch of guilt but hurriedly reminded herself that she'd known many religious people who were still able to kill someone they thought needed killing.

She rooted through the nightstand drawer but found nothing. Hurriedly, she stuck her hands under the mattress and felt for anything that shouldn't be there—a folder, a piece of paper, a book, a photo.

But there was nothing.

She stood up and looked around, taking a moment to walk to the wall and unlock the bedroom window. That was when she saw the stack of books on Toussaint's dresser. Maggie went to them and quickly shuffled through them, opening each one and flapping the pages open to release anything that had been stuck inside for safekeeping.

Again, nothing.

Knowing her time was running out, Maggie did a quick scan of the living room and kitchen. Everything was neat and tidy, the kitchen looked as if it hadn't been used in years.

Just as she was about to leave to check out the barn, she noticed there was something stuck to the refrigerator door. Maggie walked over and saw a small school photo held to the door by a black magnet. The picture was of a little girl. It was captioned by the date *1989*. Maggie studied the girl's face and tried to see any resemblance to Étoile. Or for that matter Chantal.

The year would've matched Étoile at this age, she decided. She did think it odd that the photo was just stuck on the fridge for all the world to see, considering that Toussaint appeared to treat her relationship with Étoile as a huge secret.

Probably not much of the world ever comes in here to see it.

She pulled out her phone and snapped a picture of it, mindful that whoever she showed it would know she had been in Madame Toussaint's house without permission. Then she turned and went back to the bedroom, the sound of very loud purring from Toussaint's huge cat seeming to reverberate through the small house, pausing to see if there was anything she could have missed and that's when she saw what she should have been looking for all along.

Annette Toussaint's Bible.

It was on the floor on the opposite of the bed. Perhaps it had fallen there after a night spent reading it? Maggie picked it up and flipped to the front of the Bible. She skimmed the front page until she came to the entry with Étoile's name.

And under Étoile's name were the words *infant girl 2006*.

It wasn't much to go on but it was a piece that fit the puzzle well enough. Chantal could easily have been born in 2006. This

Bible told Maggie that Étoile had had a child who'd never been named.

She pulled out her phone again and photographed the entry and then returned the Bible to where she'd found it on the floor before going to the window and easing it open. The drop into the rosemary bush below was only a few feet and would hopefully conceal any footprints or evidence that an intruder had come and gone.

Maggie perched on the windowsill long enough to work the window down as far as she could and then jumped to the ground.

Annoyed that all she'd done so far was loosely confirm what she already knew—that Étoile was Toussaint's daughter who'd had a child out of wedlock—Maggie glanced at her watch. It was after five. Things would be breaking up at the monastery by now. She pulled out her phone, saw that her battery was very low, and called Grace.

"Hey, where are you?" Grace said. "Laurent has been looking for you."

"I went to the lavender farm. Can you see if Madame Toussaint and her crew are still there?"

"Hold on, let me see," Grace said.

Maggie walked back to her car while she waited for Grace to come back on the line. She'd need to use the time she had left to go through the barn, but she wanted to grab her purse first to retrieve a water bottle.

Nervous tension had left her feeling parched. As she scanned the quiet fields, the scent of lavender was still perfuming the air, even though so much of it had already been harvested.

"I'm looking right at them," Grace said when she came back on the line.

"All four of them?"

"Yep. Enzo, Gené, Brigitte and Madame Toussaint who is talking very heatedly to Frère Jean about something."

"Maybe she's making a confession," Maggie said.

But she was glad to hear nobody appeared to be in a rush to come back to the farm.

"I wouldn't count on it," Grace said. "What are you doing at the lavender farm?"

"Just looking for whatever I can find. You know how that goes. You don't know what you're looking for until you find it. God, it's hot out here."

"They don't look like they're leaving any time soon. So have you found anything?"

"Not really. I found proof that Étoile Monet is Toussaint's daughter."

"Didn't we already know that?"

"Yeah."

"You don't really think that sweet little old lady could have killed Chantal?"

"I don't know, Grace. Maybe. I think it's possible she's not as sweet as she looks. In fact, she's actually tough as nails. And she's got secrets."

"Oh! I see Laurent. Should I tell him you haven't died?"

"Tell him my phone's about to die and I'll talk to him later at home—which is the truth."

"Makes for a nice change, doesn't it, darling?"

"Haha. Funny lady. I'll talk to you later."

Maggie disconnected and then finished off the bottle of water. Feeling comfortable that she had more time than expected, she decided to collect the doll now since she was so close, then drive the car to the barn.

She walked up the small knoll where just a few days earlier this section of field had been marked off with fluttering blue and white police crime tape. As she got closer, seeing the French flags and the flowers laid on the ground, she felt a stab of sadness for the poor girl who'd died here.

It wasn't fair. Chantal had been so young and it didn't sound like she'd had much of a childhood—and certainly no love.

As she stared at the tribute laid out for the girl, Maggie found herself surprised. Up to now she'd thought that nobody had liked Chantal. Everyone Maggie had talked to said how difficult the girl was and how hard to get along with she was.

As Maggie came closer to the memorial, she felt tears prick her eyes. She was glad for all the people who taken the time to put these things here. It might actually have been more appreciation than Chantal had ever known when she was alive.

Were these people friends of Chantal's or just people in the area who'd heard what happened to her and hated thinking of a young life snuffed out too soon?

Without knowing why, Maggie pulled out her phone to take a picture of the memorial and with a shiver saw that her phone battery had already died.

Oh well. She walked over to the mound where she could see a small baby doll sitting on top. It had rained two days ago and the doll looked like it had been out here then, although the hot August sun had since dried its hair and blue cotton dress.

Maggie leaned over to pick up the doll. When she did, the notebook Bèbè had stolen and given to Maggie fell out of her purse. A piece of paper, which had obviously been stuck between the notebook pages, fluttered to the ground.

Maggie picked up the note first and studied it. She thought it looked like one of the many scrawled grocery lists Laurent made and left around the house.

But this was no grocery list.

Without meaning to she read the first line—*Dear Chantal...*

Maggie's heart seemed to stop beating as she saw the line.

Please meet me at the southeast corner of the lavender field tonight at nineteen hundred hrs.

Give me one last chance to show you how I feel.
I love you, Enzo.

Maggie stared at the note and tried to stop her mind from flying in a million different directions.

This is the note that lured Chantal to her death.

She looked up and around. The southeast corner of the field.

This is the note that set up the rendezvous location.

She looked at the notebook, now on the ground, that it had fallen out of.

Maggie's hand began to tremble as she looked at the mound of colorful, childish artifacts. The balloons were bobbing in the bare hint of a breeze beside the plastic flowers and the doll.

It was this note that drew her to the place where she was killed. It wasn't found on her body because the killer removed it after he killed her.

So it was Enzo who lured her out here, Maggie thought as she stared at the note and suddenly blinked back sudden tears. It was Enzo who met her here, killed her, tucked lavender around her, kissed her and then took the evidence—the note he'd written—off her body.

Somewhere in the background of her mind she registered a sound and her body shuddered as if in response to a chill in the air that shouldn't be there. But Maggie was too mesmerized by what was right in front of her to really notice.

Enzo killed Chantal.

All her strength seemed to drain out of Maggie and she found herself easing down into a sitting position beside the memorial. She would rest just for a moment. Just long enough to catch her breath and get her hands to stop shaking.

She'd solved it. She'd found Chantal's killer.

She glanced at her phone still in her hand. In a moment she'd use the charger in her car to call LaBelle and tell her what she'd found. She couldn't wait to tell her that—

The next thought that came to her came from a place in the back of her brain where Maggie rarely visited. At least not consciously. It was a place where observations got registered but not yet revealed to her awake mind. She looked at the note again.

She re-read the words.

Please meet me at the southeast corner of the lavender field tonight at nineteen hundred hrs.

Give me one last chance to show you how I feel.

The words were in French but they sounded remarkably... grammatical for Enzo. Could the Enzo Maggie met have written this? Why was she doubting it? It was signed by him.

Except...

She looked again at the notebook, upside down in the dirt by the memorial. What was the note doing inside the notebook? How would Bèbè have stolen something from Enzo? He lived nowhere near her.

Curious, Maggie picked up the notebook and when she did she saw it wasn't a notebook at all but a breviary. Because she had a cousin who was a priest, Maggie knew that breviaries were prayer books, used by priests and monks every day.

She felt a tightening in her chest as she looked at the book in confusion.

What is Enzo's note doing in a breviary?

Swallowing hard, Maggie flipped to the front of the book and checked the name on the inside cover.

Luis Hernandez.

She stared at the name and felt her cheeks flush hot as the seconds ticked by. Then she turned back to the note in her hand and held it up next to the signature in the book.

The handwriting matched.

63

Her hands began to shake. The killer wasn't Enzo.

It was Frère Luis.

Frère Luis had written the note. Frère Luis had lured Chantal to the spot in the field, killed her, and taken the note back to tuck it away in his breviary.

Maggie started to flip through the breviary. In the back of the book she found another note, this time a printed slip.

Her eyes ran over the typeface. At the top of the sheet was a logo for a medical laboratory in Nice. She blinked and studied the sheet which showed three columns labeled *Test, Child* and *Alleged Father*. She held her breath as she realized what she was looking at.

Each column held a line of numbers which meant nothing to her. She skimmed to the bottom of the page and read the single sentence there.

Based on testing results obtained from analyses of the DNA loci listed at nine weeks into the pregnancy, the probability of paternity is 99.99%.

It was the DNA test showing that Luis Hernandez was the father of Chantal Lambert's baby.

She felt like her heart was going to pound right out of her chest.

I was right. The key was the father.

"Well, this is awkward."

Maggie twisted around where she sat in the grass, the breviary falling from her hand. Frère Luis walked slowly toward her, and she felt overwhelmed by a sickening sense of vertigo. She watched his eyes go to the breviary in the dirt, its pages open and moving in the slight breeze.

"So that's where that got to," he said casually as he walked over and picked it up.

Maggie scrambled to her feet.

Luis stood between her and her car.

"What are you doing here?" she asked.

Luis looked at the small memorial and then across the lavender fields before answering.

"I had a little talk with Bèbè," he said. "She wanted to tell me she was sorry for stealing some things from my room."

Maggie licked her lips.

"Well," she said. "I'd better be getting back. My husband will be wondering where I am."

Luis stepped to block her movement toward the car.

"Your husband already left to go home," he said.

He nodded at the test results that Maggie still held in her hand. "I can't tell you how much I wish you hadn't seen that."

"I'm not the only one who's seen it," Maggie said quickly, feeling the palms of her hands go clammy. "Bèbè's seen it too."

"Yes, but Bèbè is illiterate," Luis said. "I know because I've been working to help her with her reading."

Which is the reason she's still alive, Maggie thought. She didn't know what she had.

"She told me about the doll." He gestured to the tribute. "And when she told me she'd given my book to you, I came straight here."

"Look, *mon frère*, things haven't gone too far yet," Maggie said. "There's still time to fix this."

"Oh, I think two people's deaths would be considered a bit too far," Luis said. "Three won't make much of a difference if I'm caught."

"Well, you certainly will be caught," Maggie said, feeling the sweat beginning to dribble down her forehead. "I suspected you from the first. I told Detective LaBelle about my suspicions."

He smiled sadly and shook his head.

"No. You didn't." He looked around. "We can't do it here, obviously."

Things were starting to move too fast. She knew she had to slow him down. Maybe Madame Toussaint and the rest of them were on their way back even now!

"Why did you kill Chantal?" she asked.

As soon as she asked the question she realized he'd been dying to explain to someone ever since he'd killed her.

"Do you think a moment's weakness should destroy your life forever?" he asked earnestly. "Because that's all it was. One moment and a lifetime of devotion and sacrifice would be gone."

"If you're talking about the baby," Maggie said, "that wouldn't have destroyed your life forever."

"A monk gets a homeless teenager pregnant?" he said incredulously. "Being ostracized would be the best I could hope for. I certainly could no longer hope to achieve a life of quiet contemplation and service to the community."

"Where did you get the scythe?"

He looked surprised that she knew what weapon he'd used.

""It belonged to Rochelle. She left it in the monastery garden one afternoon."

"Where is it now?"

"Since you won't be telling anyone, I can tell you that I hid it in the old footlocker by Bèbè's cot. She'd have no reason to look in there. What thief expects loot to just show up?"

"But when it's found, she'll be a suspect."

"Yes. But she's a thief," he said matter-of-factly. "Are you not aware that there are consequences in this life? Bèbè thinks she can steal and lie and that we will all just continue to feed her and house her and trust her."

"That's what Frère Jean would do."

"Frère Jean is a weak fool."

Maggie inched over to open up a path on the other side of Luis. Even if she could make it to the car, he'd catch her before she could get in and lock the door. But maybe, just maybe, she could make it to the road.

If she made it to the road, there was a chance someone would come before he caught her.

"I see what you're doing, Madame Dernier. It won't work. I was a runner in school before I entered the monastery. I am very fast."

"I won't tell anyone what I saw. No one would believe me anyway."

"I know you're lying to save your life. You'll tell everyone, starting with the police. You see, I followed you last week when you came here to talk to Madame Toussaint. I borrowed Erté's binoculars and I watched you. I saw the determination in your face. I hoped you'd give up. I *prayed* you'd give up."

Maggie felt a chill thinking of how he'd been watching her.

"Speaking of Erté," she said, "you killed him because he saw what you did?"

Luis's face distorted into what looked to Maggie like true anguish.

"That broke my heart," he said. "I saw him crouching in the bushes, right there." He pointed to a berm of gorse near the road. " I couldn't believe he followed me."

"Is that why you put all those stupid lavender blossoms all

over both dead bodies?" Maggie asked. "Did you think that made it better somehow?"

He flushed.

"I'm not a monster," he said heatedly. "I cared deeply for Erté and I had a special relationship with Chantal."

"You mean the kind of relationship where your money spends as good as the next guy in line?"

"She was not like that with me!"

"Said every prostitute's john ever!"

"Enough! Thank you for making this a little easier for me—"

"You *are* a monster!" Maggie shouted as she threw her cellphone at his face and heard him howl as it hit before she swiveled on one foot and ran—toward the farm, the only possible avenue of escape.

If she could make it to the barn or the house…if she could get to some place just for a few minutes and give Toussaint time to get back!

"I'm not a monster!" he screamed. She'd hit him solidly but she knew it wouldn't slow him for long.

She tried to zigzag, knowing his arms were long, knowing all he had to do was lunge and tackle her. All she could do was try to outwit him, try to do something other than what he anticipated.

The processing barn was directly ahead of her and Maggie's mind raced trying to remember what was in it that might help her. What weapon, what—

Suddenly her foot caught in a divot in the long grass and she felt herself falling at the same time she felt his hands slamming into her shoulders, pushing her hard into the ground. Her whole body vibrated on impact.

He landed on top of her, the weight and pressure of his body pushing into her until she felt she was breathing the very earth. Her lungs couldn't expand to take a breath and she was sure she would suffocate there in the lavender field.

Stars scattered across the blackened canvas of her struggling brain and she felt herself drift away while her stomach lurched in ever widening circles of nausea.

64

Maggie woke to pain that stitched up and down her arms and legs. Luis was carrying her in his arms, her face pressed close to his black habit. She smelled the sweat and fear in his clothing.

She fought not to throw up on herself.

He was panting but whether from exertion or fury, she couldn't tell.

"Never...get away with..." she said in a hoarse whisper.

"Shut up," he snarled and dumped her on the ground.

Maggie tried to get her bearings, but the lights seemed to have gone out and the sky had darkened. She felt the ground beneath her and felt the stray stalks of lavender pressing into the palms of her hands before she realized she was in the lavender processing barn.

Luis reached down and grabbed her by the hair and tugged her up onto her knees and toward a tractor parked in the back part of the barn. On the far side was a rolltop garage door where the tractor had been backed in.

He was panting heavier now as if he'd just run a race. Maggie knew he was doing what he was going through the process of mentally preparing himself for what he was about to do. She wriggled and flailed with her hands in an attempt to free herself but he held her tightly.

"Just stay still!" he said hoarsely.

Maggie's scalp was on fire as he dragged her to the tractor and it was then she realized what he was planning to do. The tractor was parked beside the harvester, but no longer attached to it. He wasn't taking her to the tractor but to the harvester.

He groped around the control panel of the harvester.

He was looking for the power switch.

Maggie's mind raced as the world seemed to amplify in noise and color as her terror ramped up.

He has to get me up on the hydraulic ladder into the cutting floor, Maggie thought in a rising panic.

The sudden rumble of the harvester engine coming to life shook the building, its two bladed rakes at the front of the machine beginning to move slowly and then whirl rapidly.

Luis's kept his left hand wrapped around Maggie's long hair to hold her securely beside him.

"Will never...work," Maggie gasped but she knew it would. It would work perfectly.

If he could get her up to the cutting floor, it would work perfectly. It would look like an accident. A terrible accident and nobody's fault. Just a nosy American who thought she was a detective who got a little too curious and had a terrible accident.

Tant pis.

Luis pushed another button on the panel and Maggie heard the sound of the electro-hydraulic system engage. She saw the cutting floor begin to move and knew he was waiting for it to become level with where they stood. If he could throw her onto the floor, she wouldn't have a chance to scramble free of the slicing blades designed to lift and direct the lavender toward the center into the cutting system.

The cutting system that would slice her to pieces before she could take a breath.

"Don't do this," Maggie said desperately, her mind racing to outthink him, to imagine what he would do that she could counter.

He only tightened his grip on her hair.

Suddenly the cutting floor locked into place and Maggie felt Luis begin to shift his weight to throw her onto it.

Without thinking, Maggie dropped her hands from her hair where she'd been trying to pull free and instead grabbed the front of her blouse and jerked it open, popping buttons as she did.

She felt his hand leave her hair, felt his body go rigid with shock.

She didn't waste the moment. Jerking off her bra she turned to face him as he stood for one astonished moment staring at her bare chest as if hypnotized.

Then Maggie ducked her chin and rammed her head into his jaw and pushed him with both hands as hard as she could.

He fell backwards so forcefully it was as if he were being pulled from the other side.

The second he hit the harvester's cutting floor, Maggie tried to jerk him back toward her but his arm was snatched out of her grip by the momentum of the machine and its lethal blades.

She staggered backward, crossing her arms over her naked chest in horror as his screams spiraled up and out of the barn and into the sweltering August day.

65

Maggie staggered to the power panel and slammed her hand against the buttons on the control panel to shut it off. Once she heard the engine die she hesitated only briefly before snatching up her blouse from the ground and racing back across the grassy field to her car.

She fought the convulsion of guilt that rippled through her as she ran, telling herself that even if Luis was still alive she didn't have the first aid skills to keep him alive. Her only hope —and his—was to get to her phone and call for help.

She raced to where she'd flung her phone at him, scooped it up and ran to her car where she jumped in and started it up before plugging in her phone into the port on the dashboard. With trembling fingers she pulled her arms through her blouse sleeves and buttoned it while she waited for her phone to power up.

When she looked in the rearview mirror she saw a spattering of blood droplets across her face. She twisted the mirror away and picked up her phone and called the police just as she saw four figures walking down the village road parallel to the farm.

It was Madame Toussaint and her group.

After hanging up with the dispatcher, Maggie sat in the driver's seat of her car until she had the strength to get out and her phone had fifteen percent power.

Before she reached the barn Enzo came running out of it, his eyes wide with horror.

"I've called for an ambulance," Maggie said to him. "Did you move him?"

Enzo stopped running, his eyes widening and just stared at her.

"Enzo," Maggie said to him, trying to get eye contact with him. He looked as if he was about to go into shock. "Did you touch anything?"

He shook his head.

Maggie heard a long agonized moan coming from the barn which made her blood freeze in her veins. She reminded herself that it meant he was alive.

"Where's Gené and Brigitte?" Maggie asked.

Enzo waved at the house.

"Go tell them to stay inside until the ambulance comes."

Enzo nodded and then turned and stumbled in the direction of the house. Maggie pulled out her phone and called LaBelle.

"Where are you?" LaBelle asked when she answered.

"At the lavender farm," Maggie said, going to a lone picnic table a hundred feet from the barn and sinking down on the bench with the barn in view. As crazy as it sounded, a part of her wanted to make sure Luis didn't leave.

"What are you doing there? Look, it doesn't matter. You've got to—"

"No," Maggie said firmly. "You listen to me. I've found Chantal and Erté's killer."

Just saying the words nearly undid her but she forced herself to continue.

"You what?"

"It was Frère Luis," Maggie said. "Chantal's baby was his. He admitted to me that he killed her because he was afraid she would tell everyone and the scandal would end his life as a monk."

The detective didn't even pause to process what Maggie had told her.

"Do you have evidence of this?" LaBelle asked.

"Beyond his confession to me?" Maggie said in rising hysteria before taking a breath to calm herself. "Yes. I have a note that Luis wrote as if it was from Enzo to get Chantal to come out to the field that night."

"Chantal thought she was meeting Enzo?"

"Yes, and then Luis showed up and killed her. Erté followed Luis and saw what happened."

"Erté followed Luis, not Chantal?"

"Yeah. Luis was always kind to him. Maybe Erté hero-worshipped him or something."

"Where is Luis now?"

Maggie heard the sound of the ambulance and she willed it to come faster.

"Not doing too good. We had a...there was a struggle. I know I should be in there pressing against arteries or whatever but I...I—"

Maggie felt her throat close up and tears began to stream down her face.

"Maggie?" LaBelle said. "Are you okay?"

"I'm okay," Maggie whispered, wiping her tears away. "It's just been a bad day."

"It's about to get worse," LaBelle said. "I've been trying to tell you, Laurent called my cellphone to say he thinks there is a problem with your daughter."

Oh, God! Now what! Can't Mila give me one moment of peace!?

It was too much. Whatever Mila had done, if Laurent was calling the police, surely it was just to scare the girl?

"What kind of problem?" Maggie said wearily as she watched the ambulance make its way up the driveway. A motion out of her eye made her turn her head and she saw Madame Toussaint, Enzo, Gené and Brigitte standing on the porch of Toussaint's house watching.

"It seems she never showed up at the monastery when she was supposed to," LaBelle said.

Maggie frowned and brought her attention back to the phone conversation.

"So? She's with Rochelle."

"Exactly. Laurent believes that that is the problem."

66

Thank God the French drove on the right side of the road, Rochelle thought as she checked her rearview mirror. She didn't need anything more to challenge her today.

Just keep the car on the road. Take it nice and easy, she thought, fighting a relentless fluttering in her chest, unable to tell if it was terror or euphoria.

Mila reached out and turned up the radio and then began scanning the various music stations, the loud discordant sounds as the radio transitioned between stations grated on Rochelle's ears.

It was all she could do not to slap Mila's hand away.

God! The kid was annoying! How did Laurent put up with her?

She glanced at Mila who was busy switching stations and chewing gum, her cherubic little lips working in a demented ritual as she moronically focused on twisting the radio dial.

"Why don't we give the music a rest?" Rochelle said, forcing herself to sound affable. "There's nothing out here in the bergs anyway."

Mila laughed.

"Yeah. *The bergs*. For sure. When do you think we'll get to Paris?"

"In time for dinner," Rochelle said. "At some amazingly little *brasserie* where we'll have the best French fries."

"And wine, right? You said you'd let me drink?"

"Of course, dear girl. You're plenty old enough."

There would be no *brasserie*, no trip to Paris. No French fries, no wine.

Rochelle took in a breath and willed herself to think of how good things were going to be.

She was free and just days, no hours, from being with Laurent for good. Of all the people she'd known in her life, only Laurent understood the pain of the betrayals she'd suffered. Only Laurent had ever tried to help.

And now she was going to help him.

She glanced at Mila who was now looking out the window at the passing scenery and Rochelle felt a chill of excitement and expectation.

She'd seen what even his wife hadn't seen. She'd seen Laurent go from being the warm, grounded, happy man she'd met in California last year to one altered by repressed anger, rejection and confusion.

A light rain began to mist against the windshield and she fumbled for the wipers, proud of herself for finding them in the unfamiliar car. The day had started with not a cloud in the sky but it was swiftly turning gray.

She put the weather from her mind and brought up Laurent's face. Just the memory of it made her smile.

How she'd longed to reach out to him and tell him that she knew the answer to his unhappiness. That she *was* the answer. But she'd had to play it cool. Once she brought him back to where he should be, he'd see it and he'd know that only she could have rescued him.

At least the kid wasn't a magpie. That would have been

unendurable. It helped but it wouldn't save her. The sad fact was that impossible situations needed real heroism.

You didn't see that in the world anymore. She thought of that time, so many years ago, when Grandma Mary was on the brink of being forced into long-term care all because she had a cat she was too old to care for. A cat who was slowly destroying her little condo—ripping up her furniture, crapping everywhere and making Grandma Mary spend her few precious financial resources on expensive veterinary care for the cat's many ailments.

It was all her family could talk about for months. Every family dinner, every holiday when they were out of ear shot of Grandma Mary, everyone bemoaned the situation, wringing their hands with hopelessness. Grandma Mary loved that cat like her own child. It was literally the only thing that kept her going and gave her some joy in life. But social services insisted the animal created a dangerous living environment that they couldn't allow.

What was to be done?

Except to talk about it endlessly and wait for the inevitable to happen? That dreaded moment when the social workers would come and wrench Grandma Mary from her home.

Rochelle shook her head in wonder. Had anyone tried to rehome the animal? Or take it themselves? Or visit Grandma Mary more and empty the litter box or clean up after the cat?

There were a hundred different answers!

Even at twelve years old, Rochelle had seen that someone needed to step in and save Grandma Mary.

Yes, it was hard. Being a hero isn't easy!

She'd had to sneak out of her own house at a time that nobody would worry about where she was.

Then lure the cat to the backyard with food she'd bought with her babysitting money before killing it with a hammer and then stuffing its carcass in a neighbor's trash can.

But Grandma Mary got to stay in her home! At least for a little bit. Because of me!

"Are you okay, Rochelle?" Mila asked.

Rochelle turned to see that the girl was eyeing her with a distrustful look.

"Yes, of course," Rochelle said, forcing another smile for her. "Just anxious to get to Paris."

She turned her gaze back to the road and saw the sign up ahead for the train station.

So divorce, yes, of course, she thought. In time Laurent will need to divorce Maggie. But divorce wouldn't do the hard work of what needed to be done—the heroic work.

Mila would still be with Laurent on custodial weekends which would just continue to make him miserable!

Make both of us miserable.

No, the only way she and Laurent could go forward together was if they began with a clean slate.

And that can only happen, she thought, her heart filling with mounting joy as she took the exit to the train station, *if Mila dies.*

67

Within twenty minutes of the first emergency vehicle arriving, the clearing in front of the barn had been transformed into an active crime scene with cars parked haphazardly down the driveway to the main road and more than a dozen policemen and medical personnel standing about.

Maggie sat in her car and watched the activity around the barn at *La Lavandin*. Stunned after LaBelle's phone call, she called Laurent who was just dropping Jemmy off at *Dormir* with Grace and Danielle. He was now driving Danielle's car.

"Where do you think they went?" Maggie asked as she watched an ambulance open its back doors and two attendants jumped out.

She felt a numbness come over her that she was perversely grateful for. Her stomach tightened as she watched the stretcher come out of the barn with Luis's body on it—alive she assumed since his face was uncovered.

"I have no idea," he said. "Rochelle has no cellphone. She has no friends in the area."

Exactly, Maggie thought. *And that was never a tip off for you?*

As she watched the ambulance workers load Luis into the ambulance, she watched two detectives turn from the scene and begin to walk toward her.

She started her car.

"Any idea what she's up to?" Maggie asked, trying to tamp down the panic that seemed to want to leap out of her as she watched the cops draw near. She put the car into reverse and began to slowly back up. As she looked over her shoulder, she saw the two men had begun to run in her direction.

I have no time for this.

She peeled out onto the main road and accelerated.

"I am going to Saint-Buvard," Laurent said. "If they were shopping or stopped at a café—"

Maggie sped down the bordering village road, not even sure where she was racing toward. She just knew at some level that she needed to *move*, needed to find her daughter, needed to get to Mila.

"Is there any way that Rochelle might think that the two of you…?"

"*Non*," he said quickly. "Absolutely not."

"It's just that you don't always see these things."

"I see them. It wasn't like that with her."

But his voice sounded odd, strained. Was this Laurent feeling the stress about the whereabouts of his child? Or was this Laurent knowing he hadn't done all he could to make it clear to Rochelle there was no future for them?

It didn't matter. Not now.

"Maybe we shouldn't jump to conclusions," she said and waited.

He paused. "Maybe."

His hesitation told her that the conclusion they'd both jumped to was the most likely.

"Do you think they would leave the area?" Maggie asked.

Another Laurent pause. This one worse than the one before.

"I overheard Mila tell Rochelle she wished she lived in Paris," Laurent said.

"What did Rochelle say in response?"

"Nothing that I heard. They are very close, *chérie*. I don't believe Rochelle would hurt Mila."

But Maggie got an image in her mind's eye of Mila sassing her father, her face contorted and hateful. There was no way Rochelle was going to live with *that*. What sane woman would who wasn't related to the problem?

"Keep your phone on," Maggie said and disconnected.

She knew she should have said something supportive or reassuring. She knew that Laurent was blaming himself for giving Rochelle the wrong idea. She knew between his worry for Mila and his guilt, he was in agony.

She wondered what kind of loving wife she was, that at the moment, she just didn't care.

She rang LaBelle who picked up immediately. That in itself buoyed Maggie and terrified her. The fact that LaBelle was watching for her call—and taking it with everything else she had going on—told Maggie the detective was worried too.

"Are you watching the train and bus stations?" Maggie asked.

"No. Technically I can't for another twenty hours."

Maggie felt like screaming or at least slamming a door. She wished that she'd given Mila her phone back. Maggie had put a tracker on it when she'd first given it to Mila. But Mila had lost phone privileges back at the beginning of summer.

Where would they go? How long had they been gone?

"Okay," Maggie said. "I'm going to the train station in Arles. I think Nîmes is too far for them. I'll hit the bus stations between here and there."

"I'm sorry, Maggie," LaBelle said. "I wish I could help."

After Maggie disconnected she opened her phone's GPS app for directions to the Aix train station. It was at least an hour away. She felt her throat constrict as she took the entrance ramp to the highway and accelerated, her mind flying in every direction at once as she tried to imagine what Rochelle could be thinking. Was Mila in on this?

Would Mila try to manipulate Rochelle? Did she know that Rochelle was in love with her father? How would Mila react if she knew? Would she care as long as it got her to Paris?

I don't even know that they are going to Paris, Maggie thought on the verge of tears.

As she drove she typed in *bus station* in the search window of her GPS and saw five bus station icons pop up in the area as well as two train stations.

Seven possible destinations.

That is if they're not just driving to Paris which they very well could be.

Time was flying by with every mile. Every minute was precious.

Looking at the map of the five stations, Maggie felt herself imagining Rochelle telling Mila they were taking a bus to Paris. If Maggie knew her stubborn daughter, she would not agree to a bus ride when she could take a train. Had Mila gotten her passport out of Maggie's lingerie drawer? If not, there was no point in checking the airports.

If so, then she was driving in totally the wrong direction.

She called Laurent

"The cops can't check the bus and train stations yet," she said. "I'm heading to the bus stations west of us, ending with Arles. You should go to the Aix train station. If you don't see your car in the parking lot, head west and start hitting all the bus stations."

"What do you think Rochelle is doing?" Laurent asked, his voice laced with tension. The question surprised Maggie but underscored to her that he'd been going mad trying to answer this question for himself. And probably imagining answers that laid the blame for what was happening solely at his feet.

"I don't know," Maggie said. "But if I had to guess, I'd say she's trying to do you a favor."

She disconnected before he could answer.

As she drove down the highway trying to keep her panic at bay, trying not to imagine what Rochelle's purpose was, and trying not to imagine that Mila was afraid, her phone dinged to indicate that she'd received a text.

She snatched up the phone and saw the message was from LaBelle.

<Luis lost 3 fingers, and foot is badly cut but otherwise ok>

Maggie blinked at the text and was surprised how far in the past her confrontation with Luis seemed. In the last thirty minutes she hadn't given a thought to the man who'd tried to kill her.

Another text came through from LaBelle.

<he confessed to both murders>

Maggie immediately called her.

"Did you get my text?" LaBelle asked.

"Never mind about that," Maggie said. "I need your help. Laurent can't admit it but I think Rochelle might be dangerous."

There was a pause on the line.

"Tell me what you want me to do," LaBelle said.

68

The Cabriès bus station was barely visible through the thick trees and complicated stonework of the front of the station. It had taken Maggie nearly twenty minutes to maneuver into the village and wind her way down the narrow streets to where the station was set on a one-way street.

A quick sweep of the tiny parking lot by the station and an attempt at an even quicker perusal of the block around the station told Maggie what she feared was true.

They weren't here.

Screw the bus stations! They're not taking a damn bus!

Frustrated at how long it had taken to check the parking lot of just one bus station, Maggie turned to her GPS to find the Arles train station. By the GPS estimation, the station was thirty minutes away.

Twenty, if Maggie sped.

How far ahead of her were they? This was madness. She had no idea even what direction they'd gone in. She realized she could be racing down a highway in the totally opposite direction!

One thing she knew was that she had no more ideas. All that was left now was luck. Good luck on her part, and hopefully bad luck on Rochelle's.

If the train was late—*was it ever late?*—if Mila needed to use the bathroom and forced an unforeseen stop, if there was traffic in town, if there was car trouble—

She pressed the accelerator, not caring that the signs and other cars she passed were zipping into her rearview mirror.

The favor she'd asked LaBelle was to check the CCTV footage at the toll roads going south as well as the Arles, Marseille and Nîmes train stations, since they were all places Laurent couldn't easily reach.

If Rochelle was smart and had gone to the Aix station, which was the most convenient and most obvious destination, she'd have to use the parking lot next to the station. Parking anywhere else was untenable since the station was at least a mile from any other parking spots and there was no way Mila would walk a mile when she could ride.

Unless she was in the trunk.

Maggie angrily banished the thought from her mind. Checking the public video footage had been a Hail Mary in every sense of the word but this was an occasion that called for it.

With the highway sign up ahead announcing that Arles was thirty kilometers ahead, Maggie put a call in to Laurent.

"Where are you?" she asked. She wouldn't bother asking if he'd had any luck. He would have called if he had.

"Just leaving the train station," he said, his voice ragged. "I'm heading to Nîmes now. Grace called to say that Danielle had put the word out to her network to drive to the bus stations around Saint-Buvard."

"Good," Maggie said.

"Where are you?"

"Heading to Arles and then on to Marseille," Maggie said,

and then saw she was getting a call from LaBelle. She disconnected and took the call. "I'm here," she said.

"I found them," LaBelle said breathlessly. "They went through the A54 toll booth at Saint-Martin-de-Crau twenty minutes ago and Laurent's Peugeot showed up on camera at Gare d'Arles ten minutes ago. There's a train to Paris leaving from there in twenty minutes. Are you sure they're going to Paris?"

Maggie looked at her watch. She was thirty minutes from Arles.

"I'm on my way," she said and disconnected.

She didn't have to be sure of Paris. She just had to get to them before they got on any train going anywhere.

Pushing down hard on the accelerator, she gave her phone the verbal instruction to text Laurent to say that his Peugeot was sighted at the Arles train station.

He texted back that he was now behind a major accident on the highway. It looked to be at least an hour's delay.

"Why is Rochelle doing this?" Maggie said shrilly into the verbal text function on her phone to Laurent. "Does she think this will impress you?"

He didn't respond.

The next fifteen minutes were agonizing as Maggie sped down the highway and worked to keep thoughts that she would be too late from her mind.

Just focus on getting there.

Smaller and older than the Aix train station, the Arles station had no parking lot that Maggie could see. She already knew Rochelle and Mila were here somewhere so she didn't bother scouting the area to locate the Peugeot. She drove to where a line of cars were parked across the road from the station and jumped out of the car.

At worst she would be towed or have a boot put on her wheel. But if Rochelle and Mila really were here and Maggie missed them, a disabled vehicle would be the least of her troubles.

She ran into the station, not even bothering to shut the driver's side door as she pushed past commuters and travelers.

It was a Monday evening and the station entrance hall was filled with travelers, but they were almost all incoming. The platforms headed to Paris were nearly deserted.

Grateful that she didn't need to buy a ticket first before running out to the platforms, Maggie scanned the arrivals and departure board as she hurried to find the platform for the Paris-bound train.

She slowed for a moment, gasping for air when she saw the incoming train show up on the departure board. *Arles to Paris. Nineteen hundred hours. Platform nine.*

She looked at her watch.

It was five minutes until seven.

Platform nine was at the furthest point in the station, a full football field length away clustered with travelers with briefcases, roller bags, and strollers. Maggie ran down the platform, dodging the travelers until she recognized two figures ahead at the furthest point of the platform. One tall and slender, one short.

Maggie screamed Mila's name but her voice was snatched away in the blare of a loudspeaker announcing the imminent arrival of a high speed train to Paris.

Thank God. Thank God.

She let out a gasp of relief and joy. Even if the train came in the next three minutes as scheduled, Maggie could always jump on the train and wrestle Mila back onto the platform.

She slowed to a walk, a stitch drilling into her side, and allowed herself a moment to gulp in air and catch her breath. She could see the train coming now. It looked as if it were coming too fast to stop in time although Maggie knew it would.

She quickened her pace, determined that she wouldn't give them any advance warning that she was here. An image came to her of her pulling Mila away from Rochelle and slapping the woman's surprised face.

Words flooded angrily into Maggie's brain as she marched toward them.

How dare you? You're insane! What were you thinking? Kidnapping is a felony in every country! After everything we did for you!

The train was nearly to the platform now and Maggie saw Rochelle and Mila turn to face it, watching it, getting ready for it to stop.

Suddenly, all of Maggie's words of indignation and fury dissolved in her brain as she realized what was going to happen a split second before it did.

A hard thudding slammed into her chest from her increased heart rate. She started to run again as she saw the train bearing down on the platform. In something out of her worst nightmare, she saw Rochelle take a step back behind Mila.

Maggie screamed but nothing came out.

And then she saw Rochelle push Mila onto the track of the oncoming train.

69

One minute Mila was standing there.

The next second Rochelle stood on the train platform alone as the train roared into the station.

An uncontrollable shudder convulsed her as she staggered to a halt at the same moment a figure emerged from the end of the platform behind Rochelle and leapt in front of the speeding train.

Maggie blinked in confusion. Another second passed and the train rumbled past the platform, its sound deafening as it roared past Maggie.

With a hand clamped to her mouth she looked to where the mystery figure had disappeared onto the tracks and back at Rochelle who was now backing away from the train. People pushed past Maggie, screaming for doctors, for help. Maggie felt her knees weaken and she stumbled forward a few steps before falling to her knees in horror and disbelief at what she'd just witnessed.

LaBelle's sacrifice.

Her skin crawled with the cold.

Because that's who the figure was. Detective Margaux LaBelle.

Bile burned in the back of Maggie's throat. She sat paralyzed on the cement ground and stared at the train as it laboriously ground to a halt. Her brain wouldn't function, her mind wouldn't compute what she'd just seen. She could only stare at the spot where both Mila and LaBelle had vanished. Some part of her mind's eye registered Rochelle melting away in the crowd.

But Maggie didn't care. She didn't care what happened to Rochelle. Now or ever again.

A cry from the crowd behind Maggie, further down the platform toward the main terminal felt like a noise coming from within her own mind until she recognized something familiar about it. Something she knew in her bones, as familiar as her own breath.

As if maneuvering through wet concrete, Maggie turned her head in the direction of the cry and saw two figures, one big and one small, climbing up from the track at the front of the train.

Her body beginning to tremble, she watched in hysterical incredulity as LaBelle and Mila ran down the platform toward her. When she reached her, Mila flung her arms, skinned and bloody, around Maggie's neck and burst into tears as the crowd around them cheered.

Maggie looked up at LaBelle who was peering down the platform, her hands on her hips.

"Which way did she go?" LaBelle shouted at Maggie over the noise of the crowd.

Maggie squeezed her eyes closed, gripping Mila tightly, and buried her face in her daughter's hair, her own tears of joy indistinguishable from her daughter's.

70

Not even a murder attempt will stop the trains from running on time, Maggie couldn't help but think from where she sat with Mila and Laurent on the bench just inside the Arles train station terminal.

Detective LaBelle and a squad of Aix police as well as a squadron of Arles police were going in and out of the platform access, their radios crackling.

LaBelle—even though she had a suspect in a double homicide waiting for her back in the emergency room in Aix—was still on the scene, talking to witnesses, ordering her men to canvass the area to search for Rochelle.

Mila, her elbows bandaged by the EMTs who had just left, slurped hot chocolate regardless of the fact that the temperature outside the station was still in the eighties. She watched the activity around her with avid interest. Laurent had gotten up to speak to a few of the uniformed police but largely kept within a foot of Mila.

Maggie leaned back into the bench where she sat with Mila. She still didn't trust her legs to get up. And she still couldn't quite believe what had happened—Mila beside her, her chattering away, yawning, laughing, asking for French fries. *Unharmed.*

When LaBelle had learned that Mila and Rochelle were at the Arles train station she'd sped there, sirens blaring. She didn't have the authority to go after Rochelle at that time since Mila hadn't been missing long enough—but she came anyway.

Maggie put her hand on Laurent's sleeve.

"You realize that LaBelle is our hero for life," Maggie said. "I mean it, Laurent. For *life*. I don't care if she arrests Danielle for murder someday. Marguerite LaBelle gets a free pass from us."

Laurent grinned and shook his head. "*D'accord, chérie*," he said. "Of course. How did she get here in time?"

"She said she was already halfway here when she got the info about the CCTV confirmation," Maggie said. "She must have gotten here moments before me but unlike me and everyone else, she didn't come in the front way but around the back so I never saw her until she was jumping onto the track."

"Tell me again," Laurent murmured, as he cupped Mila's head with his large hand.

"She saw Mila go over the side," Maggie said, nearly choking on the words, "and she went after her because she knew there was a safety access alongside the track that repairmen and track linemen use."

"*Incredible*," he said tightening his embrace of Mila who snuggled into his arms as if she were five.

"She was able to yank Mila to the perimeter until the train stopped," Maggie said, shaking her head as if she still couldn't believe it. "And they climbed up the maintenance ladder."

Laurent lifted his head to watch LaBelle on her cellphone with her men. She was alternately talking on her phone and instructing a trio of uniformed police on the platform.

"She has news," Laurent said to Maggie in a low voice. His eyes on the detective.

He was right. Maggie could tell by LaBelle's body language that something had happened.

"I heard one of the cops say the Peugeot was still in the parking lot across the street," Maggie said. "So Rochelle's on foot. I bet they've picked her up."

Laurent kissed Mila's head and smoothed the hair from her eyes.

"She pushed me!" Mila said indignantly. "She acted like she was my friend and then she tried to kill me!"

"I'm sure it was just an accident," Maggie said. The last thing she needed was for Mila to be scarred for life thinking someone she'd trusted had tried to kill her.

"You never believe me! I hate you!"

"Do not speak to your mother like that!" Laurent said, his voice raised like he rarely did with Mila, his final button pushed for the last time.

"It's okay, Laurent," Maggie said.

"*Non*. It is not," Laurent said as he dropped to one knee to be eye-level with Mila. The girl twisted her head away, refusing to look at him but Laurent held her chin steady with his hand and forced her to look at him.

"Rochelle did try to kill you," he said bluntly.

Maggie watched Mila's eyes fill with horrified tears. It took everything Maggie had in her not to try and stop what she knew Laurent was about to say to their daughter.

"She tried to kill you," he said, "because I led you to believe you could trust her."

"Laurent..." Maggie said. She knew there was no way he *wasn't* going to blame himself for what had happened today but it broke her heart to hear him say it out loud.

Laurent held up a finger to ask for silence and then refocused on Mila.

"I was wrong to trust her," he said. "But you were wrong to run away. I know your mother wants to protect you but the truth is, *chérie*, that because I trusted the wrong person and because you lied to us, it is a miracle you didn't die today."

Maggie felt a sob erupt in her throat as Laurent put into words the thought that had thrummed through her ever since Mila had been rescued.

It had been so close...

"I don't know why I did it," Mila said, weeping. "I don't know what's wrong with me."

Laurent pulled her into his arms as Mila sobbed.

"It's all right, *chérie*," he murmured.

Maggie dropped to her knees and wrapped her arms around them both.

"I'm sorry, *Maman*," Mila said to her. "I'm so sorry."

"I know," Maggie said. "It's okay."

Maggie knew that however Mila ended up processing this terrible day—whether it led to long-lasting PTSD or increased behavioral problems—Laurent was right that letting Mila off the hook for her part in it would have eventually made everything worse. Maggie couldn't wish away the fact that it had happened. She couldn't wish away the fact that Rochelle had won Mila's trust and then tried to kill her. That fact, as painful as it was, was unassailable. At least now they would go forward together as a family with the truth planted firmly between them.

"A word, Monsieur Dernier?"

Maggie looked up to see LaBelle standing nearby, waiting.

Laurent gave Mila one last kiss on the cheek and then stood up to face the detective. Maggie and Mila sat back down on the bench, Mila still sniffling in Maggie's arms.

On the one hand it surprised Maggie after everything they'd been through together that LaBelle would reach out to Laurent instead of herself. But she realized with surprise that it didn't matter.

She and LaBelle had a connection; there was no denying that now.

~

Laurent followed the detective to a spot near the terminal just out of earshot of the bench where Maggie and Mila sat. Because of his size, he found himself leaning down to speak with her, his hands on his hips, his eyes intent and probing.

"We've picked up Rochelle Lando," LaBelle said, confirming what Laurent suspected. "She was hiding behind some trash cans and an eyewitness called it in as suspicious behavior of someone she suggested might be mentally deranged."

Laurent snorted.

The memory of the fear of having Mila taken was not gone. It simmered under the surface of his emotions, ready to torment and oppress him at any moment.

He couldn't feel sorry for Rochelle even if what the eyewitness said was true which a part of him knew it must be.

"Now what?" he asked, glancing back at Mila and Maggie.

Mila was still drinking her hot chocolate but already she was shrugging off Maggie's attempts to examine her few scratches from the fall to the tracks.

"That is up to you, Monsieur Dernier," LaBelle said as she pulled out her phone.

"Call me Laurent," he said. "And I think we are way past the *vous* form, don't you?"

Labelle ducked her head and blushed. She held up her phone and took a step away from him. "I need to take this. So do you want to press charges? Because they are serious ones."

Laurent turned back to his family and got eye contact with Maggie.

"Charges, *non*," he said. "*Mais guillotine? Absolument.*"

71

The drive home to Saint-Buvard that evening was one of the more intimate moments Maggie felt she and Laurent had ever shared.

After stopping at a *brasserie* where Mila promptly stuffed herself with *blanquette de veau, pommes frites* and *mousse au chocolat*, she fell soundly asleep in the backseat of their car. Maggie and Laurent sat in the front, Laurent periodically looking at his child in the rearview mirror and Maggie turning and touching Mila's knee or sleeve as if to reassure herself that she was really there.

Maggie and Laurent spoke quietly, bonded by their mutual feelings of relief and miraculous thanksgiving. Maggie felt there was a sense that all three of them were moving forward into a new chapter of their lives, one that would turn a forgiving eye to the mistakes of the past while hopefully learning from them.

At one point on the drive home, Maggie got a text from LaBelle.

<*Call me*>

She put her phone down and lay her hand on Laurent's

knee.

"You are not going to call her?" he said.

"I kind of want to pretend Marguerite LaBelle isn't a part of my daily round for just one hour," Maggie said.

"Call her, *chérie*."

Sighing, Maggie did.

LaBelle answered her phone with a question. "Where is the note Luis wrote?" she asked.

"I have it with me," Maggie said.

"You do understand what chain of evidence is?" LaBelle asked peevishly.

"I do," Maggie said, turning to look at Mila to make sure her voice wasn't waking her. "But that doesn't matter in this case since you can see the writing on the note matches Luis's handwriting in his book."

"Ah, very good. I will have someone come by tonight to pick it up."

"Oh, one more thing," Maggie said. "As long as I have you on the phone. Luis told me he hid the murder weapon in Bèbè's trunk."

"Very good. I'll have my—"

"Just listen to me. The weapon he used is a scythe that belonged to Rochelle."

"I see."

"And I'm pretty sure it's one that Laurent lent to her."

Laurent turned his head in a barely perceptible movement to glance at Maggie.

"The murder weapon belongs to Laurent?" LaBelle asked.

"You have a unique way of phrasing things," Maggie said with annoyance. "Anyone ever tell you that?"

"How long have you known that Rochelle's missing scythe was originally Laurent's?"

"Why does that matter?"

"It matters if you withheld information from me."

"You already knew it was a scythe! You knew it belonged to Rochelle. Whether she got it from Laurent or ACE Hardware, why does that matter?"

"You're right. It doesn't matter. Besides Laurent said as much in his interview with Rochelle last week which of course was recorded."

Maggie sputtered. "So you knew all along?"

When Maggie thought of how long she'd sweated LaBelle finding out about the fact that Laurent had given the probable murder weapon to Rochelle she had to remind herself that LaBelle was her hero today.

"As you said," LaBelle said casually, "the fact that he'd owned it first is of no real importance. Are we done?"

"One last thing."

"Yes?"

"I want you to know I will never forget what you did today."

LaBelle snorted. "I was just doing my job."

And she disconnected.

Maggie turned to Laurent. "I like her."

"I do too."

Maggie stared at his profile for a moment. His face was relaxed, his eyes alert, and yet she detected a definite air of tension in the way he held the steering wheel.

"I heard LaBelle tell you before we left Arles that Rochelle was begging to see you," Maggie said, dipping her voice low.

She saw the fury flash across his face.

"We will not talk about that," he said firmly.

"Sure," Maggie said. "But I need you to tell me one thing, Laurent."

He turned to her.

"She was only ever a friend, *chérie*. And now of course not even that."

"Oh, I know," Maggie said. "My question isn't about Rochelle."

For a moment she didn't think he would answer her and when he did, his voice was pitched so low she had to lean toward him to catch his words.

"Her name was Dauphine," he said with a sigh. "She was married to my *copain* Leo for two years. I knew them both and I saw what was happening as if I'd written the script."

Maggie wanted to remind him that he *hadn't* written the script but she'd learned from long experience with Laurent that once he started speaking it was all too easy for him to stop. She held her tongue and waited.

"He and I worked together for a year before he met her. He worked clean. He enjoyed the rewards. He was not too greedy. He would work until he had enough…it doesn't matter what his dream was," he said. "Especially now."

Maggie waited for a full five minutes and decided that instead of forming his next words in his head, Laurent was reliving those days.

"What happened?" she said softly.

Laurent took the exit to the village of Saint-Buvard and Maggie knew they would be pulling into their driveway in a few minutes.

"Dauphine was from California," Laurent said. "A *sommelier* and brilliant. From the moment they met I knew Leo's dream was not her dream. But she married him anyway. I saw the drugs as her way of controlling him, of keeping him in the game. I talked to them both but she was determined he would not quit." He paused for a moment. "Leo was destined to live out his life in a foreign prison. He was never careful enough. It was only a matter of time."

"But that didn't happen?" Maggie prompted as she heard Mila shift restlessly in the back seat.

"*Non.* I told him to take her in hand. I told him he needed to be the man and be firm with her."

Maggie didn't answer.

"The night he put his foot down with her—he called me to tell me so that I would be proud of him." He paused. "That night she poisoned his drink. And then her own."

The horror of what he said rendered Maggie speechless for a moment.

"Dear God, Laurent," she said finally. "And you feel responsible because you told him to have it out with her?"

"*Non*." He pulled into their driveway and turned off the car before turning to her.

"Because I introduced them," he said.

Maggie let the rest of the silence well up in the little car and fill every crevice and gap that surrounded them. She prayed that with their precious bundle of contrary love in the back seat —along with all the bullets they'd dodged today—that Laurent would realize that after all he'd tried to do to help Rochelle with her problems he couldn't change the past or make up for it.

She prayed that the part of her brilliant, sensitive husband that always wanted to save the world could somehow separate his guilt and responsibility for his friend's death long enough to realize that.

Maggie looked up at the front of Domaine St-Buvard. Even in the dark she could make out the black wrought-iron railing that framed a second-story balcony over the front door. Like the first time she ever laid eyes on the *mas*, a chipped stone lion sat at the edge of the terrace as if guarding it. The sight of the statue still made Maggie wistful as she wondered about its history.

The soft purring sounds of Mila's snores could be heard against the muffled sounds of three dogs inside the house barking their greeting.

"Are you okay?" Maggie asked Laurent as he took off his seatbelt and turned to look at Mila.

"*Oui, chérie*," he said with a tired smile. "I am better than I have been in a long time."

"I'm glad. And I'm really glad to be home. You know?"

He laughed softly. "You are never subtle, *mon chou*," he said and then his eyes seemed to focus on her clothing and he frowned.

"Was that what you intended to wear to the memorial service today?"

Maggie looked down at her outfit. It wasn't a black sheathe dress but it was certainly not inappropriate for a memorial service.

"Yes, what's the matter with it?" she asked frowning.

"I could be wrong but it appears as if you are not wearing a bra, *chérie*."

72

Two weeks later

The panoramic terrace overlooked the main terminal of the *Aéroport de Marseille Provence*—capturing the brilliance of the Provençal sunlight and flooding it into every nook and cranny of the stunning newly designed airport.

As Maggie looked around at the beautiful space, she knew Jemmy was too excited about his upcoming adventure in California to notice it and Mila was too cross about not going herself to care.

In the two weeks since Rochelle had shown her true colors, a lot had happened. While Rochelle still remained in France, it seemed evident that her mental health issues would keep her from serving prison time for kidnapping Mila. Maggie had some conflicting feelings about that but in an ongoing effort to *roll with it*, she was attempting to do just that.

Mila herself had shown no anticipated effects after being pushed into the path of an oncoming train by someone she thought was a friend. Both Maggie and Laurent worried about that. Maggie had never before seen her daughter as superficial or insipid, which the possibility that Mila was internalizing the trauma.

More to come on that, I'm sure, Maggie thought with a worried sigh as she watched Mila walk behind Laurent and Jemmy toward airport security.

Recently Laurent had been contacted by someone he knew in Alsace who since they started later up north was on the verge of beginning his own grape harvest. Laurent had volunteered to go up for four days to help. With Mila.

Mila was of course furious about the very idea, insisting that forcing her to pick grapes in Alsace was the very definition of child abuse. The two calls she'd made to the Aix police department claiming exactly that had resulted in a further extension of her loss of phone privileges.

Nevertheless Laurent was determined that the experience would be a good one for Mila. She would work hard and be treated no differently than the migrant pickers. He would be there to make sure of this, and also of course to protect and support her.

He didn't want to present the trip as a punishment for running off with Rochelle, but of course there was a tinge of that hanging over it. Maggie knew that Laurent didn't think the connotation was necessarily a negative.

"Either she will decide she hates anything to do with grapes for the rest of her life," he said philosophically, "in which case I am no worse off than I am now. Or she will discover something worthwhile about herself."

Maggie loved the fact that Laurent hadn't given up on trying to manage Mila. They were both frustrated of course, but giving up wasn't an option. It pleased her to see him continue to try.

A problem to be solved.

Jemmy had actually asked to go to Alsace too when he got back from California, but Laurent and Maggie both thought it would be better to just let it be Mila. It would be full-time *Daddy* time for her, especially important if, as Maggie suspected, wanting her father's undivided attention was actually part of Mila's problem. If Jemmy was still interested in picking grapes, there would always be the Domaine St-Buvard grape harvest next summer.

Laurent had agreed to give his decision to move from France at least a year before doing anything permanent.

As Laurent, Jemmy and Mila entered one of the airport gift shops to make sure Jemmy had enough snacks for the twelve hour flight, Maggie stepped toward an available bench to take a call from Grace. Zouzou was due back from her summer in Paris any moment now and Grace and Danielle had spent the weekend planning a welcome-home party for her. Maggie and Laurent and Mila were going there from the airport after they'd dropped Jemmy off.

"Hey," Maggie said. "What's up?"

"Nothing," Grace said. "Danielle and I've been cooking and cleaning like fiends and I've decided to allow myself a full thirty minutes before we go back at it. Are you at the airport?"

"We are. I've got a minute if you want to gab."

"Did I tell you that Danielle saw Étoile Monet and Annette Toussaint in Aix last week having lunch together at *Nino's*?"

"Really? Did it look like a friendly lunch?"

"Danielle said there was much sniffling and hand holding so I think it was extremely friendly."

"I'm glad," Maggie said. "At least something good came out of all of this."

"Speaking of which, after the smoke has cleared so to speak, you never told me *why* Frère Luis killed Chantal."

"I didn't? Well, I told you he was the father of her unborn child, right?"

"Yes, and how did that come about? Don't the monks take a vow of celibacy or something?"

"They do and as I understand from what LaBelle told me after she interviewed Luis, when Chantal moved to the monastery, he became smitten with her."

"Oh dear. And since Chantal was open for business with *anybody*..."

"Exactly. The only question I have is how did they keep it secret from everyone for so long."

"Well, I guess nobody would suspect a monk?"

"There's that," Maggie admitted.

Looking up Maggie saw that her family were coming out of the gift shop and heading toward her.

"What was the deal with the lavender blossoms?" Grace asked. "Why did he sprinkle them all over her? And Erté?"

"Guilt, I guess," Maggie said. "I think Luis had convinced himself he was in love with Chantal. He did kiss her after he killed her just like I'd guessed. But the salve that I thought came from the spa was actually a lip balm that Frère Luis bought in Arles for chapped lips."

"Wow. I'll bet Frère Jean is freaking out."

"Yeah, he wasn't happy. Listen, Grace, I gotta go. The big goodbye is happening."

"Just remember darling, it's only a couple of weeks. He'll be home before you know it."

"I know. See you in a couple of hours."

Maggie hurried over to her family and saw that Mila carried a small shopping bag.

"What did you buy?" Maggie asked.

Mila dug into the bag and pulled out a pink dog's harness.

"Dad bought it for me," she said. "Because Fleur is a girl and this family seems to ignore that fact."

Maggie caught Laurent's gaze and he gave a faint shrug. Maggie was careful not to smile so that Mila would see.

"Can we say goodbye here?" Jemmy said. "I already feel like

I'm going off to war or something. You know I'll be back in two weeks, right?"

After hugging Jemmy goodbye, the three of them walked back into the parking lot of the airport. Mila trotted ahead with her shopping bag, chattering about wanting to stop by Domaine St-Buvard to pick up Fleur to bring with them to *Dormir*. Maggie couldn't help but think that they'd all circumvented a nasty bend in the road that could easily have upended them.

Not that it was all over and sorted yet. Not by a long shot. And in the end, even now, they were all learning new things about each other. Maggie had come to realize that Jemmy's interest in acting felt less real to her than his insistence on making Laurent recognize his interest in it. He might be a gifted actor, but she knew her son's real gift had yet to be revealed. And when it was, he wouldn't worry about what his father thought or how he would react. Hopefully by then he'd know that Laurent's approval would eventually be there.

And Mila? One thing Maggie knew about her daughter was that in spite of how she behaved these days, pleasing Laurent was a factor for her. In fact, Maggie was sure it was one of the reasons why Mila targeted Laurent in her attacks.

Maggie could imagine that someday, after they'd all survived her adolescence, Mila would leave home. But somehow Maggie had no doubt that her daughter would come back

Perhaps she would become interested in being a *sommelier* or a wine distributor. Maggie had seen her curiosity over the years when Laurent talked of wine and how it ended up on the wine store shelves. There was something there. A spark, an interest. Maybe the Alsace trip would fan that spark. Once she'd successfully survived the trials of adolescence there would be time to revisit the spark and fan it.

With her parents always there of course to gently guide and support.

As they walked to their car, Maggie looked at Laurent, his face as usual unreadable. She smiled and reached for his hand.

One thing she knew if she knew anything was that the future would unfold as it would. Good, bad, wonderful or tragic. But no matter what the future held, Maggie knew that she and Laurent would meet it shoulder to shoulder, both oars pulling together.

And in the end that was pretty much all she needed.

∼

To follow more of Maggie's sleuthing and adventures, check out *Murder in Mont St-Michel, Book 19 of the Maggie Newberry Mysteries!*

LAURENT'S ROAST LEG OF LAMB

In Provence, lavender is often used in culinary dishes—from flower sprinkles on top of ice cream to the savory seasoning in Laurent's roast leg of lamb. A perfect Sunday lunch, leftovers from this aromatic and delicious lamb dish make for unforgettable sandwiches the next day.

You'll need:

½ leg of lamb, bone in
- 4 sprigs fresh lavender
- 4 sprigs fresh rosemary
- 1 TB fresh thyme leaves, minced
- 1.5 TB fresh oregano leaves, minced
- 10 fresh sage leaves, minced
- ¼ cup fennel seeds, coarsely chopped
- 2 bay leaves, coarsely chopped
- ¼ cup fresh rosemary, coarsely chopped
- 1.5 tsp fresh lavender flowers, minced
- 2 sprigs fresh lavender, leaves stripped and coarsely chopped

4 cloves garlic
¼ cup extra virgin olive oil
1 TB unsalted butter
Kosher salt and freshly ground black pepper

1. In a mortar and pestle, pound the garlic and 1 TB of salt to a smooth paste.

2. Add the minced/chopped rosemary, sage, fennel, thyme, bay, lavender and oregano leaves plus minced lavender flowers to the mortar. Pound the mixture until all the leaves are smashed and broken into small pieces.

3. Spread the herb mixture all over the leg of lamb, then sprinkle the meat with a teaspoon of salt and lots of black pepper. Cover and refrigerate for two days.

4. Around two hours before you plan to roast the lamb, remove it from the refrigerator and let it warm to room temperature. Remove and reserve any large herb pieces. Meanwhile, preheat the oven to 325°F/163°C.

5. Heat a cast-iron skillet over high heat for several minutes, then swirl in the ¼ cup of olive oil and place the lamb fatty-side down in the skillet. Sear all sides until deeply golden brown.

6. Put the sprigs of rosemary and lavender in the bottom of an enameled cast-iron roasting pan just larger than the meat. Set the browned meat on top of the sprigs, and pour any olive oil and rendered fat from the skillet over the meat. Place the reserved herbs and butter over the meat.

7. Insert a thermometer into the thickest part of the leg and roast the lamb about one hour until the thermometer reads 140°F/60°F for medium-rare. (160°F/71°C for medium)

8. Transfer the lamb to a platter, cover with tented foil, and let rest for 15 minutes. Then carve and serve.

ABOUT THE AUTHOR

USA TODAY Bestselling Author Susan Kiernan-Lewis is the author of *The Maggie Newberry Mysteries,* the post-apocalyptic thriller series *The Irish End Games, The Mia Kazmaroff Mysteries, The Stranded in Provence Mysteries,* and *An American in Paris Mysteries.* If you enjoyed *Murder in the Lavender,* please leave a review on your purchase site.

Visit her website at www.susankiernanlewis.com or follow her at Author Susan Kiernan-Lewis on Facebook.

Printed in Great Britain
by Amazon